# THE
# COLD CHAIN

# THE COLD CHAIN

### BY
### *NIGEL LEWIS*

HAMISH HAMILTON

HAMISH HAMILTON LTD
Published by the Penguin Group
27 Wrights Lane, London W8 5TZ, England
Viking Penguin Inc, 40 West 23rd Street, New York, New York 10010, U.S.A.
Penguin Books Australia Ltd, Ringwood, Victoria, Australia
Penguin Books Canada Ltd, 2801 John Street, Markham, Ontario, Canada L3R 1B4
Penguin Books (N.Z.) Ltd, 182–190 Wairau Road, Auckland 10, New Zealand

Penguin Books Ltd, Registered Offices: Harmondsworth, Middlesex, England

First published in Great Britain 1988 by
Hamish Hamilton Ltd

British Library Cataloguing in Publication Data

Lewis, Nigel
The cold chain
I. Title
823'.914 [F]        PR6062.E94/

ISBN 0–241–12187–6

Printed and bound in Great Britain by
Butler & Tanner Ltd, Frome and London

*For my family*

# CONTENTS

'Antinomians, so denominated for rejecting the law, as a thing of no use under the gospel dispensation: they say that good works do not further, nor evil works hinder salvation; that the child of God cannot sin . . .'

From the *Dictionary of All Religions*

# PART ONE

# BURNING

T HE FURTHEST BACK THAT ARTHUR MIDDLETON would ever be able to take it was to the day in August 1980 when the man called Snyder – or who called himself Snyder – unexpectedly turned up at his office. Middleton was the US Consul-General in Belize, a fattish man in his early forties, recently remarried. It was late in his life, both to have married again and to have been given his first foreign posting. Nor was Belize the most plum of posts. But Middleton told himself that it was better late than never, and that if he was careful he might learn to be happy and to advance his career in the service. In the meantime, Belize was pleasant enough, despite – or because of – its unimportance. While the more paranoid local politicians might regard him as the most powerful man in the country, that was not the case in reality. Until independence at least, real power was invested in the loose triumvirate formed by the Premier, the Governor and the commander of the British forces; and since independence was likely to be contingent upon a defence agreement with Britain against the military threat from neighbouring Guatemala, nothing was likely to change. The Governor would be gone, that was all. Belize was not a place of rapid change and over his year as Consul-General Arthur Middleton had learned to like it that way.

His sense of this was at once threatened when he saw Snyder.

Snyder was the sort who spends his life being a thriller character come true. His eyes were blue but – difficult, this, for blue eyes – with something piggy about them, a sort of depraved idealism. They had icy pinpoints which might have been eternal vigilance or madness. Cop's eyes which could frisk, mentally undress, or bore a hole in you as needs be.

Snyder began sentences smartly with 'Yes *sir*'. When listening he sat, hard-eyed, chewing gum. Even in tropical heat, he wore a plainclothes-style windcheater. There'd been no telex warning of his arrival – that was the first odd thing about his visit – but the ID he'd flashed had satisfactorily confirmed his account of himself as being a field man for the DEA (Drug Enforcement Administration).

So admitted into the inner sanctum of the Consul's office, he made himself comfortable on the sofa and stretched his legs.

'I'll come right to the point, Consul,' he said at once. 'I guess you're aware there's cannabis being grown in this country?'

Sometimes the Consul was alarmed to find himself feeling like a dissident, not only among his own countrymen, but within the machinery of government. The shock-horror stress which Snyder laid on *cannabis* – and what an odd choice of word – had tempted him to smile. What was coming next, he wondered: *racketeers, reefers, bebop clubs*? There was something dated about Snyder. Perhaps it was just his eager certainty; but Arthur Middleton detected a brutal, sanctimonious innocence about him which he dissidently detested from the first.

Pausing to appraise that feeling in himself, the Consul played with a pink quartz-handled paper knife on his desk. Jane had bought it passing through Mexico city, along with an onyx box whose lid, on an impish impulse, he now lifted.

'Can I offer you a cigarette, Mr Snyder?'

Snyder looked every bit as shocked as Middleton had intended.

'No *sir*,' he said. 'I don't smoke.'

Middleton replaced the lid, paused to give his next question more effect.

'Tell me, what do you think of the garden?'

'The garden?' Snyder was plainly uneasy at this, he shifted on the sofa, his eyes were wary; Snyder was the sort, the Consul noted, who felt happier asking questions.

'Yes, the Consulate garden.'

'I dunno,' said Snyder. 'Can't say I really looked. It's pretty neat I guess.'

'Isn't it? We get a special subvention for gardens, did you know that? Got to keep the iris flying as well as the flag. But you saw only the front garden, the budget doesn't extend to the back. If you'd gone round *there* . . . ah!'

'Is this some kind of parable?'

4

'Not a parable, Mr Snyder, a parallel. It's full of weeds. What do you expect? We're in the back yard of the United States. Of course I know weed grows here. Would I be doing my job if I didn't?'

'OK.' Snyder shifted uneasily again at that palpable hit. 'Don't misunderstand me, sir,' he said after a pause. 'But have you any idea how *much* is growing and where it all is?'

The shock-horror stresses again. The Consul looked at Snyder intently, as though there might be some fine-print analysis hidden in the headlines he spoke in.

'I don't believe even the government has any exact idea of that. This may not be a big country, but if I wanted to hide I'd sooner hide here than in the whole of the US.'

'Well sir . . .' Snyder smiled and for the first time the Consul detected in his accent a whiff of deep south drawl . . . 'I'm here to tell you they can't hide any longer.' He was obviously pleased with himself. He'd got to the point, or had begun to, and knew this was a lead the Consul couldn't lightly let go.

'So *that's* why you're here.' The Consul put only the faintest trace of irony into his tone, as if to suggest to Snyder that he knew already why he was here, of course he knew, was Snyder seriously imagining that Washington wouldn't have told him beforehand of this visit and its purpose? But the fact was that Washington hadn't told him, he didn't know, and something self-satisfied in Snyder's bearing told the Consul this tack was useless and he might as well abandon it at once. Not without a fight though.

He cleared his throat as if to get down to business and said, 'OK Mr Snyder, before we continue, does the NAU know you're here?'

To this, the man's response was alarmingly 'aw shucks', as if government codes of procedure were fit to be obeyed only by nancy boys. He grinned with what passes in locker rooms for charm, shook his head and averted his eyes like a shy football hero.

'Sir,' he'd said, 'I have to say that liaison with the NAU is not in my department. I just do as the DEA tells me. They sort out the paperwork.'

'You're saying the NAU doesn't know.'

'I'm not saying they do or they don't. I'm saying *I* don't know

5

if they do. I'm not here on my own initiative, Consul.'

Middleton nodded. Certainly he didn't believe that. But the Narcotic Assistance Unit, a branch of the State Department, was the foreign policy body of drug enforcement. The DEA, as an arm of the Justice Department, was required to liaise with the NAU on foreign matters. And in the field of drug enforcement, most matters were foreign in the end.

However, even the foreign busts were carried out by the DEA, albeit with NAU funding and other back-up. The NAU were essentially pen-pushers, a bureaucratic backwater staffed by officials passed over for promotion elsewhere. It was the field men of the DEA, people like Snyder, who did the dangerous work and got the public credit in the war against drugs. A grey area there, the Consul reflected, off the constitutional leash, which had also perhaps been slackened by the uncertainties of the electoral run-up. Central America, where US policy was concerned, was another grey area. Why consult the NAU in a matter of tidying up the back yard? Yes, thought the Consul, lots of scope there for departmental empire-building, career furtherance, a little maverick free enterprise. Snyder was just the shining white sort of character the bosses sent out to colonise grey areas for themselves. From the beginning the Consul had had the impression of a man straining impatiently at a leash. Well, now was the time to inject some sternness into his voice and pull that leash a little tighter.

'OK Mr Snyder, since you don't seem to know whether the NAU's been informed and since' – he might as well admit it – 'I haven't been told, I will proceed on the assumption that they haven't been. And *that* means ... I will hear you out. I'll listen, I will take notes. But I'll tell you nothing. Everything, furthermore, I will relay to Washington.'

Snyder nodded absently, as if the Consul's caveat held no interest for him and he'd been waiting for it to end.

'I think, Consul,' he said, 'that you'll be interested in what I have to say.'

Middleton said easily, 'Interest me as much as you like. Just don't try and lobby me.'

'OK.' Snyder leant forward. 'It all begins with Venus...'

Self-styled thriller character that he was, Snyder's story opened like many thrillers with aircraft and a quick weather report. And his initial arresting sentence wasn't a fake. The chain of events which were to culminate in what would be called the independence concession really did begin with Venus.

The Morning Star, Snyder explained, is bright only to the earthbound eye. Studied with the instruments of astronomy, its surface is seen to be shrouded in low and unbroken cloud cover. The cloud was of interest to scientists, suggesting rain and so perhaps vegetation. Since 1978, they had modified their ideas, however. In that year the Pioneer spacecraft began orbiting Venus and among the information it sent back was that the cloud cover contained a thick concentration of dust particles. What caused the dust? The scientists surmised that it could be from active volcanoes among the mountains which Pioneer, using radar, had already relief-mapped on the planet's surface.

A powerful enough infra-red device could 'see' through the Venusian cloud cover, picking up the heat given off by volcanoes and to a lesser extent by any vegetation that might be present. The National Aeronautics and Space Administration (Snyder said simply NASA) and the US Defense Department had combined forces to develop such a system. It was called, said Snyder, 'Daedalus, after the ancient Greek daddy who kept his distance from the sun. He was heat-sensitive too, see?'

By May 1980 Daedalus was ready for its first trials and a high-altitude ER-2 – the NASA research aircraft – took off from Fort Bragg in North Carolina to conduct them. It had been decided to do the trials over Guatemala and Belize during the rainy season, when the cloud cover was almost as thick as that over Venus. Guatemala was rich in volcanoes and, like Belize, in vegetation; Belize had the additional advantage, as an approximate model of the Venusian terrain, of possessing no large centres of population, no large factories and few internal combustion engines.

Daedalus could be switched to a variety of colour-codings, and its onboard computer printed out co-ordinates and converted the photos into data which could be fed into a mainframe back home. The purpose of the test flight was to compare results with the known reality on the ground and to compile a bank of infra-red prints and computer read-outs to serve as a basis for quick identification in the future. That first flight came up with an anomaly. Snyder showed the Consul a press report of 3 June mentioning 'unnaturally uniform grid patterns' in an area of northern Belize. They were, archaeologists thought, the remains of canals dug by the ancient Maya to drain swamps.

But a more sensational 'anomaly' was picked up by a later test flight, early in August, and here Snyder opened his briefcase and presented the Consul with a photograph.

'Hot from the press,' he said, 'and boy, do I mean hot!' The photo bore no naturalistic resemblance to its subject – an aerial 'view' of bushland. There were some patches of green, true, but they were overwhelmed by pink and yellow, and splashes of violent orange whose edges bristled with a Kirlian effect, as of a magnetic field so heavy it could move colour. Snyder pointed out the orange patches. 'Those,' he said, 'are dope.'

He explained that marijuana is one of the 'hottest' of all plants and that the orange patches fell exactly within the right heat range. The scientific truth of the heat, he said, was instinctively recognised by growers, who spoke of the ripe, growing plant as 'singing'. He pointed out the orange patches a second time.

'Look,' he said, 'that's singing all right, it screams at you. But it's not quite ripe yet. A month or so it'll be top C.

'We have,' Snyder said, 'a complete marijuana map of the north of Belize.' The south didn't matter, the rainfall there was too high, it would wash all the precious resin from the buds. 'No grower in his right mind would plant in the south. So our map can be taken to cover the whole country and, Consul, I can tell you, there's tons of it, almost ready for cutting. And all those tons are intended – you guessed it – for sale in the United States. Until we saw these photos we'd no idea so much was grown here.'

Snyder reached his peroration.

'The man on the spot should be in the know and you're the man on the spot. Now you're in the know, don't you think it would be a good idea if the government here was too?'

'Let me get this quite clear,' Middleton said. 'Are you asking me to pass this information to the Premier?'

'Yes sir,' Snyder said at once.

'To what end?'

Snyder shrugged.

'A response from him would do just fine. In the first instance, at least.'

8

'You're asking me to act as message boy for the DEA?'

'Message boy? No sir. We're asking you to, uh, communicate our concern. That's a very delicate thing which no message boy could handle. That's a diplomat's job.'

'Leave it to me, Mr Snyder, to decide what is or is not a diplomat's job.' With that, Middleton stood behind his desk as if to say 'This interview is over.' Snyder took the cue and stood too.

'Thank you for hearing me through, Consul.'

'You were right about it being interesting,' Middleton replied, 'although I'm not sure that your final recommendation wasn't lobbying. Still, I'll be sending a full report to Washington, with a recommendation of my own that a copy be shown to the NAU. If Washington wants me to tell the Premier, I'll do so. When are you leaving, by the way?'

'Tomorrow.'

'And where are you staying?'

'The Bayman Hotel.'

'Very well, stay there this evening, don't go out on the town and don't get into any conversations. Okay?' The Consul held out his hand. 'Goodbye, Mr Snyder.'

Snyder took his hand and gripped it hard. It wasn't a handshake. His eyes narrowed further.

'Consul,' he said, 'I've worked in the Guajira area of Colombia and I'll tell you, the *marimberos* there don't fool around. After Guajira this problem shouldn't lose us too much sleep.'

'Lose as much as you like,' Middleton said. 'Just don't lose more than a night's worth here in Belize. Let's do things by the book, shall we Mr Snyder?'

And that was how Middleton did them. He informed the NAU of Snyder's visit and of what had passed between them. A fortnight later, having heard nothing, he prompted the NAU for a reply and again heard nothing. The silence struck him as strange, but he contented himself with the knowledge that he had followed established guidelines and put the delay down to bureaucratic slowness. That, too, was 'by the book'.

He didn't yet know that the book as he understood it had already been, in the cliché, thrown out of the window. In the following month, September, he would find out.

*

9

It was just after lunch, the last Sunday of September. Manuel Zuniga lit a cigarette, exhaled a big cloud of smoke and said, 'I'm going to pick pineapples.'

The speaking and the smoke got in one another's way, and he coughed, couldn't stop, a paroxysm. His wife shook her head, tut-tutting. She banged him on the back; she said the sun was too hot for picking. He said, coughing, 'To hell with the sun!'

His hardware shop was shut, a cool cave of gunmetal-blue spades, buckets and innocent nails that had never known rust. He let himself out into the dazed heat of his village, Trinidad. His pick-up was in a patch of shade. Other men went whoring or gambling, kept mistresses, drank rum; Manuel Zuniga started the engine and looked forward to his land.

He had come to agriculture both very early and very late. In the hour of his birth, according to the custom, a sowing stick had been placed in one tiny fist, a hoe-handle in the other – his initiation. From earliest childhood he had seen the maize rituals – the wooden cross, the mother and father cobs of unwinnowed corn. With a torch, he'd welcomed his father and big brothers home from the *milpa* – the temporary field out in the bush where the small farmers of lowland Central America plant their beans, squashes and maize. The *milpa* farmer can rarely rest. Within three years, sun and rains between them have spoilt the soil; the jungle reclaims the *milpa*, the men having moved to begin the cycle of slashing-and-burning all over again. It is agriculture like a guerrilla campaign, always on the move. In April, the sky is dark with smoke, as the new *milpa* is burned; soon, the scorched earth is green again with ordered rows of things that men have grown, a secret encampment of plants like tents in the jungle.

Symbols, memories, all, of a destiny he'd denied; for, in his early teens, Manuel Zuniga had promised himself a better life – off the land. He'd soon gone south, to Belize, scraping and saving; by his mid-thirties, he'd raised the cash to start his shop. Trinidad was in farming country, a Mennonite settlement nearby, and, almost thirty years later, business had prospered to the point where the hold of the land was broken forever.

Then, the land renounced, he strangely began to feel the need for it. In his shop he started appraising the virgin things he sold

10

with an eye to using them, recalling the slashing-and-burning of his childhood with near nostalgia – the huge clouds of smoke seeming to reach to heaven.

A few miles from Trinidad he'd found an acre of bush – the most he felt able to manage. His application went through quickly; within the month, with help from his middle son, a power-saw and a machete from the shop, the bush had been slashed, the land laid bare. Only a small tree with a hummingbird's nest was spared; at the dry season's end, that was cut down too – then the razed land set on fire. It was April, the sky above his *milpa* dark with smoke.

He thought of planting 'God's sunbeams', as his father had called corn, but settled instead on pineapples. Unusual for the north of Belize, but it worked. In two years, they were ripe. Towards the end of that September afternoon he'd picked through the fruit of three rows – not bad for a man in his sixties.

Halfway down the fourth row, he heard the aeroplanes – a distant, demented whine, a deeper droning, a buzzing persistence in the sky to the east. On tiptoe, he could see them. But Manuel was curious. He wanted a better look. Folding his clasp knife, he climbed into the back of the pick-up.

What he saw was an air display – five bulbous-nosed Agro Trucks skimming the bush as low as lawnmowers. They flew in a tight 'V', no ragged edges; precise, purposeful flying. 'Sinister,' eyewitnesses later called them, 'like something from a James Bond film.' But that was hindsight, because the planes weren't painted black, or in camouflage, but a happy good-luck yellow, the usual strip of crop sprayers. The flight looked more like a flying circus than a mission, daredevils who might get themselves killed but never anyone else.

They were unmarked, though, and *were* out to kill – not people, but plants: the criminal *cannabis sativa* under all its aliases. Shortly before four, they had entered the airspace of Belize not far from its northernmost point, passing, astonishing for one of the world's least populous countries, directly over a man paddling seawards down the Rio Hondo. He couldn't but notice that the planes came from the Mexican side of the river, Belize's northern border.

From the few other eyewitnesses, it was possible to reconstruct the rest of the flight path. Emptying a powerful weedkiller

11

from their tanks, the planes worked their way through weed plantations in Corozal District, then down to Orange Walk, the village triangle of Trinidad, Shipyard, San Felipe: where Manuel's land was, and Manuel.

From the back of his pick-up, he could see the aeroplanes maybe a mile to the north-east. If he had a shrewd idea what was being grown over there, on the *milpa* they were spraying, that didn't worry him. Why should it have done? He, Manuel Zuniga, wasn't a weed grower; he'd nothing to fear from weed-killing.

In sudden silence, engine noise in their wake, the planes regrouped. The formation – aimed at him – fanned, fell nearer the bush, preparing for a run. What were they doing? But still he felt no fear, even when – although, instinctively, he ducked – the planes went low overhead. And then: a huge roaring, a fine mist, like the air by a waterfall, late sunlight catching the spray in rainbows, beautiful, poisonous rainbows...

They hung in the air, absurdly. Manuel couldn't believe it. He thought, 'I've been sprayed! They've sprayed me like a fly!' The planes were gone. Less than ten seconds had passed. His breath – which he hadn't held – suddenly caught. He hadn't shut his eyes: they stung. Water, he thought. But there wasn't water. He felt afraid. He rubbed his eyes, then said aloud, 'I must get out of here!' He rolled to the back of the pick-up, climbed down. The stinging eyes were worse: the poison was on his hands. The spray had settled. He could still hear the planes.

His shirt was off, he was sweating, the skin of his arms and chest was pineapple-scratched; and by the time he'd made it, somehow, home, more poison had seeped into his system through scratches and open pores. His wife washed his eyes. Already his breathing was worse. His wife kept saying, 'I told you not to go picking! I told you!' She poured water over his head, water over his body. Already – symptom of sickness – he felt detachment from his physical self. What had happened he didn't know: only that it was bad.

By eight o'clock he was in Belize City, at the hospital there, in an oxygen tent. The doctors didn't know what to do; there was nothing they could do. They did tests, they took samples. His lungs were hardening, steadily, the tissue swelling and setting.

12

They changed the oxygen cylinder. It did no good. His lungs were giving up, the dense air of the tent was rarer by the hour. Breaths were fewer – breathing was a rib-racked, deep, slow-motion sob. He was dying. They told his wife. She dialled Chetumal, her hand was trembling, she told their eldest son; come quick. She cried. Drank coffee. The room was white – walls, white sheets – a hygiene heaven smelling of spirit. Next day, the son was there. He sat by the bed. His suit was too small. He said little. The Premier of Belize was shown in, he spoke to Mrs Zuniga, softly; she cried, he put his arms round her, he spoke to her son. It was evening. A priest came. He wore black. He said words, he made signs of the cross. The church words, he uttered strongly; his own, he whispered. It did no good.

The cylinder was changed. The two young sons arrived. It was early morning, the fourth day. The family prayed and took turns to hold the dying man's hands (the room filled with nurses in white, the priest prayed, the priest made signs) the dying man, the dying man . . .

The dead man.

It was an early weekday morning in December, almost three months after Manuel Zuniga's death. Arthur Middleton sipped his coffee and studied the document which State had sent him to pass on to the Premier. It was a short note, but the big State Department typeface filled a whole page. He held the paper at arm's length like a sight test: y-e-e-s, as though the thing were being spelt out for the benefit of backward, childish people. Something anachronistic there. It made him think of quill pens, Pennsylvania copperplate – the old, honourable America.

But the document's appearance was deceptive. Rereading it, the Consul was satisfied that it was in reality a fine net of nuance through which no minnow of misunderstanding might slip. It was still a climbdown, though. 'The Government of the United States,' he read, 'proposes that it and the Government of Belize meet in the near future to discuss the growing of narcotics on the territory of Belize and their traffic into the United States, and that this matter be given high priority between us. The

President notes the communication of the Belize Government dated 3 October 1980. He assures the Premier of Belize that the United States will continue to respect the sovereignty of Belize under the charter of the United Nations, and further assures the Premier that the United States Government and its agencies will take no unilateral action towards solving this problem between the two countries.'

In State Department terms, that was outspoken. Already, the Consul knew, the document was known around State as 'the independence concession', quite a big handle for a one-page policy shift in so small an area of US interest as Belize. On this reading, the independence concession was perhaps a final product of the Carter presidency; certainly it felt like that to the Consul. Had Reagan's ratification of it, then, been obtained by Carter apologists in state who had, as it were, flown the concession under the Presidential radar? Concessions, it was apparent, didn't figure large in the new president's style. This one, then, was important. It acknowledged that there had been policy confusion and that the weed-killing flight had been a mistake. In the words of the Premier of Belize, when he'd called Middleton in soon after Manuel Zuniga's death, 'for a few acres of rough weed, you have damaged the sensitive plant, democracy'.

There were other ramifications. The flight had created ill will in a part of the world where, if the US wanted to stomp on Nicaragua, it had to tread carefully everywhere else. Belize was in a delicate run-up period to the independence from Britain widely expected the following year. An unauthorised overflight of the country causing an innocent fatality had hardly been the right signal of respect for sovereignty to send to Guatemala, Belize's warlike neighbour and claimant of its territory. Absurdly – in the light of the flight – the US had earlier that year, for the first time, come out at the United Nations in favour of Belize's right to self-determination.

What the hell was going on? The Consul had even wondered whether, on the dangerous level where politics function unconsciously, the flight had been some sort of compensation for the failed airborne bid to rescue the Iranian hostages.

Middleton slipped the document into a long manila envelope embossed with an eagle and applied consular spittle to the flap.

14

He sealed the envelope and looked at his watch. Eight-twenty. Now, where was Albert?

And where was Jane? Of course, in bed, but shouldn't the diplomat's new wife be up by now, *soignée*, seeing him off? He put the envelope into his attaché case and checked to see that, yes, the file was there. With his last mouthful of coffee he worried whether Jane's button-bright enthusiasm was dimming, purpose wilting already, love dying. Where the hell was Albert? He went to the window.

In the garden, wielding scissors and carrying a basket, wearing green chauffeur's uniform minus ridiculous yellow-frogged cap, Albert was cutting hibiscus. The scene looked, and the Consul paused, like a parody of a Japanese print. But, it occurred to him, old Albert was a parody of a chauffeur. He felt sometimes, often nowadays, like a parody of a consul. What was it about this country? The heat, humidity, something in the drinking water? It was hard to stay northern here; it was a country of parody and it parodied institutions especially. Somewhere deep in oneself one wanted to giggle all the time.

But for promotion to a better posting, the illusion of import-ance, a certain gravitas, was vital. (He *must* speak to Jane.)

He opened the window and called Albert's name. The improb-able figure in the garden, holding a spray of red flowers, looked up with a shy goldtooth smile.

'Time we hit the road, Albert.'

Albert called back, reedily.

'Jus' coming sah.'

In the bedroom, Jane was still in her Beaker burial position under the sheet. He leaned to kiss her cheek:

'So long honey, see you at lunch.' She turned and stretched. The baked-bread body smell of sleep wafted from her.

'What time is it?' He told her. 'Goodness, I must get up!' But she wouldn't yet, he knew. She kissed him absently – good morning (who are you?), see you, goodbye.

Albert was at the wheel in full Ruritanian rigout. He pulled the Chrysler out of the compound, past the early visa queue of hopeful no-hopers, then into the streets. Outside the Consulate a sign read: 'Don't even *think* of parking here.' From the start of the Iranian hostage crisis, US diplomatic missions abroad had been on full security alert, but not in Belize: it was a backwater so laid back that even the fist of American power could unclench a little. The Consul wondered vaguely sometimes about security. It would add to his own importance and be a good career move to send Washington a note employing phrases like 'soft underbelly' and asking for a security step-up. Somehow, though, he couldn't bring himself to dictate it.

There were backward glimpses of faces turning to look as Albert stepped on the gas. A boy in a straw hat riding bareback reined his horse to the side of the road. By Lord's Ridge, the tumbledown old cemetery which the Guatemalans had threatened to enlarge with black bodies when they occupied Belize, the Chrysler picked up speed and the stars-and-stripes pennant caught the slipstream. Belmopan, a Maya-style assortment of buildings and the world's smallest capital city, was half an hour away. Time to refresh memory from the file.

The Consul coded open his attaché case and fished it out. A couple of clippings fell. The headline of a local scandal sheet – MANUEL: MARIJUANA MARTYR – screamed up from the car floor as the Consul leant to retrieve them and, momentarily, he sighed inwardly over the whole sorry business. He remembered again how the Premier had stood at the window of his Belmopan office, his hand in a swearing-in sort of attitude on the head of a wooden carving of a mother-and-child, watching some kids kick a ball on the waste ground below.

'For a few acres of rough weed,' he had said, 'you have damaged the sensitive plant...' The Consul thought: So much for *my* patch here. He doubted whether even the independence concession which he carried would have the power to restore his personal relations with the Premier to their former, friendly state.


Far to the north, in the United States, the problems of independence and concession were also much on the mind of James Blythe. It doesn't much matter where he was. It might have been the apartment which he had kept on in Berkeley, or his ranch near Brownsville, Texas, or even the humbler apartment which he had taken under another name in Illinois. It was not, however, the family ranch near Sacramento; that was home to

16

his ex-wife, Mary Louise, and sometimes to his daughter by her. Two years before, when his concern with independence had first begun to press to the point where he had been forced to realise that his life, as he then lived it, would no longer be able to contain the pressure, he had settled the ranch on Mary Louise, pre-emptively, as part of their later, amicable enough divorce settlement. He had come – some would say fallen – a long way since then, but still not far enough: neither for his own liking nor, more particularly, for the liking of his second and very much younger wife, Amanda.

Over thirty years younger. Astonishing, really, that he had married her. But then, James Blythe was a man in altogether great physical shape for his age, which was just the right side of sixty, and in general women thought of him not as an old man but – which is something quite different – as an older one. He had the gift of making his age seem irrelevant. The sunglasses he wore were prescription lenses, tinted to deceive; they hid eyes in which only the very discerning could see a more than physical weariness. Sometimes, too, there was a slight, bookish stoop to his shoulders which made him 'look his age'. But his stomach was flat and his muscles toned from years of swimming and tennis and the best health clubs and resorts; and if his hair was grey, he had at least a full head of it, and the grey was *distingué*; and if his facial skin had aged, it had at least been aged as it were by Florentine craftsmen, without a hint of flabbiness.

Perhaps even more to the point in the marriage stakes, James Blythe was extremely wealthy and had been all his life. There were millions in his personal account and in the accounts of the companies which he owned or in which he held a controlling interest – his 'business bores, not interests', as he had come to think of them – many millions more. The wealth had been accumulated over more than a hundred years of family history, in which his own, he had begun to think, was utterly submerged. He had wondered whether, when one was not self-made, all that one made for oneself in the end were problems. All these years later, not even his war record as a bomb aimer over Europe seemed his own so much as a detail in the family reputation; and a family reputation, when one's own chosen family fails as his had done, can start to seem the worst of mockeries – denying life in order to look after a tomb. *Life!* Where was it? He was a trustee, of the past and for the future, and living as he would have liked, instinctively, seemed to involve a breaking of those trusts, a betrayal.

The family fortune had been founded by his great-grandfather, old Fullerton Blythe, of whom a much enlarged daguerreotype hung in the hallway of the Sacramento ranch. It showed him bewhiskered and Brunel-like, full of native energy and solidly in tune with the confidence and ethics of his time, standing beside a heap of railway sleepers. His grandfather – Fullerton's son – had diversified his inherited wealth into a broad financial base, dutifully building upon the foundations. With his father Henry, however, the family inheritance had become more complicated. He had been born into a preordained reality, his future stretching out ahead of him as immutably as Fullerton's railway tracks. It must, from the first, have been an ambiguous prospect. He had, though, done what was expected of him and at the age of twenty had been indentured into a marine insurance firm – one of his father's diversifications. When, ten years later, his father died, he had hung up his business suit and, with almost indecent haste, exchanged it for a flowing black cape and a few years of expensive dabbling in the movies. And for those few years he had, James guessed, after whatever distorted fashion, been himself.

Henry had chafed against the family bit but had not broken free. He hadn't generated enough G to pull away from his family's gravity. Henry had 'seen sense', got out of the movies, delegated control of the businesses and, a disappointed man, embarked on the more serious personal business of drinking himself to death.

This was the father whom James Blythe had known, a drunken, somewhat fantastical figure in his melodramatic cape, given to tears, rages, rhapsodies with a curious, delusive poetry about them – like his quixotic desire, often expressed, to have been 'born British'. He could remember his father being fond only once, and then he had been grown up and his father not far from death, just after the war. Then he had seen the wistful respect in his father's eyes, as though his son, by being in the war, had achieved something which had always been beyond him: a simple ambition, to be his own man among men, facing danger and death with them equally.

18

His more formative memories of his father were less fatherly ones. At the time of the first he must have been three or four. It had been a hot day, sweltering. He had reached out and touched a bottle of his father's chilled Beck's beer, so cold that he had at once pulled his hand away as if it had been burned. Then he had touched it again and, with his fingernail, peeled away a sliver of the silvery foil. Of all his early childhood impressions, of all this father's bottles of beer, why had he remembered this one? He wondered whether he had conceived at that moment the notion that reality – the hot day – was not necessarily as it seemed and the accompanying notion that there might be an abstract idea underlying all things. Then his father, laughing and drunk, had taken the bottle up and put it to his lips ...

Another, later memory was of a camping weekend and the toy compass his father had bought in Oakland. He had held it in his gloved hand for his son to see, towering above him, swaying, smiling his dangerous smile.

'C'mon son, tell me. Where's north?'

The needle had behaved strangely too, scouting the dial, spinning full circle, stopping and tensely twitching.

'True north, true true north ...'

He had thought that his father wasn't holding the compass steady.

'Son, my hand's like a rock. I'm not the problem. The north's the problem.'

It had always puzzled him (he knew now) when Daddy was drunk and now there was the puzzle of the drunken compass. The needle was fooling him into knowing where north was, then scouting again. North was the snow mountains, then the sea, north was the tent pitched under the pines. North was everywhere.

'Now you see, son, something very small and near and un-important can blind you to the big, far things. Up there at the top of the world there's true north. It matters. But here in my hand ...' his father had brought out the horseshoe magnet (it was red like the compass) concealed under his glove '... there's a little painted baby north which doesn't matter *a damn*.'

Then – his father's stranger's smile, his father's failure's smile – he had burst into laughter and his son into tears. He had been a boy: it had mattered that much to him, to be sure, to know where north was.

That act of cruelty still hurt. His father, abusing the terrible power of parenthood, had taught him doubt in the form of a practical joke. It had been part of his father's bequest to him, along with the family wealth. There had been something else, too. All his memories of his father contained an element of desperation. Perhaps he had been one of those people who spend their lives just this side of suicide. Appearances – like the flowing black cloak – had mattered so much to him, mattered desperately, perhaps because he perceived no substance. He had been like one of those party jugglers or conjurers to whom it is given to be the first to teach children that reality is relative and illusory; that it was something one could make up for oneself. The incident of the compass had been at once a juggling with appearance and a plea for the existence of something which was not merely appearance.

Perhaps every son, even a son just the right side of sixty, longs somewhere in himself to fulfil ambitions which his father was never able to fulfil. Or never dared to fulfil – because one of the lessons which James Blythe learned from his father was that when there is no acceptable framework of personal values to inherit, it is necessary to self-make one's own.

As a young man soon after his father's death he had imagined himself to have learned other things from his negative example. Consciously he had opted for the practical 'multitude of business' whence, according to the wordy-wise preacher, a dream arose, to his father's wild 'multitude of words'. He had professed certainty in whom he was and what he was doing. With the market revival of the late Forties he had resumed the direct control of the family businesses relinquished by his father and had married as 'well' as his forbears would have wished him to. A daughter had been born and he would never forget the sense of love underpinning his life when he had held her in his arms: a difficult birth after which his wife had been gravely informed that she would not conceive again. So there was to be no son – it was a turning-point which old Fullerton would have understood.

His daughter grew up, while his wife became active on dozens of local committees and a few national ones, putting her name, his name, to responsibilities and causes. Little by little his marriage, which should have been the living centre, began to be invaded by the crystalline fixity of his boardroom self; slowly, each of them became lonelier because marriage was supposed to have ended loneliness forever. For the most part he let the days succeed one another in accordance with the turning of 'the great flywheel of society', as William James called habit. But sometimes he would try and talk it out with her, to be met always with incomprehension, feigned or otherwise, or when that failed to stop him, irritability, even anger.

'Why don't you let things *be*, James?'

And he would reply, 'There's nothing *there* to be.' One day she had referred to him in his business capacity as being 'a figurehead' and he had replied, with unusual heat and to her glazed surprise, that if he was a figurehead it was that of a boat which must never, ever be rocked.

She had said, 'Yes dear, but what's the *matter*?' And he had fallen silent – because the truth of it was that he didn't know.

Under it all the compass needle span. He told himself that he would become a genial old anecdotard moving into his anecdotage, the figurehead of a flimsy craft at last floated out upon eternity, Adam Smith's 'invisible hand' on the tiller. His time in the material world would be up, his well-toned muscles would go the way of all flesh. The bubble would burst and the air inside would smell of nothing, neither sweetness nor sin, and nothing would mark where his life had been. It didn't once occur to him that this might have been the very despair which his father had experienced.

At the age of fifty-two he had delegated control of the family businesses, exactly as his father had done at an earlier age. Leisure had freed him for philosophy, but not everyone so freed is by nature a philosopher. He still did not know what to do and, without this driving force in his life, was, although he did not yet realise it, unusually vulnerable to outside influence, both evil and good. His father's demon had been drink – he wasn't going to make that mistake. His father's fragmentation, then slow disintegration of personality – all alcohol and crack-ups – had been very public. He wouldn't make that mistake either. His father had been an old ham; he was a much better actor.

Gradually, however, he had come to think that his predicament and his father's were probably essentially the same. It was rebellion without any easily identifiable cause and therefore without an easy remedy, the rebellion of the artist, but without the art – and that was another mistake of his father's, the movie business, which he would not make.

Nevertheless, his father had left him with unfinished psychological business – of that, too, he was a trustee. He had resolved that if the time came for him to rebel, it would not be a messy rebellion like his father's, but methodical and conducted by stealth.

One afternoon early in 1976 James Blythe had a chance meeting at his tennis club. Or perhaps it wasn't chance but a perception by the man Carey that, appearances and reputation to the contrary, the upright James Blythe had now become fertile ground for corruption.

Carey's confidence had been extraordinary, given that Blythe knew him only by sight. He was a man of dubious reputation who had made membership of the club by virtue of some well-placed friends on its committee and a deserved reputation, not just as a good tennis player, but as a wit. That afternoon he had entered the club and, seeing Blythe in one corner of it, alone, had half-raised his arm, as though in greeting, before walking purposively across the room towards him. Blythe had looked up to see Carey standing over him. The man's smile had been distant but also, it had occurred to James later, somewhat knowing – as though they shared a secret.

Carey said, 'Perhaps this would be of interest to you,' and handed him a roneoed booklet.

It had, James saw as he took it, the simple title *How To Disappear*. It was clearly, at first glance, a criminal production, doubtless obtained from the bad company which Carey was reliably rumoured to keep.

James had looked up from the title page, sharply, and said, 'Yes? And why should this interest me?' But it had been as though there were already an unspoken complicity between them and as if Carey had *known* that the idea of disappearance would strike a responsive chord in him – as indeed it had. (Of course, he had thought at once. Disappear. It's that easy.)

Carey had shrugged.

'It's a great read,' he'd said off-handedly, 'like a thriller, only real.' He did not make the mistake of asking James if he might join him, for if James had been suffering from the sense of a grotesque omission from things, a human gulf between himself and others, it wasn't an omission which he would have wanted filled even for a moment by a presence like Carey's.

Instead of handing the booklet back at once, James had glanced again at its title and again at Carey, and asked, 'Where did you get this?'

Carey had shrugged again.

'It costs a grand a copy, okay? But it was free to me and it's free to you. It's a joke, that's all. See what you think. So long.'

And Carey had walked off, leaving in Blythe's hands a comprehensive guide to becoming a self-made character with a secret, fictive life.

Telling himself that he would return the booklet the following day (and so, with suitably sniffy disapproval, he did) he took it home, devoured it in one sitting and photocopied the whole thing on his study machine. *How To Disappear* had begun as an early Sixties guide for Vietnam draft-dodgers, but in succeeding years editorial control seemed to have passed to the criminal classes. It had been periodically updated and enlarged, and this was the latest edition, incorporating all the latest loopholes, banking regulations, nuances in the differences between State laws, updates on extradition treaties and so on. It also listed and gave thumbnail sketches of countries – 'Cheshire-cat countries', it called them – where disappearance was easier than in others. Costa Rica was recommended; Mexico, on the whole, was not. One recommended country was Belize. James thought nothing much of the reference at first – later it would seem to him that it was there, with his reading of *How To Disappear*, that he had begun his journey to Central America.

Most of the booklet was aimed at a readership which wanted to disappear very seriously indeed – *desperados* who needed to become *desaparecidos*, on passports bearing their likenesses but the names of unfortunates who had died at an early age. He was especially struck by an ingenious warning to the effect that if you had a pet which you wished to disappear with you its name

23

too should be changed – there was the case of a man who had been tracked down by the name of his dog. It occurred to James that *How To Disappear* taught a perverted form of transcendentalism: like a cult religion, it had set itself the central problem of being 'born again'.

He mulled over the booklet for almost a year and tentatively added to its suggestions a few refinements of his own. His mulling started as an academic exercise, a mind game – he had no clear idea of implementing the idea which was, nevertheless, growing in his mind.

Then, one day in the early summer of 1977, he flew to Chicago. There he took a branch line to a place which was, as recommended in the booklet, neither too small nor too large. He had with him no credit cards nor other mark of his identity, but a large quantity of cash with which he quickly succeeded in renting a room, three months in advance, cash on the nail.

The next morning he went to apply for a driving licence. He had to steel himself: this was the first time he had lied to officialdom. It was some years, he said, since he had driven – he had moved to this area and had lost his old licence long ago. In his pocket, as 'proof' of his identity if he were asked for it, he had the rent-receipt made out to him in the name of 'William Brandl'; but he was not asked. He gave his rented room as his address and his birthplace as a small town in Texas. The clerk took down the details just as James, now becoming William, gave them and the following day William took, and passed, the driving test.

A fortnight later, returning to the room, he found his new driving licence. If the authorities had checked with the Texas town he had given as his birthplace they would have found that its town hall had burnt down a few years before, leaving no records – as *How To Disappear* had informed him.

He looked at the licence for a long while to familiarise himself with it before putting it away. He was now a criminal, in the sense that nothing connected the socially unaccountable 'William Brandl' with that other, longer standing fiction, the figurehead James Blythe.

The next step was to open a bank account, using, if necessary, his driving licence for identity. He had brought with him a hundred thousand dollars in cash. Successfully, he opened an

24

account and asked for a couple of credit cards. The manager said they would be posted to him immediately. He stayed on in his room until they were delivered. Now he had plastic money for use in emergencies and the cards were more convincing proof of identity than the licence. He withdrew some of the money and flew to New York, the capital city of US philanthropy. There – a rich man's touch – he set up a charitable institution, The Grant Foundation.

Now William Brandl's fictitious existence had a fictitious purpose to it. If Brandl were exposed, he could always convincingly claim that he had wanted to conduct philanthropy under a cloak of modest anonymity.

As yet, however, his false identity resembled one of those apartments which busy men with responsibilities will sometimes rent in the outer suburbs: somewhere to be alone, feet up and the phone off the hook, no furniture, a room whose emptiness matched his own.


Then Amanda moved in.

He met her in November 1977, shortly before her birthday and his trip to Colombia to sell gold shares which were no longer producing a significant yield. (They had been one of his grandfather's diversifications and their sale required his personal signature.)

He was at a poolside party in LA, in a circle of pseudo-Californian mid-Westerners complaining about the Los Angeles smog and an extremely ponderous German loudly telling an installer of swimming pools, whose poolside party this was, how he had first met Billy Wilder in Weimar.

On the point of going and wondering why he had come, he drained the last of his OJ and it was at exactly that moment that she – there was no other word for it – materialised. He had first set eyes on her, in fact, through the upturned bottom of his glass and seen that she was looking, and smiling, directly at him.

'Hi,' she said, 'I'm Amanda.'

Hers wasn't at all the toothpaste-ad, Barbi-Doll smile. It had spontaneity, a touch of mischievousness, something almost elfin

about it – as, indeed, her presence did. This, and her material-
isation apparently out of nowhere, made her seem like ... well
... and he said this to her, a fairy goddaughter, about to offer
him three wishes. Suddenly he found himself smiling too, for
the first time in what seemed like ages.

'But where did you spring from?' he asked. Then her smile
had changed. The brightness was still there, but pursed, the
smile of someone who has a secret and thinks it a shame, by
revealing it, to spoil the simple pleasure she has inadvertently
given.

'Upstairs.'

It was a moment before he understood.

'You mean...?' he pointed to the white mansion across the
lawn.

'Uh-huh. Charles is my uncle.'

Charles was the swimming pool installer. At that moment,
however, it wasn't this piece of information which caught his
interest so much as the extraordinary artlessness, or art, with
which she imparted it. On the 'uh-huh' she nodded gravely, at
the same time inclining her head to one shoulder, almost *lolling*
it, and enunciating the two syllables very slowly, as though she
were having difficulty with them. At first he thought she was
sending herself up; but she delivered the rest of the sentence
painfully too. It was as though she were, all of a sudden, the
American childwoman, the bright fairy goddaughter transformed into a slow learner, backward, a shy child called upon
to recite poetry to the grown-ups; or, with the unsmiling concentration with which she spoke, as though she had been dumb
in a previous life and retained the distant memory of her speech
therapy.

Someone who spoke like that all the time you would have
been sorry for; someone who evidently didn't, but who suddenly
did, you laughed at or began, ever so little, to love.

Then the bright smile was back.

'What do you think of his pools?'

'I think his pools are great, the greatest. I would like to swim
in his pools all year.'

'Could you afford one?'

'I could afford one. But why weren't you at the party?'

Her answer was astonishing.

'Neither were you.'

He paused.

'No? Am I at it now?'

'Maybe, but it's too late.'

'Why?'

'The party's over,' she said simply.

He considered that, then said, 'Well, if you had been at it, so might I.'

He had thought that, in the context of a potentially ridiculous conversation, rather a clever remark, but if she thought so she gave no sign. She said:

'I don't like parties much. I was watching.'

He nodded towards the mansion.

'Upstairs?'

'Yes.'

'And you didn't see me?'

Again she astonished him.

'I saw you so clearly,' she said, 'that I saw you weren't here.' Then she pointed to the other end of the pool. 'Look!'

He turned. A beached-out, bleached-out woman was crouched over a table, shoulders hunched, her face meaninglessly solemn, her too-blonde hair hanging loose, hands clasped to her face in a parody of prayer. The coke-snorting had begun. The group waiting around the table suddenly laughed, in unison; he didn't believe that anything said over there could have been that funny. She leaned further forward, as though something were eluding her, exactly the undignified pose, it occurred to him, in which she would probably repay the man or men in kind. He turned away.

'So?'

Something of the sort had evidently occurred to her too.

'I could only do that,' she said, still staring down the pool, 'in private.'

'Do you do it at all?' he asked, and she looked at him, not at all reprovingly, but with a distant interest, as though he had just revealed something interesting about himself. He felt he had struck a sharp, inappropriate note. She wasn't his daughter, after all, even if she was young enough to be. He smiled wryly and added, 'Anyway, at least *they're* at the party, even if we're not. Good luck to them.' (*In private*, he was

27

thinking, what does she imply by *in private*?)

She smiled (and why couldn't he keep his eyes off her mouth?) and said, 'I think I prefer your company. What's your name?'

He hesitated, then said, lightly, 'James. Yes. James is a name I've been known to answer to . . .'

He was tempted to tell her at once that if he was James Blythe he was also Bill Brandl; to start, in an access of trust, by sharing this secret with her. Secrecy begins as a reassurance that after all one's life has not come off the production line; one has something of one's own. Then it starts to swell within one, itself joining the pressures one has sought to avoid. On that first meeting, he resisted the temptation to tell his secret, but on their second, their first time in bed together, lying beside her later, he succumbed.

And what a childish secret it would have seemed if she had at once, as they lay there, laughed at him and laughed him out of it. Cured him. But he had not known how badly she was herself in need of cure. Sickness in her had complemented his, his unreality had found an echo in hers. His fake name had intrigued her. It had seemed to her romantic – he could still hear the strange stress which she put on that word: ro*man*tic.

'It could be,' she had said, 'that it's your *real* name, like the confirmation name which Catholics take.'

She had breathed her own brand of life into his fiction, had furnished it, like an empty house, to her own taste. Which had soon heavily inclined, where it had tended from the first, to the criminal. Crime too could be, was, ro*man*tic – not all crime, of course, some was just *gross*, they should line those guys up against a wall and . . .

'But it's a topsy-turvy world,' she said. 'Some of the worst crimes never get reported and maybe the worst crime of all is *not to be alive*. Sometimes in your life you just must cross a state line or two.' Astutely, she had played upon his being already halfway to crime by taking for himself a fake name. Already suggestible, she had made him more so, using her body to brainwash him. ('Lovers', she said, 'are *thieves*!'.) He would see how she had hooked him.

'The States,' she had said, 'every day we spend here is at the scene of a crime, the murder of a dream.' She had told him of her awful childhood – no wonder that she had a diffuse hatred

28

for the society of which, outwardly, her father had been a respectable, law-abiding member; no wonder that she liked to believe in a far-off romantic country where she might be redeemed as in a fairy tale.

He had been wrong, that first meeting with her. She wouldn't be his fairy goddaughter – it would be his task, rather, to fulfil *her* three wishes. And it had been nearly Christmas and she had wanted the *weirdest* presents, among them a false name of her own. He indulged her: Amanda Holiwell beame Amelia Brodie.

He would tell himself later that if he had really loved her he would have made her a gift of reality; but she had seemed to him like a child who had never owned anything and it had seemed more like love, then, to give her what she wanted.

Mary Louise, at first, put up resistance to their divorce; but at last she relented and in the summer of 1979, in Sacramento, James Blythe and Amanda Holiwell were married.

It was in November 1980, almost exactly three years after his first meeting with Amanda, that James met the Professor. He was from a university whose name James would not be able to remember at the time – just as, later, he would be unable to remember the Professor's name.

They met at a dinner in Washington, not a city which James knew well. That evening, though, it had lived up to its reputation as Sieve City, although what journalists liked to call a 'leak' was more like a seepage of information through the porous wall of people close to government.

He went to the dinner with no great expectations. Most of the twelve or so guests were known to one another, while his invitation rested upon his having known slightly during the war the husband of the hostess – as formidable a woman as he might have expected his old acquaintance to marry. They had not met up in the interim and over the gin-and-tonic quickly exhausted their limited stock of shared wartime reminiscences. So James was left to pick his own way among insider conservations effortlessly resumed from other dinner parties, rather like trying to catch the thread of an episode in a series whose earlier episodes you hadn't seen. Washington was like that. James, listening and already wondering how he might slip away early, at first paid little attention to the guest on his left, a short, square fellow in his early fifties. It wasn't until the beef Wellington that the man turned to him and introduced himself as a professor of economic science.

'Although tonight,' he added, 'I'm feeling a bit of a freshman.'

'Oh, why's that?' James asked.

'No special reason. Unaccountable high spirits.'

It seemed that he'd wielded some economic influence as far back as the Nixon administration and James casually assumed that he'd dusted himself down for the wine-and-dine circuit following Reagan's election, with an eye to wielding influence in the future. But a little later he told the table at large that he was now 'pretty well apolitical in any party sense'; he had, he said, no hopes of preferment under Reagan.

'None whatsoever,' he said cheerfully. 'I think republican economics have turned a little too, well, *violent* for my taste. I believe that as well as voodoo Haiti has some excellent primitivist painters, but I'm rather in the position of wanting to paint a *pointilliste* picture.'

That was a back-reference to a conversation about the 'voodoo economics' which would later gain respectability as Reaganomics. There was also learned stuff, which left James quite behind, about something called a 'Laffer curve'.

Nowhere in the world, perhaps, are economics discussed quite so passionately as in the United States and nowhere in the States more passionately than in Washington. But in Washington the key to the passion is power. Around the tables of influence, talk of tariffs from an ivory tower is inevitably of less interest than tariff-talk from someone who might actually effect changes. This was such a table and after his admission, James noticed, the Professor was subtly downgraded in status – a matter of nuance: his opinions weren't sought quite as eagerly, his unsought comments weren't attended to quite as intently.

It was with the awareness that the Professor was now nearer the outside, where he was too, that James turned to him and said, 'I wonder if you've read the Brandt Report?'

Yes, the Professor had read the recently published report, *North-South: A Programme for Survival*, named after the former Federal German Chancellor, Willy Brandt, who had chaired the commission which had produced it.

'What,' James wanted to know, 'do you make of it?'

The Professor was succinct. 'Like most well-meaning reformism,' he said, 'it's muddle-headed. In a world economic climate that's widely agreed to be unfavourable, it's actually asking for moral evolution in the business sphere. It's a challenge – but of course it won't be met. It isn't in big business's interests to meet it. Business – its division of labour, its dependence on differentials – is actually the biggest promulgator of the divisiveness which Brandt laments. The report talks of 'solidarity', for which we may read our old friend 'the brotherhood of Man'. With utopian circularity of argument, Brandt asks big business to show solidarity in the name of solidarity. That isn't an argument – it's a thinly disguised appeal to emotion. The Brandt Report will be discussed, the challenge will be there and businessmen will feel guiltier than before about the things they've always done. But they won't *stop* doing them.'

'I feel guiltier,' James said.

'Because of Brandt?'

'No. But Brandt has helped to crystallise the feeling.'

'A catalyst.'

'Yes,' James agreed, 'a catalyst.'

He told the Professor about a trip he'd made just before Christmas '77 – to the Colombian department of Choco, on the Pacific shoulder of South America. 'Hardly anyone goes to Choco, not even Colombians. I was with some aid workers in a helicopter and it was full of big, transparent plastic bags of footballs. Presents for children on the coast, where we were going. But on the way we landed by a river in a jungle slum. There was a shopfront which read *'Si Compra Oro y Platino'* – We buy gold and platinum. Yankee Stadium was built with gold which we mined from Choco. Inside the shop a man in a T-shirt advertising a hospital had a cigarette pack full of gold dust. He'd dived for it for months. He sold it for a song. Soon, another helicopter landed. Out jumped men with sacks and guns. The Bank of Colombia's weekly gold run. They bought all the gold the shop had, then flew off; and so, soon, did we – the jungle slum kids pleading for our footballs. *Regalos*, they said, *regalos*. Christmas presents. The Bank took their gold and we took their

31

*regalos.*' James looked at the Professor and said, 'I thought that was immoral.'

'Two worlds.' The Professor nodded, then said, 'You're sick of business. Yes?'

'I'm sick . . .' James hesitated. 'Of shabbiness dressed up as the natural way of the world. I don't believe it has to be.'

'You're an idealist.'

'I suppose. I'm certainly no economist.'

The Professor said, '*Homo mercator vix aut numquam potest Deo placare.*'

'I don't have Latin.'

'Who does?' said the Professor, then supplied: ' "A man who's a merchant won't ever please God," or stated another way, raise your moral standards and you lower the profit margin. Brandt tries hard, but he doesn't get round that one.'

'I doubt if he does,' James said, and then, 'I think it's me who's the freshman round here.'

The Professor laughed.

'I wouldn't worry. It's wall-to-wall monetarism now and if like me you think it's simplistic you don't *need* to be more than a freshman to understand it. But I'm biased.' The Professor swallowed the last of his wine, then reached for the bottle of Beaune. 'You too?'

'Please,' said James.

The Professor filled their glasses and said, 'The biggest weakness of Brandt, I think, is that he underestimates the power of the commodity countries. He's saying the industrial North has the commodity-producing South over a barrel – isn't that an odd image, by the way? Over a barrel. Well, in '73, the oil price hike, the South had the North over a barrel – of oil. Right? OK, that was an exception, but there's a lesson in it. If it isn't one world by mutual consent it's one by *force majeure*. Call it *mercator*'s projection. Merchant's projection. And what about drugs?'

'Drugs?' There was alarm in James's voice. 'How do drugs come into it?'

'How don't they?' The Professor smiled easily, confident of his case. 'The so-called controlled substances are completely out of control. I've been saying so since '72 and it's much worse now. Soon we'll be seeing an epidemic. But see it from the

32

viewpoint of Brandt's South. They're cash crops. Commodities all the more attractive to grow because they're illegal and so *can't* be controlled. Hemp for rope, yes. Hemp for dope, no. From one perspective the drug traffic is simply big business – the free market, southern style; and with drugs, the South even gets to process its own product on the spot – one of Brandt's main recommendations. But from another perspective, the drug traffic is trade terrorism, a kind of guerrilla war against the economic order. The beginnings of an international trade revolution, you could say – and why not? There've been IMF riots before – why not a riot *against* the IMF and the economic order as a whole? Why not? Implicit in the drug trade is the threat: reform or we'll ruin you. With drugs, the South is getting its own back. They're the revenge of the South. And the beauty of it is that the drug trade strictly obeys the rules of the free-market system while, at the same time, undermining the societies which practise the free market. It's an underground *danse macabre* matching step for step the dance on the floor – almost the perfect model of the free market in action. But a little too free for our collective liking, hmm? So we try and stamp it out, with the result that it responds just like any other commodity to the laws of supply and demand. The truth is, we *can't* stamp it out. The economic arguments, in the source countries, are simply too strong and economic arguments have a funny way of turning into political ones...'

As was illustrated by the example which the Professor then gave. The DEA, using as cut-out a Mexican firm of crop sprayers, had tried to kill off the dope growing in northern Belize. There'd been no prior consultation, neither with Belize nor the State Department, and all might have been well if the weedkilling overflight had been a flawless *fait accompli*. But it hadn't been: an old guy, nothing to do with dope, had been accidentally killed and his death had sparked off, in the Professor's words, 'a big political crisis in that little, unimportant country'. He underlined his point. 'Small potatoes, maybe, because it's a small country – but it is a country. And all because of one inept, high-handed attempt to stamp out drugs, what began as a localised response to the free market became first a big national political issue, then a small *inter*national one. The DEA has actually achieved something you'd have thought was impossible – linkage of dope-growing and democracy.'

In response to that linkage, the State Department – hopping mad with the DEA – had obtained Presidential approval for an 'independence concession', a guarantee by the US of non-interference for the immediate future in dope-growing in Belize. 'Down there,' said the Professor, 'dope's now halfway to being a recognised commodity, at least at source. Can you believe it? Grow weed for freedom! And if you're wondering about the weed the DEA *did* succeed in killing – it'll be sold and come here anyway, only with weedkiller all over it. So some crazy, hophead kids are going to be even crazier.'

James nodded.

'I understand,' he said. 'It's easy enough for a businessman. The economics of revenge...'

The meeting with the Professor was the decider. To James, it was as though his false identity had been lying dormant, awaiting its moment, as a seed or a disease might do. Now was the time to activate it, and to populate the empty room into which he had moved in a weak and undefended time of his life. Belize was a place where William Brandl could be himself and know himself, free of the distortions of the past.

So it was done. The thing was not thought through. It was, rather, as if the decision made itself, inevitably. Together, in a new place, they would live down the hurt and failure of the past. They would go to Belize. They would, in the Professor's words, 'grow weed for freedom' and in doing so assert the country's sovereignty, and their own. In February 1981, Amanda Blythe went on her own to Belize, for a quick research visit. Her report back to her husband was enthusiastic, even ecstatic: she was in love with the country, the people, she wanted nothing more than to be there. In March they travelled together to Mexico, to Valladolid, where they shed their old identities by depositing their passports at a bank. They decided, for greater cover, to cross the border separately, in separate hire-cars. Carrying only their driver's licences they entered Belize within hours of one another, filling in blue immigration cards en route. There was no other formality and although the Blue Card allowed an uninterrupted stay of only four months they knew that, in practice, there was no restriction. Belize wasn't a place of paper-work. It was a country whose Premier carried his papers of state in an old shoebox, having neither the mentality of a nation state nor sufficient people to man a large bureaucracy. The government machinery of Belmopan, the capital, was rudimentary; probably their Blue Cards would never be fed into it.

Both of them felt as they crossed the border the exhilaration of slipping through the bureaucratic net. It seemed to them that they had escaped and were breathing free air at last.

And now it was April, shortly before the rains, and James Blythe was driving his hired pick-up to the north of Belize, to keep a rendezvous. More than two hours from the coast, the only traffic had been a truck load of convicts being taken, pick and shovel, to mend the potholes which made driving in this country so slow and sometimes perilous a business. It was mid-day; shadows were concertina'd around the bases of the things casting them, untidily.

Just before the village of Crooked Tree, he saw the track he'd been told about. It sloped gently from the raised road, but the surface was rough; it was a delicate business driving the pick-up down to the bed of the lagoon. It was hardly a track at all; soon, with the rains, it would be unusable.

Leaving the lagoon for the bush, butterflies enveloped the moving pick-up, a tiered yellow cloud. He smiled and muttered, 'Geronimo!' The butterflies accompanied the pick-up for a while before all peeling off together back into the bush.

He turned off the track onto another which soon debouched, improbably, onto a metalled highway. It had been built ten years before, in anticipation of a promised sugar refinery. The promise had been shortlived: the highway was correspondingly short. It soon petered out, as he had been told it would, and he drove over the abrupt asphalt edge onto yet another potholed track. A hundred yards ahead, on either side, were a small gas station and a bar. He was on the way to Revenge Lagoon, a tiny community which hardly merited such amenities on its extreme outskirts. They, too, must have been built in anticipation of the refinery which had come to nothing.

He leant out to catch the name of the bar. The Downstairs Café: this was the place. He pulled onto the gas station forecourt;

there, on the far side, were the lean-tos. Under one of them was a taxi. That would be Peyrefitte. The lean-tos were thatched with *cohane* palm. A sign of good soil: the *cohane* was fickle where it grew. He parked his pick-up under the spare lean-to.

Yes, Peyrefitte: in the taxi's back windshield was the plastic Guadaloupe, hanging in mid-air prayer. He sat back; inhaled deeply, once. Ahead of him, across a yard, an old black man in a lime-green shirt was cutting grass. Remarkable, at this hour. He glanced at his watch: twenty-past. So old a man too. He must have heard the pick-up, but he had not missed a beat; his back was to him, the shirt dark with sweat.

He sat a little while, admiring the smooth flow of the machete-strokes, the grass falling in swathes. The old man was doing a young man's work; well, too. The rhythm of his cutting was of a piece with the glare, the ticking of the hot engine-block, the huge string section of grasshoppers audible through the rolled-down window.

James realised that this was his last chance to change his mind and pull back. If he didn't, now, the next few minutes would see the start of a sequence involving other people. Once under way, there couldn't be turning back; it was like that once you fostered out the child of your imagination.

He opened the door. He got out of the pick-up, shut its door and stood still for a moment in the glare. The peeling façade of the Downstairs Café gave nothing away. They were there, at least Peyrefitte was; they must have heard him arrive. But no one had come to the door. Perhaps they were giving him a last chance. Perhaps he should take it. The glare was intense, stronger than his shades.

Quietly to himself he said, 'Geronimo.'

It had all led up to this moment in the glare outside a Central American bar. Is this far enough, he asked himself, have I scared myself into self-knowledge now?

He began walking towards the Downstairs Café...


In Belize, so far, he was known simply as Bill, which was how Peyrefitte hailed him when he entered the Café.

Peyrefitte had been Amanda's recommendation as middleman. She'd found him on her research trip and, on his performance over the past fortnight, she'd chosen well. He was a real racial cocktail of a man – *mestizo*, but with some black in there as well, about thirty-two years of age. He always wore good shoes, a Citizen watch and a pair of reflecting Ray-Ban sunglasses. Sometimes his shirts were cheap, but then they were witty – one had a motif of barracudas chasing a running black man. Today, in honour of the seriousness of the occasion, he was wearing plain pale blue.

He wasn't *just* a smooth operator; there were quite a few of those. He had finesse. When he smiled, for example, which was often, it was never with that broad, knowing grin which, sooner or later, made you want to punch the guy's teeth in; there was a hesitant intelligence about his smile and when he greeted you it was always as though, in the interim, you might have decided you didn't like him after all. This made you like him more. Also, he was a good actor. When he used the name he *must* have known to be false, either to your face or to others present, he did so with confidence, conviction and subtlety – you and he might have been old friends, not just acquaintances of a fortnight.

To him, you were Bill and the name which might otherwise have been as dead as a fish on a slab became, in his handling, swimming, instinct with life; he made others, too, believe in Bill. Only once – but that might have been reproach, genuine or fake – had he pencilled light, oral quotation marks around it: when 'Bill' had pointed out that the reflecting Ray-Bans were for skiing and he'd protested, 'There ain't no snow around here! No Bill, the mirrors are so's the girls don't see my tears, when I just has to tell them goodbye!' And Bill, despite himself, had laughed.

The Downstairs Café was in cool half-darkness and full of cigarette smoke, but the Ray-Bans were still in place as Peyrefitte rose from the table and so was the middleman's smile. The other man, in half-profile to the door, turned slightly, pulling on a cigarette, cheeks hollowed, as if it were the very last cigarette from the last packet in the world. The smoke was of opium-den density, but without the sweetness, just stale, straight smoke.

Peyrefitte slid round the table towards him.

'Bill!'

They shook hands – Bill sneaking a glance at the other man; Peyrefitte, with his free arm, clasping him lightly round the shoulder in a half-*abrazo*.

'Good to see you, Peyrefitte.'

'So you made it, Bill! And how was the drive?'

'Good, good.'

He saw himself miniaturised in the reflecting lenses, two in an identical series.

'I want you to meet Pedro' – the *abrazo* became a crook, shepherding him towards the table – 'he's just about the best grower in Belize, Bill. You want to plant a coconut in Alaska? Pedro'll grow it for you!'

'Pedro, pleased to meet you.'

They shook hands. Pedro remained seated, but his mouth split open in a wide, natural grin, trickling smoke, a few toothless black gaps like cigarette burns.

'Mister Bill,' he said.

Peyrefitte laughed, lightly.

'Pedro, why so formal?' He stepped forward, his arm again on Bill's shoulder. 'Bill, come join us. Some tequila? Sit down. My, look at that ice!'

Tequila with ice was Peyrefitte's drink. On the table, by an untouched bottle of Gold Label and a saucer of salt and lemon slices, was a bowl of icemelt with a few pieces floating like old moons in their own watery light. As Bill sat, Peyrefitte reached for the bowl.

'No bar staff?' asked Bill.

'She got the day off, sick. Sick real bad. But she left the machine on' – he shot Bill a knowing glance – 'no snow, Bill, but lots of ice.'

'You should take up skating,' said Bill.

He looked at Pedro and they nodded at one another, smiling. Pedro took another long pull at his cigarette. Always, in the first instance, you sized up the other fellow from details of his behaviour and appearance. The precepts of Dale Carnegie still applied, even in the dope business. Pedro was another *mestizo*, predominantly Maya. He had the old-young appearance of the Amerindian, but was, Bill guessed, about fifty. He had the Maya nose which manages to be flat and hooked at once, and skin of

38

a coppery, burnished quality as though there were metal waiting to be mined just under the brown surface. Accidents of race apart, he looked rather like the painter Georges Braque as he had once seen him in a photograph: the same air of rocklike dignity. He was wearing an embroidered Honduran shirt, steam-pressed blue jeans of Mennonite cleanness and a pair of sandals; he had obviously made an effort and it looked as if a woman might have wet his black, straight hair and run a comb through it just before he left home.

The gestures of his hand and fingers, as he drew on the cigarette, were quite beautiful. The fingers were stubby, the hand square and, he knew from the handshake, very calloused: a peasant's hands. But their movements had a gardener's gentle eloquence. Growers had hands like that; they could break an egg over a frying pan as if it were the first time in the world anyone had done so.

Pedro smoked the Independence cigarette as if it were a joint. Then 'Mister Bill' remembered something and felt in his pocket for the wad of Job rolling-papers. Skins were hard to come by, away from the coast, and the weed-smoker's cough wasn't improved by having to inhale newspaper.

He tossed the pale yellow packets casually onto the table.

'Any use to you, Pedro?'

Something like alarm passed briefly over Pedro's face; he used his cigarette to point at the papers.

'Those for me?'

'Sure. You've got the good wine, Pedro. Have some good crystal to drink it from.'

Pedro had one of those impromptu smiles which pinned a medal on you; he reached for the papers.

'Very thoughtful of you, Mister Bill.'

'My compliments.'

Wine . . . He felt again in his pocket and brought out a small twist of paper, unscrewed it – Pedro watching him – and took two seeds between his fingertips.

'What do you make of these?'

He reached and put the seeds into Pedro's open palm. There was a complicity in the comparative delicacy of the operation, and for the first time he felt that he and Pedro had made some real contact.

39

He sat back as Pedro examined the seeds.

Wine ... Weed and wine ... the analogy seemed fair. Weed was the wine of Central America, smoking a natural strand in the rough weave of the peasant life. Something that grew, that was all; nothing evil or *risqué* about it. And to grow something well, you had to love it; the good gardener had the necessary insight, instinct, knowledge and care. He would have doubted the skill of a grower who didn't smoke – but he hadn't met one yet and didn't expect to.

Nor had he heard of a dealer who didn't – himself excepted. That was a different matter. The dealers weren't Central American peasants; weed wasn't their *vin de pays*. He didn't want to smoke, but he would have made it a rule not to if he had wanted. In the end, the dealer was a businessman, and in the end a businessman had to be tight and straight; nowhere more so than in the weed business. Most dealers were amateurs imbued with the sloppy-hippy dope ethic. They hung loose. But in business you sat tight. They believed in 'mind expanding'. But as your mind allegedly expanded, so the circles of secrecy widened beyond acceptable tolerances. The trick was to be straight without being stiff – stiffness put people off. You had to relax as he was beginning to do.

Peyrefitte reappeared from the bar area.

'You broke the ice?' he said. 'Have some more.' He placed the ice bowl on the table, sat down and seemed about to say something else; instead, he reached for the Gold Label and cracked the bottle's seal.

Pedro looked up from the seeds.

'What do I make of these? I make weed out of these.'

'Are they any good?'

'Mister Bill, your pockets are full of good things.'

'Will they grow?'

Pedro shrugged.

'Who knows?'

'They grew in Mexico last year.'

Pedro looked at the seeds in his palm.

'These from Mexico?'

'Ultimately Afghanistan.'

'Afghanistan!'

'Ultimately, but in the meantime – let me get this straight' he counted them off on his fingers – 'Holland, a home grower; Arizona, home grower; Mexico, a plantation; California; now here.'

'Man,' said Peyrefitte. 'Those seeds must have jet lag. Who's for a drink? You, Bill?'

'Pour me a shot.' He turned again to Pedro. 'They're young seeds, but you could say, Pedro, their great-great-great-grandparents were Afghani.'

'Got any more?'

He handed Pedro the paper twist.

The Afghani weed seeds were slightly longer than the Mexican ones Pedro was used to. Their colour was beige, with a speckling of chocolate, instead of the minute grey-and-brown stippling of the Mexican seeds.

Each seed – from the plant that it would produce – was worth in theory about three hundred and forty dollars, US; but more astonishing was the knowledge that something so small, dry and shiny could grow into the full plant of the season's height.

Pedro looked up.

'All I say, Mister Bill . . . if the grandmas of these babies grew in Mexico last year, no reason why they shouldn't *this* year in Belize. If they'll just take off from the ground, I'll fly them as high as they go!'

Peyrefitte laughed and raised his glass.

'Right on!'

'I'll take them away and try,' said Pedro. 'Who knows? They may be hibiscus.'

'They're all yours.'

Peyrefitte was happy. He turned to Bill.

'What did I tell you? Coconuts in Alaska.'

'Oh no,' said Pedro. 'Nature does the work and she's pick-and-choosey. I just helps her along.'

'I'll drink to that.'

He took his glass and squeezed a lemon slice into his tequila. Pedro put out his cigarette and placed a pinch of salt on his thumb joint.

'*Salud.*' He raised his glass. '*¡Salud y pesetas!*'

'*¡Salud!*'

The ice rang, as Peyrefitte raised his glass.

Why, in this heat, did Bill keep thinking in images of cold?

41

Was it simply the ice on the table? The memory of a long-distant skiing holiday in Aspen evoked by the Ray-Bans? Or was it the comparative coolness of the Downstairs Café? He met Pedro's stare and saw, or thought he saw, a fleck of iciness, which at once began to melt. Pedro looked away, leant and licked the salt from the back of his hand like summer snow.

'Something on your mind, Pedro?'

There was; you could tell from the tense, half-caste smile which the question elicited; from the deliberation of his movements as, gently, he shook another cigarette free from the pack, lit it, seemed about to speak, then inhaled instead. It was quite a performance, but at the end of it, the question still hung in the air between them.

Then he had an idea.

'Is it the weight?'

Pedro nodded. Now he looked like a small boy who has been caught out.

'That's it, the weight...'

Peyrefitte had been watching.

'Pedro!' – it was Pedro's turn for the *abrazo* – 'why don't you confide in me? Why do you bottle it up? Don't tell me. You want to grow ten tons, that right?'

Pedro's smile was still a little wan, but steady. Chuckling, Peyrefitte clapped him a couple of times on the shoulder, then reached for the Gold Label.

'I can grow it, Mister Bill,' Pedro was saying. 'Three pounds, a ton, all the same to me. But bananas, rice, sugar, you know, I think in tons, weed I think in pounds. Tons is United Fruit.'

'You grown for them, Pedro?'

Pedro nodded.

'All the big companies.'

'Then you'll know what they pay.'

'Sure. Rice, beans, sugar, citrus, whatever you throw at them – all they throw back is peanuts.' Pedro puffed at his cigarette.

'Ten cents US a pound of rice, isn't that so?'

'Uh-huh.'

'Well, Peyrefitte will have told you...'

Then he went into figures. Fifty dollars US per pound of weed, making the grower's commission a huge sum in this economy – about half of which Pedro could hope to keep for himself; the

42

rest to Pedro's team; everyone to be happy; all payments in cash, on the nail, a third to be paid out when the crop was ripe – 'Note that, Pedro, not when it's cut, when it's *ripe*! Call it my futures market.' And, in conclusion, 'You're getting five hundred times the price of rice, Pedro, *five hundred times*! An executive salary, you could say, because in my company there are no internal revenue services or pen-pushers to pay, no company reports or duplicating machines and the grower doesn't go to the wall.'

He hadn't let Peyrefitte, who'd refilled glasses as he talked, add any more to his own; now he raised it, but not to eye level.

'Worth drinking to, Pedro?'

Pedro said nothing at first; he fumbled in his jeans pocket.

'Those figures sound fine, Mister Bill,' and he brought out a crumpled, grimy scrap of paper. 'I've done some sums of my own, though, and you mayn't be talking United Fruit prices, but you're talking a lot of land.' He peered at the paper, as though short-sighted, then looked up. 'You want to see how many acres I make it?' He offered the paper. Bill took it and looked.

'That's about what I make it too.'

'Mister Bill,' Pedro pressed his point, or his attack, home, 'the weed by nature is anything but shy, but because of the law she just has to be. If she didn't worship the sun so much, you'd hide her away from the sky. This stuff's *illegal*, Mister Bill, but she's a show-off. That means you have to think small.'

Pedro paused.

'Tell me now, how you gonna hide an acreage like that?'

Meditatively, Bill turned his glass in his hand, nodding slowly – an understanding nod, he hoped: he did understand. In an aeroplane, in the sky, you could see so much that sometimes you felt like God; if you had destructive power with you, or authority behind you, you *were* a sort of god. And weed, from the air, was unmistakable. There was no way, not even by growing it alternately with sugar cane, to camouflage it properly.

But he thought of the independence concession. A direct line had led from that Washington dinner table to the Downstairs Café. Pedro the grower didn't know it, but there were to be no

43

flights like the one that had killed Manuel Zuniga. Bill wondered whether to tell him, but decided against. Not yet anyway. It wasn't the moment to give information like that.

He looked up from the café table and said, 'Take it from me, Pedro, there'll be no problem. Trust me and you'll see.' Pedro said nothing, but the obvious question – 'Why should I trust you?' – hung in the air with his cigarette smoke.

'Got a big family, Pedro?'

Pedro said warily, 'Depends.'

'On?'

'How far you go.'

'How far do *you* go?'

Pedro made a grimace, then brought his chin down in reluctant acknowledgement.

'Pretty big.'

'Well, Pedro' – he spoke slowly – 'that's how far I want to go – as far as your family. And that's how I'm thinking: pretty big.'

'What you mean, Mister Bill?'

'We've got to talk, Pedro. You'll see.'

Peyrefitte glanced at his watch.

'Time we got moving.'

They drank up. The two fingers of tequila Bill had already swallowed he had ticked off against imaginary accounts marked *Salud* and *Pesetas*. The remaining third, in an unspoken toast, he drank to *Amor* and thought of Amanda.

Bill always played these mental games, but the biggest game of all – the top table – was to pit one's sense of reality against the rest. Pedro knew Belize, but Belize was only the baize on which the game was played; the real game was in the mind and the sky was the limit.

He stood up.

'Let's go see some land.'

The heat, outside, hit him as suddenly as that from a big bonfire when the wind unexpectedly turns. Its haze, now, was just across the road and the two vehicles under the lean-tos shimmered in it.

They'd decided to go in the pick-up, but Pedro's machete and other things were in Peyrefitte's taxi. He waited while they burrowed in the back seat. The plastic Guadaloupe was still

44

praying, her robe twitched back to show the cerulean of the lining. Why did the depictions never show the red roses which had been her miracle?

The old man in the green shirt was still cutting grass. If everyone in this country worked as hard at straight agriculture as that old man, even at ten cents a pound they might not need to grow weed. The worst thing for them would be its legalisation, because then the big companies would go into it and weed would be ten cents as well...

'Why is he cutting now?'

The question – to Pedro – slipped out of him unpremeditated. He indicated the old man. Peyrefitte slammed the taxi door.

'Oh, that's Douglas.' Pedro didn't seem much interested.

'What's his hurry?'

'Snakes.'

Peyrefitte had joined them.

'A tommygoff bit his son.'

Tommygoff – the local name for the fer-de-lance. Bill turned to Peyrefitte.

'In that grass?'

'Hmm-hmm. Yesterday.'

'What happened? Was he all right?'

Peyrefitte said nothing.

'He died,' said Pedro.

# PART TWO

# PLANTING

IN THE TIME JUST BEFORE THE RAINS THE AIR IS heavy. There are days of dense cloud, banked from horizon to horizon, a bruised purple where it meets the earth rising to a leaden grey; then, the next day, one might wake up to a sky completely cloudless although no rain has fallen. It is a time of false promise, like the false spring of the temperate climes, an edgy, episodic time in which people, with the weather, must wait; a period of transition, like the hurricane season of September and October over which, uncertainly, the rainy season will become the dry. And like that later period, the weather of April and May in Central America is like a house where there's a big bust-up building. People are unusually irritable. Nothing much gets done. There is a sense of futility. It is knife-fight weather, in which small things are magnified out of all proportion. Later, they will seem as trivial as they really are, but by then it will be too late, they will have consumed the mind. It is also a time of planting, when tiny seeds are sown, later to grow tall.

In Hattieville, west of Belize City, it was one of those infuriating days in which the rainy season pretends to be the dry. Infuriating, because it was as though the weather were playing with one, arousing false hopes in people already brutalised by disappointment. The sun blazed down from a cloudless sky which might easily turn cloudy in a matter of hours and in Hattieville the sensible people who everywhere form the majority were hiding indoors. The place had the hunted, shutters-down look of a district which a loudspeaker van is visiting for an eve-of-election broadcast: cowering. Hattieville was usually so – it licked the unhealing wound of its existence. But never more so than at midday. It was then, the sun zeroing in like God's magnifying glass, that Hattieville was most abjectly aware of itself.

There was indeed a broadcast of sorts going on – not political, but as noisy. From the twin speakers of a large Taiwanese ghetto-blaster, Otis Redding was soul-urging all in earshot to 'Knock On Wood'. His lung power was great; the blaster's volume was high. The advisability of knocking on wood, the desirability, the duty, of doing so, was being heavily promoted from one end of Hattieville to the other.

There were two ends. Hattieville, between them, was two straggling strips of slum, perhaps a couple of hundred habitations all told. Between the strips was a stretch of the Western Highway, well named insofar as it was possible to travel due west on it; otherwise, it was the same old potholed laterite as always.

Hattieville was not a well-made place. The materials of its construction – peeling or unpainted clapboard, chicken wire, rusty corrugated iron – were not of the best. There were practical reasons for ignoring the Redding message. This was wood-wormy wood which, if knocked on, would very probably have crumbled to pieces; or the structure of which it was part would have collapsed. Energy was at a premium and Otis Redding seemed to be squandering it, like a standpipe left running in a drought-stricken village.

Hattieville was what its suffix implied it to be – a *bidonville,* but without the oil drums. The prefix pointed back to its origins – to 1961. In the Caribbean and Gulf of Mexico, hurricanes are named in alphabetical order as their season progresses. Hattie, that season's eighth, had been quite a lady. The breeze had been bad enough – at moments, more than two hundred miles an hour. It had blown the iron sheets from roofs, then embedded them, like throwing knives, in the trunks of trees; blown those trees, whole streetsful of telegraph poles, out of true. But worse had been the big muddy wave, after the wind. Some of those it flooded out – all of them blacks – had trailed down the Western Highway, refugees without so much as chickens and mattresses to their name. They had not gone towards anywhere so much as away, away from the coast; and far enough away, the middle of nowhere, they had stopped. Twenty years later, there they still were, on the savannah. The refugee camp had become a permanent fixture.

In 1965, Hattieville's first bar had opened. It was still there at the further end, slightly apart from the straggle, hard by the two tall coconut trees which lent the place the semblance of a little grace: a watering-hole, shaded by fronds. Topically for the time, the proprietor, Michael Pandy, had named his bar The North Vietnam, although the design – cutaway swing doors opening onto a low, shaded porch bounded by a wooden rail – was suggestive of Wild West rather than Far East. But the name was a way of identifying with world politics and old Pandy's protest at bussing in the Deep South; and a few months later the dialectic had been completed by the opening of another, identical bar, built by the same contractor, directly across the Western Highway and called, with corresponding Creole cuteness, The South Vietnam. The name apart, it mirrored the other exactly, right down to the large matronly lady – Ma Armstrong, Pandy's sister, at The North, Ma Smiling at The South – who dispensed the identical range of rums and local Belikin beer, who cooked and, in the Caribbean way, grumbled and generally ordered everyone about. One of the few discernible differences was that The South had a ceiling fan, while at The North – something else to grumble about and nag for – ventilation took the form of a palm frond which Ma Armstrong would, if you asked her nicely, wield in your face as you ate.

The North had, however – another difference – the novelty, fetching for some, that on its pool table the roles of the black and the white balls had been reversed. This had been the idea, again, of old Pandy, who was still, at the end of the Sixties, politically *au courant* enough to appreciate the nuances of Black Power. It was racist talk, he had claimed one drunken night: 'sinking the black', – it should be 'sinking the white', or 'the zac', a Maya word for 'white man' which the government wanted to popularise. And so, somehow, he'd contrived to get a big Number Eight white ball and, for the cue, a small black. This, for some players, was the highlight of pool at The North Vietnam; also, The South's table had an annoying nick in the green baize, just by the top left-hand pocket.

The clienteles, like the bars, differed only in insignificant details – like the check of the shirts which, taking up the Wild West motif, they often favoured, or the size of the hats (straw, not Stetson), which they wore. Otherwise, all were black males, of varying ages, belonging to the Anglican faith of which their

51

wives and sometimes, reluctantly, they themselves were prac-
tising members. Most men were on welfare, supplemented by
pimping, street-corner dope peddling, petty theft, mugging,
selling their blood and suchlike. Most of the youths were the
lifetime unemployed, known locally as 'base boys'. Talk of a
'black economy', in this context, was 'black' humour.

Windfalls were spent on drink and wisdomweed and, there
being no work to go to, both were consumed without reference
to the relative positions of sun and yardarm. The passing of
time was not a subject upon which the typical Hattievillean
cared to dwell; nor did he feel obliged to justify his rejection of
it in favour of an amorphous oblivion. But, if called upon to
do so, he might have invoked the Maya – those people the
government made so much fuss about, but who, as it seemed
from the standpoint of Hattieville, were mugs who worked their
asses off all day for the privilege of wearing shoes cut from
worn car tyres. Incredibly, those people had once built temples,
immense stone structures which, in their municipal grandeur,
made the new capital of Belmopan look like just another one-
horse Hattieville. But what had happened to their temples? The
jungle had pulled them back down. And why? Because as well
as growths in nature that couldn't abide great chunks of stone
as out of place as giant meteorites from outer space, there were
growths in the mind, the *mind*, that couldn't abide the edifice
of civilisation itself. And well before the baroque stones had
fallen down, the tendrils of over-particularised time – with its
calendars, stelae, sacrificial charts, days of eclipse when you
screwed your granddaughter, days of eclipse when you didn't –
had crept over the Mayan mind like a jungle; a jungle of time.
Those people should have kept things simple, but they didn't,
because they were hung up on time – and why? – because they
were hung up on *work*. Time and work; work and time. What
a life! And where had it got them? After thousands of years of
time, of work, there they were, in their rubber shoes.

Well he, the typical Hattievillean, was not about to make the
same mistake. *He* knew why the government went on about the
Maya. They wanted everyone to work for nothing. It was a con-
trick. Time, to him, had about as much ceremony as a shanty
hut and he was going to keep it so. Time, to him, was only
really acceptable in grand sweeps of years, decades, centuries if

possible, millennia if you were talking about the Maya, units of time as big as mahogany trees; anything smaller and you were chopping your way through thickets of months, days, hours, minutes, a mental jungle, eventually seconds – which were like the filigree bones you spat out when eating fish, so vexing precisely because they were hair-fine and almost invisible.

Watches weren't worn in Hattieville. But its impatience with time stopped well short of seconds. North of the border, up Mexico way, it would soon be the hour of *siesta*, the hours of the *paseo* and *tamales* to come. To tell such time hardly required an atomic clock, but here in Hattieville people sidestepped even those rudimentary Hispanic divisions of the day. Heretically, they implied an articulated conceptual shape to time – a structure somewhat more grand than a shanty. Articulation presupposed a direction, a purpose, even – worst of all – a *meaning*. Hattieville had none, and saw no reason to remind itself continually of the fact. The sun was enough: there was no shortage of that. Later, true, there would be shadows; but nothing so precise as the sundial shadow of a yardarm. Then – the relief! – right, the triumph of shadow and the best time of all: because there was nothing to nag you with the knowledge of time's passage, nothing, until you passed out and woke to the sun again, blazing away up there as always like the final shoot-out in *High Noon*.

The time for violence, however, was not noon but night. Especially dangerous were nights of full moon, when some measure of violence was a virtual certainty. It might be no more than a punch-up; but then there were those nights when rum ran, like a bore, down the racing river of one's blood; when the tide of life with no outlet was so high that banks just had to burst, one's own or others; nights when your woman had left you, you'd lost all your money, or were, simply, suicidal or murderous with rum.

On most nights you felt like that you were, by the laws of probability, in a minority of the clienteles of the two Vietnams. But on others a lot of the men, most, all of them, would be feeling exactly the same. Those were the nights when the big trouble began and traditionally you didn't make trouble in your own Vietnam: so, you made trouble with the *other* one. Those nights, the strip of highway would become as sensitive as a disputed international border. The usual Creole verbal vehemence – like the hot sauce of Creole cookery, poured over very average and often *rechauffé* conversational fare to make it more palatable – would turn from piquant to poisonous; the show-off sheet lightning of Creole behaviour, the harmless lightning which will strike no one, would turn into forked. The violence would brood for a while, like the lull before the hurricane, then, on some or other pretext, it would erupt. On several occasions, there had been fights with machetes; limbs and eyes had been lost, but no lives as yet. There was still scope for escalation of the intermittent Vietnamese conflict, but already one might have imagined that the two bars bore the deep war wounds of their eponymous republics; the names were less cute, now that they had been taken so literally, for so long.

Seeing the clienteles earlier in the day, an outsider would have been astonished to learn of the violent energy of which these men were capable. Some, by the mid-afternoon, would still be standing upright, much in the manner that Hattieville's houses still were, drunkenly leaning together; but most, by then, had been reduced to a despairing sprawl composed of various attitudes suggesting sleep, sun-stunned oblivion, terminal laid-backness. Towards the end of the day, the two porches might have been the dead-laden decks of ships that had just fought a close and bitter engagement; but then, the fun of the evening in the offing, the bodies would miraculously come back to life.

At the moment, however, as already observed, the sun was in an extremely midday-like sort of position in the sky; and that midday, unusually, there was one watch in Hattieville.

A tall, slim man in his mid-thirties, sitting out on the porch of The North Vietnam, wore one round the right wrist, because he was a southpaw, had sometimes to punch people and didn't want the watch to get hurt. In his youth he had been a boxer, butterfly and bee; standing, he still carried himself like one – lightly, loosely. His nose had once been straight; then, one boxing match, an unlucky punch had Romanised it. But you could still guess from the shape and the narrow nostrils that the black skin belied white blood somewhere in his ancestry. To some of Hattieville's more extreme citizens, it was a sort of original sin in him – that suspected rogue strain of white blood in his veins: a suspicion which his surname, White, compounded into certainty in the simplest minds. 'Officer class', they would sneer, borrowing the description some of the older blacks used of him. 'And who was the officer?' But they wouldn't sneer to his face; in the last resort, even they had respect.

Reuben White may have worn a watch; that may have been only one of many respects in which he differed from the typical product of Hattieville. He may have moved to the coast, a few years before, to be near the boat-hire business he had built up; may have been, alone on both porches, sober, unstoned, sitting upright, straight-backed in a chair, carefully groomed. But, as a child, he had been one of the original bunch of refugees to trail down the Western Highway; and, over the time since he'd moved, he'd often visited, not just because, as now, his father was sick, but for no special reason. Reuben had made something of himself and had got out; but he hadn't turned his back. He acknowledged the people of Hattieville as his own; they him, in turn, as one of them.

His Japanese alarm-chronograph chose that moment to sound off – a piercing *peep, peep, peep* like the squeal of a minuscule jungle creature in an electronically tripped microtrap. Hurriedly, Reuben silenced it.

But not before noting the digits: 12:26.

And thinking: Roll on the evening.

And not before someone had called 'Tinamou!'

People laughed. Reuben looked up, sharply. The laughter was good humoured; so, as a rule, was he; on this occasion, though, he glared about him. Whose voice was that?

'... W-O-O-O-D, B-A-Y-bee!'

He turned. At the back of The North 'Nam's porch a gangling youth was sprawled, wearing the wide-boy-watermelon-slice smile that you slap on, like make-up, when you're chewing gum. Winston: an after-Hattie baby. Reuben knew all about him, where he'd got the dollars to buy the blaster he was cradling, why he was smiling like that. A smile which started to fade as soon as he made the miscalculation of meeting Reuben's eyes with his own.

Tinamou.

'Winston, mek you shut the racket, eh?'

Reuben was indicating the ghetto-blaster; his voice had a silky muscularity.

Winston's jaw dropped. He began, weakly, to protest:

55

'But Reuben, man ...'

'I tell you: shut the racket.'

'OK; OK ...' Placatory, palms towards Reuben; then, like the smart-arse Winston was, he turned down the volume.

'Shut it!'

'Whassa matter? You don' like music?' But Winston was whining now. He switched off, then, with an aggrieved look at Reuben, stood, quit the porch and set off down the street, blaster slung under one arm.

Reuben wondered why Winston was playing soul, not reggae as usual. Down the street, the boy aimed a half-hearted kick at a stray dog snuffling in a pile of rotting vegetable matter. The dog slunk away under a shed, or it may have been a house, silently.

Otis Redding out of the way, the familiar aural backdrop reasserted itself. From the surrounding savannah, the bush beyond, the quantal stridulation of grasshoppers, crickets, God knew what, provided the backing track; against it, closer to, chickens, flies, the occasional dog, improvised clucking, buzzing and barking solos.

It is enough, thought Reuben, to drive a man mad.

Up the trunk of one of the coconut trees an iguana was climbing – slowly, intermittently, with a hunched shoulder-shuffle.

Into those trees, a fortnight or so ago, a tinamou bird had flown. A dingy brown visitant from the bush, it had perched among the fronds, the green coconuts, unusually high, preening its long feathers.

In the ordinary way of things, there is no reason to kill a tinamou. It does not peck out the eyes of animals or children; no superstitions attach to it; its flesh is not good to eat. Hattieville, not a beautiful place, might have been expected to welcome an adornment.

But the tinamou has another characteristic, unique among all the birds of the jungle, but abhorrent to Hattieville. Because of it, the species, by no means a common one, was one bird the rarer within the day.

The next morning, Reuben had called on one of his visits and found the stiff brown body under the coconut trees. He hadn't known it was a tinamou, only that, in life, it must have been

56

beautiful and then – picking it up and noticing the peppering of buckshot – that ugliness had killed it.

His people.

But sadness had swiftly been crowded out by anger. His people? No, neither his, nor anyone's, least of all their own. And, the shame of it, his father dying – no, he suppressed the thought – his father ill in this terrible dark place of the soul.

'Who done this?' he'd shouted, holding the body in his hand. 'Who done this?'; turning, from the middle of the highway, to each Vietnam in turn. But no reply had come from the porches, so Reuben had shouted some more and, this time, had really 'knocked Creole'.

'In-de-pen-dence?' – articulating each syllable – 'wha' mek we think we get *in-de-pen-dence*? You know what we is? We's *slaves*, that's *all* we is! See?' – holding up the body of the bird – ''dis was the key to we slave-shackle, bright lil' hope a future – an' wha' we do? Don' taak 'bout no in-de-pen-dence. We ak lek de Guat-e-maylans, de Guate-maylans cu' get we, kill we all! Hear me?' And so on; the most Creole that Reuben had knocked for years, a real tirade; and all the while, preparing lunch in The North Vietnam, Ma Armstrong had clucked and shaken her head, in agreement, as always, with Reuben.

Then, a little later, she had said to him: 'It was the call.'

'The call?'

Ma Armstrong had explained. The bird, she said, had whistled, with a *peep, peep, peep,* a high-pitched monotone like that of Reuben's watch.

'So?'

It hadn't been the call itself, all birds call, it had been the urgency and, above all, the regular frequency of this particular call. Ma Armstrong had outlined, without knowing the species, a peculiar feature of the tinamou – that it emits a series of whistles every half hour. Not accurately to the minute, of course, but always an average of two evenly spaced calls an hour.

The tinamou: the time-bird.

Then Reuben had understood how, from the moment of its arrival in Hattieville, the bird had been suicidally sounding its own knell. Chronometrically calling for a mate, it had been counting down the hours to its death. He understood, but didn't forgive; rather, the knowledge enhanced the beauty that had

57

died, the depth of the darkness that had killed it.

Some drunk, maddened by the bird's chronological call, had gone and shot it. But who?

'Blackjack,' Ma Armstrong said crisply.

Blackjack.

A good, accurate nickname, like a key word in a poem, can hit a number of marks at once. Blackjack's was accurate. For one thing, his skin was blacker than most in Belize, notably so – a crude-oil blackness with, when the rumsweat was on it, an aubergine oilslick shine. He might have been a Carib, to look at, but his African origins went back to another tribe and not via St Vincent. By his own account, he was a Jamaican and, since he certainly wasn't a Belizean, most people, subscribing to the Caribbean belief that Jamaican skins are blacker, were prepared to believe him. But the truth was that no one was *really* sure where he came from, or what his real name might be. And Blackjack wasn't telling; often he would talk of himself in the third person, revelling in the nickname's piratical ring, flying it like the Jolly Roger.

Also by his own account, he was a trained electrician, but no one had ever known him fix a fuse or mend a connection, or for that matter do anything which might be considered useful. He drank a lot of rum and played a lot of pool, financing the one with his winnings from the other; he was a good player – the star of The South Vietnam. As to his main source of finance – for Blackjack never seemed to be out of money – no one enquired, but it was assumed to come from the minor crime which had paid for Winston's blaster and which paid for so much else in Hattieville. But no one could be sure of that either. Nor could they be sure he was *really* on the run, as was also generally assumed. But it seemed likely, the indications pointed that way, and why else should he, six years before, actually have *chosen* to live in Hattieville?

All sorts of people on the run, from all over the world, fetch up on the Mosquito Coast; people whose previous lives have died out and left them stranded in private hells, hoping for a second or third or last chance, a way out, a way back, through purgatory to paradise, putting behind them a past which might be as small as a bad marriage or as big as history. Usually, within a few years, the present has soured into another past worth running from; but by then, there is nowhere to go, they are on the Mosquito Coast, in their last afterlife, rehearsing their pasts with themselves or one another, or wondering about the pasts of those dark horses whose hellfire flickers in secret and who have kept their lives impervious to gossip.

When people wondered what the dark horse called Blackjack might be on the run from, the speculation, sooner or later, would turn on one question: had Blackjack committed murder? There was little to go on – legally there was nothing – and the little there was was ambiguous; but still the question was asked.

Murder.

The story was Ma Smiling's, and hers alone, so the credence you gave it tended to hinge on your opinion of her. It had been late night in The South Vietnam, less than a year after Blackjack's arrival, and he was the only customer. Unusual, only one, but it did sometimes happen, and it was very late. He'd been drinking all day – rum, the dark and the white; he'd asked for another and she'd refused. Time to go home, she'd said. Home: he'd picked up on that.

'I don't go home,' he'd sneered, and a sly expression had come over his face; then something more dangerous than slyness, it gave her a cold feeling, deadly cold. He'd stood up. 'I *sends* people home, an' soon I'll send you. Now, will you pour my rum?' Still she'd refused and he'd said, 'Do I have to kill for it?' and this, she'd seen, was something more than drunkenness, more like the dangerous delusions of the alcoholic.

'You taak-in' stupid and you taak-in' ugly,' she'd said. 'Now go to bed.' Then Blackjack had stared at her, a stare, she said, she would never forget: 'There was mudder in it, I swear. You don' see look like that and live a tell tale, because it's a look which say "You dead."'

At this point in the story people began to wonder if Ma Smiling mightn't be exaggerating, but the next bit won them back. Blackjack, all of a sudden, had broken off the stare and hurled his empty glass across the bar; just missing her, it had smashed into the wall. Now she was quaking with fear, rooted to the spot. The broken glass seemed to sweep away some impediment in Blackjack – the dam, perhaps, he'd been drinking all day to break. He started pacing about the bar, babbling the while, snatches of sentences, incoherent, slurred, muttered words; it would have been comical, if he hadn't threatened her, hadn't smashed the glass and if the babble weren't ... Yes, she realised, he was acting something out, brokenly telling some sort of story, there was a violent wildness now to his stare which said that he was seeing something, like an oracle, but not in the future, the past, something which had *happened* ... Now he was creeping up behind someone. A knife, was that? Or a gun? A blunt object of some kind, leaden, wooden ... a blackjack? And what was that stain on the floor? Rum, or blood? That broken vessel – a glass, or a skull? What was he doing, seeing?

Well, not even murder is beyond the forgiving indifference of the Mosquito Coast; the easy-going Creole tolerance could extend even to a runaway killer. And so it might have been with Blackjack. Ma Smiling would not forget the killing look, but no one else had seen it and she hadn't been killed or hurt; Blackjack played ace pool and had never again made trouble in his own Vietnam. So it *had* been with Blackjack. When people recalled the story of that night, Ma Smiling's story, it was distantly. How could it be otherwise? They hadn't been present. No one had, except old Ma ...

In Reuben, however, her story had found an attentive listener. Ever since Blackjack's arrival in Hattieville – 'Hi, I's Blackjack to you! Lady, pour de boys a drink' – he'd been watching the man and quickly he'd come to the conclusion that Blackjack was bad news. A bigshot with no substance, a bigmouth who liked to boast that he had no visible means of support – 'Call me the scarlet flycatcher. I feeds on the wing!' – a man like that was the last person Hattieville needed. But that wasn't all ... He'd seen how Blackjack had set himself up an admiring court of the weakest, most impressionable men in town, cronies who'd laugh at his jokes in return for a drink, yes-men awed by the greater power of Blackjack's personality, the pilot fish around the shark. No doubt about it – Blackjack had strength, a sort of magnetism; or perhaps, better, the strength of a whirlpool's vortex, a hurricane's eye, nothing but powerful air, emptiness.

Why was it, when Blackjack was by, that he felt it was night? And why did his own certainty of insight falter in Blackjack's presence, like a sensitive piece of electronic equipment near a hidden magnet? Why was he not sure whether he was seeing things, or imagining them, half perceptions, half creations

60

mental centaurs, shapes and movements seen by night? Was he jealous of Blackjack, or was jealousy one of the negative impulses which Blackjack delicately spun into being around him?

*That*, in the end, was what he felt: that Blackjack was, in some indefinable but real way, an evil influence and that in him the negativity of Hattieville had been embodied; almost as though, thought Reuben, nature had fashioned him expressly to prove the false proposition that the colour of a man's skin is that of his soul. He had watched him, especially, with some of the younger ones – Winston and his kind: nothing you could put your finger on, a subtly goading or challenging word here, a superior smile there, but always, somehow, the angels' faces ended up dirtier. A troublemaker in the strict sense: an engineer of darkness, with others to do the dirty work. So often, when you traced Hattieville's troubles back to their source, it would be like tracing a web and there at the centre was Blackjack, the fly guy.

But ... never anything you could put your finger on and for that reason Reuben had mistrusted his mistrust of the man. There were even moments when Blackjack was glinting with jollity, or showing off his barbed but at times undeniably funny wit, when he felt he was doing him an injustice and had to remind himself *this man beats up his women*. But that ground, too, was treacherous, because Blackjack wasn't alone in that, the women seemed to like him and to stay with him, all the same, while he, Reuben, had no woman at all of his own, not one, had had none since Sibyl left. And hadn't Sibyl, too, felt herself attracted to Blackjack? Hadn't she told Reuben so? Hadn't Blackjack, in that and in many ways, put his, Reuben's, broken nose out of joint? Wasn't he, in a word, competition?

He questioned his dislike and questioned it again, but always, afterwards, it was as strong as ever. And hearing Blackjack's laughter, he would think of the surface light which makes the sea seem friendly; but below that surface, he would remind himself, there was depth, darkness, ultimately cold. Men drowned in that darkness, others were saved from drowning, but Blackjack seemed somehow to live in it, thrive on it – a big fish somehow marooned in the small pond of Hattieville. Where was he from and where did he get his money? Who the hell was he?

And then the night at The South Vietnam. Reuben could not rid himself of the feeling that in hurling the glass Blackjack had broken something more – the deep cover of an inner darkness. When would he break it again? For five years he had waited, watched, like a boxer waiting for his opponent's guard to fall, circling, sparring, seeking the knockout moment when Blackjack would reveal himself in public unquestionably to be the person he, Reuben, felt him to be. But for five years, nothing. Blackjack had danced out of reach, his guard up, his ready laughter in place like a gumshield. And how? Because he had nothing to hide, it was all in Reuben's imagination? Or because he had, and so was equally wary, light on his feet, knowing that Reuben was watching? Reuben wasn't sure. Most of the time he believed the latter and then he felt for Blackjack something of the grudging admiration one boxer feels for another's skill. How clever the man was, how hidden, how quick! In a shantytown, such secrecy!

The two clienteles also saw the latent conflict in terms of a boxing match, but more simplistically, Reuben in the red corner for The North Vietnam, Blackjack in the blue for The South. And, sportingly, they took sides, self-appointed seconds for the two men.

A few, more detached, saw the situation more subtly. If it *was* a boxing match, they wondered, wasn't it, really, Clay versus Ali? Weren't Blackjack and Reuben, really, one and the same man, or aspects of the same? In this view it was as though, in some new physics of the emotions, Reuben who had stepped back from what Hattieville was and Blackjack who had gone one step further, were the extremes which curved like light and met, negative and positive prints of one another. It was even a little ridiculous: as though, in a country so little populated, there were not room enough for the both of them, the serious light and the laughing dark!

Blackjack.

Of course. Who else?

For five years Reuben had waited, but Blackjack's guard had not fallen.

Until the tinamou.

Blackjack had shot it, so Blackjack had a gun, or the use of one.

62

As soon as Ma Armstrong told him, Reuben resolved to visit The South Vietnam. Blackjack was there, with some cronies, playing cards, expansive, laughing, relaxed, just on the point of laying down a card. Reuben stood in the doorway, waiting only a moment before Blackjack – how quick the man was! – sensing his presence, turned to him.

'Mr White!' Modulating his smile just a fraction, he paused. 'To what do we owe the pleasure?'

Now the room was silent, Ma Smiling – perhaps remembering the night five years before – silent behind the bar.

Reuben's voice was cold.

'Did you kill that bird?'

'Bird? Bird?' Blackjack, disingenuously, scratched his skull. 'Oh yeah! Quite a speech you gave out there, quite a triumph of ora–tory.'

'Answer my question.'

'Hold on, now,' – Blackjack's voice was soft, a playful pat with a practice glove – 'since when *you* tell Blackjack what to do?' He glanced round the table. 'Who to play?'

'Whose gun did you use?'

Blackjack smiled, looked at the cards in his hand.

'Mine.'

'Got a licence for it?'

Blackjack looked up.

'That's a policeman's question.' He smiled. 'You ain't a policeman, are you now, Mr White?'

Reuben went into the attack.

'So you know my name, but if you've a licence there's gotta be more than "Blackjack" written there and if you haven't got a licence I'm going to see to it, personal, that you don't have a gun.'

Blackjack's look of discomfiture lasted only a moment.

'Sure I've a licence! It entitles me! I can kill crows that eat up yo' corn, or birds that eat up your sleep. Pests.'

One of the cronies chipped in:

'That's right, we couldn't sleep!'

'None of us,' said someone else.

'That goddam bird was chiming like a public clock!'

Reuben had kept his concentration on Blackjack, who then said, slowly, capping his cronies:

63

'Yeah, man, that bird was crowding us, just like you crowds me. We couldn't breathe for that bird.' He laid down a card – the ace of clubs – then scooped up those on the table: 'My trick!'

Reuben said, coldly and simply:

'Who are you, Blackjack?' he leant forward. 'I mean, who are you *really*?'

Blackjack rolled with the punch – as Reuben had meant it to be.

'Me, man?' he said easily. 'My real name's Popeye, I yam what I yam, that's all.'

Dutiful if subdued laughter from the cronies, all but one – a kid called Sam.

'I tell you what, Reuben, here's a real problem. The country's full of birds. Always find another. But what about our ball?'

'That's right!' said another. 'What about the ball?'

The ball?

In retrospect, Reuben would later decide, this was the moment when he realised that Hattieville couldn't be saved. Nowhere was irredeemable, not even Hattieville; but this was when he saw that he had been underestimating the problem. So deep did it go that the redemptive powers of sainthood were required. Reuben did not see himself as a saint. That was why he had moved to the coast. He would sacrifice, up to a point, his time, his energy, but not himself.

With the move to the coast had come a new perspective, deepened, soon afterwards, by the onset of his father's illness. The natural bonds with Hattieville were breaking of their own accord; such bonds as would remain depended on his will power and on seeing some return for the willed investment of time and energy. The will had been there, so he had thought. But then he had seen the bird's body under the tree. The senselessness of it had overwhelmed him – a muddy wave of despair. Holding the bird in his hand, he'd been astonished by the bitterness of his reaction. Then he had felt the remaining strings of affection fraying – Hattieville becoming an utter stranger. And if the place was a stranger, the quarrel with Blackjack, a quarrel he saw himself waging on Hattieville's behalf, for his people's future, lost all point. And, it seemed, there *was* no point. Even Ma Armstrong – what had she said? – had mentioned the bird's call

64

in a spirit which suggested that Blackjack's action was entirely understandable. Blackjack had acted on Hattieville's behalf, and he and Hattieville understood and deserved one another. Well, so be it. In his denunciation, he had exhausted himself.

There was little energy left and little resistance, and all of it, he sensed, was about to be sapped by the story of the ball – a story whose dangerous absurdity he could feel even before he heard it. He had paused, minutely, then repeated: 'The ball?'

Blackjack had stayed silent, smiling; the others had spoken in a rush, spilling out the story. Such as it was, Reuben had pieced it together.

The South Vietnam's black pool ball was missing, stolen, the talk was, by one of The North 'Nam's customers. For a week, the table had been out of commission – the pool addicts were at the end of their tether. No wonder, with all the tension, that Blackjack had shot the tinamou. What could be done? Because of the two distinct clienteles, the history of conflict between them, it was out of the question that the pool players of The South should simply use The North's table. But if The South remained unblackballed for much longer there was no telling the outcome. Who was the thief? Who was he?

His father's illness, the tinamou and now ... the crowning futility, the missing ball. As a rule, when there was an inter-Vietnamese grudge brewing, he would engage in a little shuttle diplomacy, Henry Kissinger style (topical references in the Caribbean, gleaned from old back copies of *Time* magazine, are often years out of date).

No diplomacy this time: feeling empty, free at last, he had turned to Blackjack.

'Where you send the ball, man? To Jamaica?'

Blackjack had stood up, angry at last.

'If you tink I ...'

But he too seemed to have felt the sudden lack of fight in Reuben.

'Jamaica, Blackjack? Where they gun the birds from the trees?'

Then the sly expression had come over Blackjack's face. 'Not only birds, man, not only birds ...'

Reuben had stared hard at Blackjack, had seemed about to reply, then abruptly broken off the stare and walked to the door. His next action was later to puzzle Reuben himself. In the

65

doorway he had stopped, turned. Five years of patient observation of Blackjack, careful calculation, analysis and thought,
lay behind his next remark; yet he made it almost as an afterthought, on a whim and, moreover, at the exact moment when
he had given up caring – or thought he had.

'One day, Blackjack,' he had said, 'One day I'm going to get
you.'

Then he had left.

Had he meant what he said? It didn't seem so. He had meant
to go to the police, bawl them out for giving Blackjack a gun
licence, ask to see the paper and the name on it, question
Blackjack's right to have shot the tinamou. Oh, he'd meant to
do all sorts of things! But he hadn't done one.

A fortnight since Blackjack had shot the tinamou, a few weeks
more since the ball had gone missing. Sitting on the porch of
The North Vietnam, Reuben could sense how the tension had
mounted. The stare from under the hatbrims over the highway
was never very friendly. Now there was a touch of venom to it.
The black was missing and it was no use The North's protesting
its innocence, The South would not rest until it had its black
back.

To Reuben, the wave of violent envy was almost palpable
when, suddenly, The North Vietnam's small black ball hit the
pack and the sound carried across the highway. The crowd on
the opposite porch was like a cloud in which an electric charge
was building – the forked sort of lightning which must, sooner
or later, be earthed. War was in the air.

War ...

Reuben remembered that the British had once fought a war
over the loss of a man's ear, Jenkins he'd been called. Was a
pool-ball war any stupider than an ear war? Let them fight it.
He had his father to worry about, his business to build up, Sibyl
to keep in contact with. Let Hattieville have its war, if that was
what it took – severed limbs, a death, several deaths even – to
knock some sanity and sobriety into those thick heads. These
were no longer his people.

There was his father, but after that ... There and then, on the
porch of The North Vietnam, Reuben resolved to pull up such
roots as had taken in Hattieville. It owed its existence to uproot-
ing – well, true to form, he would uproot too: himself. He would

become a typical Hattievillean at last – by saying to himself, to hell with Hattieville. You did not try to build among the shattered wreckage, people and place, of a hurricane twenty years ago.

The evening rolled on. At six o'clock it was almost time for Reuben to go to Belize City, and the Bayman Hotel, for his meeting with the man who, on the telephone, had called himself simply Bill. Probably he wanted to hire a boat. If so, the meeting shouldn't last long and afterwards he would be able to see Abba. Anyway, it was good to have a legitimate reason to get out of Hattieville for the evening and the oppressive atmosphere of his father's house of sickness.

He washed, shaved and changed in readiness for the meeting with Bill and let himself out of his father's house. The tree-frogs had already taken over from the grasshoppers on the evening shift of the savannah scat-song. The sun was still just in the sky, but cooler, and most of the warmth was from below; the earth like a newly baked brick. The air was so still that the flimsiest of flags would not have fluttered in it.

In the faint hope of a breeze the swing panels of The North Vietnam's door had been propped back with chairs. The doorway formed a frame through which Reuben, sitting down in the empty bar, could see the tableau of bombed-out humanity on the porch across the highway. His father had lain as still as that in his sick-bed, so weak that he had barely been able, that afternoon, to lift a cup of water to his lips.

Ma Armstrong ducked briefly out of her kitchen.

'How is he, sweet juice?'

'He's bad, Ma.'

'Bad?'

'Bad, bad.'

In her kitchen, over a sudden squall of frying, Ma Armstrong made a clucking sound.

'Ai, ai, ai!'

'You know, Ma,' – Reuben clenched his fist – 'what this country needs most? It's medicine, Ma, medicine.'

'And the doctor?'

67

'Dr Abb? He comes. But without the medicine, what can he do, Ma?' He pictured his father again, the husk of wasted flesh, the bones coming into their own. 'It's like a snakebite, but where is the serum?'

'Ai!'

Ma muttered something – she was getting old – and waddled out with a tray.

'Stewed chicken. You like?'

'Fine, Ma.'

She took a bottle of Belikin from the icebox and uncapped it.

'Tonight I tek he one plate a dinner. Say seven?'

'Fine, Ma. But he doesn't eat much.'

Reuben helped himself to a forkful of chicken and picked up his beer. A fly intercepted, occupying the airspace exactly between the bottle's mouth and his own. He stopped, stared at the fly: it was hovering like a hummingbird, actually hovering! He moved the bottle closer; the fly flew closer. To one side: the fly followed. Reuben swore. This was precision flying. Had the fly perhaps been watching the Harrier jets down at Airport Camp? He waved it away and drank.

> There was a little fly
> He flew into the store
> He do it on the ceiling
> He do it on the floor

A calypso his mother had sung, lullaby-like. From early childhood he had known that calypso, but now it was reggae, reggae all the way. He hummed:

> He do it on the bacon
> He do it on the ham
> He do it on the head
> Of the little grocery man

Wait!

So still was The South Vietnam's human tableau that the slightest stirring showed, like a sign of life in a body one had thought to be a corpse, and Reuben had seen, not one, but several stirrings. To the unpractised eye, they would have been almost imperceptible; to him they were as apparent as a freshly

fallen leaf to a tracker. Then, remarkably, one of the prone
bodies first sat up, then stood up! On The North 'Nam's porch,
too, there was movement. What was it, the first shot in the war
of the black ball?

Then someone shouted:

'A car!'

A car.

Reuben returned to his stewed chicken, asking himself, dis-
gustedly, what kind of country it was where an item of traffic
on a so-called highway, a solitary item, could be considered a
noteworthy event? He knew the answer: it was the country
which hadn't the medicine to save his father's life.

A car. Two or three times a day, on average, this would
happen. First, the intermittent whine – Reuben could hear it
now – the car still hidden round the jungle curve towards the
coast. Then the hurried bets on its colour and make; there were
even established odds and men who acted as bookmakers.

The car gave a long blast on its horn and, as always on the
curve, the engine noise appeared to deepen. Quite a few drinkers
got up to stand at the rails of the Vietnams; money was changing hands; windows opened and people looked out, waiting; children appeared, poor man's gold, Hattieville's future blown like
sudden dust into the doorways; then the car must have rounded
the curve because, from both porches, a hoot of derisive laughter
went up, and a man in the field of Reuben's vision slapped his
thighs and yelled:

'Man, will you get a load of *that*!'

The reaction was strong, unusually so, and Reuben, too, was
interested enough now to go to The North 'Nam's doorway. It
took only a glance to understand; on this one, the bookies would
make a killing. In the heat, the car seemed to tremble, wobble
slightly as though out of control. Was it an optical illusion? No:
but why, then, was it pink? A Thunderbird, Reuben guessed.
Thoughtfully, he chewed his mouthful of chicken.

The car drew closer, a big saloon, lines cheekily raked, chrom-
ium flash catching the sun, a wheeled pink palace of Caucasian
ostentation.

On the porch of The South someone was capering, brandishing a rum bottle.

'How much white ass you got to kiss to get so much dollar?'

69

he shouted, and manically laughed.

But then the car was upon them, horn sounding, an apparition in the late afternoon. Children and chickens scattered as it swept through Hattieville, raising a high plume of the red laterite dust, driver and passengers staring stonily forward like important people in a motorcade. The man shouted:

'Belize done bruk up bigger circus than *that* one, boy!'

The saying was an old one, a jaunty formulation of futility, popular in Hattieville. It took a sort of perverse pride in the Belizean inertia which made a nonsense of enterprise, although when you thought about it there was nothing particularly enterprising about a circus; nor, to anyone's knowledge, had a circus ever visited the country – you don't start a zoo in a jungle. The sort of circus that *did* visit Belize was, for example, the oil camp down south, with its air-conditioned trailers, its generators trailing wire and its tall derricks like scaffolding with the Big Top yet to be canopied over them. In five years of drilling, they'd found a jamjar of oil. A circus. Belize, Blackjack and his kind, would break it up. The pink car, Reuben wondered, was that from the oil camp?

In the wake of the car's triumphal progress, a dog strayed into the no-man's-land between the Vietnams. The car was gone, its only evidence the slow cloud of settling dust; the show was over, the tableaux back in place on their porches, the children back inside.

Reuben sat to finish his meal. Was a pink car any flashier, he wondered, than his own Honda trail bike? On it, when he was away from the roads and the danger of potholes, he could hit a hundred in seconds. A lot of people thought that flashy, too.

'YOU BETTA KNOCK' – BANG BANG BANG – 'ON – W-O-O-O-D!'

Reuben stiffened. Covertly, over a forkful of chicken, he looked across the highway. There, on the porch of The South, grinning broadly, was Winston, ghetto blaster cradled in his arms.

> The little grocery man
> Get out a Gatling Gun
> He swear that he will get the fly
> Before the day is done,
> Before he can count
> From one to ten

70

The little fly he do it
On the grocery man again.


Fat Al was driving the pink car, Pym was in the passenger seat, Pudney was in the back having problems with the plastic wrapper of a six-pack.

'Hey,' he said as he wrestled, 'crazy niggers, what's with them guys? They ain't seen a T-bird before?' Pym said:

'They haven't seen a *pink* T-bird.' Pym's eyes were pale; his skin looked like he should be ginger but he wasn't. From his face and general demeanour you could guess he'd been making brutal decisions a long while. His lips were thin and in formal company he could sometimes manage a smile – but with Pudney he was as near himself as could be and wore the diluted scowl which was his relaxed expression.

'Still seems kinda excessive,' said Pudney, and broke the wrapper. It wasn't that he knew Pym – no one knew Pym – but he knew how far he could go and that Pym even liked him to go that far. Pym and Pudney had been in some bad places together and Pudney knew that without him Pym could lose contact and be repatriated to Mars or wherever. The dynamic of their relationship – Pudney had actually said that once to Pym, 'the dynamic of our relationship' – was the never settled question of who-was-the-tougher, quiet, steely Pym or noisy, brassy Pudney. Even Pym had once quietly admitted that he and Pudney were 'a good double act'.

No answer.

Pudney said, 'Who's for a beer?' and pulled the tab on a Lite. He passed it to Pym, who said with a hint of a whine in his voice, 'I don't want your gassy piss.' Pudney smiled. Pym didn't like things with too much fizz about them. For him the jet of spontaneity was an enemy aircraft to be shot down in flames.

'Not you,' Pudney said. 'Pass it to Al.'

Pym took the Lite as if it were a snake or laboratory specimen and Fat Al disengaged his left arm from its elbow-out-the-window driving position. It was a mystery to Pudney. Fat Al saw a lot of sun but the one bit of him that went brown was his left forearm. Pym at least went red and then he looked as angry as Pudney knew him to be. But Fat Al, never; he was like pizza dough that never got fired but for that crust of left forearm. Pudney noticed these details and got fun out of them. It was all part of the chemistry of being on the road.

Fat Al took a deep, satisfied slug of his Lite and said, 'Hey, ain't those bars something?'

Pudney said, 'Which bars?' and popped the tab on another Lite.

'Back there.' Fat Al's greasy black forelock fell over his fat-man's eyes as he shook his head in the general direction of Hattieville.

'The Vietnams,' said Pym without turning round.

'What's that?' Pudney gave Pym an alarmed glance, then said again to Fat Al, 'Which bars?'

'It's weird, man,' Fat Al said. 'Two bars back there, middle of fuckin' nowhere, and one side's The South Vietnam the other's The North. Can you beat it?'

'I didn't see names,' said Pudney.

'There aren't any,' said Pym. 'You know their names or you don't.'

'And you know, huh?' Pym said nothing. Pudney hunkered down awhile in the back seat with his beer, then said, 'It can't be right. Can't be right to call bars by the names of the 'Nams.'

'It isn't right,' Pym said.

'Still,' said Fat Al. 'I'd like to visit. You know?'

'Man, that's niggertown,' said Pudney.

They drove maybe a mile in silence, until Fat Al suddenly said, 'Other day, I go to this Lebanese joint to get new spark plugs, see? I'm there and there's this round red thing in a showcase, leather it looks like, red and shiny but with cracked veins like a wino's nose. And there's stuffing coming through the stitching. I ask the Leb, "What is it?" He says, "A cricket ball." What's that now? What's a cricket ball?'

Pym was looking straight ahead.

Pudney said, 'You being funny?'

'No,' said Fat Al.

'It's a game.'

'Yeah?'

'Cricket's a game the British play.'

'Well,' Fat Al drawled, 'that ball was *dead*, man. No one's

72

ever gonna play "cricket" with it.'

Pudney chuckled and said, 'Yeah, it's round and rolly and cracked like you, Al, and no one's gonna play with you tonight either. Want another beer, boy?'

In his cubbyhole at the Bayman Hotel in Belize City, Abba was shining a shoe when he heard Reuben's motorbike roar. He looked quickly into the foyer, then jammed the tinlid picture of a flightless bird back onto the polish. He jumped from his stool and burst into the foyer, making the guttural noises that were queer and scary until you got to know Abba. The white man in the too-white suit turned, frowning, from his talk with Maria at reception. The Bayman's foyer was full of light and reflection. The giftshop lady was shutting up, importantly rattling her bunch of keys.

Out on the forecourt, the motorbike had stopped, Reuben still in the saddle. It gave one last very loud roar like awful animal pain, puttered briefly, then died. It was dark. Tree-frogs croaked. The smell of jasmine was lovely after the toe-cheese shoes, the stuffy cubbyhole air. Reuben's back was to Abba. The spotlight by the old Spanish anchor cast grotesque shadows which looked like a masque of murder being committed – Reuben, kicking down the rests, pulling the bike up to park it.

Abba dragged himself fast as he could over the forecourt. Dark or day, spotlight or sun, no shadow could out-grotesque him – Abba, body broken forward from pelvis, from waist sidewise, head lolling useless to shoulder, arms and hands in limp, stick-insect position. Abba, mongol mute, shoeshine man. But the discerning saw too a disconcerting beauty, purified from the purgatory of his body; no one more joyful than Abba.

Near enough, now, to grunt.

'Mnyeh! Mnyeh!'

Reuben, seeing him, called cheerily:

'Hey, Abba! How's the world treating you?' He swung from the saddle; then Abba was beside him, one hand plucking his sleeve, the other gesticulating. 'What's the problem?' Now Reuben was intent, genially puzzling Abba's meaning. Abba waved, jabbed his hand at the hotel, threw back his head, mouth

73

open, gargling the words that wouldn't come. Reuben gave up. 'All right, Abba.' He made a move to the Bayman. 'Let's go see...' But Abba held on; he grunted, grinning. What did he want? Then, Abba had an idea. Reuben could see it, clear as a cartoon thought-bubble, an idea lighting in Abba's mind. Abba picked, roughly, a Rose of Sharon, took Reuben's hand – it was a single Sharon, pale pink, drained white by the spotlight. Abba, excited, gibbered; he closed Reuben's hand round the rose. He looked at Reuben, appealing, as if to say 'See?' But Reuben didn't see. Abba opened Reuben's hand, closed his own over the rose squashed between; strongly shook Reuben's hand.

'See?' said his look. 'See?'

Then Reuben threw back his head in delighted laughter, spontaneously, the dumbshow understood. Of course! Oh, what a poet was Abba!

'Beautiful,' he said through laughter. 'Pink and black. You got it Abba! A white man's waiting to meet me ...' But no; Reuben was about to throw away the rose and Abba wouldn't let him; Reuben stepped towards the hotel, but Abba's grip said 'Stay.' What now? Gently, Reuben said, 'He's waiting, Abba. Mustn't keep the white man waiting. Hmm?'

Reuben's mind, as he entered the foyer, was on the meeting with the man; how long would he, the Bill man, want a boat for? Would he want Reuben with him? What would he pay? He was concentrating on the next significant instalment of the present, not the familiar furniture of the foyer – the reception girl, Maria, her ponytail, the peachy fabric of her dress, nicely setting off the gold breath of her skin. His mind wasn't even on the unfamiliar white man wearing white, talking to Maria a little too emphatically; people were always passing through; Belize itself was a sort of foyer.

'Sorry,' Maria was saying, in a bored, buffing-the-nails sort of voice. 'Sorry Mr Palmer, but I can't help you.'

A couple of seconds more, Reuben would have been in the cheapskates' bar, out of earshot; but hearing Maria, he stopped, double-take dead, turning slowly to face the reception. What was that?

'Please!' The white suit man flattened his palm on the desk. 'There are rooms upstairs. Why am I on the ground?'

Maria said, 'You're checked in there.'

'Move me.'

'Ask the manager.'

'He isn't *here*!'

Maria shrugged.

'Ask in the morning.'

The man gave an exaggerated sigh.

'By then I'll be mosquito meat.'

'Sorry, Mr Palmer.'

Palmer: but the same name didn't mean the same family. Not after all this time. Or did it? Belize was small. The Englishman was evidently new – the unburnt skin, the clean suit, the room at the Bayman. Was he as new as he seemed, though? The name suggested not. And, if he wasn't . . . ? Reuben was confused. He was, he realised, shaking; his legs felt watery, like being on land after sea. He must sit; and so he did, staring at the reception, sinking into a foyer sofa conveniently nearby.

Palmer: could he be a son, *the* son? (He was about Reuben's own age and Reuben seemed to remember a son.)

'My dear,' the stranger told Maria, 'you aren't half as sorry as I am.' He left, Reuben watching closely. Yes, the face might be the same – but if, and then . . .? He would ask, make sure.

There was something else. The father or – slow now, slow – the other Mr Palmer had taken the witness stand just as this one had stood at, *taken*, the reception desk. He'd also worn white, he'd stood straight; he too had been high-hand haughty with servants. Reuben had not forgotten that pose, chin raised, as though born to the bar; this one had stood the same. It might not have been Maria, not her at all, the man was . . . *instructing* just now: but more than twenty years ago, his mother in the dock, her flowered dress, her Sunday hat of black raffia, devout servant diminished by her shame, before God, for stealing, and before the Englishman, being caught . . .

And what had she stolen? The shaking was worse. The past hurt like a powder burn. Reuben shut his eyes, covered them with his fists. But his seeing was inward, a memory: policemen, crowbars prising up the floorboards, his mother crying uncontrollably . . . He shook his head, hard, as though memory could be dislodged like water from the ears. Useless, he knew. The bad past, in bouts like these, had to be lived with till purged . . .

He feared madness in these moments. Hadn't his mother . . .?

But who, he reasoned, wouldn't, having seen her like that at the asylum window, shaking her fist through the bars, shouting, cursing, not knowing him, her son? (And the boys, not knowing who *she* was, had laughed and kicked the ball along the fore-shore . . .)

Who in their senses would thieve – not jewels or gold, shoes or silks – but *roses*? The policeman had pulled them from their hiding place under the floor, dead red, white and orange, the Palmers' roses shipped out at great expense. Their maid his mother had kidnapped and killed . . . What? Reuben still wondered. More than roses. Something symbolic, surely. England, perhaps, or their wished-for corner of it; or her servitude to them. It hadn't come out at the trial. Something, finally, locked up with her in the asylum. A very colonial crime – perhaps.

Reuben lowered his fists, eyes open. Abba was there – at the door, quite still, looking at him. And what was his face saying? It was Abba's foot-of-the-cross face, Abba was sorry for Reuben, Abba *knew*. Then Reuben saw what the dumbshow had really meant. For a moment, he marvelled, oh, what a poet was Abba! – then slowly opened his hand . . .

It held a dead rose.


'You want to *what*?' said Reuben.

'Save Hattieville,' said Bill. But he laughed. 'No, that sounds too grand. "Do something to help it save itself" would be better.'

'And I thought you wanted to hire a boat!'

Reuben tossed the butt of his Colonial cigarette into the sea; the water boiled briefly with catfish thinking it was food. They were on the harbour wharf, among coiled cables, the smell of oil, planed planks of Santa Maria ready for export. For the meeting with Reuben, Bill had reserved a table in the Bayman's restaurant, but Reuben had said, 'That jumped-up joint with the Silvikrin sauces! Save your money,' and suggested the foreshore instead, then the wharf. It was a strange setting for a business conversation. Bill was tired and would have preferred somewhere more conventional. There was a fresh breeze off the sea and far out a big ship was anchored, silhouetted against the dark. The lighthouse on Fort George punctuated the night with periodic flashes.

Reuben glanced at Bill and said, 'How do I come into this?' His tone was frankly suspicious.

'You come into it,' said Bill, 'because you're well known to care about Hattieville and you're the only guy in the whole place who seems to have got his act together.'

'I got it together,' said Reuben, 'by getting out.'

'They'll listen to you.'

'I'm not sure I've anything to tell them.' Reuben paused. 'How much money is this foundation of yours, the, er . . .?'

'Grant Foundation.'

'How much money is it thinking of laying down?'

'That depends. Come up with a relevant, workable, cost-effective project, we'll consider it.'

'And you want me to be your consultant, right?'

'That's the idea.'

'It's too late,' Reuben said bluntly.

'Too late for what?'

'Too late for Hattieville, too late for me.'

'What do you mean by that?'

Reuben walked to the edge of the wharf.

'You've come pretty well prepared,' he said. 'But there's a lot you don't know. Me, for example. Do you know that I once worked here?'

'At the wharf? No.'

'Yeah.' Reuben laughed briefly. 'On that donkey engine there, stripped to the waist like a black man in a "B" movie. I was young, it was fun, good training for a boxer too. I come here sometimes when the day's been shaky, look at the sea . . . I'm grateful to the sea. She got me out of Hattieville.'

'What about the people still stuck there?'

'It isn't so much a place,' said Reuben, 'as a state of mind. This now, this wharf, is a place. You said it seemed shady, right? *On the Waterfront,* all that. But to me there aren't shady places, there are shady people. It's people make places shady.'

Reuben climbed onto the base of the donkey engine, sat in its bucket seat. 'You missing the well-lit streets of the north?' he said, and flicked a switch on the engine's controls. From an overhead gantry light blazed onto the wharf. Its glare leaked

77

into the estuary, highlighting the rusty, dinosaur-like dredger – the 'sandpiper' Reuben had called it – festooned with pipes. Bill asked himself what Reuben was playing at, what all this was leading to. Certainly tonight he didn't seem the stable, reliable figure Amanda had assured him he was. As though reading his mind and wishing to set it at rest, Reuben chose that moment to say, 'Don't worry, I'm only playing. We used these lights for night-time unloading, see? It's night-time, it's light, let's unload. Tell me this. Why should a respectable American citizen come waving a cheque book and wanting to spend money on a hellhole he hasn't even seen?'

Bill said, 'Okay. First of all, it's not my money but the foundation's. I spend other people's money for them. *I'm* a consultant who wants to consult you. The adviser wants advice. Is Hattieville the wrong place to spend it?'

'What makes you think it's the *right* place?'

'Because,' said Bill, 'it sounds so goddamn awful. Even philanthropists aren't averse to seeing a little dramatic return on their money. In Hattieville it sounds like any little change for the better would be dramatic.'

'There's worse slums,' said Reuben. 'Worse in Central America and maybe even Belize.'

'In Belize? That's not my information.'

'That's another thing,' said Reuben. 'Where do you get your information?'

'Visitors, government officials, asking around. It isn't difficult.'

'You mean blabbermouths,' said Reuben.

'It's a democracy. That's another reason we've chosen to back projects here. Most Central American citizens are too terrified to be blabbermouths, but not in Belize. This country could be a conveniently close model of democracy, teach all those hornets' nests with their blue and white flags how to be beehives. You've heard the one about the dog who crossed the border for a bark? Well, maybe blabbermouth Belize could open the sealed lips of Central America a little. The people are so silent and suffering, their music's so mournful. A little *costeño* calypso could liven things up no end.'

'That's a nice speech,' Reuben said after a while, 'but is it true?'

'It could be,' said Bill. 'In the foundations they call it "high ground". Imagine you're on a wide, sea-level plain and you're looking into the distance at high ground. The aim is to cross the plain and climb that high ground.'

'Oh yeah?' Reuben turned in the bucket seat. He shook another Colonial free of its pack and lit it. 'Well, we don't have many foundations round here, let alone high ground. I don't have to imagine I'm standing at sea level and looking into the distance – I am. But all I see is a whole lot more sea level and a whole lot of sky – with just a little bit of pie in it and a pig with wings, and a fowl with teeth that's trying to avoid the pig and eat the pie. We've got a saying here, sir, "When fowl got teeth," and another one, "Belize done bruk up bigger circus than this." You're talking American-pie idealism and that's wine that don't travel.' He drew on his Colonial.

Bill passed a hand over his eyes. The light hurt them and he felt very tired. The light from the gantry suggested a giant interrogation in which the suspect was the whole country or perhaps just himself.

'So,' he said at last, 'you don't give a damn.'

'Your US dollars travel,' said Reuben. 'You US dreams don't.'

That reminded Bill of something his father – the fervent Anglophile – had been fond of saying: 'The British, my boy, *dream in reality*. That's the British Empire, a dream made material, a spirit with a body; when the British go only the ghost will be left. But they start with the dream while we start with materialism and Marshall Plans, and try as hard as you may you can't endow them with spirit.' It was odd, on the wharf, to picture and hear his father so clearly.

'I'm an American,' he said. 'I dream in dollars.'

'So does Disney,' said Reuben easily. 'But in the end that's just celluloid. Look, it's good that you want to help, sure' – but Reuben sounded far from sure. 'In the end though,' he said more strongly, 'you're no different from the guy who comes here smelling a big oil strike or amazed at all the empty land. Real estate: but it isn't real. They stand on the silver sand beaches and imagine old folks' homes or holiday complexes. That's *their* "high ground", and for a while they fly there on a mix of idealism and greed. "Untouched Belize", the tourist brochures call it, but that's double-edged. The visitors see nothing: they imagine everything. They think they've found paradise and they just can't wait to turn paradise into paydirt. But Belize can't be touched like that and soon they're back to earth with a bump. This is sea-level country: it doesn't do to dream.'

'You sound bitter.'

'Bitter? No. But sure your informants told you the truth – except the date-stamp on their information has expired. I used to want to help, but I gave it up. Idealism's like ice: it don't keep in the warm. Mine melted. You got to be a blue-eyed, glacier-faced northerner to keep on dreaming of a better world. Mix dreams and money you go mad. Like Bogart. *Treasure of the Sierra Madre*. Remember what the old prospector tells him? "If I don't hit paydirt here I'll go down to British Honduras." That's you – dreaming of spiritual paydirt. But no, this country's empty of gold and full of Clark Gables: no one gives a damn. And pretty soon if you've any sense you won't give a damn either . . .'

Bill said, 'I'll quote you back at yourself: "That's a nice speech, but is it true?" And shouldn't we turn those lights out?' The wharf raised above the water bathed in light felt like the stage of an open-air theatre; as though they should not be talking but acting – but across the estuary the Southern Foreshore was empty of audience and dark except for a few veranda lights.

Reuben laughed briefly.

'Not till we've finished unloading,' he said. Then he told Bill about Hattieville, Blackjack, the tinamou, the problem of The South Vietnam's lost Number Eight ball: 'Do you understand the *mentality* of these people?' Bill nodded: he felt that he did. Reuben said, 'You talk like money was a tide comes in and washes the Man Friday's footstep of history from the sand. But it isn't so. History stamps itself not in sand but like a die in metal. The coin of colonialism's two faces are still the same, master and slave. It'll be centuries before those images are erased and there'll be new ones in their place by then. This isn't something you can buy off or make better by the medicine of money.'

'But what if . . .?' Bill began.

'What if what?'

'Money were sometimes medicine.'

'Yeah? Tell me about it.'

80

'It's crazy,' Bill said. 'The world's crazy. Half of it's sick or starving in spirit, half or more is sick and starving in the flesh. Each world is the other's sickness – but also the other's possibility of cure. In a hospital in El Salvador a few years back I saw a boy with a Ryle's tube in his nose and a huge scar in his side where peritonitis had rotted his guts away. His name was Buenaventura, Oscar Buenaventura, and he was just old enough to know that for him the good adventure had scarcely begun but was already over. It was in his eyes. But money could have saved that boy – and saved me too: from the despair of having to accept that my moneyed world was meaningless because it had not used its means to save him. Oscar Buenaventura ...' He stopped. It seemed all of a sudden strange in this place to be talking in this vein. Produce from the rich North arrived at this wharf, but he was trying to import an idea and in this climate ideas were more perishable than ice. 'I'm a man of means,' he suddenly said. 'What if I saved your father?'

Reuben said nothing at first, just inhaled on his cigarette and stared. The dusk was gathering now. At last he said softly, 'So, you know about him too.' Bill nodded.

'It's nothing magical. Just information. And there's nothing magical about the means that could save him – just medical technology paid for with money. The magic is elsewhere.'

'Can it be done?'

'Dr Abb thinks so.'

'You've spoken to him?'

'I took that liberty. He didn't break any oaths.'

'Mister,' said Reuben – and now his voice had a hard edge, as if he suspected a trap baited with hope – 'for a stranger you sure talk a lot about salvation. What you want to do? Pay the national debt?'

'No. Just my own. But damn, yes, I am talking about salvation – not of the soul, unless I mean my own and a bit of America's, but a life, a life or two, your father's, Hattieville's, life. I want ... to inoculate myself against the meaningless. There. The US has done enough harm down here – let my foundation do a little good.'

'You talk like good and evil were commodities that could be traded here on this wharf.'

'I'm not trading,' said Bill. 'I want to give and I want to take.

Give what I've lots of, take some of what you've got.'

'Hattieville?' Reuben laughed – openly now. 'I'm sorry for anyone who goes to Hattieville trying to find a meaning, man. But then, you haven't been there.'

A little later, Reuben switched out the lights. In the dark on the way back to the Bayman he was quiet; as well – thought Bill – he might be. At one point on the foreshore he said, 'You really think my father can live?'

Bill said yes, then, 'You quoted some local lore about hen's teeth, but haven't you another proverb? "One-one okra full basket"? You reach high ground one okra at a time, my friend, but miracles like hen's teeth happen all at once. Help me to the high ground. I'm asking you to join me.'

Outside the Bayman they shook hands and said goodbye. Bill was turning to go when he took Reuben's arm and said, 'Oh, I almost forgot. Give this a good home, would you?' His hand was in his jacket pocket. He put something round and hard into Reuben's hand. Reuben gave a low whistle.

It was a black pool ball.

'Man,' said Reuben, 'I've got to admire your homework.'

'Home,' said Bill, 'has nothing to do with it.'


It was the following day. Alan Palmer, the Englishman whom Reuben had correctly recognised in the foyer of the Bayman hotel, had just crossed the swing bridge over the Belize River when he saw her. She was walking down Queen Street, holding a parasol in one hand, a white ice in the other. From the nearby police station the odour of impounded Colombian marijuana mixed with those of open sewers, rotting fish and other produce in the market, the yellow craboo berries in the street vendors' trays smelling like English silage.

Amid the great gouts of local colour, the eddies and swirls of activity like a tropical Topolski, she was cool and perfectly turned out in a red silk skirt and a T-shirt top blazoned with a macaw whose tail was below her belt-line.

She was licking her ice when Alan saw a guy step from the crowd and stop right in front of her. His eyes were futureless, full of nothing. She stopped, frightened that God had turned

82

over a stone and let this hop-headed insect crawl out.

'Hiya baby!' he hollered. 'You like corn-cream?'

She stammered, smiling, 'No, this is prickly pear.' Alan noted that her accent was American.

'You like ice, baby? Like to lick ice? Do ya lick black cock like you suck white cock like you lick and suck that ice?'

She blushed then, her poise rocked, then recovered and smiled slightly as at a risqué cocktail party joke.

'Thank you, I prefer prickly pear.'

She sidestepped, but so did he, licking lasciviously and gesturing towards his flies which, Alan thought, were probably well named.

'My pear's prickly, baby, lick my prickly pear. No? Me you then, your squashed tomato in my hot chocolate lips, lick you girl, lick you . . .'

It was mean-street time, and Alan stepped forward in his shining white Airey and Wheeler suit. He went to the girl's side and said, 'Go on, leave this to me.' She looked him full in the face, frankly, her pageboy black hair framing her face and, for a moment, it flashed through Alan's mind that the crazy might have a point.

Alan turned to the man, hoping he wasn't carrying a knife.

'Are you looking for a licking? Because it's hot today and I don't think you should accost women and that's the police station just over there.' He spoke loudly so that a knot of people gathered. Alan thought, They can't *all* be crazy.

'Shit,' the man spat out through piano teeth in a fluent stream like chewjuice. 'Go fuck yourself, white ass.' He cackled crazily. 'Just 'cause you want the bitch.' Some honest citizens demurred at this.

Alan said, 'Mistah Kurtz he alive and kicking,' and he Uncle Tommed the crazy, who Eldridge Cleavered him, and after a while it died down. When Alan turned round she had gone.

A week later he saw her again. He was on the club veranda overlooking the Barracks Road, cradling a cold scotch and hearing the ice cubes chime. It was early evening, the moon applying cold cream to the day's sunburn. It lit up the sea, the

83

scrubby mangrove, like the floor of a huge disco where no one would dance tonight. The sound system was faulty, full of bugs, the tweeter and chirrup of tree-frogs, woofer and howlaround of dogs, barking at the moon.

It was her walk which he recognised first, a jauntiness he had noticed the first time, a touch perhaps of false confidence. He marvelled that she was out alone at night, walking the Barracks Road as if it were the Promenade des Anglais, the Côte d'Or and not the Mosquito Coast. It wasn't, he thought, the walk of someone who really belonged.

He stood so that she would see him. He called to her. She stopped and asked, 'Who is it?' and her tone of voice suggested that if there was danger tonight then he might be it.

'Me,' he said, and thought, How foolish, the vanity of the voice wanting to be recognised, hollow in the night as though in an empty theatre. 'The other afternoon, you remember? By the bridge?'

'Oh, that fool!' She laughed. 'Him, I mean. Thanks for your help.'

'Are you coming up?'

'Not now.' She paused minutely, then said, 'I've got to hurry.'

'Are you safe out there?'

'I doubt it.' She laughed again. 'But there's a moon.'

And that was all. She went on. Alan wondered what could possibly be hurrying her – in this place haste was almost ridiculous. He thought of her moment of hesitation and clutched for a straw of significance. Was something worrying her? What had fetched her up here, so young, on the Coast? He feared for her in the night, potential prey in a zoo without bars, muggers and rapists, knives, stings, fangs. Was she simply unaware of the dangers, or did she have their measure?

He thought: I wish to protect her.


It was later on the veranda. Alan's scotch was icemelt. A car's engine died in the yard below, its fanned headlights folded. It was night again. A car door slammed, footsteps crunched on gravel, there was stumbling up the stairs.

A man appeared at the stairhead, stood swaying there, looking at Alan. He grinned, held out his hand and lurched unsteadily forward. Alan didn't know him. He'd never seen him before in his life. He got up hastily. The man's eyes were deep hollows in his thin face – he stared with a pock-marked, poleaxed lack of expression. Alan knew that this wasn't just drink, and that somehow this man could be both cracked and very cunning. His teeth were discoloured, uneven – his bleak grin was unsettling. He still held out his hand.

'Alan Palmer,' he said with a slurred drawl. 'Well, well, I heard you were back in Belize.'

This was the past. Alan realised that he must think again. From the games room came a frantic twitter of poker chips, sudden loud laughter.

Alan took the stranger's hand and said, 'You came just now in the car.' After twenty-five years out of the country he was playing for time, hoping that memory would pull from the wreckage the image of a child he once knew. But that kind of time couldn't be played for and sure enough the stranger's grip loosened, his grin faded, his face fell as though a plug had been pulled.

He said 'You don't remember.' His tone was hurt, accusing.

'I'm sorry, but ...' said Alan, and stopped there. The precarious grin stole back on to the stranger's face. 'It's been so long,' said Alan. 'No, I don't remember.'

The stranger said quietly, 'Then I'll remind you.' It sounded like a threat and Alan said so, only to be brushed aside with 'Know something? If I try real hard I can even remember my own name. Now ...' He snapped his fingers. 'Got it! Mike, Mike Sharp. Remember? I am and will be, while my liver lasts, Michael Sharp.'

'I remember.'

'Shall I freshen up your memory? You need a scotch.'

Mike Sharp. But the name resumed nothing to Alan except itself – a name. He tried, while Mike was at the bar, buying, to conjure up a specific memory of him, if only a moment, a peace offering of past to give him on his return. For him, evidently, some continuity was still in force from the time of seesaws and sandpits. But for Alan it was broken. He could remember nothing but the bare bones, that Mike had been born here, too, British, but that unlike himself he had stayed.

Mike Sharp returned with the drinks saying 'What do you give us, Al? C or D? How d'you rate the backward birthplace? The old but just about to be new country? Pass or fail?' Alan replied that countries couldn't be marked like essays. The childhood stranger's laugh was mirthless. 'I get it. A for effort. But you were top of the class, Al. Isn't that why you went? To get educated?' Alan nodded. 'Well, well,' said Mike. 'And where did you get the white suit?' Alan told him, Airey and Wheeler, London. 'London,' said Mike. 'I've never been to London.' He raised his glass. 'Here's to the tropical moon!'

They drank, then Mike got down to reminding Alan how he broke his nose once playing baseball; Mike was catcher, Alan swung back the bat. He leant forward and touched the bridge of his nose.

'There, can you see the break?' He told Alan about a birthday party he had had in the clubroom behind them where men were playing poker, the cake was shaped like a ship, the game was pin-the-donkey's tail, Alan's blindfold slipped and he cheated. Mike laughed. 'Think of it, jellies and jungle juice! If you had a birthday now I'd hire a Carib whore to come sit on your face. Do you remember?' No.

Alan was getting restless, at once bored and disturbed by this both deep and shallow stuff. It seemed to him that they were splashing about in a sort of paddling pool with piranhas in it – little sallies of sarcasm, unfathomable moments of bitterness. His glass was at his lips when, on impulse, he said, suddenly, 'Do you hate me, Mike?'

That surprised him. He lowered his glass, looked at Alan strangely.

'Hate you?' he slurred through a bombed-out smile. 'Why? What harm have you done me? Oh' – and he touched his nose – 'except the once.'

'I mean, hate me for who I am.'

Then Mike's smile turned sly.

'But *who* are you, Alan Palmer?'

'Mike, I'm the person who got out of the backward birthplace. Who' – he corrected himself – 'was sent out.'

Mike looked away, shaking the ice in his glass.

'Oh, it's not so bad here.'

'I didn't say it was. I like it. I feel that people haven't sacrificed so much of their humanity to the state. They're more themselves. I used to be one of those people. More myself. I have roots here.'

'Oh yeah?' Mike stared, frankly sceptical, then took a long pull at his scotch. That seemed to decide something in him, and he leant over the table. 'Look, that birthday ship of yours turned out to be real. You took it across the Atlantic. You cut from here and you cut your roots.'

'*I* didn't cut. It wasn't *my* decision.'

'Something tells me, Alan, you don't make many big decisions. Hmm? But some things are so big a lot of things look small afterwards. You may not have taken that decision to cut, but you took the rap for it.'

'I see.'

'Don't blame me.'

'It seems to give you satisfaction.'

'Oh, don't get me wrong. I took the rap too, a different rap. Look at me.' He shook the ice in his glass. 'You think I drink like this for *joy*?' Alan said nothing. Mike was suddenly serious. 'Al, this is pirate country. You could say our parents were pirates and pirates should maybe stay childless. Yours cut you adrift. Mine marooned me.'

Oh yes, thought Alan, our parents were pirates of a sort, not the ones who first settled the country, for fustic, logwood, fool's and Spanish gold, but the buccaneer-businessmen who came later, the quick-buck people, mutineers against the 'tween-decks life, England, its class system, the slump, its weather, way of life, you name it, who came to pirate their place in the sun.

They had roots, all right, so many they were practically potatoes – root-vegetable people. Roots were their problem; they tied them down in the clinging dark. So they *up*rooted themselves and came to the colony still earthy with England.

Alan thought of saying to Mike that England was the phantom limb he had never had, whereas his, Alan's, ghost life and ghost limb were here, in the colony; that both of them, from differing angles, suffered the same problem of cultural identity and what funny suffering it was, not quite real, mourning for nothing. He wanted to say that Mike had kept what he had lost by going.

Mike said again, lugubriously stretching the 'O's like Ben Gunn in *Treasure Island,* the word 'marooned', then, in one go, saw off the last of his scotch.

'Come,' he said, 'let's take the lovebug and go to Raul's.'

'Raul's?'

'A place I know.'

'Can you drive?'

'What's the matter? You squeamish? So what if we squash a child or two on the way?' Alan looked at him, but he wasn't smiling; then again, perhaps he wasn't joking. With Mike it was hard to know, and perhaps, it occurred to Alan, Mike himself didn't know . . .

In a parody of home sweet home, the words 'Raul's Rose Garden' were intricately wreathed in red and green like roses round the whorehouse door. The clapboard walls had been spray-painted. One picture showed a girl playing a bongo drum, her hands beating like a humming-bird's wings. In another a man was dancing, his hands hallelujahing. On the blue-lit veranda above, a woman was fanning herself, a real painted lady, looking out over the clearing. In it were parked a pair of army landrovers, a Transit, a stretch-bodied pink saloon and, now, Mike's 'love-bug'.

He pulled it up beside the pink car and said, 'T-bird. God, what an ugly colour!' They got out. The ground underfoot was slippery with guava fallen from a tree nearby. Alan stooped to pick one up. Its pale green skin had split neatly to reveal the pink fruit filled with seeds. In the wash of light from Raul's it shone stickily as though lacquered. It smelt sweet. He tossed it to the ground again. The tree, he supposed, had been planted by the house's original owner and whoever he was, here in this lonely jungle clearing, he had actively sought solitude. Now people came actively seeking its opposite.

The barman let them into a low, half-lit room.

'No music tonight,' he said. 'The jukebox broke. Now, what are you having?' Chivas for Mike, a Belikin beer for Alan. He looked around. Four men were talking quietly round a corner table, two tables were full of Gordon Highlanders. A man was at a table alone. A soldier was reaching the noisy punchline of a joke.

'"Tonight,"' he said, '"our Holy Father is a very happy

88

man".' They laughed. It was works-outing laughter which told Alan of the tenements they'd grown up in, the days spent kicking ball against hopeless walls. One of the boys – they were no older – had "Rangers Forever" tattooed on his forearm. Another wore a T-shirt which read "For God's sake, Scotty, beam me up."

'C'mon,' said Mike. They went to an empty table. Alan looked at the man who sat alone. He had seen him at the Bayman Hotel. He was about forty-five and to judge from his sweat the heat was affecting him badly. He wore a seersucker jacket on one of whose lapels a smudge of ink was sported like a badge and his shirt had a seethrough patch where sweat had adhered it to his sternum. He took out a handkerchief and mopped his brow with it. His slightly puffy jaw hung open like a fish fighting for oxygen in the high humidity; probably, there was an oxygen which was always just beyond his gasp.

Five girls sat in a demure row at the bar. Mike told Alan they were whores from El Salvador, refugees. One of them took a tray and loaded it with their drinks. She was smiling directly at them, but even from across the room her eyes were hurt, wary. She came to their table and Mike said, 'This is Linda. And you are too, aren't you? *Muy linda*.'

Alan introduced himself and she said '*Señor*' and served their drinks. If she was *linda* she was a little *gorda* too, Alan thought. In the tropics, people ripened fast, fell, rooted or rotted. Alan thought of the guavas. If the predators were plenty, so were the seeds, girl or guava, guava or girl.

'Linda,' said Alan, 'I'm drunk. Join us.'

Still smiling, she sat at their table.

'You want her?' asked Mike.

Slowly, Alan shook his head.

Linda said, 'You don't like me?'

Mike laughed.

'Sure he likes you. He's English, that's all.'

'I'm in love,' Alan lied.

'Ah,' said Linda, nodding. 'Love.' It was as though she were puzzled that a man in love should be in a whorehouse.

Mike turned to Alan.

'I'll bet you never got laid in the backward birthplace. Right?'

'I was too young.'

89

'Well man, down to it. There's lost time to make up and nothing else to do. Rum, bum and concertina – education out the window! Go on, she's good. And the army quack sees she's clean.'

Just then one of the four in the corner called, 'Hey, Mike! Mike Sharp!' The man knocked over his chair in eagerness as he stood and made for their table. 'Where've you been?' he was saying. 'What you doin'? Still the same old streetwise?'

'Oh-oh,' Mike had muttered, but then he said out loud, 'Blackjack, old son, what brings you here from The Vietnam?'

'Me man, I'm on the razz is all. Whassa matter, ain't goin' to say hello to Blackjack?' They did the pimp's handshake, the man called Blackjack laughing throatily like a stage gangster. He looked at Alan with yellow-edged eyes. 'Who's your friend, Mike?'

'This, Blackjack, is a blast-from-the-past Belize boy called Alan Palmer.'

'That so?' said Blackjack. 'You born here?'

'I believe so,' said Alan.

'Ha,' said Blackjack. 'That's rich, eh? He believes so. Now Mike' – he lowered his voice a notch – 'maybe you'd like to come do business with me and my friends here.'

Mike glanced at them.

'Who are they?'

'Oh, spear fishers is all. You know the kinda thing, come to "Untouched Belize" to ogle the coral, kill jewfish, all that crap.'

'They drive the pink horror parked outside?'

'They do.' Blackjack's voice was reverential. 'Man, that's one helluva horsepower!'

'The colour,' said Mike, 'looks like it was manufactured by cripples. What sort of business?'

'With them guys?' Blackjack tossed his head to signify the spear fishers. His eyes were on Alan, though, hard as a small town police chief's. 'Oh,' he said lightly, 'a little breeze is all.'

'Breeze?'

'Sure.'

Mike gave an exaggerated sigh. He turned to Alan.

'Okay. I'll leave you to the lovely Linda.'

He got up and Blackjack called to the men at his table 'Boys, meet Mike.' They met him, handshakes and hiyas all round.

Mike seemed diffident, almost shy. Alan glanced at the three men from the pink car, lounging loose-limbed on their chairs on Big Mac bums fattened by billfolds. There was, to Alan, an arrogance about their ease, as though they were the self-styled top table and the rest of the room were low-life losers. They were smoking Marlboros. Alan thought, I'm judging by appearances, but don't they ask to be? Why is their car pink? In it they had come south, spear-carrying conquerors from the consumer society. Sun, rum and women were on their shopping hit list. If they liked the way it moved they would buy it cash on the barrel. They would talk brand names, cc's, calibres, mph, dollars, machine and female horseflesh.

'Mind if I join you?' Alan turned. Linda was back at the bar. The man from the next table was pulling up a chair. 'I've seen you at the Bayman,' he said. 'Hi.' He held out his hand. 'Fuller's the name,' he said 'Wyler Fuller.' Alan introduced himself. The man mopped his brow, and Alan caught an elusive odour of mass-production deodorant and the ammoniac smell which it had been intended to counteract. Wyler Fuller had the wary, lacklustre eyes of a man who has spent too much time in the company of complete strangers, too many stopovers in air-conditioned hotels which were immobile extensions of the pressurised aircraft cabins in which he travelled.

'Is it me?' he said, 'or is it really so hot it here?' Alan said that it was but at least the jukebox was off. Wyler Fuller sat down and said, 'Jeez, do you *believe* this joint?' He mopped his brow again. Alan wondered how much of his sweat was heat and how much worry: he seemed a worrier. 'I suppose,' he went on, 'that if they opened the windows there's no telling what horrors might fly in.' Alan wasn't sure there were windows.

'Dens of vice don't have views.'

'That's true,' he said. 'A single crucifix on the wall would shut this place down. Perhaps I shouldn't write about it. But it's here. It's part of the story.'

'You're a journalist?'

'I write features. And you?'

'I used to teach, but my heart wasn't in it. I'm waiting to decide what to do next.'

'I see,' he said. 'Hanging out.'

'That's it. Hanging out.'

Fuller fiddled with his almost empty glass, staring into the ice.

'How long you here for?'

'I don't know. Until I decide to go.'

'I leave late tomorrow.' He drained the rest of his drink. 'Another?'

'I've had enough.'

'Your friend hasn't.'

'I'm not sure he's my friend,' Alan said.

'Meaning?'

Alan didn't reply. Wyler Fuller asked:

'You were born here, weren't you?'

That shook Alan a little, but to keep the dialogue snappy he simply said, 'You move fast, Mr Fuller.'

'I'm a journalist,' he said. 'I suffer from the catkiller.'

'Meaning?' Alan mimicked.

'Curiosity, it's my editor's word for curiosity. I'm a black hole of facts. I notice things. For example, just now I saw you wondering what "breeze" was.'

As a matter of fact, thought Alan, he was perfectly right, but he said, 'Was I?'

'"Belize breeze",' he said. 'It's smoke, slang for marijuana. Amazing what you can find out in a fortnight. If you're curious, as I am. As you are.'

'Something else in your little black hole book?'

'You'd make a journalist. Ever thought about it?'

'I don't think ...' Alan paused. 'Don't think I've ever thought in terms of career.'

'There you are,' he said, and despite his flat delivery he spoke with something like triumph. 'You *are* a journalist. Now,' he glanced at his watch, 'it's getting on and I reckon I've had enough too. What say I drop you off at the Bayman?'

'That's an idea.'

'I've checked Raul's out.'

Alan felt, suddenly, terribly ashamed.

'So have I,' he said, and got up. He called to Mike, 'I'm going.'

'So soon?'

To Alan, Mike's grin at that moment seemed the bituminous expression of a cynical, tarry soul; in the drunken half-light his face danced before him like a devil's. Perhaps he sensed wha

92

Alan was feeling, for when he came to bid goodbye there was the same apologetic, foot-shuffling shyness as when he'd met the spear fishers.

Then he nodded at Linda.

'You missed your chance, Al,' he said. 'Next trick around gets to mix with soldier sperm. See you at the club, okay?' And he sloped off.

'An edifying gentleman,' Wyler Fuller said when they were outside. 'Seems to spend a lot of his life among fluids, if you follow me.'

'He's destroying himself,' said Alan. 'He's destroying himself, because that's the only show in town.'

They got into the Transit. Wyler Fuller drove in silence for a while. They had reached the main road before he turned to Alan and said:

'Tell me, you met a guy called Bill Brandl?'

'Who?'

'The hotel ledger gave his name as Brandl.'

No, Alan hadn't met him, but Fuller said nothing at first. Alan glanced at him. He was leaning over the steering column peering out into the night.

'What the hell's that?' he said.

'A nightjar.'

The bird's eyes were glowing balefully from the roadside as they passed. Alan was proud to have remembered; nightjars had scared him as a child.

Fuller said, 'I'm not used to all this night life, bet it's crawling with crap out there. Anyways, Brandl, big guy, tall I mean, fifty-something, staying at the Bayman. At least he *was*. Come to think of it, haven't seen him lately. Going grey the way TV personalities do, distinguished, must be the rays, I call it television hair. Ivy League kinda guy.'

'What about him?'

'Well, that's just it. I don't know. But –'

'Yes?'

'I smell a story.' He paused, Alan said nothing. There was, he thought, lots of interpersonal fishing under way. 'You know how it is,' continued Fuller, 'you get a hunch about something. Guy like that, wouldn't look twice at him in New York, LA. But what's he doing here? You know? It's a loose end. Trouble

93

is, I'm leaving tomorrow, no time to tie it up.' He left that hanging in the air a while, then said, pseudo-lightly, 'How'd you like to follow it up for me?'

Alan said, 'What sort of story do you smell?'

'You'd be paid.' Fuller gave him another quick glance. Alan was irritated by the implication.

'I don't need your money,' he said. Ahead, the headlamps lit up the road pocked and potholed like a moonscape.

'It's not a crime,' said Fuller. 'And you might find it interesting. Why not?'

Alan paused. Indeed, why not? It would do no harm to have a bit of purpose while he was in Belize. At last he said, 'Okay.'

'Great. I'll give you more details when we get back. Keep closemouthed about it, eh? But the word is he's some kind of philanthropist. Here to spend money.'

'Belize could do with some money spent on it. Good for him.'

'Sure, sure.'

Again he gave Alan one of his nervous, puffy-jawed glances. 'But this is Central America, see? A lot of stuff goes down here. Whatever he's doing it's still a story. Good or evil, they're both done on the sly. If he's doing some sly good I'd like to know about that too. A better story maybe, if you get my meaning ...'

'I get it.'

'But to find out what *he's* doing on the sly *you've* got to be sly. Will you do that?'

'Be sly? I'm not sure.'

Half to himself Wyler Fuller said, 'I've got to trust you. There's no one else in the whole goddamn country ...'


'Frankly,' said Dr Abb, 'I just had to guess.'

Carefully he steered his Morris Minor off the Western Highway and onto the airport road. In ten minutes the Air Florida flight was due to arrive and with it the radioactive iodine for Reuben's father. Dr Abb had never worked with radioactivity before – it seemed like science fiction that he should be doing so now, at his age and in these backward circumstances.

Tropical medicine was his speciality, in so far as the war had allowed him to specialise, and hyperthyroidism, a disease usually of the developed world, he'd last heard about as a student – until old Mr White, Reuben's father, contracted it. He was well aware of his lack of experience and of up-to-date equipment. For all these reasons he felt nervous and as if they weren't enough there was the nervousness he always felt with the relative of a seriously ill patient – especially when it was Reuben, with whom Dr Abb felt ill at ease at the best of times. The habit of diagnosis dies hard and in Reuben the doctor had long ago detected a trace of latent hysteria. It was catching, which was why the doctor had chosen to say only, 'I just had to guess.'

Reuben nodded, then began, 'What if . . .?'

'If my guess is wrong?' the doctor supplied. 'If I haven't prescribed enough rads he'll still be hyperthyroid. If I've pre-scribed too many he'll be *hypo*thyroid – his thyroid will be underactive, not over. But underactivity is much more easily contained. One thing's for certain,' and Dr Abb paused. 'If he isn't treated now he'll die very soon. But the point is, he's going to live.'

'Thank you, doctor,' said Reuben. 'Thank you. You're doing very well.'

To the right of the road a khaki radar dish was rapidly moving back and forth, scanning the western border for Guatemalan aircraft. With equipment that sensitive, thought Dr Abb, I could diagnose a host of diseases I haven't the means to cure; but at Airport Camp down the road, under camouflage netting, multimillion pound Harrier jets were a ready remedy to the Guatemalans. The usual absurdity of war and well-being, death and health. But Dr Abb cared even less for war than most men do. In a sense war had ruined his life.

In 1938, as a mature student, he'd managed to wangle himself out of Nazi Germany into a posting on the Mosquito Coast to treat and study tropical diseases. When war was announced, he'd been in Belize playing cards – as in a bar-room joke – with an Englishman and Frenchman. The radio was on. When Chamberlain had finished speaking there'd been no comment, nothing at all, and then the Englishman had quietly said, 'Raise you five.' Dr Abb would remember that as long as he lived: 'Raise you five.'

Sooner than intern him, he'd been allowed to get away to

Colombia. With the war's end he hadn't contemplated a return to Germany but had drifted back to Belize. He hadn't completed his studies, but on the Mosquito Coast where measles could kill, a half doctor was good for most problems and better than no doctor at all. It was also, Dr Abb had considered, one of the few areas of the immediate post-war world where a German could feel at home.

Grateful for Reuben's silence he turned into the airport forecourt. A police car was waiting – he'd been told there would be a police escort. Pulling the handbrake, he told Reuben 'Wait here,' and got out. A policeman from the car came and introduced himself as 'Brute Flowers'. He showed Dr Abb to an airport desk where a large and sweaty man sat under a sign telling 'entertainers, boxers and so on' to fill out Income Tax Exit Certificates.

He signed a duty-free import form and in a few minutes – ahead of schedule – the Air Florida jet had landed and taxied onto the apron, the steps were in place and passengers were alighting. The courier would be the young man. He hoped yet again that he'd got the rads right. He'd done the dosimetry calculation, but in the dark, guesswork on whose accuracy the future health of Reuben's father would hang – and also, possibly, his own authority as a healer. It wasn't often tested this dramatically.

'Heinrich Abb, sir?' It was the young man. He handed over a lead-lined film bag from his briefcase and a larger bag containing the protective clothing. 'If you'd just sign here, sir,' he said, and then, looking about him, 'Boy, this is the weirdest courier job I ever did!'

Dr Abb smiled as he signed and said, 'It's just as weird for me, I do assure you.' He checked inside the film bag; the lead box was there. 'And the clothing?' he asked.

The courier said, 'Mask, jacket and gloves, they're all there.'

Dr Abb took his word for it, wished him a good flight back and retraced his way through the airport building. He asked the policeman at his side, 'What did you say your name was?'

He said with a shy smile, 'Brute is short for Brutus.'

'Well, Brutus,' said Dr Abb, 'I don't see there's much for you to do, but come along for the ride.'

96

Reuben was waiting. Dr Abb tossed the bags into the back seat. Reuben looked at them doubtfully. As though they could contain his father's survival! But Dr Abb knew better and was exhilarated. It flashed through his mind, not for the first time, that the undeveloped world provided the philosophical under-pinning of the developed. Perhaps that was why he loved Belize so much – here his identity was secure. In this context, where the workings of the body were less scientifically understood, or not at all, and the intervention of death more readily accepted, materialism not only made sense but attained the status of magic. Reuben would see. Medical procedures which Dr Abb would have gone through mechanically in the north he would here go through, not so much as Heinrich Abb, half doctor, but as Abb the medicine man. It wasn't what they called professional to think along such lines, but God it was good to feel one's power sometimes!

Reuben wouldn't be immune to the sense of magic, but at the same time he was sophisticated enough – this was the doctor's fear – to put an obvious question:

'Doctor, if this is possible now, why wasn't it possible before? Why didn't you tell me? I could have tried to raise the money. Why did you treat us like children?'

To that question Dr Abb had no answer that did not implicate him in professional negligence. No one of course would make the charge, not formally. But he had emerged from self-criticism with the clear conclusion that over the years he'd lowered standards to match the resources available. Radioiodine! Here! What a collision of worlds!

But how could he function if in every case that came to his surgery he were to reflect that there was a cure or at least more effective treatment for it in the developed world? Where would the money come from? Constantly to compare the two worlds across the huge material gulf between them would result in a sort of madness, although for the moment an American phil-anthropist's money kept that madness at bay.

The police car followed them out of the airport forecourt and as they hit the potholes Dr Abb asked Reuben, 'Would you mind holding that bag on your knee, the small one? I'm worried about the bumps.' Reuben reached behind for the film bag and placed it gingerly on his lap, again looking at it doubtfully.

97

Perhaps he was afraid. 'Hold it carefully,' said Dr Abb. 'Remember there's radioactivity in there.'

Soon they were on the Western Highway heading for Hattieville.

Reuben said, 'How does it work?'

'How . . .?'

'The iodine.'

'Ah.'

Dr Abb didn't much want to go into medical detail, but he said, 'What we're doing is killing off cells to reduce the activity of the thyroid. We're killing to cure . . .' A couple of miles from Hattieville, Dr Abb was explaining that the thyroid did its work by releasing into the system hormones containing iodine. 'In simple terms, when too many hormones are released the body's balance is lost and it starts consuming itself. But the thyroid, in secreting its hormones, needs iodine – What we do is use this attribute to smuggle into the thyroid, along with the iodine, radioactivity which kills cells. It's an exercise in atomic smuggling. Do you follow?'

Reuben nodded.

'I think so,' he said. Then, after a pause: 'You remember Sybil? She's a nurse in New York now, right? I wrote and asked about this thyroid thing. But she didn't reply yet.'

'I didn't know she'd trained as a nurse,' said Dr Abb.

'You never saw her in the hospital here?'

'I must have missed her.'

They rounded the corner into Hattieville and stopped outside the house of Reuben's father. Children came running; passersby and streetcorner loungers came slowly strolling over. Two cars at once!

Dr Abb got out and told Brute Flowers through his rolled-down window, 'You can keep those people away.' With radioactivity you didn't take chances and today he wasn't prepared as usual to tolerate people peering round doors into rooms where he was working. That was the Third World for you: a medicine show where children were the young hopefuls who might just make it as extras. 'What do you want to be when you grow up?' 'Alive.'

It was dark in the house. The front room, one of two, smelt of sweat. The curtain was drawn. Dimly, blinking after the glare

98

outside, Dr Abb made out Ma Armstrong rising from a chair, the old man in bed under a single sheet.

Outside, Reuben called 'Leave us be now, hear?'

Ma Armstrong said, in a hushed tone which doctors and priests are used to hearing, 'He hasn't eaten, doctor.'

'No?' said Dr Abb, and then, 'I'll need light. Would you open the curtains?' He turned to the old man – but he was old too; why did one think of the ill as older than oneself? – and said, 'Hello Jimmy.'

'Doctor . . .'

Ma Armstrong opened the curtain. The man in bed shut his eyes; light hurt him. Reuben carried in the bags. Dr Abb started taking off his jacket and said, 'I was going to ask you, Jim, how medicine was different from the movies. It's this. In medicine, when the cavalry comes you know it's *not* the last reel.' He said to Reuben and Ma Armstrong, 'In a moment I'll have to ask you to leave.'

Reuben nodded, then went to his father's bed. He put a hand on his head and said, 'You'll see, Daddy, it'll be all right.' Dr Abb opened the bag containing the clothing. He took out the protective vest and slipped his arms into it, straitjacket style. It had a low apron to cover his crutch and it was weighted in front like a shield. He asked Ma Armstrong to do up the straps at the back, then fumbled in the bag for the lead-lined mask and gloves. He slipped them on and then, when Ma Armstrong had finished strapping him in, signalled that they should both go to the door.

'Outside now,' he said, his voice muzzy behind the mask. He put the film bag on an upturned tea-chest and took out the lead box.

In this outfit he was in space-age contrast with his surroundings. Twenty years ago, before Hattie, old Jimmy White had been a fisherman. It hadn't been long before that that Dr Abb had last treated him – a fishhook had lodged in the flesh of a finger. From the roof hung one of his nets, complete with the coloured glass floats the fishermen called 'Portuguese'. On another upturned crate was a hurricane lantern and a King James Bible.

He broke the seals on the lead box and carefully removed the lid. What a disaster if the liquid should spill now! Inside the

box was a bottle, again sealed, containing a red liquid as artificially bright as cherryade.

He said, 'Now Jimmy, are you hearing? I'm coming to you
and I want you to keep absolutely still. You're having that drink
I told you about. Do you understand me? The old man gave a
grunt of assent. Dr Abb took the bottle from the lead box and
sat on his bedside. He said, 'You must understand that if we
lose this liquid we've lost your treatment. You've got to keep
still and drink it all down.' Dr Abb broke the seal on the bottle.
He felt like a priest in a heavy metal alb, serving nuclear mass
in a shantytown hut. The new life he had to offer was not
metaphysical but a material certainty. He removed the glass
stopper and imagined beta particles fizzing to the room's
corners. Holding the bottle tightly by the neck he carefully
brought its lip to those of his patient.

'Drink, Jimmy,' he said. 'Careful now . . .'

The old man drank. Dr Abb was aware of Ma Armstrong,
Reuben, the policeman looking in at the door; but he didn't
turn, this moment was too important. The old man drained the
bottle down to the last drop that wasn't filming the inner surface
or darting for cover among the hairs on his chin. Dr Abb realised
he'd forgotten the drops that would spill and called without
turning, 'A cloth, fetch me a cloth.' He put the stopper back on
the bottle as though to corral any leftover beta particles, then
used the cloth which someone had put beside him to dab the
transsubstantiated iodine from the old man's chin.

'That's it,' he said. 'That's it Jimmy. Go to sleep now. And
wake up healthy . . .'


Nothing and nobody, but *nobody,* was going to spoil Mister
Bill's big day. That was how Peyrefitte had put it to Pedro that
morning when they met up again in the Downstairs Café –
Mister Bill's Big Day – like the title of a learning-to-spell children's book. But when he got out of Peyrefitte's car, a few hours
later after lunch, there was a bounce, a spring to his step. And
although the car was a beaten-up old taxi, you'd have thought
it was a chauffeur-driven limo. And although it was parked in
parrot country – the middle of *nowhere* – Mister Bill got out of

it as if onto a smart, big city sidewalk, as if he were arriving for a gala première, bulbs popping, arc lamps, cameras whirring, the works.

And the funny thing was, he looked the part. He was dressed for it, in jungle-cred green safari suit and sunglasses which Peyrefitte, a connoisseur of these things, knew to be better than his own. And draped on his arm was the obligatory mollish-looking woman much younger than he was, Amelia, she called herself; but then he called himself Bill, didn't he? She played her part too, looking at him wide-eyed from time to time, while he was casually proprietorial of her, the promising juvenile whom he, the star, had taken under his wing. Peyrefitte couldn't find a chink in his ego-armour; he'd got his act together just fine. Anyway, what was he supposed to do? Call him? It was his money. It was his *show*. So Peyrefitte went along, played his role too. Or rather his roles, because a dope farm foreman was lots of people. Mister Bill expected to be noticed? Well, he would be. Mister Bill acted as if there were cameras recording his every move? Well, Peyrefitte was adaptable; he would be attentive, bend to his will, court and flatter him like a camera. Mister Bill came on like a head honcho? Okay, Peyrefitte would play henchman. But he made a mental note: cameras are unforgiving too, and Mister Bill had better remember that one thing Belize and all the hot countries weren't short of was banana skins to slip up on. Better not screw up, Mister Bill, because dodgy enterprises like these float on the head man's high; he loses confidence, so does everyone else.

It was this doubt that had had him say to Mister Bill, in the Downstairs Café, 'You've come a long way, Bill.' He meant his remark to probe, to test, if possible to prove.

'Oh yeah?' Bill stopped in mid-forkful. 'What does that mean, Peyrefitte?'

Unfazed, Peyrefitte said, 'I mean . . . it's like you were worried last time. Like you weren't so sure of yourself. You know?'

'No,' Mister Bill had said, 'I don't know. What is this, Peyrefitte? Marking my grades?'

Peyrefitte laughed – a laugh he didn't feel. 'Man, you were top of the class first time! It's just . . .'

'You're talking,' Mister Bill had said quietly, 'bullshit,' with a smile to bandage in advance any hurt his remark might cause.

Well, Peyrefitte happened to know that he was giving with no such substance; but, ritually, he agreed, and said, with a big, stagey sigh, 'I guess you've hit it. My big mouth, you know.' He'd made his point, though, and Mister Bill, he'd noticed, ate silently for a while after that, as though thoughtful about what Peyrefitte had said.

But if doubts had troubled Bill then, none seemed to now, as he stood in the clearing, his arm round the shoulders of his moll. She was, Peyrefitte had decided, no baby doll; those shoulders of hers had a good head on them – and maybe, thought Peyrefitte, if I'm smart she'll give me some of it. Her good head. And, as he watched, she inclined it to look upwards, where Mister Bill was looking, at the sky. Yeah, it was quite a sky. Peyrefitte too looked at it. The cloud was low, unbroken, the clouds grey except for their edges, which were the colours of a black eye. Over to the west the light was an end-of-the-world violet; the horsemen would ride tonight. Rain? But the sky had been like that for days, the cloud lower every day, more leaden looking, until it seemed impossible that it should float up there at all.

'How does he know?' Amanda was asking Bill. She meant Pedro, who in the Downstairs Café had confidently predicted rain today. Bill shook his head.

'Beats me,' he said. 'Maybe he's psychic. Or maybe he's a Maya bullshit artist.' But that was Bill being untrue. He wanted rain, not just to soften the soil so planting could start, but for more metaphysical reasons. This was his big day. In an imperfectly worked-out synthesis which, however, impressed him powerfully, he'd made a connection in his mind between rain, planting and self-renewal. No one is such a slave to his unconscious as the man who, having denied it all his life, suddenly gives it free rein; mystics, usually, are muddled thinkers. Planting, it seemed to Bill, was the start of life, a challenge, and the man who plants is intimately part of the cycle of renewal. When you planted you went, every season, back to the beginning and affirmed the triumph of life over death; symbolically, you were young and full of hope again. As he'd felt since splitting from the States; as he felt today. The *milpa* they were going to see was razed and waiting. And if it was ready, so was he. His boats were burnt; his past was behind him, blackened. Everything was ready but the rain, but Bill took

102

heart from Pedro's calm confidence that it would fall today.

Softly, he touched the side of Amanda's face and said, 'Come. It's *milpa* time.' They went to the edge of the clearing where Pedro, Peyrefitte behind him, had drawn his machete and waded into the bush. They followed and were soon in dense vegetation, succulents with fat leaves like flash-fry steaks. It would be a hike of maybe a hundred yards, Pedro had said, through the bush to the *milpa,* but the short distance was long and dark enough for some irrational fears to form and Bill was soon interpreting low clumps of undergrowth as crouching jaguars, rustles as slithering snakes. Pedro, of the four of them, was the only one at home in these circumstances; he seemed to know his way almost instinctively, using his machete, not to cut, but to sweep branches and leaves aside with the flat of the blade, as though there were a preordained path known only to him. He lives here, Bill thought, while we are escaped zoo animals whom he's teaching all over again what wilderness is.

Bill had just begun to tire of the jungle stuff when he smelt the *milpa* and knew they must be near. A burnt, acrid smell and then, ahead, light breaking through the last wall of leaves where the vegetation thinned out at the *milpa*'s edge. He broke through it and there was Pedro, already in the open, sticking his machete into his belt, Peyrefitte brushing himself down, getting back his cool. They'd seen the *milpa* before, but this was Bill's first time, and he stopped, put his hands on his hips and breathed the one word, 'Jesus!' It seemed enormous, a waste of burnt stubble and strewn, black branches. This was all down to him. Astonishing – so much land, so well hidden; and . . . what was that over there? He shaded his eyes against the glare. Yes. Over a brow in the land, two *cohane* huts, two *chozas*, so recent that their palm roofs had yet to turn brown; and near them a trestle table, people around it looking their way, the planters.

Peyrefitte said, 'What you make of it, Bill?'

He nodded. 'This is quite something. You've worked hard. Is that your team over there, Pedro?'

'That's my team.'

They set off across the *milpa*, their feet crunching on stubble and charcoal. Bill counted five around the trestle table and said to Pedro, 'Are there enough of them?'

Pedro shrugged and said phlegmatically, 'They're hard

103

workers.' Bill was aware of the sort of image they might be presenting to the planters, Pedro walking beside the American money man – a real venture at last, something of *substance*.

'So you're sure it'll rain, eh?' he asked. Pedro nodded.

'Pretty sure,' he said, and from behind them Bill heard Peyrefitte:

'He's a walking weather station, aren't you Pedro?' Then Peyrefitte laughed briefly with what sounded to Bill surprisingly like sourness. What was it with him today? But he chose for the moment to ignore it.

The planters were young men in jeans and T-shirts. Bill looked quickly at their faces. They were the faces of boys, the frames of their bodies were boyish, but Bill knew from experience how difficult it was to gauge an Amerindian's age; you had to adjust sometimes upwards, sometimes down. In other parts of Central America, he reminded himself, these apparent boys would be gun-toting guerrillas, or prematurely aged in the authority of an army uniform. He smiled at them, a smile which he hoped was friendly and as impartial as sunlight, while they stared back, by no means with hostility, but with a disconcerting self-possession and unanimity. Bill, as an employer, had experienced that stare before, if not so openly. There was anxiety in it, a wish to see into the mainsprings of the employer's character – on which, eventually, your security depended; but this stare also said, quite clearly, that it was him, Bill, who was the unknown quantity here; it was up to him to measure up to the standards of *their* world and not vice versa.

'Okay, this is Mister Bill,' said Pedro. Then, very much the man in charge, he summoned them to be introduced. One by one they stepped forward, Juan and Bartolo (Pedro's sons), José (his nephew), each smiling shyly or grinning broadly as he took Bill's hand and then, after Bill, met 'Amelia'. The fourth boy, another nephew, was simply 'Coffee'. Bill wondered why, and Coffee and all of them laughed at Pedro's reply.

'Because he coughs all the time.' Then Bill knew it was only a matter of time before he discovered each of the planters' personal attributes, like Coffee's weed-smoker's cough. He began to feel easier.

'And this,' said Pedro, 'is Rafael. You know about him, no? Manuel Zuniga's boy.'

'Oh,' said Bill with real surprise. 'So you're out here too?'

'Yes, Mister Bill,' said Rafael. He spoke woodenly, as if by rote.

He shook Rafael's hand and said, 'Rafael. Pleased to meet you finally.'

The trestle table was spread as though for a party with bottles of the local, unlabelled rum, Belikin beer in buckets filled with chunks of ice, tequila. There were straw baskets of corn chips and cold tortillas, and a bowl of refried beans – campfire food. Now Pedro went to the table and lifted from it a large earthenware jug of water.

'Here,' he said, and offered it to Bill. Bill was puzzled, felt a surprise was being sprung on him, but keeping up the geniality he asked, 'This is for the drinks?' and took the jug from Pedro.

'No,' and Bill could have sworn there was a mischievous twinkle in Pedro's eyes. 'We drink soon, but first you pour this. No?'

'Pour...?' Bill looked around for guidance and Peyrefitte stepped forward, was about to speak, but Pedro, rocklike, simply pointed to the ground.

'There,' he said. Bill had trouble deciding what his tone was – somewhere between polite and firm. He glanced at the boy planters. Now their stare was more frankly curious, as though a test had been set and they were waiting to see how the *Americano* would do.

Bill said, 'You want me to pour this on the ground?'

'It's a ceremony,' said Peyrefitte, 'like champagne when you launch a ship.'

'Ah,' said Bill. Now he understood. But had Pedro expected him to intuit this?

He glanced at his grower, who said imperturbably, 'Then we drink.'

'Sure,' said Bill, 'sure.'

One of the businesses which he had left behind him in the States was a meat-packing plant near Brownsville, Texas. He had flown down to open it and the manager had presented him with a cowpuncher's hat on which he'd then turned up the brim, to indicate a cattle baron. He'd kept a photo of himself that day, grinning, hat brim raised, scissors poised near a ribbon. He remembered that photo at this moment in the jungle, as,

105

holding the jug in both hands, he leant towards the ground. He didn't dare glance at Amanda – in case he laughed. He saw that the boys were smiling. But at what? The ceremony, or the fact that he, the gringo, was performing it? But Pedro wasn't smiling; that was what mattered. Bill, his face composed, paused with what he hoped was due solemnity, then, having created a moment of respect, tilted the jug. Water splashed at his feet, a noisy, embarrassing splashing which was an added temptation to smile.

Bill found it difficult to keep up with the rapid tacking through cultural crosswinds. Was this serious or wasn't it? Or was it both at once? When the planters, the jug emptied and following Pedro's lead, laughed and broke into applause, clapping their hands as though something really quite delicate and clever had been achieved, he couldn't resist the notion that he'd been out-manoeuvred, in some subtle fashion made a fool of, and said, 'Is that it?' with a nervous snigger which he at once regretted. He knew that he, the man with the false name, had struck a false note and for a moment the laughter of the planters hammered him home in a sense of aloneness. He glanced at Amanda, but she was smiling as though nothing untoward had happened; perhaps nothing had. He replaced the jug on the trestle table.

Then Pedro shook an Independence cigarette from his pack and said simply, 'It was holy.' He lit the cigarette and sucked in his cheeks as he puffed.

'Holy?'

'Hmm,' exhaling smoke. 'Holy water. A priest said a blessing for us.'

'Jesus, I'm sorry,' said Bill, and regretted that too. Jesus was someone hereabouts; people called their sons Jesus; it wasn't just something you said. Bill took a hold on himself and said, 'I hope I handled the water okay.'

'You handled it fine, Mister Bill.'

'Peyrefitte, you didn't tell me it was holy water!'

'I didn't know myself,' said Peyrefitte.

Pedro turned to the trestle table to fix drinks, leaving Bill with the feeling that he was walking a minefield of observances which he not only didn't share and couldn't properly grasp, but which he couldn't even see in advance. The water had been holy; for all he knew the drink on the table was holy too. Certainly there

106

was ceremony in the way Pedro was handling the bottles – or was that his gardener's hands, ennobling the things they touched? Carefully, like an old-fashioned pharmacist, he uncorked the rum and levered the caps from the beer, and when he broke the seals on the tequila he seemed to do so as reverently as a librarian with a rare first edition. And now Bill came to think of it, perhaps the drink *was* in some manner holy. When the Maya drank alcohol didn't they appoint a pourer, not out of optic-minded meanness, nor, exactly, out of fairness, but because tradition and religious form required an equal distribution of spirit? Was Pedro, then, the pourer? No one but Bill was watching him, but something about him suggested a silent blessing of the alcohol. And yet, no one was watching Coffee either, as he went, with similar concentration, through the ritual of rolling a quite enormous joint. Was that holy too? Was *everything* holy? And had the priest known the purpose for which he was blessing the water? Probably it hadn't mattered. At the convent school in Belize City Bill had seen children filling water-pistols from the holy water stoups and had imagined them playing a made-up game called 'Bang! You're blessed!' Whatever the water supply in these parts, a lot of it was holy.

Bill drank beer from misted bottles sweating ice-water. He drank tequila from little thimbles of plastic which were the transparent Sacred Heart colour of Catholicism. He took a couple of tokes of Coffee's joint, and soon felt a spurious sense of interconnectedness and warmth.

A little later, Amanda said to him, 'You know that wasn't the *real* ceremony?'

'Oh, I'm glad to hear it. When's the real one?'

'Later, or they may have had it already. Who knows? We're not invited. It's a ceremony of their own, really Maya, you know, with some Catholic stuff maybe thrown in, incense and prayers, all that, maybe even a *brujo* – you know, a magic man?'

'How d'you know this?'

'Peyrefitte told me.'

So the ceremony with the jug had been as it were watered down for his benefit. Bill wondered about that and felt obscurely cheated. Hadn't he, after all, paid the full price of admission? Wasn't it his show? Then Rafael passed by with a tray of tequilas. Bill took one for Amanda and one for himself.

'How are you feeling?' he asked her.

'Great.'

'Was this what you imagined?'

'Better than I imagined.'

He briefly raised his tequila, then drank it down in one shot. He said, reflexively, 'Brr!' – as if the hit of firewater at the pit of his stomach had felt cold and not hot. Then – what was this? He looked more closely at the red plastic cup in his hand. Inside it, just under the rim, was a tideline of white rime, like salt. Then he realised. He flaked some of the rime away with his thumbnail and said to Amanda, 'I don't believe this.'

'What is it?'

'Look.'

'There's nothing in mine.' She took his cup and examined the rime. She looked up at him and said, 'It's wax.'

'That's right. Wax. Do you get it?' His eyes were bright.

She shook her head and said, 'No.' He laughed and said 'Someone up there, or down here – is overdoing the symbolic stuff.'

'I still don't get it.'

'These are holders for votive candles,' said Bill. 'The nightlight type. You see them in all the churches.'

*It's all holy,* he was thinking. For a few cents, this cup once held the hope of health or heaven.

'You're right,' said Amanda, examining the cup in her hand. She looked at him. 'Isn't that the strangest recycling you ever heard of?'

'I bet they came from the priest,' said Bill. 'The same one who blessed the water.'

Then Rafael was with them again.

'Mister,' he said. 'Come see. I show you.' He pointed to the *cohane* huts.

'He wants to show me the stuff from the States,' said Bill. Rafael was already walking away. He gestured that Bill should follow and called again, 'Come see.'

Bill followed. Rafael, young as he was, was a key figure in the operation, who had become involved as a direct result of his father's death. After Manuel's funeral his eldest son, who was a clerk in Chetumal, had returned to Mexico, while responsibility for his hardware shop had devolved on his wife

108

and second son, Rafael. And under Rafael things were going to be a little different.

His father hadn't countenanced weed-growing. Over the years he'd often resisted approaches by growers wanting to use his hardware store as a conduit for equipment. Such deals would have carried no danger for him. It wasn't illegal to import on request ten trash compacters, say; but that request could have only one purpose behind it – the compacters were used to press the weed into blocks which kept the precious buds intact but which were easy to handle, wrap and export. Manuel had *known* and his conscience had not permitted him to comply.

But if, Rafael had reasoned, his father, who had been no doper, had yet died a doper's death, why should his son have the same moral qualms? His father had been too good, too trusting; Rafael wasn't going to make the same mistake. He had gone straight to Pedro, negotiated with Peyrefitte a larger than usual retailer's commission, and evidently cut himself in as a planter too. Rafael had his head screwed on. His father's death had severed the connection his father had felt between making money and morality, and Rafael, without those scruples, would make a lot more money than his father had done. Bill thought of his own family. Manuel Zuniga, like his great-grandfather Fullerton, had founded the family fortune; Rafael, like his grandfather, would diversify and this *milpa* was seeing the first of his diversifications.

He followed Rafael into one of the huts. He removed his shades. It was cool and dark under the palm roof, smelling slightly of creosote. When Bill's eyes were used to the half-light he saw that it was surprisingly roomy. To one side was piled a high wall of plastic sacks – the Miracle-Gro fertiliser ordered through Zuniga's. Miracle-Gro was well named – it sent plants soaring and also, importantly, tended with weed to produce a predominance of female plants; it was the females you wanted. A sack was open, as though for his inspection. He dipped a hand into it and let the green crystals trickle through his fingers. He remembered the Guadaloupe in Peyrefitte's back windshield. 'I know where she got her roses,' he suddenly thought. 'She used Miracle-Gro.'

Rafael was explaining in his broken English that the weed would be planted as maize was, the planters walking the *milpa* with fire-hardened sowing sticks and shoulder bags of seed. Bill listened absently, then pointed to a shape under a cowling.

'Is that the pump?' he asked. From outside he heard a peal of laughter from Amanda. Rafael pulled away the cowling and Bill lowered himself to his haunches, at eye level with the diesel pump. Weed while it grows is thirsty and this would supplement the water supply if necessary. Abstractedly, Bill listened as Rafael explained that there was a stream in the bush behind the huts, dry now, but when the rains came they could run a hose up from it and ...

Then the young *mestizo* saw the rich American do the thing which his mother had done that day in Belize Hospital when his father died and again at his father's funeral. He sank from his haunches to his knees on the earth floor and both hands flew to his chest; he threw his head back with a groan and bared his teeth beseechingly in what looked exactly like impassioned prayer, an involuntary overflow of emotion with no other outlet. But the American?

*Ice.*

'What is it, Mister Bill?' asked Rafael.

*This was it. He was going to freeze to death.*

'Are you okay?'

He gasped and his hands clutched, as though they could still pull out the axe which had been buried in the exact centre of his chest. But it wasn't an ordinary axe and this wasn't ordinary pain. He'd felt as much before, but nothing so strange; and his fear of the strangeness was mixed up with the pain. Because this was an axehead of solid ice and the pain it caused wasn't bloody, sharp like a blade; it was intensely cold and it had come from nowhere he knew. Rafael half stepped forward, wide-eyed with alarm, frozen indeed; only a moment, then he ran to the door and shouted, '*¡Venga, venga! ¡Pedro, el Americano! ¡Algun ha ocurrido!*'

Now he imagined the stock attitude of Rafael in the hut variously replicated among those outside it, bottles of beer and those crazy Sacred Heart cups in the act of being raised to mouths from which the smiles and laughter had suddenly died, disbelief as they registered the ghost at the feast. And on Amanda's face? Fear, or knowledge?

'*Venga, venga ...*'

Then the hut was full of people, Pedro first, kneeling beside him, then Peyrefitte, then Amanda; *pesetas* followed by *amor*. Pedro said something in Spanish and Bill caught '*córazon*' and shook his head before Pedro had translated himself.

'Is it your heart?' he said. Amanda's arm was round his shoulders and how could she bear to be near such cold as he felt?

Peyrefitte had already let go, moved back slightly and now Bill heard him confirm, coolly and as though from afar, 'No, it's not his heart.'

Bill looked at him and through the pain his eyes said, 'How can you *know*?' And in Peyrefitte's eyes was, 'Mister Bill, you're an old and a sick man and you've fucked up . . .'

It was all happening very quickly, but very slowly to him. Now Amanda's hand was rubbing his chest and she'd found where the cold was but didn't understand that she couldn't reach it, not only because, unmistakably, it was *under* his breastbone, but because, in some other sense, it was *his* cold, *his* pain and *no one* could reach it.

'What is it?' he heard her quietly ask him, and he managed to say the one word: 'cold'. Then he heard *fiebre,* but no, this wasn't hot-and-cold like fever, but a bitter, localised cold, a block of frozen north he'd brought with him at his centre, the last to defrost. Then two of the planters were in the hut with a folding camp bed and next thing, somehow, he was on it, rolled over onto his side, someone had tossed a poncho over him and Amanda held his hand. It already felt better. The stabbing sensation had gone and his body was going into shock, the cold dispersing through him. There was a little space of silence, then, like voices inside his own mind, he heard the hospital whispers of the planters:

'*¿Que es?*'

'*Puede que esté cansado.*'

'*Es viejo.*'

No, he wanted to object, he wasn't old; but now he'd started to shiver, uncontrollably, his body was shaking.

Amanda asked, gently – how uncannily calm she was! – 'What is it?'

'I don't know,' he managed to say through chattering teeth, 'I don't know, don't know . . .' It was a voice touched by frost.

111

She said, 'It was cold. You said cold. Where is it?' and in answer he moved his fist against his chest. She rubbed there again and said with the no-nonsense efficiency of a nurse, 'It's something you've picked up. You must sleep.' She turned to the others in the hut and said, 'Leave him to sleep.' She was in charge; with courteous expressions of concern, they went.

Now it was winter throughout his body; his feet and hands felt cold. 'It'll be okay,' she said, and put her hand to his face, 'Sleep and it'll be okay.'

'We're alone?' he asked, and she said yes; but light still slanted through the hut's half-open door. He asked her to shut it and when she had done so said from the darkness, 'Tell them it's the war, shrapnel, metal in my chest from the Germans.'

She seemed to hesitate, then said, 'Okay, I'll tell them.'

He said, sharply, 'You understand?'

'I understand.' Then she was near him again, her hand on his skin. 'Go to sleep,' she was saying, 'you need to sleep,' and somehow her repetition of 'sleep' was tied up with the warm darkness he could now feel welling up inside him, a dark tide of sleep at last overwhelming the last consciousness to which the mind clung.

He awoke fresh from a dream which might have been hours or seconds before. The cold woke him, but this time it wasn't his own but a chill in the air, rising from the earth floor. He pulled the poncho up over his shoulders, then moved again, as one might move to test the mend of a broken bone. But he was fine, refreshed by his sleep like any healthy man. He wondered what time it was; a bluish light filtered through cracks in the hut walls.

Then he thought of what he had dreamt.

He had been at a fairground where an unnaturally fit old man was riding a bucking bronco; there was something almost frightening about this old man's air of health – his cheeks were red like apples injected with dye. Then he'd looked down and realised that he was himself on a horse, not a bronco but a painted merry-go-round mount, and he had heard the meaningless, repetitious tinkle and grind of fairground music.

Another man whom, with the certainty of dream, he had known to be his father, was under a striped awning feeding dimes into a fruitless fruit machine. Bells and flashing lights, the machine had gone through the retching motions of coughing up: but nothing.

Then he had found himself in an empty corner of the fairground; the tents and stalls and wheels were some way off now. He was with someone wise – he could have been Pedro in dream-disguise. This shadowy man was telling him, very gravely, how to plant a seed.

'Why do old men garden?' he'd asked, and answered himself, 'Because they long for the earth they're not long for.' The horrible old bronco-breaker had appeared from somewhere, grinning, rude with health. A tannoy-voice was saying, 'Some people are never happy, some people are never happy,' over and over, round and round, and the old man was saying it too, the shadowy man was saying it, all of creation was saying it, 'Some people are never happy, some people are never ...'

He shuddered. The sense of the dream was still upon him, with an unaccountable sadness. Then the hut door opened with a slight creak. It was Amanda framed in the doorway against what he could guess to be moonlight – but he was in a temporary ward where tricks had been played with time. He said from the dark, 'Amanda,' whispering.

'James, you're awake. How do you feel?'

'Fine. How long did I sleep?'

'Hours. Did you hear the rain?'

'There was rain?'

She was still at the door as though it were that of a study which he, a person of authority, had not given her permission to enter; the seizure, the collapse, whatever had happened, had the weight of an embarrassment between them.

'A huge thunderstorm,' she said. '*Huge.* You must have been completely worn out, *cansado* like the boys said.'

'*Cansado*,' he repeated, and then, 'I wonder what it was?'

'Some bug,' she said with a stranger's cheerfulness. 'There are crazy tropical bugs. An amoeba, maybe.'

'It felt like a fist,' he said, 'a fist of ice in my chest.'

'We'll go see Dr Abb.'

He said, gruffly, 'Come to me, will you?' And in a few steps she was beside him, half knelt on the earth floor by the bed, her head on his shoulder and his arms were around her, and she

113

was saying, 'It's okay, it'll be okay,' then, 'Oh, it's so beautiful outside. You should see.'

'Are we staying here the night?'

'Hmm. The boys start early. Pedro was right, wasn't he?'

'Right ...?'

'About the rain.'

'Yes,' he agreed. 'Pedro was right. Where is he?'

'He and Peyrefitte went home.'

'And the boys?'

'They're in the next hut.' She laughed quietly. 'Drunk and high.' He tried to pull her more closely to him, but she laughed again and said, 'Careful, the bed will collapse!' and when she kissed him, on the mouth, it was a kiss in which there was the last tight restraint of a smile. She broke off and said, 'Come and see,' rising to her feet. 'Put the poncho on.' She went to the door and stood there, looking out. 'Beautiful,' she murmured, 'beautiful.'

He joined her. There was the spectral stillness of new moon-light after rain, as though a wand had been waved over the landscape. He, too, caught in its spell, was still. But there was nothing cosily pastoral about the scene. At the far side of the black *milpa*, sleek now with rain and light, someone was walking with a pitch-pine torch – the one human focus. But the yellow flame only served to intensify the sense of darkness. He had never felt a greater sense of the world's vastness than at this moment in this very small country. And it was, strangely, a good darkness, in which no irremediable evil was being per-petrated. The bush walls of the *milpa* were outlined against a sky from which the rain had removed all anger and hurt, but already, to the west, a concentration of cloud was building, as though the next day's consignment of rain were already being stacked for delivery.

Amanda said, 'But look at the stars!' He looked up. It was the fantastic balancing act of the Southern Cross, poised upon Acrux, its brightest, southernmost star, just above the horizon. He stared wonderingly at the cross of stars standing out at the far limit of imagination, against infinity and beyond understanding. Then an idea occurred to him. He walked out onto the *milpa* a little way, Amanda following, and when he was far enough out turned to face the huts; face North.

114

It was there too, just over the horizon but sharing the same sky, the Pole Star, the constant companion of the North. And he remembered the spinning compass and, all the years before, his father saying 'North *matters*.' There is no civilisation, he had read, without the plough and now, looking at the constellation fully visible, he wondered if his father had meant, not the North Star so much as the Plough which pointed at it. The Maya had died out in one theory because they had not invented the plough; thus the *milpa* surrounding him now. But he had spent a lifetime behind that plough of northern civilisation.

Then he knew that whatever had caused the cold sensation at the very centre of his chest, the cause had not been tropical, southern. No, in some mysterious manner it had emanated from *there,* the North, the Plough. He turned around. The North had imagined a plough, the South a cross. He turned again to the North. A plough. And the South. A cross.

Amanda said, 'What is it?'

He said, 'Amanda ...' then hesitated. All his time with her he had been or had played the protector, the older man, indulging her, revealing some truths while hiding others. But there was something pitiless about this sky, the configuration of the stars on this night, as pitiless as the cold he had felt.

'What is it?' she asked again, and he turned to her, bracing her with an appearance of courage he didn't feel;

'Amanda,' he said, 'I'm going to die.'

# PART THREE

# GROWING

On the Southern Foreshore you might chance to see, haphazardly piled against the seawall, mounds of an off-white substance looking like unglazed porcelain; you might pass as it is being landed from a lighter, fresh from the seabed, one of the spits or the shallows of the offshore islands called cays, wherever the lightermen find it. Go closer. Pick up a piece. It is a hollow, slightly curved shell or stone, a fossil perhaps or colourless coral. The mound as a whole is a giant's plate of pasta, steaming as the seawater dries and having the sea smell of *vongole*.

In due course convicts will come from the Gabourel prison and shovel the mounds onto PWD trucks. The trucks will drive around town or up-country and the convicts will use the 'pothole pipe-clay', as the locals call it, to mend the roads. The poor state of the roads is the national despair, an obsession, significant because beneath it lies a primitive anxiety that the land is only just real. On the coast it has the feel of naturally redeemed swamp, which much of it is; the sea is the absentee landlord who might at any moment repossess. The abiding reality is the sea and the life of the sea.

Every hurricane season it is rubbed home how tenuous the shore is. Most years it is only the landlord rattling the locks; but sometimes, possessed, he breaks the doors down. The sea builds itself into a wall; the land cowers after the storm, waiting for the tidal wave. Then boats will float in the streets and shacks drift out to sea. The coast along its length is submerged. All over again the land is mud and it'll be weeks before the beer truck gets to Punta Gorda.

But go into the interior and the land is solid enough. Find the tropical hardwoods and learn a marquetry of names, Mylady and Silly Young, Santa Maria and Billy Webb, Provision and Bullet trees. Go in a dorey, a hollowed-out log, down rivers and

119

creeks lined with Madre Cacao. Disembark and go deeper, you might find a fustic or logwood – the trees used for dyeing which first brought the British timber buccaneers to this stretch of coast. With the decline of the dye trade, another wood kept them there. 'King Mahogany' was cut and floated downriver, over the sludgy shallows of the estuary and then to the roadstead offshore, where ships of oak from the mouth of the Thames filled their holds with mahogany logs to be milled, carved and sanded into the cabriole-legged furniture of Chippendale and Sheraton.

There was no formal agreement to cut mahogany. Spain agreed a concession, but demand was growing, and soon the buccaneers or 'Baymen' were wielding their axes deeper inland and further south, in virgin forest far outside the concession's terms, on the Rio Grande, the Moho, the Sarstoon, chopping a territory out of Central America, pirating land as well as wood. A boundary agreement was drawn up with Spain, in which practical considerations of woodcutting figured large. To north and south the borders were the Hondo and Sarstoon, rivers to float the logs down; the western border was determined by waterfalls, Garbutt's and Gracias a Dios, over which logs couldn't be floated. Looking at that piratical early map one half expects an 'X marks the spot'. It was a new, larger concession, but not yet a colony, although a superintendant's report of 1840 refers hesitantly to 'this settlement or Colony of British Honduras'.

But there was no 'British' Honduras as yet except in so far as the territory was not Spanish either. A glorified logging camp is not a country. Yet the British by then had been on the coast two centuries, long enough for 'Wallace', the name of the first buccaneer, to have been polished by Grimm's law and corrupted by Spanish into 'Bullys', 'Bellese', finally 'Belize', the name of the coastal town.

Traditions had grown up, a distinctive brand of English, a speech-pattern, attachments. Generations of blacks, Hispanics, runaway Mexicans, Maya and Kekchi and whites had interbred. There were *mestizos*, half-castes, second- and third-generation settlers who in the snooty imperial phrase had been 'country born', entering the world under a mistaken sky. There were Anglophone octoroons. There were fast-bowling, freed slaves

All these people were stuck in somewhere without recognition, fictional country requiring blind-drunk dreaming to give it the semblance of reality. The settlers were far from Britain – insecure and uncertain. The pirates wanted respectability. The mistress – Miss Mahogany – wanted marriage. But she had to do the proposing. In 1850 the settlers petitioned Britain asking for colonial status.

They got their wish in 1862, when British Honduras was declared a colony; Britain would still be regretting that decision more than a hundred years later. But the Empire at its height reproduced itself effortlessly, almost automatically; it was the same old story, only this time in a pirated edition.

The settlers symbolised their new-found security in a colonial emblem. Pride of place on it went to a stylised mahogany tree, with, below, the legend *Sub umbra floreo*. Indeed the settlers had flourished under the broad-leafed shadow of 'King Mahogany'; but the colony was born under another shadow too – that of its aggressive neighbour, Guatemala. And in 1945, in a new constitution, 'the Guats' declared 'Belice' to belong to them.

By 1981 British commitment to Belize's defence had taken the form of six vertical-take-off Harriers and seventeen hundred Gordon Highlanders. The jump jets were under camouflage netting at Stanley Field, the airport; the jungle jocks, the Scotsman Wallace's successors, breakfasted on malaria pills in a variety of sweltering, mosquito-tormented camps around the country.

The timber industry had declined. Mahogany was now just one of a variety of trees sawn into planks up-country or floated down to the docks, the boatyards, and the saw-mills whose high-pitched scream filled the evenings. There was ironwood for marine pile-driving; men outside hotels sold sailing boats and sharks carved from two-toned ziricote, the novelty wood; planks of cedar and pine were used to build boats and houses.

The houses were timber-framed, as was the colony's history, and supported above rats and floods on wooden piles like boats in dry dock. The older ones were close to the sea, straggling from the Barracks to Fort George, then again along the Southern Foreshore to Government House, on either side of river mouth and docks. The seafront was cooler and healthier, but the irresistible impression was of the houses as starting-blocks, their

121

inhabitants ready for a rapid getaway from the 'resting, not abiding place'. With fading optimism the houses looked out to sea and faraway Britain, like old men in rocking chairs, backs firmly turned on the interior where the worst diseases were and the storm cloud of Guatemala which might at any moment overwhelm the western border as the sea might overwhelm the coast. There was still no real security. Belize could not forget her beginnings as a concession; she had come into existence as a kind of favour and was still there on sufferance.

The house Bill Brandl had taken was not on the seafront, but back from the Southern Foreshore on Regent Street. Baskets of orchids hung from the veranda, which faced the Wesleyan school and a corner where a perished whitewall truck-tyre lay on its side. Passers-by would use the tyre as a sort of impromptu love seat, sitting on it facing outwards and talking jivily to one another over their shoulders. Behind the house was a vat which collected rainwater for drinking and a lawn of Bermuda grass.

One mid-morning in July Bill was at the foot of the lawn picking limes, placing them one by one in a blue-striped mixing bowl he'd brought from the kitchen. He felt something less tepid than happiness, a muted joy, light-headed and calm at once. Sunlight fell across the garden and the air under the tree smelt sharply of citrus. He had never felt better and he asked himself again whether he really needed to make the trip to the States which he had planned. It had been Dr Abb's suggestion. Returning to Belize City after the *milpa* he had gone to see the doctor about the phenomenon which he had described to Amanda, and then described to him, simply as 'the ice'. But it was hard to describe and when Dr Abb had asked for his symptoms in more detail he had simply dried up. The doctor, too, had been mystified and suggested a check-up in the States, where there was the diagnostic know-how. Bill had begun to comment on the parallel between himself and Reuben's father, when Dr Abb cut him short with 'Jimmy White's illness was serious. Yours may be nothing. It sounds a little like a growing pain, but of course it can't be. Anyway, let me know if there's a recurrence.

But there had been none and Bill had begun to wonder whether 'the ice' had not been a figment of his imagination. Perhaps it had been a growing pain after all, or a muscular spasm hysterically exaggerated, a mysterious visitation which

122

had come and gone, never to return. Still, though, he had not been able to forget that strange, incommunicable iciness in his chest. 'The ice', he told himself, had been real; but until he went to the States he would not know whether there was an underlying physiological cause.

However, he rebelled against the idea of going north. He could stay here as long as his health allowed – and his health seemed to be fine. What he had said to Amanda on the *milpa* that night, under the terror of the stars, now seemed to him the purest self-indulgence. He had told Amanda so. Die indeed, when he felt so intensely well and alive! Still, why not clear up the last doubt? He could always keep Amanda's mind at rest by telling her he was going to the States to meet the terms of immigration of his Blue Card.

The bowl was full of limes. He crossed the lawn and climbed the stairs to the kitchen, where the floorboards gave beneath his feet with a shipboard creak. He placed a lime on the chopping board and sliced it; the juice of course went straight in his eye. He dabbed it with a corner of drying-up cloth, then continued slicing.

That morning after breakfast Amanda had asked for fifty Belize dollars. He'd given her the money and she, with a kiss on his cheek, had taken her mammy-style straw shopping basket and gone to the market. She kissed his cheek a lot these days, less often his lips. It seemed to him that her kisses were slowly moving away from his mouth to become merely creature comfort kisses of the kind you give someone lovable whom you do not love. He hoped it was only a phase. Amanda went through more phases than the moon. Her present one involved buying live turtles from the market stalls and letting them loose in the sea. Fifty dollars a turtle. She spoke feelingly and often of their faces puckered and perplexed like those of babies and little old men. People had harder shells than turtles, she said; there should be people soup and humanshell combs. Every week she would save a turtle's life – their 'turtle tax', she called it. Well, he would indulge her. He usually did.

When all the limes were halves he started to squeeze them and pour the juice into a jug of ice cubes and sugar. He was doing this for the third or fourth time when he realised how silent it was. The hubbub of car horns and bicycle bells had gone quite still, leaving an oppressive silence broken only by a distant rat-a-tat-tat. It was a drum. He stirred the juice and poured some into a glass. Mmm, it tasted good. He put down the glass and went through the dining room. It would be a march of the Belize Defence Force, the BDF or 'Bloody Damned Fools'; it would be a parade of some sort or a demo by BAM, the cartoon acronym of the anti-independence Belize Action Movement; it would be a procession of floats carrying the finalists of the 'Miss Beautiful Belize' contest. He opened the louvre doors on to the veranda . . .


So close had Reuben's father been to death, so widely had it been assumed he would die and so dramatically did he prove them all wrong, that news of his recovery travelled with a rapidity matching that of the recovery itself. Having been unable to get up one day, unable to perform even the most basic functions unaided and barely able to talk, by the next evening he was sitting up in bed and looking around him at his familiar and shabby surroundings as though he'd been transported to a wondrous new land. While still gaunt, he yet seemed positively refreshed – more like a man plucked from the jaws of sleep than death. And he was still sleepy. After asking for his Bible and silently leafing through it for a few pages, after eating the dinner Ma Armstrong had prepared for him, he took his blue, Portuguese glass float and lay down in bed with it, holding it like a baby, or as if he were the baby and it were his comforter. Perhaps it was a former fisherman's memory of buoyancy as a life-saver. Reuben had been touched by that simple gesture – how eloquent human beings can be *in extremis*, when their egos are out of action. So, the second day, had he been touched when his father said, 'If not for God, I would have been bones back there.' He knew all over again how much he loved the old man, how much more alone in the world he'd have been if he'd died, how grateful he was that he'd lived. And his father, too, had been grateful. But by the third day the wonder had begun to wear thin; he'd put on weight already, and on this day, for the first time, he bawled out the people who gathered outside and peered round the door for a glimpse of the Miracle Man. What

124

people called 'his old self again', and Reuben already subtly liked his father less.

He was, though, intensely grateful that his father's life had been spared and that afternoon he rode his motorbike to Belize City intending to thank Bill. On the way he stopped at the post-office and found waiting for him in his box a letter from Sybil in New York. He thought that before going to Bill's he would visit Mom's Triangle Restaurant across the way and read the letter.

From its first words Sybil's tone roused his suspicion. Her letter recalled a 'perfect day' they had spent together two years or so before, on the beach at Placentia; the sun, the fine white sand, the smell of citrus and taste of rice-and-beans cooked in coconut milk. Reuben licked his finger and turned to the next page. More in the same vein. And the next page. Still more. Something was wrong here. Too much past, no present or future. And had that day at Placentia been anything special? They had quarrelled, if he remembered rightly. What was 'perfect' about that? He knew about Sybil's delicate footwork. This was to get him to feel strong for when her body blow came. What was the blow to be? When would the bee-sting show, under the butterfly's wing?

'What can I get you, Reuben?'

It was Mom, an overweight American lady in a striped apron.

'Uh? Oh, nothing thank you Ma.'

'*Ma*, Reuben?'

'Mom I mean.'

'Ma's in The North 'Nam,' she teased him. 'Mom is in Mom's.'

'I get confused,' said Reuben. 'It *is* confusing.'

She laughed. 'Poor boy,' she said, and went.

Now Sybil seemed to be getting to the point. In New York, she had written, lemon-scented bath-scourer was the closest you came to the blossom smell of Placentia. How ugly the big city was – why, only last week a man came to casualty with his face cut up with razors. A bigger, nastier jungle than Belize and none of the beauty. But even so the city sucked you into its life, a fast current which swept away the past and its observances. And Reuben was alas part of that frail past. How remote he seemed to her, now; but come to think of it, hadn't he seemed remote

125

even in Placentia, on that day which was itself so distant? Wasn't he, Reuben, in himself a remote man? Her feeling for him had always been half fear. How could it endure the distance between them, the time apart, the struggle to survive in New York, her need for a man by her to help in that struggle?

And there was someone now, a man. It was funny: he knew all about life for the moment; he didn't brood on the past, like Reuben; and yet he had come from further back in her past than Reuben ever had. Most of all he was there, in New York, and had come there specially to be with her; and he had money; he made her laugh; he knew about big city life and she felt strong with him by her. 'And Reuben, I have to say,' Reuben read, 'all the time I was with you it had never died out between me and Peyrefitte . . .'

So that was it. Reuben folded the letter. The North and money had saved his father's life: he had lost 'his' woman to money and the North. Peyrefitte was a shyster. How could Sybil think she might be happy with him? How could she think he had gone to New York 'specially' for her?

There, she was accusing him. Reuben had not gone to her, after all. At least Peyrefitte was there, a warm body in the night, a charm against loneliness. While Reuben, in another of the battles of will which he fought on all fronts, had counted on her returning to him. And he had lost: Sybil wasn't going to let herself fail so easily . . .

Reuben, for the first time in earnest, asked himself whether there was something about his personality which did not make sense. Something excessive, or something missing . . .

'Mom,' he called across the restaurant, 'a Belikin beer. Fetch me one, will you?'

After the beer he had gone to Bill's, to the number in Regen Street which he had been given. Only at the gate did he realis it was the house where his mother had worked as a maid, i whose garden the roses had grown, the tyrant's castle of hi childhood memory. So, his benefactor lived here, where th Palmers had lived. He took a deep breath and slipped the latcl

Bill, hearing him from the veranda above, looked over and called, 'Reuben! Come on up!'

On the veranda, Reuben looked about him and said, 'This is a nice roomy place you have.'

'Old colonial mansion,' said Bill. 'My father would have loved it.'

'Your father?'

'He doted on anything English. Care for a beer?'

'That would be fine.'

'Amelia's out. I'll go and get it.'

'Amelia? So you know Amelia.'

'We, ah, met out here,' said Bill. 'She's lodging with me.'

'She was in Belize alone a few months back,' said Reuben. Then he made the connection. 'Of course. The pool ball. I told Amelia. You knew it was missing from her.'

Bill gave a half smile.

'Maybe. Did it do the trick?'

'Like magic.'

'Well,' said Bill, 'let me get you a Belikin.'

Once upon a time, thought Reuben when he was alone, someone on this veranda would have snapped his fingers and my mother would have brought the beer. Bill came back, the Belikin already poured, and told Reuben to take a seat. Reuben sipped his beer, sat down and said to Bill:

'I came to thank you for my father. The cure worked like magic, too.'

'Dr Abb told me,' said Bill. 'Good. It's nice when things work out.'

'Nice?' said Reuben. 'It's the kindest, most generous thing I ever heard of. Down in Hattieville now they're calling my father the Miracle Man. No, I want to tell them, it's you, Bill, who's the Miracle Man. Don't worry,' he added quickly, 'I won't tell. But the point is I don't know how I can thank you enough.'

'Please,' said Bill, 'it's nothing. A little money, that's all. What's that against a life? And like I said on the wharf, I did it for myself too.'

'And you? I heard you'd been poorly, too.'

Bill seemed embarrassed.

'How,' he asked, 'do you keep a secret out here?'

127

'You don't. The country's too small for secrets. Big secrets, anyhow.'

Bill, with that, seemed still more uncomfortable and Reuben said, 'What's the matter? Did I say something wrong?'

'About me being "poorly"?' said Bill. 'No. That's nothing either. An old war wound. Some shrapnel over Germany. It plays up sometimes.'

'You should get it seen to,' said Reuben, 'like you saw to my father. Charity begins at home. Have you seen Dr Abb about it?'

Yes, thought Bill, I have and it is probably from him that Reuben has heard; but I said nothing to Dr Abb about shrapnel and if Reuben speaks to him again about me they will both wonder about that. And something else: if Reuben thinks some more about 'Amelia' and me he'll guess that I must have known her before – because where in Belize could I have bought a black pool ball?

He said, 'If you don't mind, Reuben, I'd rather not talk about it. Tell me your news.'

'My father?'

'Your other news.'

Reuben hesitated.

'Well,' he said, 'on my way here I just picked up a letter. I had a girlfriend in New York called Sybil and she's left me. I mean she'd already left me for New York, but now she's *left* me left me, if you follow.'

'I'm sorry to hear that, Reuben.'

'No more miracles up your sleeve?'

Bill smiled.

'A little money and medicine can sometimes save a life,' he said, 'but not love.'

Reuben nodded. He said, 'I can't really blame her, can I? All those miles between us. It was already getting kind of theoretical. And she must have been lonely. But who's she left me for? That's the crazy thing.'

'Who? Do you want another beer?'

'No thanks,' said Reuben. 'A no-good guy from here called Peyrefitte. He must somehow have sweet-talked the Consul into giving him a visa, then sweet-talked his way into Sybil's apple-

128

pie order bed. I wonder if the Consul knows he's let another maggot into the Big Apple.'

'Peyrefitte?' said Bill.

'You know him?'

'Wears Ray-Bans? Guadaloupe in his back windshield?'

'That's him. Con-man. Ex-con. Could sleepwalk Gabourel jail and not trip up once. Well, fancy you knowing Peyrefitte.'

'He ...' – Bill hesitated – '... did some driving for me.'

Reuben laughed and drank the rest of his beer.

'I bet he overcharged.'

Bill paused. His mind was racing. Peyrefitte had done more than overcharge. He'd done a runner from the dope farm, with *his* money. It was difficult to hide from Reuben, who was quietly agitated enough on his own account, his agitation at this news. If Reuben went to the Consulate and moves were made to extradite Peyrefitte, what might the consequences be for himself and 'Amelia'? But Reuben owed him a favour.

He said carefully, 'Reuben, I don't think you should go to the Consulate.'

Reuben looked at him, surprised.

'Bill, I don't think you understand. This guy's a criminal.'

But so, thought Bill, am I.

He said, 'Is that your real motive, Reuben, civic duty to the United States? Isn't it really revenge and wouldn't you really be revenging yourself not on Peyrefitte but on Sybil?'

Reuben laughed again.

'My father says things like that. Very Matthew, Mark, Luke and Dear John. But I find, turn the other cheek it gets slapped too.'

'Think about it, Reuben. You may not have the temperament for revenge. Think about the good things. The future. Think what we can do for Hattieville.'

'I've been asking around down there ...'

'And?'

'You'll never guess what they want.' Bill waited. Reuben said: 'TV.'

'Come again?'

'Television. Even my father wants it. Maybe he's a little bored with his Bible.'

'TV,' said Bill. 'It seems a strange sort of philanthropy.'

Reuben shrugged.

'Boredom is a disease too.'

'And Hattieville's got it and TV could cure it, eh? What would it cost?'

'Not so much. There's already electricity. A satellite dish, a TV set . . .'

'High-tech in Hattieville.' Bill smiled. 'But is it "high ground"? What would the benefits be?'

'Keep people off the street. Smarten their act up a little. Remind them they're in the big wide world. Who knows? But that's what they want.'

'Then,' Bill said decisively, 'let's give it to them. And Reuben . . .'

'Yes?'

'There's a little something I want too. A favour.'

'Just say the word.'

'Don't go to the Consulate.'

Reuben stared.

'Is that all?'

Bill nodded.

'All.'

'Done,' said Reuben. 'But I hope you're going to ask some more from me than that. I owe you, Bill, I owe you . . .'


Bill was a good friend, thought Reuben as he climbed on his motorbike, but a new friend, and what he needed now to help him get over the shock of Sybil's letter was an old one; what he needed was Abba.

He kick-started the bike and thought how strange his relationship with Abba was. Unique. Its strength derived from a bonding of their disabilities, Abba's physical, his emotional. Reuben was fiery and argumentative – but you couldn't get into slanging matches with a mute. Abba was a good listener too and above all now Reuben needed to spill things out. You could trust a mute to keep your secrets.

No, that wasn't right. Reuben told Abba his secrets and Abba respected them, out of love. And it wasn't as if Abba couldn't communicate. Sometimes, Reuben thought, he communicated more eloquently than those gifted with speech, as with the dead rose that evening; or when he'd gone through an elaborate mime of being born – he had been telling Reuben it was his birthday. Others were quickly bored by Abba's charades, but never Reuben. To him, Abba was a blessed oasis of silence in a desert of words which people picked up and threw at each other like sharp-edged stones. Words were weapons. Words hurt. Abba's gentleness had something to do with being mute.

Reuben parked his bike outside the Bayman; he went into the foyer and looked into Abba's cubbyhole. Abba wasn't there. On the bench was a brown shoe in the middle of being shone and a small vase of Roses of Sharon picked, Reuben supposed, from the bush outside the hotel.

When he turned around Maria had returned to the reception desk. And something was wrong. (Who had put roses in Abba's cubbyhole?) Reuben sensed it at once from the way that Maria stood, how she looked at him, with hurt of her own and with fear of hurting him.

She spoke first.

'Reuben . . .'

And stopped.

'Maria, what's the matter?' said Reuben. But he knew the answer already.

'Bad news, Reuben.'


Miracle Man. Ma Armstrong had said that about Reuben's father on the first day, and crossed herself like a Catholic, hurrying off to spread the good news in The North Vietnam. A miracle – so much more colourful an explanation than a glass of souped-up cherryade. Reuben could understand it, but at the same time he was uneasy. All this talk of God made him uneasy. Why were people in the dark places of the world so inclined to belief in divine dispensation? Was it the celebration of those who had no choice? Was spirituality always rooted in ignorance, like insanitary conditions? 'No Ma,' he'd wanted to say, 'it's money and the modern world is all.' But he'd promised not to elaborate; to protect Bill from importuning petitioners and to protect the authority of Dr Abb's practice, he would say nothing.

The policeman had promised too, but he'd said enough for a story of gobbledegook gossip, garbled science, to spread along with the miracle explanation. It said, in essence, that the old man had 'drunk the juice of an atom bomb'. And there were, of course, the usual stories of a hex lifted by magic. Magic. Some of it had rubbed off on Reuben, too, enhancing his prestige, but at the same time sickening him with the knowledge that life-and-death issues could resolve themselves into a sawdust secret like those of the stage magician who won't reveal how he cuts the woman in half. It's money, that's all, that's what he wanted to say. How did doctors endure the hokum gap between their own and others' knowledge? How did priests stand the suspicion that God was only people's fear and foolishness made meta-physical? Delighted as he was with his father's physical recovery, it also came as a philosophical shock. The world had made sense for once – that was all. And they called it a miracle. But he said nothing, himself enduring the bullshit, except on the occasion when Ma Armstrong, who'd grown into the habit of calling his father Lazarus, actually called him that to his face, and he actually smiled and accepted it! As though they'd both stepped out of the well-thumbed pages of the old man's Bible! Then Reuben had demurred and said:

'Lazarus? He's New Testament, Ma, but my father, he's Old, very Old, aren't you Pa?'

'I like to read the Old Testament more,' the old man said. 'The words are prettier.' And he had licked his fingers and turned a page, looking, Reuben thought, mightily pleased with himself.

Ma Armstrong said, 'Now don't you go exhausting yourself, hear?' She wrung a grunt and nod of assent from the old man; then Reuben thanked her for coming, she grumbled to herself a moment, she went. Silence in the room. Reuben picked up a copy of *Brukdown* magazine. 'Is Nicholas Ridley bluffing?' asked the front cover. 'Can Belize afford to find out?' He opened the magazine and read:

The second round of Anglo-Guatemalan-Belizean nego-tiations slated to begin in London June 15 was postponed. The real hang-up, according to sources in Belmopan, was that the Guatemalans are insisting on the right to establish naval

132

bases on the southern cays. Whether or not a treaty is signed plans are going ahead for Belize's Independence Day celebrations. A bipartisan committee has been meeting weekly to plan the details of the Big Event.

'It isn't Lazarus.'

'Mmm?'

Reuben looked up from *Brukdown* to see his father intent over his Bible, a finger firmly pressed against a page. He turned to Reuben, on his face the look of muted triumph he wore when he caught someone out on a point of pedantry. It is strange how a pettifogging pedantry accompanies old age, as though only then does one get around to examining the fine print of the contract. Behind his father, through the open door, Reuben caught a glimpse of a small boy with no clothes on using a stick to bowl a bicycle wheel down the road.

'Ma Armstrong,' his father said.

'What about her?'

'She *say* Lazarus, but she *mean* the man with the palsy. It troubled me, see? Lazarus was dead but ...' and his father laboriously followed the words with a finger '... the man with the palsy was sick because of he sins. And they let his couch through the roof and the Son of Man forgive and cure him. Jus' like that!' His father shut the Bible with a satisfied thud. 'I tell her nex' time.'

'You tell her, Pa.'

Reuben couldn't remember a time when his father had been ordinarily devout. He must have been once – church on Sunday, grace at meals, that sort of thing, a relaxed faith that hadn't been tested to destruction. What had gone wrong? Had he lacked the mechanisms to deal with what life threw at him, or had life simply thrown too much? Or had he loved too much? Was that a sin too? Perhaps so. Because when you loved someone like that – as his father had maybe loved his mother – when they died you died in spirit with them, your unconscious wanted to be with them where they were, dead or mad it didn't matter. And his mother had both gone mad and gone and died. And when she'd been put away his father's sanity had gone on sympathetic strike. He'd got God bad. It had begun then – nearly thirty years ago. The house where Reuben grew up had

133

been strewn with holy-roller tracts – an out-patient extension of the asylum, where God was the polite name for the high-pressure pain his mother was feeling raw. His father had matched her madness with mania – was this Lazarus talk the prelude to a new bout of it? Lazarus. Reuben had an idea – he saw an opening. Should he follow it now, was the time right? He went to the door. The boy was bowling the wheel back up the street. It was taller than he was and he couldn't run fast enough to keep up. The wheel wobbled, out of control, toppled and hula-hooped briefly in the dust. Reuben said, absently, 'More ways than Lazarus to come back from the dead.'

'What's that?' The flash of alarm in his father's face gave him for a moment the pop-eyed look he'd had when he was ill. Reuben took his time.

'Alan Palmer, you remember?'

'The Palmer boy? What about him?'

'He's back in town. That's kind of back from the dead, no? He's walking the streets, but there's no bandages on him. Maybe he's well or maybe he's ill. I don't know. I haven't enquired after his health. But I know this Lazarus opens old wounds.'

'What you saying, boy?'

Reuben shrugged – but he wasn't the sort to shrug things off.

'I don't know what to do is all.'

'Do? What should you do?'

'Don't we have a quarrel with him?'

'No,' his father said firmly. 'No, but you have one with me you not careful. What's a matter with you, boy? Why do you quarrel-quarrel all the time?' His father was staring at him, as though his question had an answer and he wanted it; Reuben said nothing. His father said, 'You're never happy, are you? An' now you go vexing me when I'm ill.'

There was great tiredness in his voice and Reuben said, 'I'm sorry. I figured you were well enough to hear.'

'Well enough?' the old man burst out. 'It's you's not well enough, boy, sometimes I think you got bad trouble brewing in your mind and that don't cure easy. What's a matter? The Palmer boy, he was just a little *boy* when your mother steal the roses. You want a visit the father's sins? You want mine? Let bygones be.'

Reuben said, 'Some moments, they're never bygone. They

134

stand still forever, some moments, they burn in your mind always.'

'Boy, you're talking crazy and you don't be careful that's what you go. Like your ma. Crazy and quarrelsome and obsessive. You play the good boy, but the man goes mad, he goes bad, all the same. What you thinking of? A killing him? He has roses to steal? You steal the boy's roses, repeat the past? No, you do nothing. Hear? Don't fight the moon.'

It was a reference to a long-ago episode from Reuben's childhood – a family story he'd often heard. It told how they'd been out on the cays one night, fishing, and Reuben had held up his arms at the sky and said, 'I want to fight the moon!' It had been a full moon, very large, and perhaps, for a child, intimidating. By its light his father was mending a net. He'd laid his work aside and sat his child on his knee, where again he'd shaken his fists at the sky and challenged the moon to a fight.

'No, sonny,' his father had said, 'you can't fight the moon. That's God's moon – see? – an' you can't fight it.' The moral was plain – but what, Reuben thought, if one had been born fighting and born to fight? Some people were boxers by nature and instinct: they existed sharply only through conflict. But the flesh-and-blood opponents of his boxing days – how much easier they'd been than this shadow boxing where the ring was one's mind!

Reuben said, 'She was driven crazy. The Palmers – they *drove* her crazy.'

'No boy.' His father's voice was full of sadness now. 'She *was* crazy. Or she drove herself. Or God drove her, God put her craziness there just like he put the moon and no one knows the reason.'

'She was *driven*,' said Reuben, and if his father had recently been near death he was still going to make this point. His father knew it, too; in his eyes he was backing down. Reuben said, 'It isn't always God, Daddy, who does everything. Sometimes it's life and bad luck. Sybil goes to New York and sleeps with another man. Abba is hit by a truck. Your best friend is killed. Love is killed off. *You get driven crazy.*'

It hung between them, a horrified pause. And then the old man said, his voice small, 'Did all that happen?'

'Yes, Daddy.' Reuben felt a little ashamed. 'Life's been rolling on while you've been sick, rolling on like a runaway truck.'

'Abba? He's dead?'

'If he isn't then it's a live man they'll be burying tomorrow.'

'No. No.' His father closed his eyes; he wrapped his arms about himself.

'I didn't want to hurt you.'

'And Sybil?'

'That too.'

'Oh son,' the old man said, 'son, I'm so sorry for you ...'


The drum was still being beaten. Bill went to his veranda rail and looked down Regent Street. It was a funeral. Perhaps a hundred people in black were following a horse and cart with a coffin on it. The street was silent except for the grinding of wheels in dirt, the shuffle of feet, low murmurs, the unmilitary tapping of the drum. Passers-by had stood aside and were waiting in respect for the procession to pass. The street-corner whitewall tyre had been vacated. Four men stood beside it, looking down the street. One held a carboy of rum. A mother held the hand of a pig-tailed little girl with a satchel over her shoulder. Bill felt the reality of death rolling towards him as a rheumatic might feel the onset of rain.

Bill had seen the horse and cart on Regent Street a few days before. Then it had been taking a used fridge somewhere; today it was a horse and hearse. He'd been struck then by the yellow sign on the side of the cart saying simply MISTRY: REMOVALS, and by the sight of its driver up on the box, Mr Mistry himself one presumed, an old East Indian with long grey hair and a face so fixed that its owner could have hidden the existence of a handful of aces. Mistry's head had been bowed in mimicry of his broken-down nag's in profound misery or indifference and on his head had been a straw hat which might have belonged better on the horse. Passing the veranda the old man had turned and stared up at him – a frosty, strong stare but oddly without curiosity.

Today, in honour of the dead, Mr Mistry carried no whip, but the same mask of suffering nothing was on his face and the sign saying REMOVALS was still in place. Seeing him the other day Bill

136

had reflected that he might have been witnessing the funeral of a fridge; Mistry had been so solemn. Fridges in the tropics were expensive and heavily taxed. There was to the south a waterfall called Poor Man's Fridge. This one was a vintage Coldspot of the 1930s; its door with the lock broken had swung as the cart moved. Today's removal was the waste disposal of a human being. Dump or cemetery, it was perhaps all one to a mover like Mr Mistry.

The coffin, in this country of fine timber, was not of cedar but of some rough wood crudely hammered together. It was a shantytown coffin headed for the marshy Yarborough cemetery. Whoever lay inside would be lucky to get the 'dry hole' which was the last ambition of the town's poorest people. This person looked to have been very poor. On top of his coffin it was poignant to see the tools of the trade he'd followed, a shoeshine box filled with brushes and tins of boot polish. Bill remembered what he'd once overheard in a small midwest town: 'Nothing so sad as a dead man's dog, unless it's a dead man's glasses.'

The turnout was good though, the women sticking out their chests like veterans, the men in ill-fitting suits shuffling and shifty like small boys dragged off to church. Then Bill saw – why hadn't he seen at once? – that each mourner carried between his or her lips a green leaf pressed like a host. Well ... nothing about this funeral was expected. He guessed that the leaves enjoined silence and symbolised the soul. In something like wonder, Bill stared from his veranda. Such acceptance and faith were moving, and there too was – who was that? Yes – among the mourners, the tall figure of Reuben. Someone Reuben had known, then, and he was subdued with them all, leaf-lipped, to this simple, powerful expression of resurrection.


There's a crowd round Reuben but he hardly knows it. He's numb. This is the hardest corner he's fought. He's concentrating with all his might on the leaf between his lips. It mustn't fall. It is helping Abba to heaven. It is the risen soul. Was this what it had been like for Abba, being mute, a leaf between the lips? Reuben's frightened that if the leaf falls he might shout what a lie it all was, there were no miracles or risen souls; the leaf is the last papery wall between silence and screaming. Submit, boy. Shut your mouth and move with the crowd. Otherwise ... when the leaf fell, was that madness? Had his mother spat out the leaf and let out the scream? Spit out the leaf, you're behind bars screaming obscenities at the huge obscenity outside. You're alone with the truth.

Now the tail end of the procession was passing Bill's veranda. A fat man in the uniform of the BDF was beating the snare drum which stuck out against his big bass belly. The Bloody Damned Fool at the end of the shaggy-dog-story solemn funeral might have been as funny as a punchline, but there was, rather, a zany and self-confident poetry about his presence and no one, least of all Bill, was laughing.

There was, anyway, a much stranger apparition just behind him. He wore a dark suit and tie, and sat upright on the saddle of one of the large tricycles with wooden carriers of the kind used by delivery boys. His hands in white gloves steered the handlebars, his feet in black shoes pedalled with circus-turn slowness.

As with the East Indian carter there was a confusion of associations which might have been grotesque but was somehow impressive. This man's errand today was unusual and yet an errand nevertheless. Loaded in his carrier were not brown paper bagfuls of groceries for delivery but a heap of wreaths and sprays of flowers already wilting.

What most held Bill's attention, though, was the contraption like a rimless top hat with eyeslits which the man wore jammed over his head and face. What the hell ...? It looked like a full dress version of a hangman's hood, but he could hardly believe that to be the intended effect. He stared at it fascinated, torn between dismissal and acceptance of the imagery forming in his mind.

Had the shoeshine man belonged to some sort of sect of which the apparition was the high priest? No, there'd been a conventional priest in white following the cart. Was it, then, a quaint local custom or clumsy attempt at deep mourning? Heavy-handed symbolism? But if so, symbolic of what?

138

It was all very anthropological – voodoo, duppies, the Black-heart man. Death. Instinctively, Bill's hand stole to his chest. But he thought, No, Reuben is there; that reassured him. Reuben would have no part in black magic. He would speak to Reuben ...

Alan said, 'The person you saw was the Box Man.'

They were on Bill's veranda, about five minutes after the funeral procession had passed. The Englishman's white suit was a little grubby, but arriving as he had so soon after the black-clad mourners and the hangman-hooded apparition, Bill still saw him as an envoy from the light side of life. There was, however, something about his manner that Bill did not quite like; it had to do with the way he stretched his legs and leaned back as he sat; with the way he held his glass of lime juice; with his accent.

In his absorption with the funeral Bill had forgotten that Alan had, a week or so before, buttonholed him in the cheapskates' bar of the Bayman and asked to see the house he was renting. It seemed he had lived there as a child – an odd motive, but Bill knew nothing of the brief to find out about him which Alan had from the visiting American journalist, Wyler Fuller. He did not know that Alan was having a go at being 'sly'. He had been happy enough to have him round and pour him a glass of lime juice. And if it did disturb him a little that Alan's manner suggested ownership, not only of the veranda where they sat, but somehow of the whole country, that was at least less dis-turbing than the mystery of the hooded tricyclist which Alan was about to explain.

'The Box Man,' said Bill. 'Tell me.'

'I would see him from here,' said Alan, 'this very veranda. I called him the Box Man because of his carrier, perhaps, or his hat-helmet. Then in England over the years I started to think I must have made him up. The man himself. Surely there could not be a Box Man? But there was. There is. This lime juice is excellent.'

'And the hood?'

'Shame,' said Alan. 'Shame. His face is terribly scarred. Once

139

I saw him with his hood off. Have you seen ziricote wood? His face was like a carved stump of that. Two-tone. Black blotched with a sort of yellowish white. The story goes that he poured acid over himself.'

'Out of shame?'

'So the story goes.'

'Why, for God's sake?'

Alan shrugged.

'Information like that is at street not veranda level.' He used his hand with the glass of lime juice in it to indicate the veranda rail. 'On national days,' he said, 'the Queen's birthday, we would pin bunting there and sit up here like mine-owners while the parade passed by. A cut above. Fantastic now to think of it. But the real fantasy was down there. On the street. The Box Man scared a little English boy like me out of his wits and out of his little white skin.'

With a touch of malice Bill asked, 'Is that why he did it, you think?'

'Did . . .?'

'Poured acid over himself. To scare you?'

Alan looked Bill in the eyes and said evenly, 'Doesn't he scare you too?'

Bill hesitated before agreeing, with a slight nod of his head, 'Yes, he scares me. Forgive me, but I thought you sounded a bit flip. Can I fill your lime juice?'

Alan said, 'Yes please,' then sat back in his chair looking, to Bill's eye, a deal too pleased with himself. ('This limey,' he would later tell 'Amelia', 'he sat there drinking lime juice.') 'Flip,' Alan repeated, 'Hmm. Well, I'm sorry, but you've just seen something I can't help thinking of as a dream. Something *imagined*. I know the Box Man is in the street, real, but he's also in my mind. How much in my childhood the sight of him must have enriched my unconscious. And that's fairly near faith, isn't it? I don't mean the faith that's artificially induced in churches. I mean, I grew up in a church. The street down there was the central aisle. The Box Man was the high priest.'

'Lucky man,' said Bill.

'And you?'

'Me?'

140

'He has obviously made an impact. What does he mean to you?'

Bill was thinking how pompously sure of himself the Englishman was. 'Enriched my unconscious' was a phrase he found particularly irritating: as though colonialism could claim mining rights even to the local psyche. That was it: this Englishman, whom his own father would automatically have admired, was a colonial. But Bill had to admit, too, that Alan had a point.

'Yes,' he said carefully, 'I must say that when I saw him I thought of death somehow. No death in particular. An abstract, slightly mediaeval idea of mortality in general.'

'Coffins.' Alan nodded. 'Maybe that's why I called him the Box Man. But tell me . . .' Alan was about to steer Bill onto the territory which had intrigued Wyler Fuller – who was he? what was he doing here? But then he saw, coming down Regent Street towards them, the American woman he had last seen from the clubhouse veranda. Today's instalment of her apparently extensive wardrobe was a clinging avocado green creation in what looked like silk; she carried a gone-native mammy bag which she swung to and fro as she walked, looking brightly about her. Alan smiled and said, 'So there she is again.'

'Who?'

Bill followed Alan's gaze, glanced quickly back at Alan and then at his watch.

'Ah, Amelia.'

'Amelia?'

'My lodger. She's quite an apparition too, isn't she?'

'But better looking than the Box Man,' said Alan.

Bill could not resist getting a dig in and said, with the necessary smile, 'The old habit dies hard, eh? Sitting on this veranda, enriching your unconscious from the street below.'

Then she was at the gate below, unlatching it, calling up to the veranda, 'Hello!' and to Alan, 'Oh hi, did you look round the house?'

'Not yet,' Alan called back.

She climbed to the veranda and set down the bag. 'Oh, that market is *crowded*,' she said, and Alan noticed that she had picked up a little of the local Creole accent. To Bill she said, 'I bought red snapper, okay?' She sat down and at once stretched her arms above her head. 'The heat!' she said.

Bill got up.

'Red snapper, yellow snapper,' he said. 'All these fish taste the same to me.' To Alan he said, 'Do you find there's not much choice to the food here?'

Amelia said, 'At least it's real. Not plastic-wrapped, processed garbage.'

'I'll get some more lime juice,' said Bill. 'But have you met Mr Palmer? I told you he was coming, didn't I?'

'You told me,' said Amelia, and Alan, taking her hand and saying, 'Hello Amelia. I'm Alan,' noticed the tone of companionable irritation in her reply to Bill. This didn't feel like the usual landlord-lodger relationship. And hadn't there been something like domesticity in her announcement of red snapper for lunch?

She said to Alan, 'Has it changed much?'

'Belize or the house?'

'Either. Both.'

Alan shook his head.

'Neither,' he said.

'It's all in the mind, eh?' said Bill, and laughed. 'Or is it? Wait until you look round a little. You may be surprised.'

He went inside the house, and as he did so Amelia stretched again, yawned and said, 'In this humidity I feel like a damp rag.'

'You don't look like one,' said Alan. 'That's a lovely dress.'

'Oh, do you like it? Thank you.' She sat up. 'I wish I could paint. All the colours in the market, the fruit and the fishes, and the poor turtles on their backs. But I can't paint them, so clothes are my paintbox instead.'

Alan said, 'I'm making a trip to the cays. Will you come?'

'The cays?'

Her voice had quickened. Alan saw alarm in her eyes; but not only alarm. He said, 'St George's Cay. It's cooler there. We could spend the day.'

'When?' she asked.

'Next week. Thursday. Will you come?'

But she wouldn't be pushed. She examined her nails and said, 'Tell me what you do here.'

He looked away from her. 'Not a hell of a lot,' he said. 'But I have an idea of writing a little history of the far end of this street. The Cathedral. Government House.'

'That's a cathedral?'

'That's how they sanctified it.'

She said, 'It looks like a little village church.'

'It was built from bricks which came here as ballast,' said
Alan. 'A bricklayer was sent out from England and as he laid
the bricks his family died of disease, one by one, and were buried
in the churchyard of the church he was building. Then he
finished it, and died too and was buried with them. And Government House, opposite. The other evening the Governor was
there in his ostrich-plume hat and a bugle blew as the flag was
lowered. It's a forgotten corner of colonialism. Like St George's
Cay. You will come, won't you?'

He wanted this settled before Bill came back. She paused and
on her lips as she studied her hands was something like a smile.
Then she raised her head and in her eyes, as they coolly met his,
was a look very near to determination.

'If you like, yes,' she said. 'I'll come ...'

Two days later, Bill was on his veranda reading a mildewed
airport novel. Reuben sat nearby, humming and looking out
over Regent Street, but from time to time looking intently at
Bill as though there were something he wanted to ask or tell
him, but he wasn't sure how.

Bill laid down his book and asked, 'Okay Reuben, what is
it?'

'What is it?' Reuben repeated.

'What's eating you?'

Reuben smiled, then asked: 'You ever meet the Black Power
people?'

'A few. In the States. But that was back in the Sixties.'

Reuben nodded.

'I was a kid then, but they changed me just the same; for the
good, but not just for the good. I'm a fighter. I used to fight
with my fists' – and Reuben made his hands into fists and
paused – 'but then my hands joined church' – and he touched
his fingers and made his hands, as in the children's game, into
a steeple – 'I fought for acceptance, work, peace.' He held the
steeple a moment, then lowered his hands and looked at Bill.

143

'Now,' he said, 'I'm not sure. Maybe I've wasted my time. We have a saying here: when a black man steals, he steals only *some*, but when a *bakra* steals – a *bakra* is a white man – he steals *everything*. You'll never understand the black man until you understand his belief that the white man has stolen his identity, his history, *everything*.'

'Is that what you believe?'

Reuben held up his hands so that they made a frame for his face.

'What colour am I?' he asked, as though that settled the matter, but his smile was ambiguous. He said, 'Sure. I grew up angry too.' He pointed to the garden below them: 'Roses grew there, years ago. English roses. Well, my mother stole them.'

'Your mother . . .?'

'Stole them.'

'Roses?'

'The roses that grew down there.'

'You mean – I'm sorry, Reuben, this is hard to follow. Your mother picked someone else's roses?'

'She didn't *pick* them. She dug them up. An English family's roses.'

Bill made the connection.

'There's a guy in Belize at the moment . . .' he said.

Reuben nodded.

'Alan Palmer.'

'It was his family?'

'My mother was their maid. But he wouldn't remember,' said Reuben. 'No more than a horse remembers the bug he crushes under his hoof. And this is between us, okay?'

Bill said, 'Of course. But does it *matter*? A few roses?'

'My mother went on trial,' said Reuben. 'She was committed and sent to the crazy house. Those roses, you see, were property. And my mother dug them up and buried them, under the floor of our house, in a kind of slave-dungeon. My mother wanted roses and so, with a cracked kind of poetry, the courage of her confusion, she stole them. And I'm confused too. I've been overambitious. The Black Power thing, for instance. I valued its self-assertion, but I thought those people had thrown out the baby with the bathwater, too, the brain with the brainwash. In this bit of the world, black experience was slave experience.

There was slave wit, slave wisdom. There were calypsos, the *bakra* couldn't take all that away. In fact we owed it to the *bakra* for making us slaves. So Black Power rejected it. But I wanted to keep that slave wit and wisdom *and* have the new self-assertion. Overambitious, see? Better if I'd been more stupid. Better if when I was a boxer I'd been knocked out more, had some more brain cells killed off. Because I may not be very bright but I'm too bright for the situation I'm in.'

They laughed. Bill said, 'Did you ever get knocked out?'

'Once,' Reuben said. 'I was a southpaw. My trainer always told me – look out for the left hook. That's what would get me, a left. And every fight I believed him. I had that left on my mind so much that, sure enough, it was a right that got me. There's a moral there maybe, but who's looking for morals? I want action.'

'Sometimes,' said Bill, 'action only makes things worse.'

'Well, we'll see.'

'You have something planned?'

'Planned?' Reuben shook his head. 'You don't spread architect's plans in a storm. I'm a child of the hurricane. I remember that Hattie blew houses down but not coconut trees, because they bent with the wind. That's my plan; bend with the wind. This is hurricane country. No, sir, float me on the sea breeze and where it blows is where the pelican wants to be.'

'And where's it blowing you?'

'Your direction.'

Reuben returned Bill's stare and it was suddenly clear that all he had said had been an oblique spiel leading to this moment. He had been preparing the ground; but what for?

Bill, momentarily speechless, then managed to bring out, '*My* direction?'

'Yours.'

Reuben's stare was still stony. Bill smiled nervously and asked, 'And what direction is that?'

'I think,' said Reuben, 'you're a man of principle who wants to be a man of action. I think you have enough undertow of despair to wash a swimmer out to the Atlantic. I think you're in trouble and I want to help you. Just like you helped me. You stepped in and I'm going to step in too.'

Bill was silent. He stared at a page of his airport novel,

numbly, so as not to look at Reuben. 'Too, he wanted her in his loins like fire,' he read. He shut the novel and laid it to one side. His mind was empty and then he thought of the toy compass of his childhood, an instrument of certainty becoming an instrument of confusion, the needle spinning, his father laughing. To stop the memory he got up from his chair, abruptly, and walked across the veranda. His back was to Reuben, but he knew Reuben was watching. At last he turned and met Reuben's steady gaze. He said, 'Tell me more.'

'Sybil wants me back,' said Reuben.

'Is that a good thing?'

'She thinks she wants me back,' said Reuben, 'but what she really wants is what, at any one time, she thinks is the best she can get. And each time she thinks that *that* was what she really wanted all along, as though she weren't just another pelican at the mercy of the sea breeze. Really, she's confused, and she has the courage of her confusion. And it is perfectly normal and perfectly crazy.'

'So,' said Bill, 'she's written to you . . .'

'Yes.'

'And Peyrefitte?'

'She came home one night from the hospital. Peyrefitte was there with another guy. He said she should 'go with him'. Peyrefitte wanted to pimp for her. She threw him out. Now she wants her revenge. Just like I did, remember, when you asked me not to go to the Consulate? And now I know why you asked me not to.'

'I see.' Bill glanced at Reuben. He walked to the rail of the veranda and grasped the rail with both hands, looking across the street to where the usual wastrels sat around on the perished whitewall tyre drinking rum. That passed for their normal life; this passed for his. If a passer-by had looked up, he might have caught in Bill's eyes the wistful, caged expression you see sometimes in the eyes of waiters or shopkeepers, when business is slack and they stand at their doorways soaking up the life outside – as if it were over *there*, life, so near yet so far. He turned to Reuben and said again, 'I see.'

'Yes,' said Reuben, then, abruptly, he asked, 'you're "Mister Bill", aren't you?'

'Yes. That's me. Mister Bill. And have you told Sybil?'

146

Reuben shook his head.

'I won't tell her anything. But I don't understand. What's a man like you doing, growing dope? Don't you know it's against the law? But it isn't that. Isn't it against your law too? What the hell are you *doing*?'

'A seed,' Bill said, too quietly for Reuben to hear.

'What's that?'

He said more loudly, 'A seed was planted. And it grew, and grew . . .'

Reuben was silent a moment.

Then he said, 'Maybe it's time to dig it up.'

'For what reason?'

'Your own good.'

'Dope grows, Reuben, in what it pleases religious people to call God's earth. What's evil about it?'

'God also imagined the anopheles mosquito,' said Reuben. 'That doesn't mean men should breed them. Man must multiply what is useful to Man. Maybe we were meant to look at marijuana, not smoke it.'

'Dealers in tea used to be denounced like heroin pushers today,' said Bill. 'Where would Assam and Darjeeling be now without their tea? And where will this country be in a few years without its marijuana? It's a cash crop, Reuben, and it'll grow, grow, grow.'

'Why not go to Pakistan,' said Reuben, 'and grow white poppies? Or Bolivia and grow coca? Or Columbia and deal in cocaine? But a little dope growing in dear little, safe Belize, growing trendy Sixties marijuana; that's okay, is it?'

'And Hattieville?'

'What about Hattieville?'

'I should tell you, Reuben, that I'm not in this for the money.'

'Then why are you in it?'

'Why did your mother uproot the roses?'

'Because . . .' But Reuben stopped.

'Because she was crazy?'

'Look,' said Reuben, 'commit crime if you want, but don't disgust me by moralising about it.'

'Maybe it was self-disgust that got me into this,' Bill said. 'Self-disgust, self-destruction. Kill or cure.'

'Like my mother,' said Reuben.

'Maybe.'

'Oh yes, except ...'

'Except?'

'With her it was roses. With you it's weed.'

But what Reuben had really been about to say was that his mother's action had killed, not cured her. They were silent. Then Bill asked:

'Well, what are you going to do?'

'I'm going to help you,' Reuben said. He spoke strongly. 'You're in a bigger mess than Hattieville. You need some charity work done on you.'

'And how will you help me, Reuben?'

'By seeing you through this, whatever you decide. It wasn't the law saved my father's life. It was you. I owe you. And you'll be needing a header, won't you?'

'A header?'

'You don't know what they call a foreman in the dope trade? Well, I'm going to be the only black header up there in brown man country.'

'Do you think it could work? What about your beliefs?'

'I have none,' said Reuben.

'But just now ...'

'And earlier I said almost the opposite. Or didn't you hear? Don't you realise? I'm like you, two men in the same skin.'

'Maybe we're crazy,' said Bill, 'with occasional moments of lucidity.'

'Sounds just like life,' said Reuben.


Bill awoke to find himself with his knees tucked into the backs of hers, in the position of sleep which Amanda called 'spoons'. It must have been around four. In the dark he heard the hum of the air conditioner distilling the humidity into the pool of water which would be there when they got up. Suddenly, he sensed that Amanda was awake too. She had not moved, but nor was there the easy breathing of sleep; a low frequency tension of her muscles held her apart from him. He propped himself on an elbow.

148

'Amanda?' he said. 'Are you awake? What is it?' She sobbed then, once, and deep in her throat, and 'Oh no,' he said quietly, 'You're crying.' He held out a hand to touch her face. 'Darling, what is it?' he asked, but she turned her face into the pillow, hiding, and shook her head strongly as if to say, 'I can't tell,' or 'Better you don't know.' Her shoulders shook. Helplessly, he touched her cheek, but this wasn't the kind of crying he could make better by touching or holding her.

The rain started then, a few scattered drops at first, pattering on the tin roof which sloped above the bed; then lightning and thunder and, without prelude, a roar of rain, a demented pounding, as though upon a theatre thundersheet, the rain machine in overdrive, water sluicing down the corrugations, filling the gutters and flashflooding them. He thought 'The vat will be full tomorrow.' The air conditioner's hum was drowned; Amanda could have cried her eyes out and he wouldn't have heard. But outside, rain and a sudden wind shook the coconut leaves, and he heard their tinny rustling; it sounded oddly dry in all the wet.

He tried to exorcise his desolation. When the rain died down a little he leant to her and said, 'Shall I turn on the light?' and her voice in the dark saying 'No' in a small, remote voice sounded lonely. So much of Amanda was secret. She was crying about her father perhaps, or her past, or his, or him, because he was going away, or her fear of their future, the child she had been or the child and childhood she had not yet had; or because it was raining tonight and things had been dry too long. He moved his hand on her face and thought how human life would be a desert of dry stones and hard-heartedness without the wetness of tears, and touch, and the body of a woman. He was disappointed that she had sneaked off without him and taken sorrow like a lover.

That was it. The rain still fell. His hand lay still now on her cheek. He stared numbly into the dark. It was like staying with the victim of an accident until the ambulance arrived. But who had been hurt and who was staying with whom? He heard himself say, 'Would you like to hear a story?' That surprised him. He had no idea where in himself the idea had come from and no real idea where to begin.

She turned her head slightly on the pillow, as though

149

acknowledging that it was his turn now to be comforted. She said, 'A story?'

'Yes, let me tell you a bedtime story ...'


'Once upon a time on the Gulf there was a wise old fisherman called Young. This was a long time ago when Venice was just a lagoon, before reptiles and paper money, when people were still warm-blooded. Joe Young could swim like a fish but better and could harpoon a barracuda a whole boat's length away. But what he liked best was to catch the big and tasty grouper fish out on the reef.

'The groupers waited under the coral ledges to keep cool. Joe could see them through the glass bottom of his boat which he'd renamed *Cry Baby* when his son was born. The groupers fanned with their fins to stay suspended in the water, and fat and blotched as they were with God's thumbprints and liver marks they looked for all the world like shrewd old rentier dowagers who never made a bad deal yet. Until Joe caught up with them. And they didn't know it but that was why they were waiting – for Joe to catch them up.

'Because the groupers had a weakness and Joe knew what it was. They liked candy. Their candy was conch and Joe kept a whole confectionary store of it in the seawater well of his boat where his bait was.

'The rim and deep inside of the conch shell was the breathy pink of a Homer's dawn and in it the conch was a muscle like the heart. The shell had the blush of the woman you would know, but the conch itself was the woman you *did* know.

'Joe took his ice pick which had never broken ice and Trotsky'd the back of the shell to break the hold of the muscle, and the shell's suction. He pulled out the conch by its scythe of cartilage, then tugged away the beard which was like a mussel's, but bigger.

'He took the pearl if there was one from its tiger lily-like sac and cut the conch into pieces, pink creams from the very best selections. He threaded a piece on the hook and drop-fished it from the side of his boat; the bait hung dangling not far from

150

the coral caves. He tied the line round a sort of pommel on the gunwhale of his boat. It was a warm afternoon ...'

'This is a long story,' Amanda said half into her pillow.
  'Are you bored?'
  'What's it got to do with bedtime?'
  'Maybe it'll bore you to sleep.'
  'It's too interesting, I'm too sleepy,' she said sleepily.
  'Sleep will win.'
  'Go on about Joe Young.'

'Joe's sails were down. For anchor he carried a big brain-coral but he didn't bother to drop it. He took a shot of rum. It was warm, the waves were lapping gently against the hull of his boat, the blue was pounding distantly against the reef, the light was flashing on the water's surface, his boat was moving gently with the swell. He began to feel sleepy, as sleepy as you do, no, sleepier, sleepier, he was drifting into sleep like a boat that hasn't been anchored, back into the blackness – and this is a bedtime story about a man who shouldn't have fallen asleep told to a woman who should.

'Joe woke or dreamt that he did. The sea was big and high and no longer blue but grey. The living brightness had gone as from the scales of a fish. It was cold. The air was now like eggwhite after it's whipped, but dirty grey, the cataract colour of dead fisheye or jellyfish out of water. The air was like smoke but cold. He could see his breath and it scared him.

'Then out of the mist a net fell over him. It had him, as they say, in its toils. He struggled but that made it worse. Then the net tightened around him and he felt himself hoisted from *Cry Baby*, hanging over the sea, dangling, then swung through the mist like so much cargo. Now Joe Young was really scared.

'In the mist loomed a black shape low on the water the length of Fisherman's Town, a ship unlike any he'd seen or had imagined in his wildest dreams. But this *was* his wildest dream and it came from the deep. It was a submarine, a super-modern

151

slaver, not of body but of spirit. On its conning tower was the name, *"Secret Sorrow"*.

'They swung him into the tower's mouth and gaffed the net with boat hooks, then lowered him into the tower where men in suits grabbed him tightly as though he were a tarpon and might fight.

' "We've rescued you," they said. "Now you'll be rich, wet back!"

'A doctor arrived and took his temperature.

' "Good God," he said, "98.4! The fellow's feverish!" Then he filled a syringe and injected – this is a nasty bit – pure ice into Joe Young's veins.

'When Joe came round he was bobbing in a small boat that wasn't *Cry Baby* any more at the mouth of the St Lawrence River. He thought, How perverse, that water so cold had been named after a saint who'd been roasted to death and knew that that was the last thing he would ever wonder. Wonder was dying in him, feeling being frostbitten, compassion freeze-dried, the ice in him was a crystal crust over all he had known and loved; and love was dying too, it had once been necessary but so had the appendix.

'He thought, "Of course! What do you do with a man when you've caught him, what do you do with a fish? What could be more logical? I'm in the deep freeze!" And that was the last thing he would ever think. His thinking cap was becoming an ice cap; thought was icily scientific and was done by the management-minded fishers of men in their human cold; there was no more room for Joe Young in the world ...

'Then he wanted to die or destroy, it didn't much matter which, destroy or die, anything but life in the ice. His pick was still by him; if he still had strength he could put it to the use for which it was intended. He could smash the ice into floes. He could kill. He could die. Or ...

'He lifted his ice pick, then paused. He was looking at his feet. He wore no shoes. There were gaps between his toes from a lifetime of going barefoot. They reminded him of something he couldn't remember – something on the tongue-tip of the mind. Memory. Who are those two 98.4s in bed together? A man and his wife. What depthcharges secret sorrow? Love. Why do sharks not sleep, but turn forever in the waters

152

and cut through the nets of the fishers? Why won't salt freeze? How do you catch a grouper fish? So a man at the sea may remember that Man once swam, or on top of a high building feel a twitching in his toes and know that Man once flew; whatever we evolved from ...

'The ice pick dropped from his fingers. The imprint of wholeness was in his brain and bones. Memory of wholeness was tearing him apart. Desire to die and desire to live were snarling his soul. He was hooked. He would kill. He would die. Or ...

'Ice melts as well as breaks. There's the St Lawrence but there's the Gulf. He could cry. Secret sorrow could empty its tanks and surface. And who would have thought, when the old man cried, that he had so much water in him? The warm Gulf Stream that's in us all flooded his eyes, the world's damage was repaired and grieving for lost wholeness he was whole again, back on the Gulf once upon a time ...

'And that's it, baby, that's why we cry: neither to kill nor to die but to melt the ice and be back where we belong. It's been so cold where we've come from, we've been so damaged, we went cold in order to cope.

'And it's melting in me, too, I could cry ...

'It's like ... deep in the soul there's an order which life messes up sometimes and when we cry we put things back where they belong ...

'Amanda?'


But Amanda breathed evenly beside him, asleep, against the jetflight hum of the air-conditioner, audible now after the rain. From overhangs and branches, rainwater dripped heavily.

He stared into the thick dark which abstracted him from his surroundings. Downstairs, his luggage waited, packed for the journey which he was to begin making, later that very day, to the United States. The thin fiction between him and Amanda was that he was going to get more cash and renew his Blue Card. On the way, he would take Reuben – who would drive him there – to the *milpa* and introduce him to Pedro as the new 'header'. Reuben would restore confidence if it had been shaken by Peyrefitte's desertion and allay any anxieties arising from 'Mister Bill's' visit to the States. Oh, there were plenty of

153

plausible reasons for going north, but, of course, the real reason was his medical check-up.

This felt unworthy to him. He had made his decision and turned his back on the North. But now he was on the point of turning *to* it. If one went it alone against what a society in its wisdom or folly considered to be in its best interests then one was an enemy of that society; and one does not ask an enemy to dress one's wounds.

In the dark, he saw clearly that he no longer needed the *milpa*. Its purpose in his life had been served. But the *milpa* had an objective existence now. Its crop was ripening, growing. There were financial obligations, to Pedro and the planters, to Hattieville; other, more obscure obligations to Amanda.

He should have kept it all in his imagination. Was the imagination outside time, as theologians said the soul was? Perhaps imagination and soul were synonyms for the same elusive thing, the unconscious or God – the Gulf Stream or molten core – but God help the human being in whom it cooled. It had cooled in him, in the States, and warmed again here in the tropics.

He visualised the expression he had seen on Peyrefitte's face in the *milpa* hut. There had been a contemptuous pity in it, but also perplexity, as Peyrefitte saw the patrician American, the mandarin playing the coolie overseer, brought low to the dirt floor. 'The ice' had been the death of Mister Bill, the part he wasn't up to playing, and it had put him back where he should always have been, trying to find reality and solve an inner problem, not in the outside world but in himself.

The societies of the South are used to being out-patient clinics for the emotionally and psychologically damaged people of the North. But in Peyrefitte's face had been an inability to see what Mister Bill was suffering from, a realisation that this American didn't come from the usual left field. That was the trouble. He was too honest, too decent, fundamentally too *conventional* for the situation into which, in despair, he had put himself. Peyrefitte's face had seemed to be asking, '*Where you coming from, man?*'

It was a good question which now, in the dark, he put to himself: *Where am I coming from?*

And he had no answer either . . .

*

154

There would be no more sleep for him tonight. He got up, went downstairs and dressed. He made instant coffee and took it to the living room, where his luggage waited in two green leather suitcases. This would be a long day and he was starting it before sunrise. Time passed quickly. When the first fingers of sunlight felt their way into the room, he opened the blinds and looked down the garden to the lime tree. In minutes, the heat of the sun was enough to start the Bermuda grass steaming, as last night's rain was dried away. And minutes later he heard Amanda's footsteps down the stairs.

She was wearing the blue silk dressing gown and running her fingers through her hair.

She said 'How long have you been up?' and yawned luxuriously.

He didn't answer.

He said, 'Amanda, I want you to come with me.'

Abruptly, she cut short the yawn and glanced at him.

'Is there coffee?' she wondered aloud, and went into the kitchen. He made a gesture of silent exasperation and followed her. He stood by the kitchen door, watching as she filled the kettle and placed it on the gas. She took coffee beans from the fridge. She did not look at him. Her actions had a quiet, domestic ruthlessness.

'Did you hear me?' he asked.

'Yes.'

'Well?'

The taut monosyllables attenuated the unspoken tension between them, which she acknowledged with a guarded smile and a quick, sceptical glance – as if to say 'Do you want to get into this?' But she said nothing. Instead she augmented the tension into a key of her choosing, shaking the coffee, with a tinny rattle, into the grinder and depressing the switch. The cacophony stood in for her answer: this, her actions implied, was normal life.

She released the switch and said, 'You mean the States? Go with you all the way to the States?'

'You think I'd ditch you in Tampico? Of course all the way.'

'For a while, or for good?' She tapped the top of the grinder.

'For good.'

She nodded, as though to question what good there could

155

possibly be in such a return, then asked, 'And what about here?'

'Here,' he said, 'should be us.'

'And we,' she replied, 'should be here.'

'I thought that too. Now I don't.'

She took off the grinder's dome and replaced it with a dunce's cap, the inverted cone of a coffee filter. She shook coffee into the filter and said:

'I don't get it. The crop will be ripe soon and now we've got Reuben everything's fine.'

He shook his head.

'It isn't fine to me.'

'What's wrong?'

'*It's* wrong,' he said.

'You're frightened.'

She stared at him – a challenge. He didn't deny her charge: he *was* frightened. But he had a question for her.

'Why did you cry last night?'

'Oh yeah,' she said. 'I cried, didn't I?'

'Why?'

'Because I'm a woman and crying is one of the dumb things women do.'

'Because you're lost,' he said. 'And your brave face slipped. You're lost and you're frightened too.'

'I'm not lost. I've never felt so good in a place, anywhere. And I'm not homesick for the United States, I'm just plain sick of the United States.'

'But you belong there ...'

She shrugged.

'Maybe. I have a US passport.'

'You belong there.'

'I'm not going back,' she said, looking at him with a level, unblinking stare, 'not now, not yet and maybe not ever. It's funny, in fact, because I was going to say to you this morning that you should stay here with me. Screw your check-up – that's why you're really going, isn't it? Get a check-up in the States, there'll always be something wrong, because being in the States is wrong. You go back there, even for a while, and you're the one who'll be lost.'

'I don't think so.' But he spoke without conviction. Amanda had no scientific basis for her remarks – they were pure witchery;

156

but even so, or for that very reason, they carried a curious authority.

'You'll be lost because you'll have gone back as a loser,' Amanda said. 'You won't have seen this thing through. Have as many doubts and fears as you like, but see it through. Treat it as an experiment then. If you don't finish it you'll never know what the result would have been.'

'I have my result,' he said. 'For me the experiment is over.'

'No,' she replied. 'It won't be over until the dope is ripe, cut, wrapped and shipped to the States. Then you'll know the result, but not before. What you think of as your result is just fear – fear of that thing in your chest you called "the ice". But you've got to go further. You've got to win.'

'What a very American thing to say.'

'Sure, I'm an American. But so are all the people here. America's bigger than the States. Are you seriously trying to tell me that those assholes at the DEA who killed Rafael's father are right because they're citizens of the United States? And that Rafael, Pedro, the planters – some of the gentlest, sweetest people I've ever known – are evil?'

'No,' he said quickly. 'But what I can say, having reached this point, is that somehow the *milpa* is okay for them, but it isn't for us. Because they belong here. We don't. They were born and will die here and this is their way of life. We weren't and won't, and it isn't ours. The *milpa* fits their perspective, it doesn't fit ours.'

'What you're describing,' she said, 'is just fear.' The kettle was starting to steam. She looked at it and said, 'And maybe I will die here.'

'Christ, you can be tough sometimes.'

'Tough,' asked Amanda, 'or strong?' Then again, 'Tough or strong?' She turned from him. 'No, since time began' – and she said those words with an ironic, exaggerated drawl – 'it's been the job of woman to encourage her man. And a woman likes to see her man hard. Conscience is the soft cock the morning after – feeling guilty for the night before. But I like the night before.'

'There's always the morning after.'

'Then it's . . .'

But she stopped, then she came to him, put her arms round him, her head upon his chest. He put his hand to the nape of

157

her neck and stared beyond her into the kitchen. He knew what she had been about to say: that the morning after was when it was too late, or over. Their marriage had been predicated upon the basis which he was now threatening. He might or might not be fighting for the truth, but she was certainly fighting for *them*; because, if it was the truth he was advancing, they had married, not just in spite of it, but in direct denial. They were two worlds, too, in uneasy union, held together, not by the dynamic of inner need, but by the outer framework of shared secrecy, necessity and intensity – the *milpa*, their false names, being outside the law – which they had made and which was, essentially, artificial. Once again he was a figurehead. And that was what she had meant by the necessity of their staying *here*. The adventure which was their marriage would not survive outside the context of this Central American adventure. He was proposing another, organic alignment between them, but – he knew it in his heart as well as she in hers – their relationship would not sustain it. For them, it was the night before or nothing.

'Come with me,' he said, and at once felt, although he could not read her face, her alertness, her wariness of him – like a half-tame animal that will feed at the cabin door but not come in; then, stiffly, she shook her head.

'No,' she said, 'no.' Then she looked up, looked into his face. 'Stay,' she said, 'or, if you must go, come back quickly.' She smiled broadly, but it wasn't a happy smile. 'I do love you, James, and do look after yourself. I'm your wife and it scares me to think of the dangerous country you're going to.'

He smiled at that, too, and then they heard a knocking at the front door. Reuben had arrived. They kissed goodbye. Bill went to open the door, and Reuben came in and helped with the luggage. They kissed goodbye again. Reuben and Bill carried the luggage downstairs and across the road. Bill got in. He felt heavy, old. Reuben got in on the driver's side and Bill said to him, 'Reuben, I've been a little less than truthful with you. It's time I told you a few things.'

'Lots of things, Bill,' said Reuben, 'but slow now, slow. There's lots of time, too.' He grinned and started the engine.

Bill and Amanda waved goodbye . . .

*

It was in late March that Fat Al had, on Pym's instructions, gone down to Mexico City and bought a car. At a dealer's he'd seen the reconditioned 50s T-Bird and known at once that he wouldn't be able to resist buying it. This was the car for him. A T-Bird had been the first car he'd owned and once, in his early twenties, a whore in Oklahoma City had done some really *rude* things for him in the back of it. This car was also within the budget Pym had set and what was really wild about it was its colour. Some of these reconditioned Hispanic cars were so patched and pieced with different coloured fenders, hoods and doors, their chromework was such a cross of makes, they were practically psychedelic; but he knew that Pym would never have stood for driving around in one of those, although Pudney, whom Fat Al semi-secretly liked a hell of a lot more, would probably have thought it a gas. Fat Al knew all about the tension between Pym and Pudney though, and, like Pudney, he liked to rile Pym a little while staying just this side of strict professional standards. A bright pink T-Bird, he thought, was just the way to do that and, hell, if Pym *really* didn't like it they could always get it resprayed in this parrot and alligator place, Belize. Nowhere was so wild you couldn't get a respray.

So he'd bought the car and, as Pym had told him he should, got his Blue Card at the Belize border and driven to Belize City where, Pym had told him, they would meet up again on the Southern Foreshore. On the day Pym had said, he'd gone there and, sure enough, there was *The Mary May* – a thirty-five foot Delta Spearfisherman; the motor yacht – although 'yacht' was pushing it just a bit – on which Pudney and Pym had sailed down from Miami. Just as Fat Al had thought, Pudney had loved the car, while Pym had disapproved. He hadn't hit the roof or anything, though, just scowled and said, 'That the best you could do?'

'With the right suspension and chassis,' Fat Al had replied. 'You know how bad the roads are here.'

'It's too loud,' Pym had said. 'Get it resprayed.'

So Fat Al had gone around town looking for someone to do a respray, only to have to report back after a couple of days that there was scarcely a place in town worthy of being called a *garage,* and they'd be lucky to get spares, let alone a respray.

They'd driven around the country in the pink car while *The*

159

*Mary May* had remained at its mooring on the Foreshore. It had been there for a time now and the locals were starting to speak of it as 'a duck' – a boat which stays in port, like a baby's toy plastic duck stays in the bath. It was getting a shade suspicious – spear fishers who didn't spear-fish – and Pym, six weeks or so before they were due to sail *The Mary May* north, had decided that they had to do another trip before that, just like real, water-loving spear fishers. He had decided they would visit the reef.

The problem was that Pym didn't know a shit about sailing and Pudney did. It was Pudney, not Pym, who had done the real sailing down from Miami. So Pym, sitting in *The Mary May*'s stateroom one day, and poring over some charts of the cays and the reef, was feeling a little frustrated at Pudney's apparent lack of interest. Pudney was lounging half on and half off the edge of a bunk, his feet bare, drinking an iced Lite.

At last Pym turned from the charts to Pudney and said, 'This is your side of the deal. You should be planning this.'

'I'll plan it,' said Pudney. 'No problem.' He drank beer and said 'You get yourself too nervous, Charlie. I want to get out of this stinkhole just as much as you. The reef would make a change. Be nice to breathe some air don't smell of shit for one thing.'

'Then do it,' said Pym.

'I'll do it,' said Pudney. 'Stop brooding like an old hen over those charts. They're no use, anyway.' He finished the Lite, then said, 'Jeez, how did the British stand it?'

'Stand what?'

'Their Empire. Huh? I mean, three hundred years in this fucked-up-never-come-down hole. Why did they do it? What did they want? Did they get it and if they didn't why are they going?'

'It's running the world,' Pym said. 'You've got to understand that. If you're running the world you've got to be everywhere. Even the places as don't count – in case, all of a sudden, they do. The outfield.'

'And us? What about us?'

'You know why we're here.'

'I don't mean us, you and me. I mean us, the States. Huh? Is
160

Mr Arthur Middleton our man in the outfield? Running the world?'

Pym nodded. 'He's our catcher here.'

'Shit!' Pudney strode to the icebox, opened it and pulled out another Lite. 'The guy can't even hang onto his wife. Our catcher here.' He pulled the tab on the Lite, drank some, then asked Pym, 'Charlie, what do you think of Jane?'

Pym looked at him – a level stare. His eyes were pale grey, but they looked colourless.

'I think that Jane is the wife of the US Consul-General,' he said, 'and I think that you think of her more than is seemly and of women too much in general.'

'She's supercooled,' said Pudney. 'She's an ice maiden, and I can see the red roses frozen up inside her and she knows I can see, and she wants me to melt those roses for her. Middleton can't melt her. He can't hold her roses in his hand. He may have married her, but he hasn't caught her. No, sir.'

Pym pretended to concentrate on the charts for a moment.

'It's none of our business,' he said, 'not just your business, *our* business. We're here as a team, don't forget that.' He was wondering what Pudney was getting around to.

'Yeah,' said Pudney, and Pym, stealing a quick look at him, was alarmed to see a certain expression in his eyes. Pym had seen that expression before – a sort of brutal dreaminess. 'Man to man,' said Pudney, 'you ever seen such a boudoir body, such bedroom eyes, such boredom with her guy? That lady is one class act. She's a big white cat, caged, waiting to pounce ...'

Pym waited, then said, 'What is this?'

Pudney gave Pym a quick glance, then drank some beer. Pym knew that he would answer then and so he did.

'Charlie, she's coming with us.'

'*What?*'

'That's right,' said Pudney, and Pym detected the tone of voice Pudney used when he really meant business. What was going on here?

'The Consul's wife? Going with us? You've got to be crazy.'

'It's her idea,' said Pudney.

'Hold on. Let me get this straight. You're telling me the Consul's wife wants to go to the reef with us?'

'Not the reef. North.'

'For a piece of *spear-fishing*? That so?'

'She knows who we are, Charlie,' Pudney said evenly.

'And what about you?' asked Pym. 'Does she know who *you* are?'

'Yeah. She knows who I am.' Pudney met his partner's eyes. 'She wants out, Charlie. I think she wants out. She and Middleton have been arguing it the last two days.'

'She told you that?'

'I already said: it's her idea.'

'Encouraged by you, right?'

Pudney smiled and said, 'I certainly didn't put any resistance her way.'


When Alan got to the jetty for the trip to St George's cay, Amelia was already there talking to Reuben. She wore a straw hat whose floppy brim was of Bloomsburian proportions; it seemed too big to have been packed and he wondered where she could have got it. Amelia's wardrobe was already a puzzle to him: he realised that he'd not seen her in the same clothes twice. Today it was a red silk blouse which 'played Paree' to her down-on-the-farm blue jeans; her sunglasses hid eyes doubtless as full of amusement as her mouth was when she saw him and returned his kiss on her cheek smelling of Nivea.

'Love the hat,' he said.

'Well, thank you,' and there was a hint of a curtsey in her voice. 'Women who don't wear hats, their faces turn into crocodile handbags, their breasts sag, their slacks wrinkle round the crotch. I wear a hat.'

He laughed and said, 'A couple of Mexicans could siesta under it.'

Reuben had stood aside. Now he said, 'So you know one another?' and in his voice and manner Alan caught a guarded, watchful note, something almost proprietorial; his face was distinctly humourless, as it had been when Alan had hired the boat.

'Only just,' he replied, injecting a bit of lilt into his voice to jolly the proceedings along; he didn't look forward to a day

162

with dourness at the helm. But Reuben just turned away and said, 'Okay, let's get moving.'

Alan glanced at Amelia. To his surprise she seemed embarrassed; her face which she kept from the sun was actually blushing. Why? Was it Reuben's question or his own reply? He thought: to hell, I'm hiring the boat, it's my nickel.

'You loaded the cold store, Reuben?' he asked, and if he'd been doubting the other man's attitude his response now left no doubt.

'Yes, *sir*,' he said, saluting with a quick forelock-touch – not so much as a look, let alone a smile. He stepped lightly onto the deck of his boat, then into its well.

As he took the wheel Alan said quietly to Amelia, 'What's eating him?'

She shrugged and said simply, 'He gets uptight.'

Reuben pressed the starter; the engine fired first time, with a cloud of diesel fumes. When it was running smoothly he came aft and helped Amelia aboard – an act of selective gentlemanliness which showed that he knew very well what good manners were. Then, compounding Alan's confusion and confirming his impression that he was being singled out, Reuben called roughly, 'Untie the ropes!' For a moment he considered protesting, but Amelia's conspiratorial smile advised against. He thought how lovely she looked, seated like a queen under the narrow awning at the back of the boat. 'I'll do it for her,' he thought, and untied the ropes. Reuben pulled from the jetty giving him scarcely time to jump aboard and scramble under the awning next to Amelia.

'I don't understand it,' she whispered. 'He's normally so nice.'

'How d'you know him?'

'Oh, from my first visit. He was very helpful.'

'Why were you embarrassed?'

'When?'

'When he asked if we knew one another.'

'Then? I wasn't embarrassed.'

'You blushed.'

She smiled – as guardedly as her full lips could manage – and said, 'You don't know what I was thinking.'

'What were you thinking?'

'Dirty thoughts,' she said, with a glance which recognized that he might find her reply rather shocking. He didn't, exactly, but nor did he know what to make of it. 'Not about anything or anyone in particular,' she said. 'I always think dirty in the dawn.'

'It isn't dawn,' he said.

'It just *was*.' And she said this as though falsely accused of something; the inflection was wrong. He remembered the odd American tendency to make statements sound as though they lacked confidence by adding question marks to them. Is it because she's her, he wondered, or because she's American? Whichever, the effect was both to charm and to disconcert. She had perhaps a repertoire of inflections, more limited than her wardrobe, from which she chose at random, or almost so.

'Well,' he said mildly, 'I'm sorry I wasn't around at dawn.'

'You got it,' and she laughed. 'I'm like the writer who gets her best ideas in bed but I don't keep pencil and paper by me.' Her laughter was full of fun, but he wondered why she talked in this vein. Is she, he asked himself, simply playing, as a porpoise does, for the sheer delight of play? Or is she playing with *me*? Compounding that little doubt was a cultural uncertainty: she was perhaps an American of a recognisable type – but if so it wasn't recognisable to him. Conceivably she talked like this with everyone. But what had she said? 'I always think dirty in the dawn.' That was surely unusual, issuing from under the brim of a Bloomsbury hat. Wasn't it? Then he tired of analysing what were, after all, only his own hypotheses, speculating about her as though she were possible life on another planet instead of a woman sitting next to him. Why not ask her?

'What do you mean?' he said, but the boat was picking up speed now, the engine-noise was louder, and she leant to him and said 'Mmm?'

He cupped his hand round his mouth and called, 'What do you mean?'

The smile still played around her lips, but now she looked him in the face as frankly as sunglasses allowed and with something like seriousness; at any rate, with a steadiness he hadn't seen before.

'I mean,' she said, 'that I haven't got a man.'

'A man,' he said. 'He's the pencil and paper.'

'I got that wrong. I'm the paper, he's the pencil and sure as hell he'd better have some lead in him.' And she laughed again,

164

then pointed and said 'Look.' They were passing under the rust-streaked stern of a big freighter, one of four or five ships out on the roadstead. A seaman was staring down at them over the rail; they looked up into his face. The features were broad negroid, but the skin was the muddy colour of coffee with not enough milk in it; the man's hair was ginger and his eyes blue. Amelia gave him a half-hearted wave, but he didn't wave back. Then Reuben gunned the engine, the boat's hull slapped on the next instalment of swell and they were past the freighter facing open sea.

'Did you see that face?' asked Amelia.

'Yes.' Alan flipped the catches on the cold store. 'Like a painter's palette, mismatched colours in conjunction, not like a finished picture.' He fetched out a can of Swan and pulled the tab. He took a long draught of the beer, then offered the can to Amelia, who asked, 'It's a little early, isn't it?'

'It doesn't make any difference,' said Alan. 'I feel drunk already. Maybe it's the diesel. Let's go up front.'

Out of the estuary the water was a milky green; the boat bucked more strongly on the bigger waves. The water was quieter as they passed through some mangrove. Around the stems of the plants, at tide height, were Elizabethan ruffs of baby oysters. Alan helped Amelia to cross the well of the boat, then helped her onto the gunwhale. As her jeans had faded, so they had learned to hip-hug her exactly. She held down her hat, leaving only one hand free to help herself along the boat to the bow.

He looked into her face, and said, 'Shall I take your . . .?' but before he could get to the word 'hat' the wind had got to the hat itself. It flew from her head, a straw flying saucer, and she shrieked as it went spinning, bowling over and upwards, propelled by slipstream and breeze, then settling crown upwards on the water in their wake.

'Oh hell!' shouted Amelia. Then, as Reuben revved back the engine and turned the wheel, 'Leave it, it's only a hat!' It was a scene from a seaside postcard, and Alan smiled when they reached the hat and he lifted it from the water: not at her dismay, but because, for a quick moment, her face had been undeniably *her*.

He left the hat to dry and joined Amelia at the bow. It was quieter there.

165

'Is it ruined?' she asked, facing forward and her voice far away.

'No,' he said. 'Are you sure you won't have some Swan?' She took the can without replying, took a deep swig, and gave it back to him. He finished the beer and threw the can into the sea; Amelia said 'Litterbug!'

'See over there?' Alan pointed to a mangrove swamp off their left bow. 'That's Stake Bank. The boats from England carried bricks as ballast. Stake Bank was where they ditched the bricks. The mangrove's rooted in it. Stake Bank's a Regency rubbish tip. And there – see that strip of land? – that's Gallows Point. They hanged people there.'

'How wonderful,' Amelia said. 'It's like pirates,' and he remembered Mike Sharp saying 'Our parents were pirates.'

Amelia said, 'Where I grew up the most interesting landmark for miles was the big grain silo. Never go anywhere that's the breadbasket of anywhere else. Breadbasket equals boredom.'

'Where was that?' he asked.

'Illinois. A little railroad stop. But here we are with your past all around us. Don't let's talk about mine.' She faced the bow and said, 'Maybe a shrimp will make his home in your beer can.' He noticed how she shied from talking about herself: why had she come to the Coast?

The skin of his face felt tighter; the sea breeze was caking it with salt. He must be careful: in the sun he went an angry, English red, while Amelia's shoulders, he saw, the top of her spine and nape of her neck, were finely tanned with a flue of gold. There was sadness about her shoulders, though; something defenceless. In this back view he saw something of her which she couldn't dissimulate. Her smile – jaunty, brave – appeared to be open but it was intended to disarm and prevent difficult questions: it was literally a front. And suddenly he longed to see her naked, out of that wardrobe of hers.

But Amelia had no hat. Alan took off his own and placed it on her head; she turned and smiled. He lay on his stomach on the deck. The roadstead and Stake Bank were behind them; they'd left the waters of straight commerce and entered those of piracy. The strongest reminder of the twentieth century was their diesel engine; staring into the clear water one could imagine oneself out of time altogether. Gallows Point and the rule of

166

law were behind them too; ahead lay the magical region of the cays. Already they were out of the weak gravitational pull of the colony. As for Britain, thought Alan, from this distance a society so structured seemed somehow preposterous.

The islands still belonged in spirit to the pirates – even St George's, which had a name and houses and a cemetery, and which had been the old capital. But many were nameless and none – St George's apart – had a recorded history. Such history as there was was sketchily suggestive, as one would expect of the pirate period at the dawn of empire. Alan had boned up on it – a skeletal history in which, however, skulls and crossbones had played a discernibly large part. To the south in the Sapodilla islands, there was Hunting Cay – its name came from *hontin*, old Dutch for 'ghost'. That, he thought, was apt: the pirates haunted the cays.

But otherwise the pirates were anonymous. Individualists and rebels though they must have been, they were not in the flux of acknowledged history; they weren't respectable – a consideration when it comes to naming. Who, for example, had been the unfortunate dead man after whom no fewer than four of the Sapodilla cays were named? Deadman's Cay. Alan wondered: how did he, or they, die? And was there truth in the centuries-old story of buried treasure on the Deadmans?

That would have been the treasure of Vera Cruz. Just before the war, an Englishman had died on the Isla de las Mujeres, off the Yucatan, looking for it. He'd been murdered and buried under the sand, which an incessant easterly blew into dunes twenty feet high. It was, Alan thought, the most desolate, weirdly beautiful place on earth and he clearly remembered his father saying of the murdered man, on a childhood visit to the island, 'I met him a few times. He came from Surbiton.' Surbiton – the suburbs. Years later, passing through Surbiton on a commuter train, he'd stared through the glass at the rainy platform and remembered the Isla de las Mujeres, where nothing was built up but the dunes, the only houses the tunnels of the land crabs, the only human presence the grave of the unknown treasure hunter from Surbiton. And he'd thought, 'You're lucky, Deadman, like the old pirates you ran from respectability, you renounced a salary and went looking for treasure.' The train had pulled out towards Esher and he'd remembered himself as

167

a child on the island beach off Mexico, thinking that it wasn't a bad place for a burial, in the sea spray, among the call of the seabirds and the boom of the big waves, in the sand whose whiteness the amazing Yucatan moonlight doubled by night into beaten silver. And the wind. Of course the wind. One day, perhaps, it would turn, to reveal the bones picked clean by crabs, the watch stopped but boots and knapsack still intact: the man from Surbiton shut up forever in the Great Outdoors.

Alan said so Amelia could hear, 'Isle of Women.'

She said dreamily, 'Mmm? What's that?' How tomboyish her face was under the snap-brim of his straw hat – not in the English sense of a freckled horsiness: there was a frontier, fuck-you quality to her expression.

'The Isla de las Mujeres, Isle of Women, a cay off Yucatan. It occurred to me – you see? – its name must come from the same source as Mauger's, Mauger's Cay, Mauger – from *mujer*. It was a pirates' landfall. They'd taken women hostage at the sack of Bacalar, but on the way to Mauger's they must have put in at the Isle of Women.'

Amelia said, 'What's the sack of Bacalar?'

'The sack of Bacalar? You don't know what the sack of Bacalar was?'

'No.'

'Neither do I.'

'And what happened to the women?'

'Don't know that either.'

'They got raped,' said Amelia. 'The pirates sacked Bacalar, then put in at the Isle of Women. There they put the women in the sack. Then they put in at Mauger's and raped them all over again.'

'How d'you know?'

Amelia shrugged and said, 'You don't have to be a historian to know things. Rape, that's history, isn't it? But how come *you* know?'

'Know ...?'

'This history stuff. You remember it from way back?'

He shook his head.

'No, I got it in London. Books. I ransacked libraries. There wasn't much but I knew there'd be some. There's always some history.'

168

'History's sad,' she said, and her face and voice were again far away, as when she'd asked about her hat.

She shrugged. 'Sometimes countries get in the way of the world. You know?'

'Yes,' said Alan, 'I know.'

Reuben suddenly pointed and called, 'There she is!' They turned to the bow and saw a smudge of green which, as they watched and came closer, grew steadily larger. It was the island, like a fleck of green paint which had stained the surrounding water. They saw buildings; white houses which replicated those on the mainland, tumbledown huts where the fishermen lived, disentangled nets hanging between poles. Then they were in shallow water, floating over white sand, and Reuben gunned back the engine to make white water at their stern. Ahead was a jetty and Alan stood unsteadily at the bow, ready to be the deckhand. No one had appeared from the houses or huts.

They tied up at the jetty, and landed the cold store and their things. They would walk the length of the island, to swim and picnic at the far end. Reuben said he would have a drink in the bar – he pointed to a building in the other direction – then wait there or in the boat. They started off, then Reuben called Alan to him.

'What is it, Reuben?'

'Look after her, hear?'

'Of course I'll look after her.'

'Not just for yourself,' said Reuben. 'I've a feeling, you know, that lady's maybe spoken for.'


They came to a sandy hollow where the grass was just beginning to bind the sand into something more permanent than an encirclement of dunes. In time, if wind and sea allowed, that sand could become real land.

'Look!' said Alan, and pointed to the barrel of an old cannon which lay at the hollow's centre. They supposed that it had once faced the sea, but had broken away long ago and rolled to its present position.

It was understood that this was where they would stop. Alan started down, carrying the cold store, Amelia following with her hat which had yet to dry out. The cannon was rusty and barnacled as if it had spent time in the sea. They sat on it side

169

by side and it occurred to Alan that history was evidently not going to let them go so easily.

Amelia asked 'How old is it?'

'Eighteenth century?' suggested Alan.

'It should be in a museum.'

They marvelled at this evidence of history so casually abandoned. Alan opened the cold store and brought out sandwiches and another can of Swan. Amelia started to roll a joint with sinsemille from a little enamelled box ...

All in the senses, then; later, all in the mind. It was their first wild place, but the cannon gave it a civilised feel, like a piece of garden furniture, the work of some English smithy in the shires. Later, Alan would consider that he had been high even before Amelia's joint and that in his high he had been dizzily thinking of 'we' – the insidious little pronoun which few people can long restrain themselves from using, so pleasing when it applies but so painful when it doesn't.

Looking back on the hollow he would try to remember it as the grave of something, not the cradle of the idiot child called hope; not the place where, pursuing a reckless instinct for permanence, he had begun like the grass in the dunes to put down little roots of feeling for her, the tentative start of a shared history, feelers to bind them together and make land out of the sand which (he would tell himself) he had really tried to build upon.

On their journey to the cay he had been rather admiring of the pirates. It was hardly Amelia's fault if he had to discover the hard way that he was a law-abiding lover after all.

'Reuben said a funny thing back there.'

'Oh?' Her tongue tip touched, teased, the gummed edge of the rolling paper.

'He said you were spoken for.' She stopped in mid-lick.

'Spoken for?'

'He said maybe. You were maybe spoken for.'

She said, 'Maybe we all are. Like lots in an auction.' Then she added with a smile, 'I speak for myself.' She licked the paper again.

Alan said, 'I wonder what he was getting at.' She shrugged. In one of her shrugs she could resume an entire outlook on life.

'I can't imagine.' Then, as an afterthought, as though wishing to be helpful, 'Maybe Bill Brandl?'

'Bill Brandl?'

'Hmm.'

'But he's an old man!'

'Not so old,' she said. But the joint was ready. Alan held out his lighter and clumsily, after several flicks of the flint, got a flame and lit it. When the fuse tip was ash she knocked it away and put the joint to her lips, drew on it deeply; and if Alan had imagined a frown on her face it was now a mask of concentration. She held down the smoke and passed him the joint, then said as she started to exhale, 'I mean, not so old that he can't be a little sweet on me.'

'And is he sweet on you?' Alan took his first turn at the joint. She nodded.

'I think so. And Reuben's a friend of his.'

'Of Bill's?'

'Hmm. Naturally Reuben would root for him.'

'Naturally.' Alan considered this, then said, 'It would account for Reuben's behaviour to me this morning. Wouldn't it?'

'It might.'

'You aren't convinced.'

'Reuben's hard to figure out,' she said. 'I don't know what he means about me being "spoken for". But if he doesn't want Bill's feelings hurt, I don't either. He's been like a father to me.' Alan hesitated, but the opening was too good to miss.

'And what about your own father?' He wasn't really expecting a reply so, when it came – and what a reply – he was the more taken aback.

She gave him a quick glance in which he read reproach, vulnerability, then looked away and said simply, 'My father molested me.'

Alan sat absolutely still, amazed, not just at the brutality of her revelation, but by the sing-song obedience with which she spoke it.

Another revelation quickly followed.

'I was born deaf,' she said. 'My mother's amnion was around my head. The Vedal Cap, they call it. They say it's lucky, but all the time I was in the womb wearing my Vedal Cap my father was out there in the world, drunk as a skunk, waiting for me. And when my mother sewed bells into the hem of my dress, so she could find me, that told him where to find me too. And later, I wanted to kill him, but the alcohol got there first.'

She continued to speak in a sing-song rush, the joint unsmoked between her fingers, her eyes looking past Alan as though no privacy they might share could be as private as this. Alan was remembering what she'd said about the Isle of Women and rape.

'That's history, isn't it?' Just like that. No wonder, he thought, that she found it sad. Perhaps she didn't live for the moment as it came so much as for one or a few moments always.

Then she puffed quickly on the joint and said, that strange reproach in her eyes once more, 'It happens, you know.' She handed Alan the joint.

'I know it happens.'

'A slice of bread from the loaf,' she said. 'A slice of life from the breadbasket.' She smiled – and Alan smiled. 'So you see,' she continued, 'I grew up with a distorted idea of men and, you know . . .' She tailed off there, then said strongly, 'I knew a man like Bill, Bill's age, in the States. Bill's age or my father's. And he showed me gentleness. He always used to give me roses on my birthday.' She smiled at the memory. 'But my feeling for him was tied up with . . . my distorted view, my problem. And gradually, as I began to see straight, under his influence, as the problem began to go, my love for him was less intense, while all the time my gratitude to him grew greater. It's crazy, really. He saved me, but not for himself. And if he hadn't saved me I'd still be his. That's love, isn't it? He probably knew. And that made me even guiltier, till I couldn't stand it. So I came here.'

Alan said, 'Does he know?'

She shook her head.

'No, he thinks I'm still with him. It'll hurt him like hell if he finds out . . .'

' "If"? But the . . .'

'I mean "when". But you see what I mean when I say Bill Brandl isn't too old? After all, I've been sweet on someone his age.'

'I see,' said Alan.

'And I don't want him to be hurt either,' she said. She stubbed out the end of the joint.

\*

172

Sinsemille is cannabis sativa at its most powerful. It is Spanish for 'seedless'. If marijuana is a woman called Mary Jane, then sinsemille is her sterile sister. There will be no little sinsemilles. And that's why she packs such an instant punch – because she's all for now, none of her strength set aside for the future; like the grasshopper in the parable. Of course the point of the parable is that the ant wins in the end. The boring bloody ant, on good terms with time.

It's an ant's world, out there in objective reality ruled by time; cold and forbidding, bleak. Drugs warm it up wonderfully for a time, which at the time seems timeless. Under sinsemille, everything in that sandy hollow seemed all of a sudden marvellously alive to them, even the preposterous iron cannon, and especially, one thing leading to another, the sea lavender where they later lay, sharing, or seeming to, the same subjectivity. As people feel when they are in love, or have anyway just gone – with surprisingly practised hunger, given their inexperience of one another – through the immemorial motions of it. As people feel when they have taken together the spurious sacrament of sinsemille.

They lay there not daring to believe that they'd really got away with the ordinary thing they'd just done; not daring to believe their luck and still expecting to be found out. That was why they lay without moving, saying nothing. They'd stolen a precious piece of time and somehow felt that they were at the top of the 'most wanted' list. But if they kept very still and silent they might be missed and make their getaway. And the lavender was deep and their eyes were shut, like babies who hide their eyes and think they therefore can't be seen. The most grown up of acts had returned them to a child's world where the grown-ups would never find them. They would prolong this moment for as long as they believed it would last forever.

Then Amelia was disturbed by something. Perhaps it was a thought. Perhaps it was simply an ant crawling across her skin. Or perhaps she felt on her shoulder the hand of time, the arresting officer. But she moved and the spell was broken.

If the bad side of Amelia's being American and generous was a mercurial over-instantaneousness, Alan would come to think,

173

the bad side of being himself, English and relatively stable, was a certain meanness of spirit. He would wonder whether she ever thought of him, as he sometimes did of her, as a clone of his culture. What occasionally astonished him was that someone as concerned with freedom as Amelia had so little awareness of what a prison language could be. He did not see her as being an adventurer of the mind. To him, however far off the beaten track she might be, she was, in her spirit, always on the Pan-American Highway.

One night in Belize City, she suddenly asked him, her finger on a page of the book she was reading, 'What's this guy?' She meant a word she had not understood. Alan stared at her.

'A word can be called a *guy*?'

She shrugged. 'Sure. A word can be a guy, a girl can be a guy, if you're lucky even a guy can be a guy. Didn't you know?'

Alan said, 'In England a guy is something you burn on Fireworks Night.'

She looked at him, wide-eyed, and said, with comical gravity, 'But that's weird!'

It was words like these – words like 'weird', or words like 'guy' in weird contexts, or familiar words like 'body' weirdly accented to 'baady' – which would bring it home to him how mutually alien they were. There were parts of her which had been colonised beyond his power to reach or change her. His judgement would be that Amelia the woman he understood instinctively; Amelia the human being moved him; but Amelia the American was always ahead of him or beyond.

His sense of a cultural gulf began for him on that first day on the cay. After a time, they climbed from the hollow and were facing the sea. A jetty led out to a *kraal,* an enclosure of pimento stakes driven into the sandy seabed against barracudas and jellyfish. They walked down the jetty, took off their clothes and jumped into the *kraal.* Wet-haired and laughing, Amelia called to him, 'Isn't skinny-dipping great?'

Skinny-dipping. Later, Alan would be unsure whether he was hastily rewriting history or whether he had really, at the time, found that phrase (which he already knew) cringe-making. Perhaps there is a certain jealousy at the root of a sense of cultural gulf for, as he would realise, the idea of skinny-dipping carried the burden of a context he had never shared – proms

174

and graduation dances, dates and drive-ins and screwing in the backs of cars. But to him her flip encapsulation also deadened his sense of the uniqueness of what they were doing.

When they had finished swimming and were drying out on the *kraal*'s edge, she suddenly asked, 'What if I threw my birth-pills in the sea?'

'The sea? Why would you do that?'

'To be free!' Then, with sudden vehemence, she said, 'Taking the pill's like being a pedestrian instead of jaywalking. It makes me feel like a cow on a farm with a big, high biological fence all around. Like just now, swimming in there with stakes all round us. But I want the sea! How good people always are at making playpen-prisons for themselves. But it isn't wild, it isn't real, it isn't free! It's always safety and too much safety kills.'

He was looking at her, wondering at her outburst.

'Is that so?' he asked quietly; but she was still in a bleak, disappointed place. 'Is too much safety killing you?'

'No. Not now. But ... it would have.'

She looked at him then and her eyes told him she was in different territory. In them was a look which men call animal and indeed, under some hormonal illusion, her face did seem she-wolfishly swept back, the features somehow flattened, the nostrils flared and her eyes narrowed.

It wasn't some sort of grotesque transformation scene, but a suggestion of transformation, no more, momentary but unmis-takeable; and in that moment Alan felt that he was seeing the eternal murderess or mother in a woman.

She said, 'It's all yours, Englishman.'

'All mine?' he asked.

'All yours.' And then, 'Take it, Englishman. Take it again. Now ...'

That *fête champêtre* on St George's Cay was the start of a six-week campaign, an animal idyll. Alan took what she called 'it' there again on the cay and again in Belize City where, the next morning, they hired a Transit to travel the country. All lovers should travel in a Transit.

Wherever they went it was, to Alan, as though they were staking claims not just to one another but to the virgin country as a whole. One evening in Xunantunich, the Maya ruin whose name means Maiden of the Rock and which was still the highest building in Belize, they saw the Pole Star low over the jungle and, in the same sky, the Southern Cross going into winter hiding under the horizon; there under the stars they made their earthly constellation.

Another night near Benque Viejo they heard drifting over the nearby border the sound of automatic fire – some skirmish between Guatemalan troops and guerrillas. Listening, they tried to imagine the horror they were hearing, as though a final reality eluded them.

'There go the barracudas. And here we are, still penned up in the *kraal*,' said Amelia, with something near regret. Then they made love again, and again in Punta Gorda, on the Sarstoon River which was the southern border; everywhere except Pascó, where making love was too much like making babies for a world which did not want them . . .


'That first day,' she said, 'the dirty-talking crazy. It made me horny as hell. Right then I wanted you. And you? Shall I tell you where I'd been? To the market. To buy a turtle and let it back into the sea. They have eggs, turtles, people eat them and drink their blood, make their meat into soup. I've even seen toucan soup here, the Indian villages, a big pile of beaks outside a hut. Toucan soup! Toucans, turtles, are beautiful and I'm behind on my turtle tax. There should be more money moving around, they should sell more drugs and the sky and sea would be dark with toucans and turtles.'

And another time:

'You're my drug. You're so white, if I had a spoon I would snort you, so white, my long line of Englishman, my Union Jack, red where you've caught the sun, my British possession, my *bakra*, your blue eyes go red when you drink, bloodshot blue, the bits of you where blood is close by the surface, the Vedal Cap I was born with, my Copperfield caul, butcher's shop blue, blue rose of my womb, Blue Grotto they call blue hole here, the flue of blue membrane round your corona, poisonous-looking, prussic, the blowfish spine, the bad mushroom, silver goes blue when you boil it, it oozes blue when you cut it, yolk of boiled egg blue, but yellow inside when you bite it, like all

176

men, yellow inside; albumen come, come, I can't talk dirty when I'm a racoon.

'Red, white and blue. My special relationship. We're here eating – a red frank from a white bun under a blue, blue sky, and over there, under Communism, there's a little grey man, in a little grey room, and he's eating a little grey potato, and on the walls are bad pictures of volleyball players, and the sky outside is grey, and it's raining, raining ...'

But she could, thought Alan, be cold, too.

'It's like, normally, all I see is a square,' she told him once. 'A goddam great square, staring at me. Some days I get up and maybe there's a rectangle, or a triangle, but they don't last long. The square is soon all-powerful again. But when I come, ah, when I come ... Then I see all kinds of geometric shapes. Parallelograms. Rhomboids. If I'm lucky, a trapezoid.'

And he could be cold. They were near Xunantunich, waiting for the Mexican boatman to come and take his *mordida* out of them. A young man with a harpoon stood by the river, patiently waiting. He stood there quite still, his harpoon poised above his shoulder, while the muddy riverwater rushed by. He wasn't looking at the water just below him, but further out, and Alan couldn't understand how he could hope to see anything through the mud at that angle of parallax. Then he threw and speared a fish, which he brought to the riverbank. In the mud, it shone, wriggling. He held it up and it flashed in the light like a silver dollar, and Alan thought of Amelia, America, impaled upon him ...


Against advice they went to the rain forest in the rainy season, when rivers flooded and roads became impassable. In the morning they bathed in Five Blue Lagoon, before driving into the cooler air of the Maya Mountains. The low cloud cover, which made it unsafe for the army helicopters and put a stop to military exercises in the rains, hung over the Norfolk pines.

On the far side of the mountains Alan cut the engine. Staying in their seats like Sunday drivers, they looked from on high into the jungle of Toledo. Down there, in the country's south-western corner, was the waterfall of Gracias a Dios – Thank God Falls.

They had the vague intention of reaching it by nightfall.

Then rain fell over the jungle from clouds which were lower than they were, and the light broke into fantailed spectrums like those of waterfall spray.

Amelia said, 'It's like a display put on just for us.'

Alan started the engine. They drove on and soon the foothills began to flatten out, as their road became little more than a *chiclero* trail. They were in a dank tunnel of vegetation, the mud so bad that sometimes they had to lay a carpet of palm fronds – as though for a triumphal progress – so that the wheels could gain some purchase.

They were in deepest Toledo, where the idea of Belize as a nation was even more notional than it had been at Punta Gorda, on the coast, on an earlier stage of their travels. There, some children had asked Alan to take them to the Royal Wedding, while a drunken quadroon had taken him aside and whispered, 'We don't want to be Guatemala. Go tell your government.' In a shop, a cricket ball had been on sale, its leather perished into a craquelure like broken blood vessels. Here and there had been portraits of the Queen left behind by long-gone district commissioners.

But if the paw of the British lion had lain lightly on the coast, here in the jungle it had been barely a playful pat. It was not the presence of Britain that they felt but the magnetic pull of Guatemala, whose largest department, El Petén, ran the length of Belize's western border.

In Belize's Anglican 'cathedral' Alan had seen a memorial to Charles Henry Hadley, of Lee, London, who had died 'while marking out the Western boundary of this Colony'. Probably, thought Alan, of the 'country fever' against which he and Amelia were protected by vaccination, and certainly in country like this not far from where they were. It occurred to him that there are other kinds of 'country fever' and that if Hadley had not himself been vaccinated he had been instrumental in politically vaccinating the country – with his sextant, as it were – against Guatemala.

That had been in 1885. Almost a century later the boundary he had died for was still in dispute, but still held, in spite of all the strains upon it – a magic shield like vaccination. The border was the *cordon sanitaire* against the reality obtaining on its

178

Guatemalan side, the death squads, summary rapes and executions, the predatory soldiery – jungle where one would sooner meet a jaguar than a man.

Towards three that afternoon they broke from the jungle on to scrubland. Here the road was raised. Its surface was better and dryer. They came to rice fields, then, a few miles further on, saw a Range Rover pulled over to the roadside ahead of them. To their right, the jungle jutted in the shape of a widow's peak on to the scrub. On its near side was a clump of trees. It looked to Alan's unpractised eye as though this land had been rudely landscaped once, perhaps to grow rice. A bluff ran from the road to the trees, which were on higher ground and which looked to have been planted on purpose, for fruit or shade, or as a windbreak. Alan slowed and they saw at the trees' edge a 'trash' hut with a caved-in roof, apparently abandoned. Then a solitary little girl, an Indian, walked from the trees and stood looking at them.

Something was wrong. Why was the little girl on her own and not waving to them as everyone had done on their route? The beige Range Rover with no one near it was like a doctor's car on call. Instinctively, Alan pulled up the Transit just ahead of the Range Rover. Inside the trees, momentarily, he saw a watery shine which glided briefly, then disappeared. He tried to point it out to Amelia, but it was already gone.

Then a man appeared from the trees, walking briskly. He stopped and stood there staring frankly at them, his hands on his hips, his attitude – even at their distance – conveying suspicion, efficiency and territoriality in about equal parts. He reached out and ruffled the hair of the little girl. She didn't move or react. Then he walked to the bluff and started along it, as Alan and Amelia got out of the Transit to meet him.

Alan saw a man of about the same age as himself, white, but short and stocky with strong forearms. His hair was pale brown and his face untanned. He wore jeans and a grey, short-sleeved shirt. He looked to the ground as he walked, only looking up and facing them – but with no welcoming smile – when he reached the end of the bluff.

'Where you going?' he called.

Alan called back, 'Nowhere special. Just travelling.'

'You're English?' He started to climb the incline which led up to the road.

'Yes.'

'With the army?'

Alan found it strange to undergo questioning from an interrogator in motion.

'No,' he said.

The man was now on the road and Alan saw that on its comparatively level surface his walk was slightly rolling. He held out a hand and said, 'Hi. I'm Jay Peurifoy.' They introduced themselves and he said to Amelia, 'You're American,' in a tone so near to accusation that it made Alan say, 'So are you.'

He glanced at Alan.

'We had an American here a couple of days back,' he said. 'I think he was from the Consulate.' He asked Amelia, 'You from the Consulate?'

'No.'

'Funny time of year to come down here.'

'We're funny kind of people,' Alan said.

He glanced at them in turn and perhaps reached a decision. Anyway, his manner noticeably altered.

'Have you food?' he asked. 'Or fresh water?'

'Both,' Alan said.

'Bring them. There's people could use food and fresh water.'

'Who?'

'Refugees.'

'Over *there*?' asked Amelia, pointing to the trees.

'Over there.'

Alan remembered Benque Viejo and the fighting they had heard, and asked, 'From Guatemala?'

'The Petén,' said Peurifoy. 'I'll tell you about it. But bring what you've got.'

Amelia was looking at the trees. She asked, 'How many people?'

'More than you would think,' said Peurifoy. 'But it all helps. Have you any spare clothes?'

'Let's see . . .'

They pulled their bags to the open back of the Transit and started to pick through their things. Amelia asked again how many people there were in the trees. Peurifoy shrugged.

180

'Every day it changes,' he said. 'Some arrive, some reckon it's safe to return and go into the jungle, some die.'

'Die!'

'Sure. It isn't a picnic.'

Amelia and Alan exchanged quick glances. Alan at least was thinking of the picnics they had shared. Peurifoy said, 'Today there's maybe a hundred and fifty.' And all they could see was a little Indian girl.

Alan repeated, 'A hundred and fifty?'

Peurifoy nodded.

'About that.'

'Are you from an aid agency?' asked Amelia. She tossed the red blouse she'd worn to St George's Cay on the pile of rummage.

Peurifoy gave her a glance as if he suspected a trick question. Then he said, 'Nope. Would that I were, but I'm not.' Alan asked what he meant. He said that he would 'brief' them and, hearing that word, Alan realised that Peurifoy had the no-nonsense brusqueness of an army officer or aid worker, used to command and to thinking of men and misery in the mass. He didn't explain – he briefed.

He began his briefing as soon as they started to descend the incline to the bluff, carrying armfuls of their things. Peurifoy told them that El Petén, as well as being Guatemala's largest department, was its most remote, least populated and least developed. It was also perfect guerrilla country. In February, extra government forces had been drafted into El Petén and shortly afterwards a major offensive had begun. A war against guerrillas is never easy to contain, said Peurifoy, but this one had been unusually savage and uncontained even by Guatemalan standards.

One of the first government measures had been strict enforcement of the 1954 regulations on identity cards, which had never been fully applied in remote Petén. Now, to get his ID, the peasant had to go to his birthplace, but if he attempted the journey without ID and was stopped on the way, he could be shot on the spot as a guerrilla or guerrilla sympathiser. Soon, government forces had abandoned even this crude effort to distinguish between combatant and innocent civilian. Every peasant was suspected of giving the guerrillas 'moral and logis-tical back-up' (Peurifoy's phrase), feeding them when hungry and hiding them when hunted. No one was innocent. 'Original sin in action,' Peurifoy called it, 'the *conquistador* mentality.' Recently, in Melchior de Mencos, just over the border, the heads of murdered peasants had been displayed impaled on stakes in the main square. In retaliation for the shooting down by guerrillas of an army helicopter, a village had been napalmed.

'These people,' said Peurifoy, 'are running scared. That's the reality, but in Guat City they've manufactured a "reality" of their own at tyranny's service. These people, they say, are "subversives", "Communist insurgents". Screw geopolitics! But wait till you see . . .'

By this stage of Peurifoy's briefing they were near the trees. Ahead of them, faintly, Alan heard a baby crying. They walked in silence, Peurifoy leading the way. The little girl still stood there, staring at them fixedly and yet without curiosity, as if they hailed from another planet which, however, she knew only too well. Their footsteps were noisy in the scrub. Alan caught up with Amelia and put his free arm around her, and she broke off from staring at the little girl to give him a smile. It was forced, guilty, and Alan realised that if he had been at Amelia's centre he was so no longer. The little girl, the predicament of the people in those nearby trees, had replaced him. Quickly, he took his arm away. There comes, he thought, a Copernican revolution in the life of every individual when he has to accept that the sun no longer shines from his arse.

At the end of the bluff Peurifoy said, 'Welcome to Pascó.'

'Pascó?'

'They call it that. Don't ask me why.'

The little girl ran into the trees. Amelia watched her go, and said, 'She's frightened of us.'

Peurifoy ignored her. He looked at them in turn and said, 'Okay, before we go in. There's something you've got to understand.' He pointed to the trees. 'Guatemala knows these people are here and has asked for them back. Belize knows they're here and would, ideally, take them in. Britain knows they're here. Most days, an army helicopter on the way to Cadenas lookout detours this way for a looksee. The US knows they're here and while it's committed to tagging along with Guatemalan anti-Communist rhetoric it is also committed to helping Britain help Belize to become independent. This is a sensitive time. Talks

182

are under way about Belize's independence and future. These people could become an issue on the negotiating table. Already the heavyweight weeklies are carrying stories saying the guerrillas get their arms through here. All Belize needs is a story saying it harbours "Communist insurgents" too. So, a formula was arrived at.' Peurifoy paused. 'We aren't here.'

Alan tried to take that in, but couldn't and prompted Peurifoy, 'I'm sorry?'

'Guatemala's been told that there are no refugees,' said Peurifoy.

'But you just said that Guatemala knows that there are refugees,' Alan objected.

'Of course it does,' said Peurifoy evenly. 'All the interested parties know. But this isn't to do with truth. If Belize had returned refugees which it knew very well, as Guatemala must know too, not to be Communist insurgents, that would have set a precedent and extended the influence of Guatemala's fictitious 'reality'. At the other extreme, if Belize had rejected the Guatemalan request out of hand and taken these people in, Guatemala would have another cause for complaint at the negotiating table. It would have been able to represent Belize to the United States as too weak to exist, a conduit for guerrilla guns and a hideout for subversives. Hell, I can't help wondering about the timing of the Petén campaign, just before independence. Were refugees created on purpose, to compromise Belize? Anyway, to avoid being compromised Belize has agreed to a compromise and Guatemala has the satisfaction of knowing that it is important enough in the region to be worth telling diplomatic lies to. There are, officially, no refugees and that is why they're here, in hiding, instead of on the coast, where there are hospitals and they can be fed properly. If Belize looked after them, Guatemala would know at once and pounce on it. So, the refugees are left to rot. And they're very perishable. Welcome again to Pascó, the humanitarian bait on a political trap.'

'It's incredible,' Alan said.

'It stinks,' said Peurifoy. 'But it could be worse. Come ...'

It was dark under the trees. Most of the refugees were on the far side of the clearing, under a large polythene canopy hung from the branches of a tall hardwood tree at the clearing's centre. What Alan had seen from the road had been light

183

glancing from the polythene sheet as a breeze rippled it.

Nearby, separate from the rest, sat a man and a woman with a baby in her arms. The man lowered his head to Alan in sombre greeting and Alan was troubled by the sense that although these people outwardly resembled the Maya and Kekchi Indians they had seen on their travels, they were, somehow, inescapably *foreign*. Then he realised why: what was foreign about them was their fear.

To be among these refugees was like being the one clothed person in a room full of human beings who have been forcibly stripped. Clothing was more than a matter of the garments they had brought with them. It was, thought Alan, all the protections of civilisation. He had his passport, his vaccination scar, his rights under the law, a multitude of layers between himself and whatever these people were experiencing. But the impression, rather, was that life was a freezing cold day, which he was dressed for and they weren't.

'What's that?' asked Amelia, and Alan followed the direction of her gaze towards the foot of the hardwood tree. A white box lay there, unmistakeably a coffin the size of a child.

'A kid died yesterday,' said Peurifoy. 'We were about to load him when we heard your pick-up.' There was, to both of them, something terrifying about that 'load him'.

Amelia asked quietly, 'What did he die of?'

'Measles,' said Peurifoy.

'*Measles!*'

'I think so. Or malnutrition. Or dehydration.'

'With all this water?' asked Alan.

'Diarrhoea,' said Peurifoy. 'Water isn't always clean when you get a lot of people together and soon the rains will be over. I'm no doctor. I don't know. He's the twelfth so far.'

'*Children!*'

Peurifoy nodded.

'By the time they've made it through the jungle they're very weakened. Then they get here and there's little or nothing for them. And they aren't vaccinated. That's what I most want to do. Vaccinate them. All of them.' He paused, looked at them in turn. 'Are you beginning to get the picture?'

'This needs an aid agency,' said Amelia.

'I've tried,' said Peurifoy. 'Don't think I haven't tried. But the international or Pan-American agencies can't just move in like that. First the problem has to be admitted and aired in open forum, otherwise it's political interference and I've already explained why it can't be aired. The refugees who made it to Mexico, they're okay, because Mexico's big enough to tell Guatemala to go take a flying fuck. They exist as refugees, but with these there's a danger of their existing, officially, not as refugees but as subversives. I'm repeating myself, but this thing drives me crazy. As for the private agencies, they're so Commie-bashing they wouldn't touch this one.'

'What about the British agencies?' Alan asked.

'Maybe,' Peurifoy said doubtfully, 'but they're so far away and anyway ...'

'What?' Alan prompted.

'There are spies,' said Peurifoy. 'Hard to believe, out here, but there are spies. There's a guy comes most weeks, from Benque Viejo, and I know he's reporting for Guatemala. He brings a little food each time. Then there was the guy last week. I'm sure he was from the Consulate. And if any aid agency got officially involved that would be breaking the terms of the formula. I've thought of trying to place these people in small groups around the country, but that would be noticed too and the figures would dwindle.'

'How are they living?' asked Amelia.

'With difficulty,' said Peurifoy.

Somewhere, there was a shriek of a bird. Peurifoy turned sharply, away from the main body of the clearing. 'Come,' he said again.

He took them to the family Alan had noticed sitting nearby. The father, seeing them approach, made to stand up, but Peurifoy impatiently waved him down. He greeted the family in Spanish and crouched beside them, his attention on the baby in his mother's arms. Peurifoy had said he was no doctor, but his bedside manner was practised and suddenly the clearing seemed the ward of a teaching hospital which they were touring.

Alan and Amelia crouched beside him, and Peurifoy said, 'These people came two days ago. The little boy's sick.' The mother's head was inclined towards her baby in perplexed concern. Peurifoy asked her permission and gently unfolded from the child the thin piece of cloth in which he was wrapped.

185

Alan had already seen that the child's face was blotched with a violent rash, his eyelids gummed tight together. He had heard his rasping breathing – incipient pneumonia. Now he smelt his pre-pubertal smell and saw, under the cloth, his thin legs and swollen stomach – malnutrition, the lean calf which comes at first in the guise of the fatted.

'Measles again,' said Peurifoy. 'But as you see, there are complications. So many that it would be hard to say just what this kid is dying of. Complications,' he said again, and then, 'You see my point? If the Guatemalan army don't get you, some stinking little virus will . . .'

Amelia was reaching her hand towards the child, slowly, looking in turn from Peurifoy to the mother for permission.

'Can I?' she asked, and touched the baby's forehead. 'He's feverish,' she said.

'He's *everything*,' said Peurifoy. 'He needs to be rehydrated, fed properly and medically treated. I'm taking him to Punta Gorda.'

'With the coffin?' Alan asked.

'You got it. Hearse and ambulance in one.'

'We're coming with you,' said Amelia.

'You are?' and there was acquiescence in Peurifoy's question, as though he had relinquished command to Amelia. It occurred to Alan that Peurifoy had been alone too long. He covered up the baby and said, 'Well, that would be useful.' His voice was suddenly that of a tired man.

'It's the least we can do,' said Amelia. 'I wish we could do more. *Can* we do more?' Peurifoy, tucking up the baby, opened his mouth to speak, then seemed to think better of it. Amelia asked again, 'Can we?'

'That coffin . . .' he said uncertainly.

'What about it?'

'It cost thirty-five dollars, US,' said Peurifoy. 'These people live in shit, but they die in style. The boy in there had little life to speak of, but he'll be buried with the full rites of the Roman Catholic Church, by a priest wearing vestments, in a thirty-five dollar coffin. His family is Maya. When he was born they buried his birth-string near home, so he would stay there. They didn't reckon with politics . . .' He stopped and Alan prompted him.

'Go on.'

Then, before he could continue, Amelia put in, 'You want us to pay for the coffin? No problem. We'll pay for it.'

But Peurifoy shook his head and asked, 'Do you know what the cold chain is?' looking at them in turn. They didn't know. Behind Peurifoy, under the polythene, the Indians were in Dantesque half-darkness.

'They say that life is cheap,' said Peurifoy, 'but they forget to add that death is expensive. Five dollars would have saved that kid's life. Less than a dollar a disease. Life is cheap. But there's a snag. Vaccine has to be kept cold. In a hot country that isn't always easy. You can air-freight it from the north and an hour in the sun can kill its power. It's like a balancing act. As long as you stay between zero and eight you won't fall off. You need isothermic cases, temperature monitor cards, disposable syringes or air compression injectors, a kerosene or solar-powered icebox for storage. I've looked into it a little. That's the cold chain. The kid in the coffin was baptised. He'll go to heaven. But if he'd been baptised by the cold chain he wouldn't be going in such a hurry. You follow?' Peurifoy's eyes were gleaming. He paused. 'A cold lifeline,' he said, 'to a hot country. I don't know why, but that does something for me.'

Amelia nodded.

'And me,' she said, and her tone was almost fervent. 'It does something for me, too. But you don't answer my question. What can I do?' And Alan noticed that she no longer spoke for both of them: 'we' had become 'I'.

Peurifoy gave her a look in which he seemed to be asking himself whether she was serious, or could be trusted, then said in a hard voice, as though he regretted speaking so much, 'Do what you can. What you must. I don't know.' Then he glanced at his watch and said, 'It's getting late. Time to be going.' He started to get up and said, 'Are you really for Punta Gorda?' but Amelia grasped him by the forearm.

'No,' she said. 'Wait. *What do you want?*'

Alan thought of what she had said on the cay: 'It's all yours, Englishman ...' In Pascó, another passion was beginning to claim her.

'What do I want?' Peurifoy lowered himself again. He said, 'I want to get the cold chain to this place. I want to look after these kids, then make this a cold chain base for Petén and do the kids there. I have contacts . . .' They knew he must mean the guerrillas, or people who were in contact with them. They had come a long way since Five Blue Lagoon that morning and the day wasn't over. Soon they emerged into the light where some women, standing over the things they had given, thanked them effusively. Then the funeral procession carrying the child emerged, then the family whose child was sick. They trailed along the bluff. It had been agreed that the sick child and his parents would travel with Peurifoy and with Amelia, who wanted to know more about the cold chain. The Transit would be the hearse, driven by Alan.

No one cried on the way to Punta Gorda, and there was little conversation between Alan and the Indians. At one point he asked the father why the bivouac in the trees was called Pascó.

'¿Porqué Pascó? ¿El nombre, porqué?' He thought that his poorer than pidgin Spanish got through, but the man just shook his head and smiled. Perhaps he didn't himself know, but Alan thought that it was a secretive smile and wondered whether, if so, the secret was among his last remaining possessions.

The act of naming was a part of dignity too, a shelter against experience, like the polythene sheets. Perhaps Pascó didn't name a place, but a period of their suffering.

Then Alan thought: this is no time for amateur etymology. I should simply be human . . .

Pascó wasn't marked on the map which Alan carried but later, in Punta Gorda, he found the place and put a cross there.

A kiss, a gravestone, a place of buried treasure: a cross can mean many things. One day, perhaps, he would know.

TELEGRAM *Bill to Amelia Brodie*, PO *Box 23, Belize City, August 21, 1981* THE COLD CHAIN IS A GREAT IDEA. LOVE IT AND WILL DO. SEEING SPECIALIST TOMORROW. WILL WRITE. LOVE BILL.

UNSENT LETTER ONE *William Brandl to Amelia Brodie*.

Well, well, there is something the matter with my thymus. The specialist thinks it may be fatty. 'My *what*?' I hear you ask.

'What is a thymus?' It is a gland, situated just behind the sternum, high up, the anterior-superior something, midway between the lungs, not far from the heart but definitely *not* the heart. Where 'the ice' was. You will tell I've been talking to a specialist, but I hope my cheerfulness comes through.

It's hard to exercise a thymus. You can't just flex the thing like a muscle. Perhaps that's how they get fatty. But the thymus (specialist again) hides out in an intact capsule of muscle and fat, so there's some fat there anyway and muscle to turn into same. This capsule is hermetically sealed – like, it occurs to me, a thermos. There'll be more of these words and their relations, and although I'm feeling playful, kiddo, it isn't word-play. I have the obscure but distinct feeling that someone, somewhere, is picking on me with words; taking them, not only literally, but literally *out on me*.

Naturally, I asked about the Big C. The specialist guy shook his head and said he didn't think so. 'Apart from anything else, Mr B., that would be a most rare occurrence. In the thymus? Most rare. But of course . . .' Then he proceeded to tell me how rare it was that I had a thymus at all. Jocularly – if that's the word I want – he showed me a textbook entry. I took it down: 'From birth to puberty it doubles in size to reach a maximum and thereafter gradually undergoes involution' – 'dwindles away' to you and me. 'In someone your age,' the specialist said, 'it would usually have involuted completely.' ('Would have' is specialist-speak for 'should have.') 'But,' he pursued, 'with you it hasn't involuted at all. It's still at maximum.' His leaden jocularity was infectious. I said, 'You mean I'm the eternal adolescent?' His laugh was like a symptom, dry and hacking. 'It means,' he said, 'you're lamb dressed up as mutton.'

He spoke more truly than he knew; or perhaps he did know. I am fond of research, as you know – the fondness often shown by men of imperfect education, like myself, who go in some awe of specialists and professors. Knowledge is dignity when you are up against those to whom knowledge is power. To me these people are like puppeteers. I want to grab hold of a few of the strings, seize the reins, so to speak. So I thought I would look a little into 'thymus'. And what do I find? A bigger, more powerful puppeteer.

I assumed at first a connection with thermos, not just because of the similarity of sound (I am not that imperfectly educated), but because of the connection with heat and cold. The ice. I thought the thymus might be the body's thermostat, as it were, and that mine might have been turned down to compensate for the tropics. I let go of this idea with reluctance, but let go of it I must, because little as is known of the thymus it *is* known that it isn't that. It is evidently, or probably, something to do with the autoimmune system – but scientists aren't sure. Have you got that? *They aren't sure.*

Nor is there an etymological link. Thymus is related, descriptively, to thyme; the gland physically resembles two bunches of thyme flowers, a double posy. Lamb of course is good cooked with thyme; but lamb is also killed for sacrifice and, etymologically, the two posies in my chest, unwithering *eternelles,* were picked from the Greek root *thymon,* or *thymos,* whose root in turn is *thiein* – to burn or sacrifice (we are a silver Christmas ball's thickness from 'thermos').

How much the stranger, then, to have felt such intense cold there; but of course the self-contained capsule of a thermos contains cold as well as heat and the specialist did assure me (so this isn't, this *can't* be, all in my own mind) that intense cold is a discomfort one might reasonably expect from a thymus disorder. They aren't sure, they don't really know ...

One associates sacrifice with burning, fire; but why shouldn't one, or someone, sacrificially freeze to death? Here comes the most curious fruit of my 'research'. It seems that the superquack of the ancients, Galen, thought the thymus was the seat, or site, of the soul. Can you beat it? This thing comes on like gangbusters. What is this? Something is wrong with something I shouldn't have, there are associations with soul and sacrifice, I should have grown out of it (and perhaps Dr Abb had a point, 'the ice' was a growing pain).

This induces in me a quiet hysteria. Does one, then, grow out of the soul? Is it 'normally' left behind at adolescence? Or is the soul rather the thing that grows out of some people and not others? Perhaps this is not after all some awful symbolic ganging-up against me; perhaps *I* am the one who is taking this too literally; but the symmetry of it floors me. Do I have a cold soul? A fatty soul? An eternal, overgrown, adolescent soul? What sort of disorder, exactly, do I have?

190

'Let me state it like this,' the specialist stated it like this, 'if the odds are high against a fully grown man having a thymus, the odds against him having a carcinoma of the thymus are much, much higher. It is a very rare complaint indeed. So, don't you trouble yourself, Mr B., don't you trouble yourself ...'

TELEGRAM *Bill to Amelia Brodie*, PO *Box 23, Belize City, September 2, 1981*
COLD CHAIN COMING ALONG. ALMOST IMPLEMENTED THIS END. TELL P. LOVE B.

UNSENT LETTER TWO *William Brandl to Amelia Brodie*

You said just before we left the States, 'Avocadoes are eighty cents apiece. We inject our meat with water and our apples with red dye. Abattoir. Fake Health. Snow White. What earth isn't metalled is under cultivars, fertilisers, pre- and post-emergent herbicides. Everywhere I look I see the man-made not God-given. We eat Big Macs. Help us. I don't like Civil War cemeteries. I do like swamps. In so many tons of silo wheat so many rodent droppings are allowed. I want *dirt*!'

In Washington, when I came back from the dinner party and the Professor, the huge Santa Claus high-kicked on the façade of the department store opposite. There were snowballs on the sidewalks, and I don't mean the white kind but the snowball cocktails made with egg-nog, yellow splatters of secretarial vomit, very Christmassy. Santa was all lights, his cheeks were apple-red with rude health, reindeer piss, or dye, his boots were white and his leggings were red, and in computerised innocence he kicked, a dulled lighthouse scattering against our curtains, kicked in high spirits for those who were happy family, kicked in the crutch those who had never had childhood. The tyrannous happiness of Christmas America. Our hotel. You were crying. You said, 'The States is so sad sometimes. Pink grapefruit grow with price tags on them. Be happy and buy. Buy, buy. Feed the beast.' I know why you cried, A, I know why you cried. 'Feed the beast . . .'

UNSENT LETTER THREE *William Brandl to Amelia Brodie*

Metastasis. In its rhetorical sense it is a device to make them sit up, a sudden, apparent change of subject which is, in fact, the same subject relocated so as to be seen in a new setting or approached from an altogether different direction. It starts by seeming to be a digression; then, gradually, the rhetorician shows it to be relevant. It had seemed at first to be a completely new idea – but it is only the old host idea in a new form, under new colours, so to speak; and the host idea has not abandoned its metropolitan base, merely established a new, subsidiary base elsewhere.

A metastasis, in rhetoric, is very like the colonisation of another country, or the occupation of land which then evolves into a colony. (You will start to see the drift of my metastatic start.) I am examining the idea of metastasis metaphorically. Let me try another metaphor. We, A and B, are on a journey *from* A to B. Most of the stops on the way we speed through, but at one, to refresh ourselves and gain strength for the journey ahead, we get off. This is a metastasis on our journey. In stopping there, precisely because we have stopped there, it will become in our minds as like to A, our starting point and host idea, as B will be once we have got there; one is, as it were, the envoy of the host, its rep, and although the place one stops off at will seem new at first it will not seem so for long. We violate everything new with our old host idea. (In Salvador once, I travelled with a Gillette rep up-country on a sales drive. The little shops were metastases of the razor-blade war; over every counter Gillette and Wilkinson Sword were at daggers drawn.)

Belize, dear A, a metaphorical metastasis in its own right, was also ours. Looking there for a cure, we took the host disease with us. The British disease, the US disease, the Belize disease . . . I do not believe that the soul occupies the body as a bird does a cage, or as the thymus occupies its capsule. I do not

192

believe that the cage decays and the soul flies away to where it has always wanted to be. I believe that the soul occupies the body as the colonising power occupies the colony, and that when it goes it's an uhuru hopper; the good times are gone, the sun has set on the sundowner day, the place has gone to ratchet, and it's getting a little too dodgy and dangerous for the soul to stick around. I think the fatcat soul is in the body, its metastasis, for its own parasitic purposes and that when those are served, or when it can't get servants any more, it slinks away from the place where it should never have been ...

Enough of this outburst. You'll gather I've been doing 'research' again. Sorry about that. Well, I didn't send my last letter and I doubt I'll send this one. Most letters, mine included, are rubbish. But where was I? Ah, metastasis. Now, in its medical sense, metastasis means ...

TELEGRAM *Bill to Amelia Brodie,* PO *Box 23, Belize City, September 12, 1981*
ALL CLEAR. COMING HOME. MEET VALLADOLID. SAME PLACE. SIX PM SEPT EIGHTEEN. LOVE B.

To Alan, back in Belize City, it was as though their brief time in the wild had unfitted him and Amelia for even the most rudimentary society. Their relationship seemed awkward to him, less natural. He wondered, too, whether the experience of Pascó had not upped the ante between them to a point where continued play would soon be out of the question. He realised that, with Pascó, the central core of Amelia's preoccupation had subtly altered and that he could not join her there. It was as though she had had a child and their honeymoon was over.

Amelia's first act on returning to Belize City was to pack up her things and move out of the house on Regent Street she had shared with Bill. And, thought Alan, what a lot of things! Later, he would conveniently adduce the size of her wardrobe as evidence of the triviality of her nature. She was, she told him, 'with him' now; it was inappropriate that she should stay on at Bill's, although she asked him not to say anything to Bill on his return.

With him. But in fact, to Alan, it felt as though they were drifting apart, as though the hand which they had previously played together, pooling their resources, had become a hand which she hid from him. He felt that they were relating not directly to one another so much as to their relationship and it occurred to him that for every relationship which dies of neglect or insensitivity there was probably one which died of self-consciousness.

From Bill's, Amelia moved to a frame house in a back street further from the foreshore called Pickstock. All day, an old lady called Ella, the house's owner, sat on the veranda, sewing and observing the comings and goings of the street. Amelia and her clothes occupied the front room of the house.

One evening Alan called to be told that Amelia had gone.

'Oh?' he asked Ella. 'Gone where?' His heart was beating faster and he was anxious that Ella should not see his fear. Already the situation seemed to him to have been, all along, inevitable.

'Perhaps this say,' said Ella, and handed him a sealed envelope. 'She left it for you.'

Alan took the note, glanced at it and said, 'She's left town?'

Ella shrugged as if to say that Alan should have got the message by now.

'Uh-huh,' she said, and dropped a stitch. 'Sudden. She said she had to go sudden.'

'Did she say why?'

'Perhaps her letter say.'

'Yes.'

Alan glanced at the envelope again. It read simply 'Alan', in Amelia's sloping scrawl. A thought – or a hope – occurred to him.

'And what about her things?' he asked Ella.

'She packed them and moved out,' said Ella. 'Paid my rent and I don't ask no questions.'

Alan thought of pressing her, but restrained himself. Ella was a formidable gossip, but there were others in Belize he could ask about Amelia. He thanked Ella and went downstairs, and

194

knew that she was watching him as he walked down the street. Studiously, he waited until he was around the corner, in Douglas Jones Street, before tearing the envelope open.

Amelia's note, he thought, was so like her.

It is time to go now. You should go home. It is all finished here. Now you see me now you don't. I love you but don't try and follow. Take it light. When you're in England I'll write with the good news.
Love, Amelia.

Alan had just crossed the Swing Bridge and turned into Queen Street, and was standing at almost exactly the spot where he first saw Amelia, when a clerk came out of the post office and asked him if he was Alan Palmer. It was 18 September, 1981, two days after Ella had given him Amelia's note, and three before Belize was due to become independent.

Alan said yes, and the clerk handed him a letter carrying a US stamp and a form which he asked Alan to sign. Alan did so and gave the clerk a fifty cent tip. He considered the writing on the letter and, wondering who could possibly have sent it to him, opened it.

It was from Wyler Fuller, the American journalist who – it seemed an age ago – had suggested to Alan that he should be a journalist too. His first sentence was to tick off his 'stringer' for not reporting back to him. But he had a piece of information for Alan, too, which he suggested that Alan might use as a basis for gathering more.

Wyler Fuller had been digging and Alan was astonished, if not particularly impressed, by his persistence. But more astonishing was his piece of information. He had found out that a man called William Brandl, whose age and other details fitted with the William Brandl who had lived in Regent Street, had been issued with a charge card in early August 1977 – four years ago – and that the following month he had registered a charity – The Grant Foundation – in New York. The seed capital had been small, only three thousand dollars, but much odder had been the business of the charge card. Or lack of business. What kind of small-time philanthropist is it, Fuller wanted to know, who gets himself issued with a brand new charge card at the age of fifty-four? Odder still, Brandl had used his card only once in four years, in Bogotá, Colombia, to have a bunch of roses sent to the United States. (Fuller gave the florist's name: Alvaro, of 15 Calle Marmoriás, 'just by the cemetery'.) The roses had been sent on 6 December.

Roses. Alan remembered what Amelia had told him about the man of Bill's age who, she had said, was 'sweet on her' in the States: 'He always sent me roses on my birthday ...' He remembered his unease at the time, on St George's Cay, when she had talked about Bill, or whatever his real name was. Could he have been the same man who had been 'sweet on her'? Alan remembered, too, that curious moment of domestic intimacy between her and Bill on the veranda, in Regent Street, just after he had told Bill about the Box Man. Hadn't there been, also, something rather over-elaborate about her concern that Bill should not know about their affair?

Alan's mind was starting to reel under the hail of questions and implications in Wyler Fuller's letter. There was another disturbing detail, too: the roses had been sent to one Amanda Holiwell, of Bement, Illinois. Wyler Fuller was working on that, but he hadn't traced a phone number and he was based in New Mexico. He couldn't always get away when he liked, and had, he confessed, quite failed to interest his editor in this 'story'. But if Alan were to come up with something ...?

The Bayman Hotel had a Reader's Digest atlas. Alan consulted it, remembering what Amelia (whoever she really was) had told him, that the biggest local landmark had been the grain silo: Bement was a tiny railroad stop in the heart of grain country. 'Illinois,' she had said on the way to the cay, 'a railroad stop ... *He always sent me roses on my birthday ...*'

In his letter, Wyler Fuller had added that he had found no records of any philanthropic activity by The Grant Foundation. But Alan was asking himself how, if Bill Brandl were in Belize, as Wyler Fuller had put it, to do some 'good on the sly', that would involve Amelia's taking an assumed name and pretending not to have known Bill before Belize. Could he really bring himself to believe in the idea of Amelia as a philanthropist? But if that wasn't her purpose here, what was?

He remembered that Amelia had once told him about a dark Colombian dope called 'wacky weed'. 'It's legendary,' she had said. 'It makes everything look crazy. *Everything!*'

Now Alan was beginning to ask himself more questions. Why had Amelia consistently refused to let him photograph her? Why had she consistently evaded specific questions about her past?

Wacky weed. Alan was starting to feel as if he had overdosed on it.

UNSENT LETTER THREE *William Brandl to Amelia Brodie (continued)*

... Medically, onco- if not ontologically, a metastasis is a secondary, just as Belize might be said to be a secondary of Britain. A colony of the Big C. The thymus is rare; cancer of the thymus is a rarity visited upon a rarity; cancer of the thymus with metastases is, largely, because of the self-contained capsule, a meta-meta-rarity.

When Galen's soul is cancerous, the treatment is simple. The sternum is cut open, vertically, as one might use kitchen scissors to cut a chicken's breastbone, and the pesky pair of posies is removed. After all, it – they – shouldn't be there anyway. The treatment is only effective when the disease is confined to its host. But when there is a secondary, ah ...

There. The figure is complete. What began as a rhetorical metastasis has ended as a medical one. In plain terms, last Thursday the specialist told me I had carcinoma of the thymus; today he said it had a metastasis – my spine. I think of the Roman Empire collapsing under Christianity – the Big C. The word has spread and is being spoken elsewhere, in a pidgin version; I try to stop The Word with words. I have cancer of the soul. I will die of a disease which began in something I should never have had.

I will die not like an ancient Roman but a modern American, guns blazing if necessary at nothing or no one, at the sky where God used to hang out, a shoot-out, a showdown with the showman whose angels have pulled out and who refuses to show; litigious to the last, I will bring a lawsuit against life for shutting down on me. I am an American, which is to say a spoilt child whose last technological toy will be the life-support machine. A freeborn son, I will have my last fist-fight with fate.

I am scared. I am so so scared.

# PART FOUR

# CUTTING

Two Central American literary stereo-
types – a drunken priest and a drunken consul – sat at the
club bar getting drunker. It was two days before independence
and Mr Arthur Middleton, Consul-General of the United States,
had never been seen at the club before in any other than an
official capacity. Now he was being seen at the club incapable.
Several people, themselves drunk, had sought to take advantage
of the opportunity to buttonhole him. But the Consul, who
wore an open-necked shirt tonight, had simply stared at the
newcomers, while the priest had discreetly caught their eye and
made a slight movement of his hand suggesting they should go.
And so they did, wondering what was eating the Consul tonight
that he should appear among them in this state.

The priest knew what the Consul's problem was, but was
bound to silence. He wore a little crucifix in his lapel and his
collar was worn the wrong way round, and even in this place
and with the priest in this condition, the iconography was strong
enough to lend authority.

Alan Palmer had come to the club looking for Mike Sharp.
He'd quickly found him in his preferred place at the corner of
the veranda, staring out to sea and nursing the inevitable scotch.

Mike had looked up and said, 'Well, if it isn't the old babyhood buddy! Siddown, Al.'

Alan had done so and come straight to the point: 'Mike, can
you help me out . . .?'

Mike had stared at him.

'Help, Al? Help you *out*?'

'Is that so strange?'

'You need a drink,' said Mike.

'Oh, I haven't a thirst tonight.'

Mike leant closer to him.

'Who's talking about a thirsty drink, Al? I'm talking about a drink-drink, a let's-get-a-little-drunk drink. What's your worry?'

'I'm trying to trace someone.'

'Who?'

'She's called Amelia Brodie,' said Alan. 'Amelia . . .'

'Oh.'

'You know her?'

'Like . . . like I know you. But I mean – you've got woman-trouble, hmm? But that woman *is* trouble, if you're sweet on her.'

'I'm . . .'

'She's a fast-lane lady, Al, and you're a slow-lane man. What happened? You moved out into the fast lane; got run over; that so?'

Alan smiled ruefully and said, 'Now you know why I come to you, Mike. You hear all the hoofbeats, don't you? Fast lane and slow. You could have heard some hoofbeats I haven't.'

'Who's talking about *horses*, Al? I'm talking about *cars*.' Mike lifted his scotch and drank the rest of his glass. 'Tell me, what's England like? English girls? They good? You ever bedded a real blueblood? Studded a brood mare? England . . .' Mike shook his head. 'To think I could have been English! But my blood's too thin, born here. I couldn't take the cold. And yours, Al? Isn't yours thin, too? How do you take the cold?'

Alan shrugged.

'I take it,' he said.

'And the warm? How do you take the warm?'

'I sweat a lot. But . . .'

Mike laughed.

'That's the problem. Keep warm in the cold, cool in the warm.' He held out his glass and shook it so the ice tinkled. 'Ice,' he said.

'I don't get it, Mike. You talk in code all the time.'

Mike stared at him.

'You're the one who asked for help, Al. So I gather you're in a hole. Maybe you fell in, maybe you climbed in. Hmm?'

'You're still talking code.'

Now Mike leant forward, his face close to Alan's. He held up a finger and said, fiercely, 'This isn't England, hear? Don't be fooled by the flag which flies for two more days. If you're in a position to help someone here, and you do, likely as not you hinder someone else. Get me? And that means you're a double agent and double agents use code. This is *my* territory.'

The finger Mike was wagging in Alan's face seemed all too likely, at any moment, to form a fifth of a fist and Alan, although tempted to say that Mike was *still* using code, resisted the temptation and sat back in his chair.

'Okay, Mike,' he said. 'Okay . . .' and he raised his hand, palm outwards, in what was intended to be a placatory gesture. But it was a few moments yet before Mike relaxed his position, then put his hands on the veranda rail and looked out to sea.

'I need a drink, Al,' and Mike's voice was weary. 'You need a drink. Go get a bottle, will you, and we'll talk.'

Later, much later, Alan would believe that Mike had spoken with regret as well as weariness. At the time, though, he had only the impression that Mike was proposing a linkage between some heavy drinking and any help he might deign to give. He did as he was told, and returned from the bar with a bottle of Chivas and the trimmings, saying as he set them down, 'There's a pissed priest in there.'

'Oh, the father,' said Mike, but he didn't sound too interested. All his attention was on the scotch. No sooner was the tray on the table than he poured himself a large slug of it. His hand was trembling; his fingers – Alan stared at them, fascinated – were clutched clawlike around the glass as if it were a grail which might suddenly be taken from him, so tightly that even in the poor light one saw the white knuckles. Perhaps the tight grip stopped the trembling. He looked up to see Mike watching him and if his hand trembled his gaze was steady. 'All this way,' said Mike, and shook his head as though over a hopeless case, 'you've come all this way only to live in your own head.'

Perhaps the fear of imminent independence was getting to people, but there was a hectic, unstable atmosphere in the club that night. Laughter was that little bit too loud and a lot of people were drunk – the desperate drunkenness which, like a faulty argument predicating too much upon too little, will end up flat on its face. But what possessed Mike was something nastier and more calculated. As drink succeeded drink, he looked at Alan over the rim of his glass and said, 'So you got laid in the backward birthplace, eh? With the fast-lane lady. But she's bad news, Al, she's going to hurt you real bad. You should have taken my advice, gone with Linda at Raul's. But you would have to dress it up as love first, wouldn't you? Your glass is empty. Pour yourself one.'

Alan obeyed. He said, 'I don't like whoring.'

'Whoring?' Mike asked. 'Or paying for it?'

There was a tense pause. Alan stared hard at Mike, who returned the stare, coolly, almost with amusement – but with the same strange regret, as though this was a job he had to do. Alan raised his drink slightly.

He said, 'I should throw this in your face.'

'Don't, Al,' Mike said quietly.

'And stop called me "Al", will you?'

'Michael says, "Don't", for three reasons,' said Mike. 'One: you'll be very sorry if you do. Two: it isn't worth it because you don't love Lady Fast Lane. Three: you think you love her and you want my co-operation in finding her, and that means keeping me sweet. Right? Right.'

'I said "I should". I didn't say I was going to.'

'That's it, Al – Alan. We're going to have a nice, uncivilised drink, okay?'

'I don't believe you *can* help.'

'*The pink car, Al.*'

'What's that?'

'I'm trying to help you.'

'You mean the spear fishers?'

'I told you, Al' – and from Mike's tone it might equally have been 'I warned you' – 'you should have gone with Linda.'

'Where are they?'

'The spear fishers? Why, the spear fishers are spear-fishing,' said Mike. Then he added, 'I imagine...'

'Tell me, Mike.'

'They have a boat, *The Mary May*. They've taken her north.'

'And Amelia?'

Mike shrugged. Alan waited.

'Well?'

Mike smiled.

'I guess she slipped anchor too, eh?'

Alan remembered what Amelia, Amanda, whoever the hell she was, had written in her note – 'Take it light': that had had the guiltless guile of a woman who's taken another lover, who knows somewhere in her back-brain that she's caused hurt but who, in her wildcat strike of happiness, simply doesn't care. Mike was right: she lived in the fast lane. He tried to take this in.

'She's with *them*?'

'Did I say that?' And Mike spread his hands in the age-old gesture of the guy who wasn't even *near* the scene of the crime.

'Well? What *did* you say, then? What *are* you saying?'

Mike leant forward with aggressive confidentiality.

'I'm saying, Alan, that if you let your blindfold slip, ever so little, and cheat a little all over again, you just might get the donkey's tail on the donkey's ass. *Follow the pink car!*'

'Down the yellow brick road,' said Alan. His head was spinning with the scotch. Where was the stress? he was wondering. Did Mike say 'Did *I* say that?' or did he say 'Did I say *that*?' Unsteadily, he tried to stand.

'Down the potholes,' said Mike.

'Thanks.' Alan put his hand on the table to steady himself. 'I'm not sure what for but thanks.'

'Don't mention it,' said Mike, 'and I mean that, okay? Don't mention it. You never met me.'

Alan shook his head.

'I never met you,' he said.


Later that night, in bed at the Bayman, it occurred to Alan that it was perfectly possible to be a human being without ever gaining full admission to the human race. It was a matter of what were called roots. Man *was* a root, a mandrake or forked, thinking radish. It was in his power to move, physically, and to travel in imagination and thought. But somewhere in himself he needed, however much he moved, to be still, rooted. If every individual was a forked, thinking radish, he was also in the radish patch along with all the other forked thinkers. The radish patch was society. There was such a thing as placing too much emphasis on the individual. Man was a social animal, too; more than that, his identity as a sexual animal was somehow tied up with his social being. A sexual relationship could not long survive away from the sustenance of society.

Freud suggested that every act of sexual union was participated in by at least six persons, the two individuals directly concerned and – in spirit – their respective parents. Psychologically, all sexual activity was group sex. But why limit the figure to six? Why weren't one's grand- and great-grandparents there too, one's former lovers, the bank manager, the milkman, one's neighbours? In this one contact, all one's contacts could be said to be resumed and no act is more ancestrally social than that of sexual intercourse. In a sense, it was a whole football crowd rooting for this one or that, waving their favours and banners. The thing might just as well be Match of the Day. One is mistaken to believe oneself entirely alone with another person.

He and Amelia had imagined themselves alone together, outside society. They had imagined that they might root themselves in one another, apart from the radish patch. It had been their joint rebellion, for him the latest of many rebellions, at the end of all of which he had found himself back where he started, rootless, contemplating his continuing rootlessness. To that history of rebellion he now addressed himself. What, really, was it a rebellion against? *Really?* The easy answer was society; but the truth was surely subtler. He saw that the apparent rejection of roots which underlay his rebellion was an elaborate stratagem designed to cover up, from himself and everyone else, the fact that there were no roots to reject. He could not be still in himself, with another, in society. Neither could Amelia. That was why, instinctively, they had travelled, to preserve for as long as possible the illusion that they might have a rooted future together. Benignly, they had deceived one another. Less benignly, he had deceived himself – although he wasn't sure that that was true of Amelia. If she was Amelia. Because if she wasn't, if, as seemed likely, she was Amanda, then she had doubly deceived him.

The fear that she had done so was an added humiliation. There was already the humiliation that she had left him, for one of the spear fishers. And what had Mike suggested? That their relationship had, anyway, been no more than a glorified whoring? In the limited sense that they had not been prepared to submit it to the tests of society that was, he supposed, true. But Mike, on another occasion, had said something more to the point: he had been cut adrift as a child and that made it harder, almost impossible, to root himself now. And Amelia? To her,

roots represented the boredom of the breadbasket, the mol-
estations of her alcoholic father. They had travelled together;
but, more importantly, they had both separately travelled *here*.
To this country which would tomorrow (for it was well past
midnight) become independent. Then, little by little, it would
become a nation and the matter of belonging to it or not
belonging, the vexed question of roots, would become para-
mount here as well. For another day, though, in this mongrel
non-nation, he could enjoy the illusion that being rootless he
was free. That would have to do. He would never settle down.
Social commitments required roots. Amelia had been another
of his false starts in the human race.

He rolled over in bed, and thought how unfair that one should
have drunk so much and still, however imperfectly, be capable
of thought. The anaesthetic had not worked; truth probed like
a scalpel.

Never worry. By daybreak the mind's own morphia would
have gone to work. Moments of truth were all very well by
night, when one was effectively out of commission. They were
a sort of seasoning; but when one had not lived by the truth,
when the truth was a killer, one needed more filling if not
sustaining fare to keep going by day ...

Lies, lies, lies.


So far, Mike's clue was checking out nicely. On the Southern
Foreshore, he had called at the car-hire office and found that a
boat called *The Mary May* had indeed been moored there, and
five days previously had indeed sailed north. Moreover, as Mike
had intimated, there had indeed been on board a young and
attractive American woman, with dark hair cut shortish, just
like Amelia's. But as Alan had extracted this detail, the car-hire
man had become suspicious and tired of questions. Alan had
wished that he had a photograph of Amelia to show. At the
time, her refusal to be photographed had struck him as shyness;
now it was another detail fuelling his confused suspicion of her.

The rainy season was over and the lush growths of those
months, among them his feeling for Amelia, were now to be
tested by the direct and unrelenting heat of the sun. It beat on

the Transit roof; but, mercifully, the humidity was lower; the steam bath was now a sauna and the further he drove north, in pursuit of the boat and the pink car, the dryer it was. As the thermometer climbed, so did his jealousy. In pursuing the clue from Mike, he realised, he was acting automatically, reflexively. How much, rationally, was there to go on? Little or nothing. But his reason was not in the ascendant. He told himself: the facts fit, face them. As to the matter of what he hoped to achieve by this pursuit, that he would deal with when he came to it.

And it looked now – towards two in the afternoon – very much as if he had come to it. There before him, perhaps two hundred yards away all told, riding easily at anchor in a small bay visible from the coast road, was a boat resembling the idea he had formed of *The Mary May*, an expensive white motor yacht on still, blue water, the picture of self-possessed purity. He felt tired and thirsty, and wished he had brought cold beer – binoculars too, so he could read the boat's name. Nor would he mind a swim in that tempting water. Well, he would investigate. He drove off the road down a short track, then drew up at the edge of the white beach which fringed the bay, just behind some trees, so people could maybe see him, maybe not.

Now what? He wasn't sure how to handle this. He got out of the Transit and mopped his brow with a handkerchief. He looked at the boat. Was she there now, sniggering at him from behind a porthole? Or was she a spear-fisher groupie, 'with' all of them? This was madness. No, it was possible. Anything was possible. He remembered how she had been at Pascó. Had her decency there been a deception too? Surely not. Why not? He found himself saying, 'Oh Amelia', then remembered that he didn't even know her *name*. What was wrong with her? She must be ill. He would save her from herself. No. He would see her damned to hell. As long as he saw her, as long as he saw her...

First things first. Was this *The Mary May*? He shaded his eyes and screwed them up in an attempt to read the name on the hull; no use, he was too short-sighted. But wait a minute. His eyes still shaded, he looked to the end of the beach. Was that ...? Yes ... under the ... yes. A small, ramshackle hut, set back from the beach under trees. Strewn outside were things suggesting occupancy, a chair, some crumpled-up plastic that

208

could have been a dinghy or child's paddlepool, a Coca-Cola cooler.

Skirting the trees so that he couldn't easily be seen (or was this skulking? – should he be seen and precipitate things?) he walked to the hut. It seemed to be some terminal place of amusement for, as he drew closer, he saw that it had a signboard which bore, in peeling paint, the name 'Mr Fruits', no possessive apostrophe. Well, perhaps it was a Dutch bar. He was really feeling most odd. Perhaps it was the combination of sun and raging jealousy, or – and he thought of his peculiar chain of thought in the Bayman last night – perhaps the stimulus was in himself. The door of the hut or bar was ajar. He stepped up to it and peeped inside.

Asleep in a chair, his head thrown back and his arms crossed over his lower abdomen, was the smallest, strangest-looking man he had seen. Not counting dwarves or midgets; because, although very small, this man was somehow neither and if he was a manikin he had none of the dapperness which that description suggested. He was shabbily dressed and very ugly, with a knobbly face, greasily desiccated, like the walnut which no one ate last Christmas. His mouth hung open, more than half empty of teeth, and all the remainder black; to top it all he wore a porkpie hat made of leather surrogate. He looked like a creature of folk imagination, a Rumpelstiltskin; or a degenerate strain of monkey on which experiments had been performed and which had escaped the laboratory.

On the wall behind the creature was a Pirelli calendar – last year's – turned to the wrong month, a beautifully proportioned woman posing on a Bounty Bar beach not unlike the one outside this hut. To complete the unreality, time had stopped. Alan, to attract attention, gave a low, discreet cough and when that failed, called, in an absurd housewifely halloo, 'Is any-body theah-air? Hell-oh-oh?'

The creature's eyes flicked open and perhaps he had not been asleep, so immediately predatory and on the alert was he, appraising the newcomer; Alan at once had the impression of having wandered into a web, or the mouth of a fly-trap plant, a place to waylay the unwary.

The manikin-fellow stirred in his chair and said, 'You wa' something,' a statement, not a question. His voice, from so

209

slight a frame, was disproportionately deep.

'Yes,' said Alan uncertainly, looking abut the room. On one wall hung a fishing net, Anancy's web. He forced himself to look at the man in the chair and asked, 'Do you by any chance serve drinks?'

'Order,' said the creature. 'Order.' he half raised himself on his stubby arms, 'What you wa'?'

'Beer?'

Alan ordered a Belikin and, while the man went out and rummaged noisily among the broken ice of the cooler, lit a cigarette, as though smoke might assert his presence in this place. His head pounded with the heat and engine noise of the journey.

He called out with what he hoped was nonchalance, 'I see you've a boat out there...' The cooler lid slammed shut and the fellow reappeared brandishing a bottle of Belikin.

'Americans,' he said shortly, and uncapped the bottle with a hiss. He said, 'Two dollars,' and Alan gave him the money, counting it out in coins.

'What Americans?' he asked. The little man's movements were quick, but his vocal delivery was slow, *el hondo*, dark brown, voice-over deep. His short bursts of laughter seemed to take an age.

He said, 'Men, three, a woman. Moan all day, moan, moan...'

'Really?' said Alan, although he was by no means sure what the man was getting at. He sipped his bear and thought he would have a stab at turning his dislocated dialogue into a conversation. With the back of his hand, he wiped foam from his mouth and asked, 'What do they moan about?'

The little man's eyes fixed on Alan as if he were potential prey. Alan was about to elaborate when the man laughed, doubling up, and said, 'No, no, no.' Then he looked Alan less truculently in the eyes, touched his forearm delicately with a fingertip and took a step backwards, hand limply extended. 'Jig-a-jig,' he said, and made a *moue*. Seeing the *moue*, and having noticed earlier the man's somewhat mincing strut, Alan realised that this was the Mr Fruit of the hut's signboard. But that wasn't his real name; like Rumpelstiltskin, he would keep it hidden. Was everyone in this country under an alias? 'Jig-a-jig,' the man

said again, this time with an unmistakable thrusting of his hips.
It was grotesque. Diplomatically, Alan broke off his stare and
drank beer, hoping to distance himself and impose some
decorum; but the man then touched Alan's forearm again and
said, 'No, no.' He pointed out of the hut door. 'Boat call *Mary
May*, okay? Come two days. Lots of jig-a-jig all a time, night-
time, maarnin, before siesta. Mr Pym don't like, Mr Pudney
like. Lady love and hate. Moan and scream, yell and groan every
time like he pop 'er virgin, see? Last night now, big moon, still
water, no wave. Silent. Then she moan. She only moan. And
Mr Pym only angry. Drive skiff from *Mary May* and sit wi' Mr
Fruit. All night, sit and he moan she moan. Then maarnin, fat
man come and they go. Shrimp colour shark car. More jig-a-
jig. Siesta, more jig-a-jig. Sleep now.'

'On the boat? She's asleep on the boat?' asked Alan, in no
doubt now that he had found Amelia.

Mr Fruit nodded urgently and said, 'Uh-huh, uh-huh.'

Alan said, 'And her name? What's she called?'

Mr Fruit didnt' hesitate.

'Honey,' he said. 'Pudney call her honey. She call Pudney
honey.'

Alan said, 'I see,' and put the beer bottle to his lips to disguise
his choking on these indigestible morsels of information. Honey,
he thought bitterly. She called me honey. There was a fire in
him and Mr Fruit had just poured gasoline over it. Keep cool,
he told himself. He lowered the bottle. 'And where did the car
go?' he asked.

Mr Fruit put out his hand.

'Money,' he said.

'Money?'

'Give me money, an' I tell you. Fruit nuh work fuh free.'

'You call this work?'

'If is no sleep, is work. If is work is money.'

Alan thought of protesting but this was no time to fool
around. He dug his hand into his pocket.

'How much?'

'Ten dollar.'

Not bad, as bribes go. Maybe the car's whereabouts would
be worth it. He extracted the note from his billfold and held it
by a corner, watching as greed began to work in Mr Fruit's eyes.

There was a form to these low-life dealings.

'Okay, where did it go?'

'West,' said Mr Fruit.

'West? That's not enough, Mr Fruit. We all go west. Where west?'

Mr Fruit ran his tongue over his lower lip.

'Nuh know where,' he said. 'But I hear thin man say Trinidad.'

'Thin man?'

'Pym.'

'And Trinidad?'

'Township to west. Money now.' And he actually snapped his fingers. Alan gave him the note, which was so gauzily threadbare with use that it probably held together by humidity alone. Mr Fruit licked the ball of his thumb and carefully folded the bill before putting it into his pocket. He resumed his seat with an air of self-righteous weariness, as of a man thoroughly deserving of a good rest. Perhaps he had dependants to support, but Alan doubted it. Mr Fruit's appearance was good insurance against the disaster of close human involvement.

Now what? Alan sat finishing his beer, staring out of the hut at the white boat framed by the doorway, imagining night, the moon, Amelia's moans of distracted pleasure. Over time, perhaps the boredom and beauty of this place, the sheer blueness of it, had driven Mr Fruit mad; if he stayed much longer, jealousy would send him the same route.

Absently, Alan said, 'Mr Fruit . . .?'

'What you wa'?' Mr Fruit had seemed to be nodding off, but now he was instantly, angrily awake.

'Do you have a boat I can borrow for a while?'

'Ten dollar,' said Mr Fruit.

'Okay.' They repeated the routine, he reaching into his pocket and peeling off a bill, Mr Fruit lovingly pocketing it.

'Down beach,' he said, his speech still orientally free of the definite article. 'Down beach, boat back of trees . . .'

Just beyond the trees an iron spike for braining coconuts had been driven point upwards into the ground. It was like a place of execution. Alan imagined Mr Fruit, monkeyman, raising coconuts above his head, bringing them down on the spike. Around it lay half husks and other detritus, devil's purses, seagrape, beer bottles, a severed length of heavy-duty nylon line, a Johnson's baby shampoo bottle with its teardrop-shaped label promising 'No more tears'.

The boat, a dorey, was tethered to a pimento stake. More half husks bobbed in the water around it. Alan, keeping his centre of gravity low, got in; he unhitched the dorey and pushed it gently out onto the water...


'He's coming over,' said Pudney. 'Get a look at him. Seen him before?'

He moved his head so Jane could look out of the porthole. She squinted in the light. After a pause she said, 'No. I don't think so.'

'He's using the Fruit's boat,' mused Pudney. '*And* he's wearing a white suit. Who wears a suit in this sun?'

'No,' said Jane again. 'I'm sure I never saw him.'

'Maybe he's some sort of diplomat,' Pudney said. Jane looked at him.

'Then I would know him, wouldn't I?' she said. 'And it's a very dirty white suit.'

'All kinds of people qualify as diplomats,' said Pudney. '*I* qualify. Maybe he's my kind of diplomat. Move your head, honey. Don't let him see you.' Jane obeyed.

'You think Arthur sent him?' she asked.

'I'd believe anything of that asshole,' said Pudney. 'And isn't it just the sort of trick he would pull...?'

'Sending someone to do his dirty work? It's the sort of trick,' Jane agreed.

'Well,' said Pudney, and heaved his lower bulk so he was sitting on the edge of the double bunk, 'we'll soon find out. You'd better get some clothes on, honey.'

Pudney, as he dressed, was troubled. It wasn't every day that one ran off with the wife of a US Consul and Middleton, by now, would surely have guessed that something was wrong with his marriage. It was past the date on which Pudney had promised to return Jane to the Consulate, at the end of this innocent

213

'fishing trip' on which Jane had been so eager to go. After a big bust-up, as Pudney had since learned from Jane, Middleton had given his reluctant permission, probably calculating that the three 'unofficials' would, in the end at least, bow to the Consul's authority. At first, Pudney had had no intention of posing a final challenge to that authority. Sure, he had wanted to ball the Consul's wife, but only to shopsoil her a little and hand her back. Things had progressed to a point, though, where to Pudney's own astonishment he was, or thought himself to be, in love. He, Pudney, in love! Pym had not liked that development at all, but Pudney had stood firm; their journey north had been fraught almost all the way. Pudney would have welcomed a man-to-man stand-off with Middleton. He would have enjoyed, for one thing, confronting the Consul with his knowledge, acquired from Jane, of his extremely weird sexual practices. No wonder Jane wanted out of a marriage to 'a monster', as she called her husband, a predicament in which she had seen Pudney as her 'rescuer'. Well, Pudney was going to rescue her, even if it did mean a few professional difficulties back in the States. And Middleton would be a fool to use this personal problem for professional purposes. Yes, Pudney was fairly confident he could come through this, but still he was troubled. If there was to be no direct stand-off – and, Jane had assured him, that wasn't Middleton's 'way' – there was still the Consul's intelligence and cunning to be reckoned with. Middleton would not lose his wife without some sort of fight, surely. But what sort? That was the question at the back of his mind as he saw Alan unsteadily approaching in Mr Fruit's dorey . . .


. . . extremely unsteadily. It was a long while since Alan had paddled a dorey. He was much larger now and, in the scaling-down of Mr Fruit's peculiar world, this was surely a smaller than usual dorey. It teetered and Alan had to balance carefully as he dipped the paddle, striving for the speed which, like a bicycle, it needed to give it stability. At the same time, his never very sure sense of purpose was wobbling, as he asked himself what was the point of this quixotic exercise in cockleshell heroism.

214

Nevertheless, he reached *The Mary May*, and was soon under the stern bearing its name and the registration 'Miami, Fla'. A set of tubular steel steps had been bolted into place, as though the sea were a swimming pool. Tied to the steps was a skiff. Its unladen hull made greedy slurping and slapping noises on the water. Closer to, *The Mary May* was less impressive, just the place you'd expect to find a fast-lane lady, more of the vulgarity he had mistaken for vitality. He tied up beside the skiff and climbed the steps to the stern.

The boat seemed deserted, the usual siesta illusion. They were down there, though, no doubt about it, *she* was down there. And what was he going to do about it? Swashbuckle into their cabin, their post-prandial, post-coital doze, and say to her, 'Pack your things. You're coming with me'? Like hell he was. What would her spear fisher say to that or, more likely, do about it? That was the real problem; in a discourse of doing, you had to want things badly, otherwise it was just histrionics. Did he want her that badly? Well, did he? He didn't think so, which probably meant that he didn't. He turned and had just put his foot on the top rung of the steps when, behind him, a man's voice said, 'Just hold it right there.' It might equally have been 'Freeze'. Obediently, he froze. 'Now turn around,' the voice said.

He turned around. The man in the doorway across the deck wore white slacks, no shoes, a white short-sleeved shirt with a *sportif* motif above the left breast. Alan had little difficulty in guessing what the sport was. Near the fly of the slacks was a damp patch; the shirt had been hurriedly, imperfectly tucked in. Covertly, the details aroused an animal aggression in Alan. The idea of 'Amelia' below, having just been enjoyed by this lout, that this should be the focus for the torment he'd been bottling up since Belize City . . . Had she really ditched him for a hairy shoulder-bladed hunk of rough trade?

At the same time, animal self-preservation was warily at work in him. While relieved that the man carried no gun, the many illusions he was under did not include the illusion that he might successfully take him on. If his stomach was an incipient beer paunch, his shoulders, chest and arms were powerfully muscular, and his leisurely brutality was that of someone who could handle himself in a fight. So, Alan told himself, don't get into a fight. Outwit him.

'What do you think you're doing?' the man asked.

That, thought Alan, was exactly right. He hadn't been doing anything, but he had *thought* that he was. From this ape the simple locution suggested the refinements of the sadist.

Alan gulped and said, 'You must be, um, Mr Pudney, yes?'

Pudney stared at him. He asked, 'Who are you?'

'Alan Palmer,' Alan said quickly. 'My name's Alan Palmer.'

'Well, Alan Palmer, perhaps you'd like to explain yourself.'

So, she hadn't told Pudney about him. Well, the poor sap Pudney would find out like him what a manipulator she was. Alan preferred, however, that he find out for himself, in his own time. He could still worm his way out of this.

He said, with a nervous smile which found no answering nervousness in Pudney's face, 'I thought I'd drop by, you know, but it's tricky with a boat. I mean, paying a social call...'

'*A social call?*' Pudney scathingly repeated. This wasn't going to wash.

Less confidently, Alan said, 'Yes. Isn't it? You can't phone up and there's no front door to knock on. Call round, you're already sort of trespassing. But I thought, anyway, I'd paddle over, but...'

'Hold it,' said Pudney, as Alan half-turned, ready to beat a retreat. Pudney's face showed signs of a pained impatience. Pudney said, 'Okay, we're miles from anywhere. I don't know you. You creep round the beach...'

'I was keeping out of the sun,' Alan objected.

'You were creeping,' insisted Pudney. 'Then you creep on board my boat. And start to creep back to your dorey. Except it isn't your dorey...'

'It's Mr Fruit's,' said Alan. 'And by the way, isn't that...?'

'You paid him, right?'

Oh-oh, he's got me, Alan thought. Pudney seemed to know his Mr Fruit. He nodded and agreed.

'Ten dollars.'

'Ten dollars. For a social call to people you don't know? You creep aboard my boat and don't holler for someone? I saw every move.' Pudney did a ghastly imitation of an English accent. 'Pop around for a cuppa tea did you, old man?'

People. Pudney had said people. If he didn't know who he was, then why, Alan wondered, was he so hostile?

216

'I'm not a thief or anything,' he said. 'And there are social calls and social calls, aren't there? Sometimes the social situation is quite, well, unusual, yes, and embarrassing...'

'Go on,' said Pudney. That was odd. Alan had been expecting Pudney to ask for clarification of the 'embarrassing' situation. His failure to do so seemed to suggest acceptance that such a situation existed. But ... Was Pudney subtler than he seemed? Was he pretending ignorance as part of an elaborate put-down? Or was he exceptionally obtuse?

Alan said, 'Mr Pudney, I haven't come to challenge you. To tell the truth I'm not quite sure why I've come. But certainly not to challenge you. Obviously you know nothing about me. That makes an embarrassing situation doubly embarrassing. But if I could, well, see her for a little while, that might...'

'Ahh!' said Pudney. He was nodding his head, slowly and comprehendingly, and staring at Alan. 'Now you're talking.'

Something wasn't quite right with the tone of that either.

'Yes,' said Alan uncertainly. 'I'm talking.' The penny had dropped, it seemed, then at once got stuck again. Pudney was – as Alan to his alarm could sense – restraining himself with difficulty. To Pudney the milk toast Brit's mention of Jane had confirmed that he had been sent to do the Consul's dirty work, unlikely as it might appear. Well, what was the plan? He looked nothing like a hitman. Pudney had seen at a glance that he didn't pack a piece. A knife then? Maybe. But for the moment, Pudney was more interested in the Brit saying that it was embarrassing he didn't know him. Jilted husbands did crazy things. They sent someone to knife you in siesta time; hatched weird plans involving Brit milk toasts.

Pudney said, 'Keep on talking, Mr Palmer.'

Alan had an inspiration.

'Do you remember we met?' he said. 'In Raul's Rose Garden one night? You were with your friends and I was with ... Well, I didn't actually *meet* you, but my friend Mike Sharp did' – Alan saw a gleam of recognition in Pudney's eyes; encouraged, he went on – 'Mike's one of my oldest friends and...' Impatiently, Pudney broke in.

'Mr Palmer, I don't mean to keep talking more social-call bullshit. Why did you come looking for us? Why are you lying to me?'

217

'I haven't lied, Mr Pudney. *I'm* not the one who's lying. I've told you the truth. I...' Alan, realising another dimension to this, stopped. Us. Pudney had said us. Oh no. Amelia was below. Unless she was asleep she must have heard his voice. Especially now it was raised. But ... No, this was monstrous. And what if...? Pudney had known he was here as soon as he'd arrived. Had Amelia too? If so, that meant ... What did it mean? He looked at Pudney. 'Does she know I'm here?' he asked.

Pudney wondered whether to answer that, but nodded.

'She knows you're here. And?'

Alan was straining to take in the implications.

'So,' he said. 'You do know who I am.'

'Sure,' said Pudney. 'you're a dime-a-dozen creep.'

'Insult me as much as you like, Mr Pudney. But she didn't use to think so.'

'Don't lie to me. She's never seen you before.'

Alan stared.

'She told you that? Then ... then why do you think I'm here?'

'Because he sent you,' said Pudney. 'And you're going to tell me why.'

'He? Who?'

'You're testing my patience, Mr Palmer.'

'Honestly, I don't know what you mean.'

'Her husband, asshole!'

Alan thought of Bill and of Wyler Fuller's letter. So that was it. But why...? No, this was going too far. Something was wrong here.

He said, 'Her husband?' Pudney was looking more dangerous by the second. Alan said, 'I think we have a big misunderstanding here, Mr Pudney. I haven't come representing anyone's husband. Amelia, as far as I know...'

'Wait a minute,' said Pudney.

'... isn't married,' said Alan. 'She's ...'

'Wait a minute, *wait* a minute!'

Alan waited. Brain against brawn was beginning to work. In Pudney's face was a hairline crack of doubt.

'Amelia?' said Pudney. 'You said Amelia?'

This was crazy. Were they talking about the same person? For a moment Alan doubted it. But surely this was more of Amelia's, Amanda's, whoever's, duplicity? Now Pudney was

218

looking dangerous again. It was time to get out, whatever was going on.

'She's not called Amelia?' Alan said, and when Pudney did not reply (as well he might not), continued smoothly (too smoothly for Pudney's liking). 'Well, Mr Pudney, this is obviously a misunderstanding. I'm sorry to have...'

But it was too late. If Alan had been interpreting Pudney in the light of his having been hopelessly taken in by 'Amelia', Pudney had been suspecting in Alan the machinations of Middleton. Here was the milk toast claiming to have had some sort of liaison with Jane and it occurred to Pudney that she had been unhappy with her husband before he happened along. Might the diplomat's wife have sought solace elsewhere under another name? For a moment he wondered, then thought: with this creep? No, this was Middleton's work.

Pudney reached and grabbed Alan by his lapels, keeping him at arm's length but lifting him slightly so he was forced to tiptoe if the cloth wasn't to tear.

'Okay, creep,' he said. 'I've heard enough. Now' – and Pudney used his grip to shake him – 'why are you calling her Amelia?'

'That's what she called herself,' said Alan.

'Are you *fucking crazy*?' Pudney shouted. 'When? Called herself Amelia when?'

'When I knew her,' said Alan. 'I don't know why. Ask her. Why doesn't she come up and explain? *I* don't know.'

Suddenly, Pudney saw how clever Middleton's plan was. This creep had been sent along to destabilise his relationship with Jane. But that wasn't all. Dimly, he saw the threat. What if...? Yes. Middleton was threatening to blow their cover, using as his cover this creep. And he'd be able to blame it all on Jane's having been extra-maritally intimate both with him and the creep. It would be his security leak. He took a firmer grip on Alan's lapels and bellowed into his face.

'How much do you know?'

Alan put up his hands to guard his face. Pudney, holding Alan's jacket in one hand, used the flat of the other to take a hard swipe at him. It half caught his head and half his wrist. 'Tell me!' Pudney shouted. 'Now! How much do you know?' He swiped him again. Alan was yelling.

'Nothing! I know nothing! For Christ's sake...'

Pudney was about to hit him again when a voice behind him yelled 'Peeder!'

Pudney grabbed Alan by the other lapel too and, without turning, said, 'Keep out of this, honey.'

But now she was beside them, her hand on his forearm, restraining him, and in the milk toast's face was an amazement which couldn't be acting.

'Peeder,' said Jane. 'Stop it. Wait.' Alan was giving her a bemused stare. Pudney's grip relaxed slightly, but he still wasn't sure. Alan's head was singing from Pudney's blows.

He said, 'Mike lied. He told me she was with you. Was this his idea of a joke? Jesus. I got the wrong one. I'm sorry. I made a mistake. A complete mistake. I've never set eyes on her.'

Pudney let go of Alan and took a step back. He was, though, still suspicious.

'Run it by me,' he said.

'I had an affair,' Alan said, 'with someone called Amelia. Except I'm not sure now she's called Amelia. And she looked like you,' he said, addressing the woman. 'American too, dark hair, young, maybe a little younger. Then she disappeared and Mike told me she'd gone with you, see?' he said to Pudney. 'And I was kind of crazy and didn't know what the hell was going on. It's all Mike's fault, Mike Sharp's. Well, you know him, you know what a joker he is, and . . .'

Pudney's eyes had narrowed.

'Now why would he do a thing like that?' he asked.

'He must be warped,' said Alan. 'A bit crazy maybe. He . . .'

'And this "Amelia",' Pudney wanted to know, 'who isn't Amelia. What about her?'

'I . . . she's a joker too,' said Alan.

'He's telling the truth,' said Jane.

Pudney turned to her.

'You think so?' he asked. You think he's telling the truth?'

'Well,' she said. 'Look at him.'

'Yeah,' And Pudney did look at him with, Alan was relieved to see, contempt now, not aggression. 'From the sound of it,' said Pudney, 'you're one of the ultimate assholes.'

'It sounds like it,' said Alan.

'Well, then' – and Pudney planted the palm of his hand firmly on Alan's chest – 'get off o' my boat' – and pushed him smartly

220

overboard. Alan, as he fell, knew that he'd got off lightly, in this last-moment turning of violence into farce. Thank goodness the woman ... Then he hit the water with a twelve-stone splash of white-suited foolishness and was underwater in a sane, silent world where ... Only to surface with the man and woman laughing at him over the edge of the boat, Pudney heartily, the woman with restraint. 'Asshole!' Pudney yelled again.

'I'm very sorry,' Alan called back, then took a mouthful of water and spat it out. 'My mistake...'

An hour's drive later and, despite the heat, Alan's clothes had not quite dried out. He had sat at the wheel of the Transit in his sopping-wet suit and set off still wearing it. Then he'd stopped and stripped down to his underpants, and stopped again and stripped them off, so that now he was driving naked, his body wet, not with seawater now, but sweat. At first he had felt only fury that Mike had misled him, mingled with relief that Amelia apparently hadn't, after all, left him for one of *The Mary May*'s ugly customers. He had been angry with himself for mistrusting her and for trusting Mike.

Then, more soberly, he had acknowledged that Mike had not misled him last night at the club so much as put no obstacle in the way of his misleading himself. That wasn't quite the same thing, was it? Jealously, he had jumped to conclusions. What, exactly, had Mike said? On the matter of the boat, *The Mary May*, he had been murky, but on another matter, the pink car, he had been quite clear. Follow it, he had said, *follow the pink car*. And if he altogether disbelieved Mike now and after the unfortunate misunderstanding with Pudney, then why had he automatically acted on that bit of advice and set off in the direction Mr Fruit had given him, after the pink car? And if it was still to be proved that Mike's lead had been a valid one, it did at least appear that Mr Fruit had earned his ten-dollar bribe, because there in the distance approaching him *was* the pink car. It was evidently returning to *The Mary May* and what a story Pudney would have to tell them when they got there! But why not use this opportunity to give them, too, a story to tell Pudney? In taking it, Alan considered, he might find out a little more about the evidently curious background to Pudney's half of their misunderstanding and that strange question he had asked, 'How much do you know?' He had learned, indirectly from Pudney, that there was a jealous husband somewhere and, directly from Mr Fruit, that the thin man, Pym, was exasperated by Pudney's philandering. Here were anxieties he could exploit.

He pulled up on a stretch of road where there was no room for the pink car to turn and follow him. He kept the engine running. His heart was beating fast, his hands were shaking. He felt particularly vulnerable pulling a stunt like this in the nude, but they couldn't see and there wasn't time to dress. He waited until the pink car was just in front of him, then flagged it down. It pulled up beside him, the 'fat man' (whom Mr Fruit had mentioned) at the wheel, beside him the 'thin man', Pym, and, in the back seat, Alan saw, the big, black guy who'd been with them that night at Raul's.

'Are you the guys from *The Mary May*?' Alan called over the engine noise.

Pym, the thin, gingery man, leaned over.

'Yeah? What if we are?'

'There's trouble down there,' said Alan. A cloud crossed Pym's face. He and the fat man exchanged glances. 'Big trouble, it looks like,' Alan pursued. 'In Mr Fruit's. I saw some of it. Thought you should know.'

'What kind of trouble?' asked Pym.

'Someone's husband. He's mad as hell.'

The fat man sat back in his seat and said, 'Jesus!'

'What's he doing?' asked Pym.

Alan shrugged, as if the matter were of no concern to him.

'Yelling a lot,' he said. 'Making threats. Something about if he doesn't get his wife back he'll tell everything. But looks a little violent too.'

The fat man turned to Pym and said, 'He's blown the whole fuckin' thing.'

'Shut up!' Pym snapped at him. The black man in the back seat was rolling down his window, his eyes on Alan.

'I knew this would happen,' said the fat man.

'Shut up, willya?' Pym shouted this time.

The black man called to Alan, 'Didn't I meet you some place?'

The fat man whispered something to Pym.

'Did you?' Alan said to the black man. 'Maybe. I don't remember.'

The black man furrowed his brow and said, 'It'll come to me ...' Pym leant over the fat man's lap and said, 'It seems we've got some bother. Thanks for your help.'

'Someone's been fooling around, eh?' said Alan, smiling and playing up to Pym's attempt to pass this off lightly. 'Oh, another thing. He wanted to speak to someone called Pym. That's you, I suppose ...'

'Yeah,' said Pym. 'He said that?'

'He said that.'

Pym nodded.

'Thanks,' he said. Then to the fat man 'Let's go ...'

'Good luck,' called Alan. He pressed the clutch and started off again towards Trinidad. He did a calculation. Pym and the people in the pink car would not be pleased when they got there and found out the truth. He was storing up trouble for himself, but in the short term he reckoned that he had, on these roads, three clear hours before they could return to Trinidad and catch up with him. Follow the pink car, Mike had said, but if there was substance in his lead it seemed to lie, not in literally following the car, but in finding out what the people in it were up to. Well, what were they up to?

This jealous-husband business, for example. Pudney had believed that he, Alan, had visited *The Mary May* on the husband's behalf. 'How much do you know?' Pudney had asked. With those as his clues Alan had gambled in saying to the thin man, Pym, that the husband was threatening to 'tell everything'. The gamble had come off: Pym had not queried the idea, while the fat man had been openly dismayed. So Alan had gambled again, with the suggestion that the 'husband' was waiting to settle his grievance, not directly with Pudney, his wife's lover, but with Pym, and at that very strange idea Pym had balked only briefly before taking it, too, in his stride.

What sort of jealous husband was this?

The strange thing was that he seemed to be involved, not just with Pudney and his wife, but in some way with all of them. He knew something which, if it came out, could damage all of their interests. They were all involved, then, in an activity requiring discretion and it was hard to resist the conclusion that

223

it must be a criminal activity. Pudney, by taking the man's wife, had introduced tensions which put the discretion in jeopardy. And the husband? Did he, in Alan's fictional disclosure, appear to the people in the pink car to be threatening himself too? To have gone wild with jealousy and to have thrown self-preservation to the winds? Or was he threatening only *them*?

And Amelia? How if at all did their need for discretion tie in with her? The name had meant nothing to Pudney. And Mike? How had the black man addressed Mike that night at Raul's? 'Still the same old street-wise . . . A little breeze is all.' Had the black man been, on the part of the pink car people, soliciting information from the 'street-wise' Mike, information about breeze?

Amelia carried sinsemille in a little enamelled box . . .

'They should sell more drugs,' she had said, 'and the sky and the sea would be dark with toucans and turtles . . .'

'A little breeze is all . . .'

It was little to go on. It was nothing. But it was all he had. And he was in the north of the country where, he knew, dope was grown. Last year there had been a weed-killing raid. A man had been killed.

If Amelia wasn't involved with these people, then was she . . .?

And the man who called himself 'Bill' . . .

'He's blown the whole thing,' the fat man had said. But blown what?

Perhaps he would find out in Trinidad and now he was almost there. He drove on for a while, then, just outside the township, stopped and struggled back into his damp clothes. He drove into Trinidad and parked in the main square. Or the only square. What now? When in doubt ask a cab driver or visit a bar. There wouldn't, in Trinidad, be any cabs but across the square he could see a bar. There was always a bar. From someone's open window a radio voice backed by balls box and echo chamber was advertising Independence cigarettes! 'Everyone's changing to In-de-pen-dence.' It flashed through his mind that Mike might be trying to get him hurt. He got out of the Transit.

'*Esta es Radio Belice, la voz de la nación naciente de Belice en Centroamérica . . .*' He started across the square, looking forward to a cold beer.

In the bar someone was singing:

You won't be here and I won't be here
When the hundred years are gone
But somebody else will be right in the cart
And the world will still go on.

The voice, a man's, was unmistakably English, as was the figure whom Alan then saw, the lone occupant of the bar, a dishevelled man perhaps in his mid-thirties sitting at a formica table whose surface was littered with dirty plates and empty beer bottles. The bar was full of sweet-smelling marijuana smoke and the man was holding in his right hand what the penny dreadfuls used to call 'a srange cigarette'.

'You've come to my goodbye party,' he said. 'You're late, but welcome. Do get yourself a beer.' In the empty bar, his voice sounded hollowly.

'Is there a barman?' asked Alan, taking an uncertain step into the bar. The man put his palms together and pretended to pillow his head on them.

'*Er schläft*,' he said. 'Siesta.' He puffed on the joint. 'Take what you want and leave the money.'

'I've a hell of a thirst,' Alan said. He went behind the bar and opened the cooler. There was a pause while he found himself a Belikin. The man was assessing him with a far from stupid stupefaction. It occurred to Alan that he was a re-run of Mike.

Alan looked up and said, politely, 'You're English?' Then, Belikin in hand, shut the cooler lid. He started to count out eighty cents onto the bar.

'George Bourne,' the man said, or rather declaimed. Oh no, thought Alan, a stage Englishman. His fake accent and clubbable manner wouldn't have deceived anyone in England for a moment. What a strange day this was proving to be. Alan uncapped the Belikin and drank from the neck, and perhaps his face showed his dismay, for the man then said with something like aggression, 'And you, sir? Whom do I have the pleasure of meeting?'

Alan lowered the bottle and said, 'Alan Palmer.'

'Well, Mr Palmer, pull up a pew and join me in a few. It's a longish road we have to travel before we reach the hotel-graveyard...'

'Hotel-graveyard?' Alan pulled up a chair and sat down

225

opposite George Bourne. 'I don't quite . . .'

'In Poland once. I was looking for a graveyard, a particular grave. They wouldn't let me cross the Bridge of Friendship, so I had to go the long way. I have no Polish, so went through the same mime with the taxi driver which I enacted just now' – and again he put his joined hands to the side of his head – "*Schlafen*," I said. I lay down on the back seat of his taxi and joined my hands on my chest in prayer. *Schlafen*; the place of sleep; he sleeps. Understanding dawned in the driver's eyes and he said, "Ah! Hotel!" No, no my good man, the Friedhof! "Hotel," he said again. Where you will, my man, where the wind listeth. So he drove, and we arrived and – do you know? – we were both right. They'd demolished the graveyard, just a heap of stones, and built a hotel in its place. The hotel-graveyard, you see?' He laughed briefly and said, 'Travellers' tales,' then took a deep puff on the joint.

'You're a traveller, then,' said Alan. The man nodded, still drawing on the joint. Then he offered it to Alan. 'Care for a toke, would you?'

Alan hesitated, then said, 'Why not?'

'See God,' said Bourne. 'Inject the stuff in the eyeball and see God. Yes, I'm a traveller. It's all a hotel, all a graveyard. Am I hurrying you? I stood outside that spanking new concrete hotel and I picked up, at random, a couple of stones from the pile of sledgehammered gravestones. Then I went to Gdansk and got drunk. Drunk in Gdansk. It even sounds drunk, doesn't it? Then I took the stones to my hotel washbasin and cleaned the mud from them. And I saw that they fitted. Two random stones, an exact fit. How about that? And on one stone was GO, and on the other TT. GOTT. God. The very devil . . .'

'That's a good story,' Alan said.

'Isn't it? But don't let me hurry you. One doesn't get an awful lot of company. And one's always nervous before a new journey . . .'

'Ah, you said it was a goodbye party . . .'

'I'm off,' said Bourne. 'Off to Managua. Have pocket calculator, will travel.'

Alan was beginning to warm to George Bourne. He said, 'You're going to Nicaragua?'

'Six years ago it was Mexico,' said Bourne. 'Then Belize

and now Nicaragua. I'm getting to the bottom of the Central American sock, going down the funnel into South America. And that's another funnel. I calculate that by my seventies, if I make them, I should have made it to Tierra del Fuego. There I shall tell the sheep my travellers' tales and among them I hope to have a few about my days as a revolutionary accountant, a balancer of Sandinista books, in Nicaragua! Then I shall sell up and return to Southampton where, as a little boy thirty years past, I watched the big ships come and go ...'

In a different setting Bourne's mannered self-consciousness and flowery delivery would have been simply repellent; here, however, they highlighted his extreme vulnerability. If the fellow was evidently touched, as they say, he was also touching. There was something moving about his preposterousness. That elephantine word suggests a large, fat and clumsy man, but Bourne, on the contrary, was thin and tall and nervously edgy. His fingernails were bitten very short but he had still contrived to get a lot of dirt under them. His teeth were bad and his hair was tousled. He wore a grey and very lightweight tropical version of a business suit and under the armpits were large sweat stains. Bourne was like a small, grubby schoolboy, desperately alone but pretending to be in control of his life.

'You're an accountant?' asked Alan.

'I am,' Bourne gravely replied. He offered Alan another turn at the joint, which Alan, with a shake of the head, refused.

'And you've been living in Belize, you say?'

'I've been living here,' said Bourne. 'In Trinidad. This is my farewell to Trinidad.'

'*Here?*' Alan repeated. It was barely credible.

'Oh, you'd be surprised,' said Bourne. 'I like my places out of the way, of course, but there's also work here. The Mennonites, for example. They've been my main clients, but a lot of people need things doing on the side ...' He let that hang and Alan thought: oh-oh, another marginal man – is it crime that he's referring to? It was as though Bourne guessed his thought. 'I wouldn't have told you before,' he said. 'But as I'm going tomorrow ... One reason I'm going is the drug money up here. It's bad and it'll bring bad men in its wake. That may sound funny, coming from me, sitting here with a spliff in my hand, but ...' Bourne took a last drag of the joint, then stubbed it out.

227

Alan waited. Bourne looked at him and there was challenge in his eyes. 'I'm weak,' he said. 'I admit it. A weak man. Pathetic really. Sometimes I get sorry for myself and that's even sadder. There are millions of men like me, though. People who don't believe in it all any more, if they ever did, for whatever reason. Nothing to hold on to. Despair creeps in, then weakness. I'm just a worse case of it than usual. Maybe I'll believe in Nicaragua, but I doubt it frankly. Don't you? Well, we'll see . . .'

Bourne paused, not a considered pause; more as though some temporary darkness had fallen on his thoughts and he couldn't see clearly. He was staring down at the tabletop just in front of him. Then he looked at Alan again and in his eyes now, having opened up this much, was something resembling trust, or the beginning of trust. Alan thought, 'He's been alone and silent too long. He needs someone to talk to.'

Bourne said, 'It's worse when you've been brought up to believe. The empty tomb. Isn't it strange how belief is all involved with an empty tomb? Believe in the empty tomb. But when you no longer believe, that's an empty tomb, too. Here –' and he put a hand on his chest – 'it's empty. I try to fill it with smoke and the local brand of beer, conviviality, an illusion of joy.' The hand-on-chest gesture was, Alan thought, absurdly histrionic, however sincere Bourne was being; then he lowered his hand. 'Well,' he said sadly, 'the stones spelt God, didn't they? Who knows . . . ?' Then he looked at Alan more intently, his eyes narrowed. It wasn't so much suspicion which Alan saw there as a dutiful doubt – an attempt to be suspicious of someone he was starting to trust. Then, 'You're not a nark, are you?' asked Bourne.

Alan shook his head and said with a slight smile, 'No, I'm not a nark.' To emphasise the point, he looked Bourne in the eyes. There was hardness in them at first, which soon relented: Bourne is right, Alan thought, he *is* weak.

'I hate them all,' Bourne said. 'The narks, the dealers, the pirates. Bastards all. They come to me sometimes, knowing I smoke the stuff like a chimney, wanting me to launder their money for them. But some stains don't wash out and I know I'd be lost if I did that. I smoke and I know it's a sin, but it isn't . . .' He stopped, then laughed and said, 'Anyway, what would the Royal Institute of Chartered Accountants think, eh?'

228

'Pirates?' said Alan

'What about them?'

'You mentioned pirates. What sort of pirates?'

'Dope pirates,' said Bourne, and then, seeing Alan's blank stare – half recognition, half incomprehension – 'have you not heard of dope pirates?' he said.

'Tell me about them,' said Alan.

Bourne laughed briefly.

'You arrived just a little too late,' he said. 'I had some in here just now. You could have asked them personally what they were.'

Alan realised that his pulse had quickened. He asked, trying to keep the excitement out of his voice, 'You mean the people from the pink car?'

'You know them?' asked Bourne.

'I passed them on my way here.'

'One couldn't very well miss them,' said Bourne.

'And they're pirates?'

'They're pirates.'

Then Alan remembered something and said, 'Pudney! Of course.'

'I'm sorry?'

'Pudney. He's one of them. They have a boat called *The Mary May*. If that's its real name and if Pudney is Pudney's real name. Pudney comes from *pas-de-nez* – no nose. They used to punish pirates by cutting their noses off. How about that?'

Bourne didn't appear to be impressed. He nodded and said, 'The head honcho of the people who dropped in on me was called Pym. That's an old Cornish wreckers' name. All very nautical, very piratical. Wouldn't you say? Oh well, another traveller's tale for the collection.'

'It's extraordinary,' said Alan.

'They made them up,' said Bourne, 'and it's quite ordinary. I would estimate that every second gringo I meet out here is flying under a false flag. Sometimes it's like a fantasist's convention. Especially about now.'

'Why now?'

'The dope's just about ripe. Soon they'll be cutting it. That's when the pirates turn up, too. They let other people do the growing and the paying, then steal the stuff when it's ripe and cut, ready to go. Bad hats, really bad hats. You've finished your beer. Fetch another one and one for me, and we'll drink to independence.'

Alan went to the bar. His mind was racing. Bourne must know more, but how was he going to get it out of him? And how honest should he himself be when, as was inevitable, Bourne enquired into his interest in the people from the pink car?

He uncapped a couple of Belikins and asked, 'Do you know someone called Mr Fruit?'

'Mr Fruit? My, you have been travelling, haven't you? So they're moored on Mr Fruit's beach, are they?' Bourne chuckled, as though at a private joke. Alan returned to the table and raised his bottle of Belikin.

'To independence!' he said.

'To independence,' Bourne agreed. They drank, then Bourne said, in the same amused tone, 'Do you remember the old puzzle about the Cretan at the crossroads?'

'The two Cretans,' Alan corrected.

'Yes, quite,' said Bourne. 'Well, Mr Fruit isn't at a crossroads, exactly, but he is at a junction, and Mr Fruit is the Cretan who usually tells the truth. That's probably how you come to be here, am I right?' Alan nodded. Bourne smiled and said, 'But down the road at Milepost 60 from Belize City there's a tin tabernacle, at a crossroads, and tethered outside it there's a spider monkey called Pompidou. A vicious little bastard. Bit me once. And *inside* the tin tabernacle there's a caretaker called Alfredo. He likes the dollars, just like Mr Fruit. Alfredo has a collection box in the tabernacle and into it goes money from passing strangers wanting to know the way. But Alfredo usually lies. There are only two possible ways to thrive at a crossroads, you see. Now, you will tell me truthfully what kind of crossroads you are at and why you followed the pink car here.'

'I'm trying to find someone,' said Alan.

'Who?'

'Amelia. Or so she calls herself. I have, though, reason to believe she may be called something else and that she might have got caught up with these people.'

'Two reasons to believe,' mused Bourne. 'You're doing well. So. It's a case of *cherchez-la-femme*.'

Alan said, 'But before I go on ... Can I trust you? I don't

230

want her to be harmed.'

'I don't get involved,' said Bourne. 'When I've finished here I'm climbing into that heap you may have seen parked outside and driving to Belize City. Tomorrow I'm on the plane to Managua. You don't survive in Central America by poking your nose too strenuously into other people's business.'

'That's roughly what Mike said.'

'Mike?'

'Mike Sharp. Perhaps you know him?'

Bourne nodded.

'A broken man and a very low form of life indeed. Now I'm going I can say it. But surely you don't believe anything he told you?'

'He didn't tell me anything. Not as such. But he ... hinted. He said that if I wanted to find Amelia I should follow the pink car. The name means nothing to you?'

'Amelia!' Bourne paused, then shook his head, slowly. 'I don't think so.'

'What about Brandl? Bill Brandl?'

Bourne hesitated.

'It ... *may* do.'

'It may do?'

'Carry on with your story,' said Bourne.

'What did Pym ask you about?'

'Carry on with your story.'

'Should I?'

'If you think so.'

Alan took a deep breath, then nodded, acknowledging that he really had no alternative but to trust Bourne. He told him about Amelia and Bill, and Wyler Fuller's letter.

Bourne interrupted at that to ask, 'Are you a journalist, then?' Alan shook his head.

'No, and certainly not if it involves Amelia getting hurt. One reason I'm here is to stop her getting hurt.'

'And,' Bourne volunteered, 'if it's you that gets hurt?' Alan looked at him.

'Then it's me,' he said, and went on with his story. He told Bourne about Mike and the drunken night at the club; how they had been young children together ...

Bourne interrupted again to say, 'There you are! You may

have thought my earlier remark about Mike Sharp to be rather sanctimonious. But I meant it. It isn't that he drinks and whores nor, even, that he's bitter and twisted. What's corrupt about him is the lurid loss of his childhood. It is possible, though, that his hint to you was substantially correct, and that out of his bitterness and corruption he really was doing you a favour, as he might have done as a child before he lost his childhood.'

Alan looked at Bourne and said, 'Are you saying that he did tell me the truth?'

'In a warped form, perhaps,' said Bourne. 'But go on.'

'There's not much more to tell...' Alan told him about *The Mary May* and his misunderstanding with Pudney; how it had been, possibly, a revealing misunderstanding and how he had tried to exploit that possibility in his meeting with Pym on the road.

Bourne nodded and said, 'So I can take it that you don't know who the woman on the boat is?'

'I don't. Do you?'

'No.' Then Bourne pointed out of the window to a shopfront across the square and asked, 'Does that name mean anything to you?'

Alan read the shopfront sign: ZUNIGA'S HARDWARE.

'No,' he said.

'He was killed last year,' said Bourne. His tone of voice was musing. 'By crop sprayers killing weed. Manuel Zuniga. A nice old chap. Honest, too. You've probably heard the story of how he died?' Alan nodded. 'Well, assuming you heard the correct story,' said Bourne, 'you were probably horrified, as was everyone in this little community. It was almost exactly a year ago.'

'I was horrified,' said Alan.

'Really?' said Bourne.

'Really.'

'I ask because the men from the pink car pretended to be horrified.'

'They...?'

'They were, ah – let's say unusually interested in Zuniga's hardware. While pretending not to be. While pretending, at the same time, to be unusually interested in this grass of mine. But they weren't really interested. Not in the dope as such. They were interested in money. And, being an accountant, it was natural that I should talk to them about money . . .'

'What did you tell them?'

'I lied,' said Bourne. 'I told them I did the Zunigas' accounts. I told them how badly the business had gone downhill since the old man's death. How sad it was. Now – ' Bourne placed the fingertips of both hands on the edge of the table – 'I have decided to trust you. If you betray my trust . . .'

'I just want to find Amelia,' said Alan.

'I believe you,' said Bourne. 'And that is why I am trusting you. The truth is this. The business has not gone downhill, but up. I don't do the Zunigas' accounts, but I used to. I don't any more because since Manuel's death "Zuniga's Hardware" has become a bit of a misnomer. The business has branched out into software, too, or, more accurately, dry goods, dry goods like this . . .' And Bourne picked up his pocket tin of marijuana and shook it slightly. His eyes were on Alan. 'Do you see?' he asked.

Alan nodded uncertainly.

'So far,' he said.

Bourne fixed his gaze upon him for a moment then turned away.

'I want,' he said, 'to tell you a bit more about Manuel. He was an old man, but he was also a child, with the goodness of a child. And I don't mean goody-goody goodness. Essential goodness. As a child in Southampton I watched the big ships come and go. Manuel's childhood was different. His father was a small-holder *milpa* farmer in southern Mexico and somewhere at the back of his mind he had this modest dream, just like my dream of the ships, of growing something in the earth. It was his nature, you see. Lose that dream and you might as well be dead. Keep it, they'll try and kill you. They killed Manuel well enough . . .' Bourne stopped and Alan saw that he was holding down strong emotion. The stage Englishman of their first minutes of meeting had disappeared completely. Bourne drank from a glass of beer, then said, 'When one loves someone, I think, it is the child in the other person one sees, as I saw the child in Manuel, the child and the father. He gave me good advice and I loved him, and I think his death has something to do with my wanting to leave Trinidad. But before I leave there's something I owe to his memory . . .'

233

It was clearly a cue. Alan took it and asked, 'What's that?'

'When you came in here . . .' Bourne began.

'You were singing.'

'And thinking,' said Bourne, 'about Rafael. That's Manuel's son. I was thinking that if he goes on any longer in the dope business he'll soon be older than his old man ever was. I was wondering how I could talk him out of it, but I don't think I can. It's too late now and, anyway, we all go to hell in our own handcart. But I could at least tell him – if I had the time, which I haven't . . .' He looked pointedly at Alan. 'But you have. The time and the motive.'

'To do what?'

'Go up to Manuel's land and tell Rafael about the pirates.'

'Oh . . .' Alan shook his head. 'I don't think I should get into this. I'm already deep enough in something I don't understand.'

'Rafael,' said Bourne, 'is working for an American called Bill.'

Alan stared at him.

'Bill Brandl?'

'They call him "Mister Bill". But I'd say it was the same man, wouldn't you? If "man" is the word I'm looking for . . .'

Alan tried to take this in. He said, 'And Amelia?'

'I think,' said Bourne, 'that the lead Mike Sharp gave you was a good one.'

'Then that means . . .'

'You have been most royally lied to,' Bourne supplied.

Alan nodded reluctantly.

'Well, will you go?'

Alan wondered. What else could he do, having come this far: go back to Belize City? He felt fear, but also the excitement and curiosity of the chase. To go back now would spell defeat: his victory would lie in confronting Amelia. He lowered his head in assent.

'Yes, I'll go.'

Bourne sat back with a kind of relief, the tension of the moment broken.

'Excellent,' he said, and then, qualifying his open pleasure at Alan's decision; 'I mean, now you can get to the bottom of your problem and I can leave Trinidad with a clear conscience. Birds and stones, all that.'

Alan wondered, 'Is it likely to be, ah, dangerous at all?'

Bourne pursed his lips for a moment, then shook his head.

'No. No. possibly a bit embarrassing at first, but once you've explained...'

'Okay,' said Alan. He wasn't convinced, but Bourne's reassurance would have to do. He felt quite calm. 'How do I get there?' he asked.

Bourne leaned confidentially over the tabletop.

'Go to the crossroads at Mile 60,' he said. 'Take the left. Alfredo in the tin tabernacle there would tell you otherwise, but take the left...' Alan got out a pen and took down the directions as Bourne gave them. They finished their beers, then Bourne gave Alan several more to take with him. They shook hands, semi-formally, and went to the door of the bar together. There Bourne stood a moment, his hands on his hips, looking about him. 'Bye bye, Trinidad,' he said.

Alan was looking at Bourne. He said, 'It's hard to believe. Meeting you here like this. By chance.'

Bourne said, 'Two random pieces of stone. Or apparently random. But they interlocked. That's all.'

'I was going to ask you. What were you doing, in that Polish graveyard?'

'*Hotel*-graveyard,' Bourne corrected him. 'I was looking for my father. But that, as they say, is another story...'

It was the time of cutting. The plants were close to complete ripeness, a week or fortnight away. They were tall, up to eight feet high, their heads heavy with buds. They had been well cared for, and were strong and healthy. Green crystals of fertiliser had been heaped around their roots; they had been watered; the sun they worshipped blazed upon them. They had been denied nothing except what they craved the most – to be fertilised, *really* fertilised: by the male.

Months before, when they were still seedlings, the males had been weeded out and burned. Tricked, the females had responded, as the growers had known they would, with wiles of their own. They had plastered their buds, as though with make-up, more heavily than ever with resin and applied the heaviest of perfumes. All to attract the male. But no male came.

Still the females waited, aridly obeying their imperative, and as they waited tricked themselves out the more.

Cleverly, the growers thwarted the desire they encouraged. That was their skill. The heavier the resin and perfume, the richer the smoke when the females too, bud by bud, would be burned in darkened rooms. The smoker's buzz would be in proportion to the heightened frustration of the female plant.

The growers were jealous of their *hierba*. In their loving tongue, they spoke of the plants, and to them, as though they were lovers. Each plant was 'she'. They were 'babies', 'little sweet things', *'niñas'*. Then they were expensive, pampered women whose buds the growers looked forward to 'manicuring'.

The growers were sorry for them, too. They would die like this, well fed but starved, ripe but unfulfilled, desiring, but their desire denied – *sinsemille*; and – a funny thing this – it was almost as though they knew they were doomed. As ripeness approached they lost all shame. Although their heads were heavy they did not bow them, but brazenly held them up, like the whores of Rosarito, not missing a trick. And like whores they despaired. Secretly – their one remaining secret – they knew. Then the growers saw their *milpa* in the image of a whore-house walled in by bush and under the roof of the sky. They joked about their virgin *putanas*. But now the growers had a secret of their own – a secret nagging almost like guilt. After all, the females offered themselves for free; it was they, the growers, who were getting paid.

Following Bourne's directions, Alan drove to the clearing. It had been well used. Tyre tracks from the time of the rains had hardened under the sun into bumpy ridges and where the ground was flat it had cracked like a mirror – the cracks where, as a child, he had believed lizards to be born.

He parked the Transit. In motion, the draught through the rolled-down window was primitive air conditioning. Now that he was immobile, the air was at once much hotter and the smell of marijuana, undiluted by the draught, at once much stronger. It smelt like an Arabian warehouse, rich but also dusty, an indoors smell although he was in the open. He had smelt it first, faintly, on the track leading to the clearing, just as Bourne had said he would. 'Follow your nose,' had been Bourne's parting shot, 'follow your nose...'

He got out of the Transit. He locked it. The smell came from beyond the bush ahead of him. He went to the edge of the bush, parted the screen of leaves and went in. It was as easy as that, as Bourne had said it would be. The smell grew steadily stronger. Soon he came to a tree where a fork in the lower branches had been scorched as though by a flame-thrower – a beehive which the growers had burned away: bees brought pollen. For the first time the smell seemed heavy with foreboding, but its lure was stronger too and he went on, following his nose. There was a secret here. It was, it must be, her secret and with every step he was getting warmer, warmer, until only a last, thin screen of leaves remained. Beyond it he saw a black alleyway of burnt earth and, beyond that, another wall of vegetation, paler green and evenly spaced. He broke out of the bush and on to the alleyway. Charcoal was everywhere, twigs, sticks, branches, like the aftermath of a barbecue. Here and there, during the rainy season, weeds had sprouted from the black earth – here and there weeds, and there the sheer wall of *sativa* weed ahead of him.

He crossed the alleyway. His shoes made a crunching noise on the charcoal. He felt a little dizzy – the overpowering smell, the light, the heat. And the air was not simply hot, but somehow, mysteriously, *on heat*, heavy with more than the smell of resin. Alan stopped in front of the weed. He reached up and, with his fingertips, touched one of the exceptionally large and resinous buds which dealers call a '*crème*'. Sticky to the touch, it flamed with strange beauty, purple and green, an Afghani bud which is ripe after five months. The colours were an explicit visual invitation.

It was quite silent, no birds, no humming insects. Nature gave weed a wide berth. It was no good to eat. It was no good for anything. That was why it was called weed. It was good only for money, a cash crop with a vengeance. They might have been greenbacks growing there, strangely shunned under the sun. What would this bud be worth at street level, where grubby fingers would prise it open? Money. Coming upon the plants was like walking into an open-air bank vault.

237

It was quite silent. Then Alan stood very still, the sort of stillness in the sort of silence when you really do hear your heartbeat. He had just heard a charcoal crunch like that his own footsteps had made. He listened. A regular, repeated crunching.

He looked around him. How did the land lie? To his right, the earth alleyway ran straight for twenty yards or so, then turned a corner of the dope crop. Around that corner, out of sight behind the dope, someone was walking steadily, unhurriedly his way.

Nowhere to hide. Only the bush. The bush was too far. The bush was too noisy. And no time. *Crunch*. He braced himself. Reuben White stepped around the corner.

Reuben was on a routine circuit of the *milpa*, a sort of cross between patrol duty and beating the bounds. He was the foreman, the 'header' – it was one of his jobs. He carried the rifle which Pedro had assured him you had to have if you were the header.

Pedro had put it well. A gun, he'd said, was a psychological scare technique, but for it to work people had to believe you were prepared to use it. Let it get about that you'd a gun and meant business and people would stay away, just like the birds. And Pedro had been right. It had worked. No one had come up to the *milpa*.

Until now. And who had come? He would have been startled to see anyone, but *who* did he see? A sense of inevitability stole over him. Of course ... *Of course! He's caught me out in a crime*, was the refrain running through Reuben's head, *like his father caught my mother, Palmer the father, Palmer the son. He's come for me* ... The remoteness of the spot where they were – everything wild but the weed – gave conviction to his fear. It possessed him and he panicked. Here were no social restraints, as there had been on the boat trip – and then, too, Reuben had been guided by his father. On the contrary, the bias of the *milpa* was in the opposite direction – anti-social. If there was to be restraint it had to come from Reuben himself and, in his fantasy, he would murder the man who was facing him.

It was the most dangerous moment, morally, of Reuben's life, and physically, of Alan's. Alan didn't know it at first. It was all happening very fast, but there were rapid reactions before the fear hit him; surprise, at seeing a black man in brown-man

238

country; more surprise, recognising it was Reuben; the memory of Reuben's dislike for him and of Amelia saying he was Bill's friend; and only then the shock of – *Jesus*! Wha ...? Reuben had a *rifle*. He had the thing at waist height, at the ready. *He was pointing it at him.*

Still, it wasn't quite real. Weakly, Alan said 'Reuben ...' and did the done generic thing: reached for the sky real slow. Then it hit him that the rifle was real. There were bullets in it, for Christ's sake. And the set of Reuben's face and his stance, feet planted apart, and his voice, not the voice that Alan remembered, saying, 'Okay, stay there Palmer. You. Now tell me what you're doing ...' This was for real.

Alan couldn't tear his gaze from the gun. He said, 'Reuben, the gun, please ...'

'*Tell me!*'

'I ... I came to warn you, Reuben.'

You can warn someone as a favour or, as Reuben heard it, as a threat.

'Warn me! You! Warn me! *I'm* the police round here!'

Reuben was shaking. Perhaps to overcome it he shook his rifle at Alan. That made things even scarier.

'Please ... I'll explain ...'

'I don't want your explanations. It's too *late* for your explanations ...' But Reuben's tone was different. If still hostile, the dangerous high tension had eased off a little and the sense that he was out of control. And now he lowered the rifle so its barrel pointed downwards. He tossed the rifle to his right hand and held it by the stock, so his finger couldn't steal back to the trigger.

He shouted, 'Keep your hands up,' and started towards Alan.

Now Alan's relief that the rifle was off him was succeeded by fear of Reuben coming towards him. He felt exposed with his hands up but it was better not to lower them and risk the rifle again. He spoke in a rush.

'Reuben, I didn't even know you were here. George Bourne told me about Rafael, and pirates, American dope pirates, the people from the pink ...'

But Reuben wasn't listening and what he heard meant nothing to him. He kept on coming. He knew why Palmer was here, at this place where he, Reuben, was least himself, most himself.

239

He'd come in some sense for him. No other possibility entered his mind.

Reuben kept on coming, nearer and nearer, narrowing the gap of nearly thirty years...

'They're dangerous men, Reuben, Bourne said they...'

And now he was near enough. Reuben used his left, the southpaw, to punch him hard in the solar plexus. One fast and fluid movement. Manuel Zuniga had gone down on this land; Bill Brandl had gone down; Alan followed them to his knees, clutching his hands to his stomach. Desperate to double up and roll over he struggled to stay on his knees in case Reuben meant more violence. But Reuben meant no more. The fight had gone out of him, all at once, although Alan couldn't know it; all the fight. Alan fought for his breath, his eyes open and on Reuben – who stood there, above him, looking down.

His silhouette blocked the sun. It fractured the light which fell from the sky behind him.


It was night. Alan lay on the camp bed in the *choza* where the stores were kept. In one corner were a few sacks of Miracle-Gro fertiliser; in another, several stacks of the five-gallon white plastic buckets in which pigtails were imported into Belize. That was easy enough to work out – on some of the buckets were cartoons of 'Louisana Hogs' perplexedly turning to look at their tailless backsides. As to their purpose here, Alan guessed (rightly) that they were to contain the dope when it was cut and compressed ready for export. In the *choza*, the homely smell of garden shed fought with the dope smell of the *milpa* for possession of the enclosed space, and lost.

Not that the *choza* was entirely enclosed. If he was under detention, Alan had decided, it was evidently a downmarket form – hut- if not house-arrest. Leniently, as a concession to the heat, he had been allowed to sleep with the door open. It let a lot of moonlight in, but on balance the light was worth the few tepid breaths of night air which occasionally entered too, even if they did smell of dope. It wasn't the dope smell, though, or the moonlight, which were keeping him awake, but the novelty of the situation in which he found himself, the sense of danger

240

which still attended it and his calculations of the reality of that danger.

Outside, for example, in the moonlight, the young grower called Coffee sat on an upturned crate cradling the rifle which Reuben had made such a point of handing over to him. He was chain-smoking joints, although, one presumed, he was on guard duty. The point of the rifle, presumably, was to shoot the detainee if he should make a run for it. Alan didn't like that idea at all. At the same time, however, he couldn't believe that Coffee, who had earlier, with a grin, offered him a toke of his joint, and taught him *choza* and *milpa*, could actually bring himself to shoot at him. It was surely a show of strictness, rather than the reality, but Alan was of no mind to test that theory. From the camp bed, he glanced through the door. Coffee was stubbing out a joint, the rifle across his lap like a newfangled farm implement of whose application he hadn't the slightest notion. For a moment, the young grower lurched unsteadily forward on his upturned crate. No, Alan decided, Coffee was more likely to fire accidentally than on purpose.

How serious were these people? Or was it not a matter of seriousness so much as of their relative relaxation, their laid-backness – Reuben apart – regarding the dodgy enterprise on which they were engaged? Alan had formed the distinct impression that of the people on the *milpa* the uptight one was Reuben and that if he had chanced to bump into Rafael, or one of the other growers, he would have been given a quite different reception – even a friendly one: for had he not come to the *milpa* armed with useful information?

After punching him, Reuben had brought him up to the *chozas*, where he had sat nursing his stomach and watching from a distance as Reuben and Rafael talked together; or rather, whispered, the two of them in a sort of heated huddle – heated, anyway, on Reuben's side, to judge from his gesticulations. Rafael, by contrast, had seemed quite calm – glancing occasionally at Alan. Then he had come over, followed at a few paces by Reuben. Rafael had held out his hand.

'Rafael Zuniga. You already know my name, no?'

'Yes,' Alan had said, standing, and offered his own hand in return. 'Alan Palmer'. They shook hands.

'Sorry about this,' said Rafael, and Alan was struck by the

241

officer-class idiom, even if it was strongly accented: '*Sorr-ee aboud dis*. George Bourne sent you?'

Alan nodded.

'That's right.'

Reuben was now standing just behind Rafael, stroking his chin and looking down at the ground, or into the half distance (all that the height of the dope plants allowed) – anywhere, Alan guessed, rather than at the man he had punched. Reuben, he realised, was ashamed.

'You want to tell me the story?' Rafael prompted.

'Sure. I was driving about the north, sightseeing. On the way to Trinidad a pink car came my way, with three men inside...'

'You know who they were?'

'There was a thin man, American. He calls himself Pym. And a fat guy, he was driving. In the back there was a black man. Oh, and there's a fourth one, Pudney. He was on the boat they have, *The Mary May*, which is moored by a bar called Mr Fruits. I'd stopped at Mr Fruits for a drink – he told me their names – and the pink car stopped *me* to ask a direction.'

'Then, in Trinidad, you met Señor Bourne.'

'Yes. And he told me about their interest in your hardware shop and how he thought they were – pirates. So I did him a favour and came up here.'

Reuben looked at Alan now and asked sharply:

'Nothing else?'

Alan said:

'What else should there be?'

'And the black guy,' asked Reuben, 'in the back. You know his name?'

'I've been trying to remember,' said Alan. 'I met him one night at Raul's Rose Garden. Black-something, Black...'

'Blackjack?'

'That was it. Blackjack.'

For the first time Reuben seemed impressed. Rafael turned to him and asked: 'You know him?' Reuben nodded slowly.

'If I needed one piece of evidence that they really were pirates,' he said, 'that would be it: Blackjack.'

Rafael, looking at Reuben, asked: 'Yes? You're sure?' but he was thinking, 'Why didn't you wait to find that out from the *inglés* before hitting him?' He turned to Alan. 'One more thing.

242

George didn't tell my mother?'

Alan looked perplexed.

'He didn't mention your mother.'

Rafael nodded, accepting Alan's reply. But he thought, he would have had to tell her in an emergency and it was an emergency until this Englishman came along. His mother, like Bourne, disapproved of his venture into the *hierba* business and news of the pirates would not only have frightened her, alone in the hardware store as she often was these days, but frightened her on his, her son's, behalf. He should, really, they all should, be grateful to Señor Bourne and his *compadre* for this warning. Rafael asked himself again why Reuben hated the Englishman as much as he seemed to. He would talk to him again about it, get him to see sense: to relax. Reuben had none of Peyrefitte's cool, but he was still 'Mister Bill's' header – for better or, probably, like 'Mister Bill' himself, for worse – and if Reuben wanted the Englishman to stay, well . . .

Rafael had said to Alan, 'Would you mind to stay the night?'

'The night?'

Alarm must have shown on Alan's face, because Rafael reached to touch his forearm and said, 'Don't worry. Is no problem. But I regret . . .'

Now, staying the night, Alan was wondering about that abrupt question of Reuben's, 'Nothing else?', and remembering what he had said on St George's Cay, 'I've a feeling the lady's maybe spoken for.' If Bourne's 'Mister Bill' really was Bill Brandl (and Reuben's friendship with Bill, vouched for by Amelia, suggested so), then Reuben would be wondering at the coincidence of Alan's having turned up, apparently only as the bearer of a message from a stranger, at this out-of-the-way place which was the dope farm of people whom he, Alan, knew. From the boat trip, Reuben knew that he and Amelia were friendly; but, on the boat trip, apparently in defence of Bill's interests, he had seemed to suggest that Alan shouldn't get too friendly with her. Reuben would be wondering about all of that, thought Alan, and perhaps he was insistent that Alan should stay the night because he was waiting for Bill, or Amelia, or both, to come to the *milpa* so he could find out what they thought . . .

But his stomach muscles hurt; his skin was salty from Pudney's pushing him overboard; his face had caught the sun badly.

And the dope smell was strong...

It was almost tomorrow, Independence Day. He would see it in under hut-arrest.


In the other *choza*, Reuben was also awake. This was the day on which he had nearly become a murderer.

He shuddered at the memory with retrospective horror, as if, in his mind, he were actually carrying through the thing he had almost done. That was the power the mind had over the body. He drew on his Colonial cigarette, then transferred it to his right hand. By its gleam, he examined the index finger of his left hand. He waggled it a little. It was his mind that told his finger to waggle. Today his mind had told that same finger to squeeze a little on a trigger. It had begun to. A tiny bit tighter and the rifle would have fired. A tiny bit tighter.

This was the nightmare flickering tonight across his mind. It made a change from the weed. Often over his weeks on the *milpa* bad dreams of the weed had awoken him. He had seen it in even more vivid versions of its true colours, growing with even more nightmarish speed, like the time-lapse effect in *The Living Desert*. He had smelt it and woken to realise that the dope smell of his dream – a smell like rotting – was not the *milpa*'s real smell. Could one dream a smell? The mind could. When it was filled with fantasy not thought, when you didn't use it but it used you, the mind could do all sorts of things. It could bring you to the very edge of murder.

It could turn your life upside down in a little over six months. He had been a respectable citizen, a slum boy made good, socially responsible and concerned, engaged to be married, worried about his father's health. Then all these traits had gone under and the unconscious mind come out on top. For his personality to have been so rapidly dismantled it must all along have been a lightweight, shantytown construct, not the strong house on firm foundations which he had imagined himself to possess. It had been a fantasy, not nailed together, unshakeably, by true conviction, but tacked together by will power against odds like Hattieville and its life. To cohere, he had needed enemies like Blackjack. His moral poise had been that precarious. Then, with his father's illness, he had begun to lose faith in the idea – which had inspired him – of social reform and with it his moral balance. His father, in principle, was right – lose faith and you fell. Then the unfair odds and accidents had invaded the centre of his personal life. Sybil's desertion, Abba's death, the memories of his mother's pitiful life which had revived with Alan Palmer's presence in Belize. A few serious blows like these and his shakily constructed personality had blown down like a trash hut in a hurricane.

To complete the mix of powerful, irrational forces, there had been added his ambivalent gratitude to Bill for saving his father's life. His one piece of good fortune in the past few months had come from a dope grower and Reuben felt gratitude to him with the force of a debt of honour. It wasn't 'society' – the same society which had condemned his mother – which had saved his father: it was someone 'outside society'. So, his 'respectable' personality demolished, his former fantasy of himself in ruins, he had fallen in with someone else's fantasy – Bill's – and come to the *milpa*. Here he was, its header, in the dark.

It was easy to see now, at the end of the steep curve which his life had described in only six months; but each stage of his decline had been imperceptible to him. If he had used his mind at the time to think, none of this might have happened; only now that it had happened did he think. Despair had blinded him. And gratitude. There was, though, a limit to both, as there was to a debt of honour, and if anything was beyond the limit it was murder.

He stubbed out his Colonial on the earth floor and reached a decision. He had already gone through the questions which a real header, like Peyrefitte, his predecessor on the *milpa*, might have asked about Alan Palmer. Had Palmer really come to the *milpa* by accident, or had he followed a trail? And if so, what trail was it? Did he know that it was Bill's *milpa*? Had he got involved with Amelia and if so had he come in pursuit of her? And, if it was pursuit, what sort of pursuit was it, vengeful or simply lovelorn? And if it was vengeful, would he too, Reuben, be included in the revenge? Did Palmer plan to report him, as Palmer's father had reported his mother? Was Palmer some sort of spy? The permutations seemed endless. But, Reuben had decided, he was not going to ask the questions, neither of

245

Palmer nor, any more, of himself. Because they were a header's questions and when he saw Bill he would resign as the *milpa*'s header. No. He had resigned as of now and when he saw Bill he would tell him why. Whatever happened, it would be in the lap of the gods – the leaf between the lips: submit. He would, without looking for an explanation from Palmer, explain himself to him and perhaps Palmer would understand, and leave things be and go his way.

No, that wasn't quite good enough. Already he felt better for his decision, but there was a way to feel better still. He got up – he was still in his work clothes – and tiptoed across the earth floor so as not to wake the two growers, Bartolo and José, asleep on its far side. He picked up Palmer's holdall, which he had taken from the Transit after parking it in a safer place. He opened the holdall on the ground, unzipped it part way and felt a twinge of shame for having searched it. He felt in his pocket for Palmer's car keys and popped them inside the holdall.

Coffee was half asleep, but at Reuben's approach he awoke and started to reach for the rifle before recognising his header. Reuben remembered what Pedro had said – if you carried a gun you had to be ready to use it.

He said, 'It's me, Coffee.' The young grower, well blasted, mumbled something, while Reuben glanced inside the *choza*'s open door and saw Palmer asleep on the camp bed. He went inside the *choza* and placed the holdall on the floor just by the door. He glanced again at Palmer. He was breathing evenly. He was alive.

Reuben went out of the hut and said to Coffee, 'Time to sleep now. Come, Coffee, and give me the gun.' Coffee didn't move, but gave Reuben a glazed, uncertain smile. 'The gun, Coffee,' Reuben said again, but Coffee asked:

'Now, you don't plan to kill him?'

'Christ, no! I plan to go to sleep and let him sleep, and let you sleep. I don't plan to kill anybody.'

Coffee got up from the upturned crate. He gave Reuben the rifle. They started back towards the other *choza*. Coffee asked, companionably, 'You think it's a crime, no? The *hierba*?'

Surprised, Reuben stopped.

'Coffee, sometimes I think it's evil.'

They walked on.

246

Coffee said, 'The *hierba* is good, good to smoke, good money.' He tapped the side of his head. 'Evil is in there.'

They went into the *choza*. Coffee lay down in his clothes, while Reuben undressed.

Tonight, he would not dream of the weed.


Alan was woken early by the sound of hammering. He wondered where he was, then realised. He got up from the camp bed and went to the door. No one was on guard.

Yesterday he had noticed two tall pimento stakes driven into the ground. This morning the growers were putting a rack of wooden poles between them. Coffee was one of them, and his was the hammering that he had heard. The rack, although Alan didn't know this, was for hanging the cut buds of weed to dry. Over it would be built a *cohane* roof to stop the direct heat of the sun, making a kind of *choza* without walls.

Coffee, nails between his teeth, turned from his hammering and briefly waved at him. Alan reflected how rare it was in Belize to see people, not only busily working but, as the growers were, working cheerfully. Like the bloody seven dwarves. He half expected them to burst into song.

Alan wondered whether he might not be better advised to tell Reuben the truth about Amelia and his visit to the *milpa*. It might be easier to convince Reuben he meant no trouble for anyone if he could show that he meant none for Amelia. Why not tell him the truth? As long as he didn't tell it to Bill...

Then he saw his holdall. It was partly unzipped. He undid it and looked inside. Someone – Reuben – had gone through his things. He took them out one by one – his socks, T-shirts, his Sony portable radio – and laid them on the earth floor. Then he found the keys to his Transit. What was going on? No one on guard, his keys returned. Did this mean...?

He heard footsteps outside the hut and then Reuben was in the doorway. He was carrying a pail – a pigtail bucket – of water. Reuben came into the hut and stooped to set the bucket on the floor.

'This is to wash your face and brush your teeth. And there's a canvas latrine round the far side of the *milpa*.'

247

Reuben's manner and tone of voice let Alan know that his misadventurous quest for Amelia had moved into another key. Since yesterday, the vocabulary of violence had apparently been purged from Reuben's body language. He entered the hut more like a supplicant than a jailer. The fierceness was gone from·his face. The change was so abrupt and extreme as to be almost more alarming than no change at all. Was this his psychotic, good-cop routine?

Alan said, 'Thanks. And thanks for my keys.'

Reuben nodded.

'How does your stomach feel?'

Alan wasn't going to give Reuben the satisfaction of knowing that it hurt.

'Okay,' he said, 'thanks.'

'Sorry about that,' said Reuben. 'I broke the Queensberry Rules. And you weren't to know...'

He let that hang.

Alan asked carefully, 'What wasn't I to know, Reuben?'

'Why I hit you.'

It hadn't occurred to Alan that there might have been a hidden motive. He asked, 'Why did you hit me?'

Reuben didn't answer at once. He asked in his turn:

'Are you planning to tell on us?'

Alan shook his head.

'No,' he answered truthfully. 'I wouldn't know what to tell, who to tell it to, or why to tell it. I went to school in England, Reuben, where the main thing you're taught is put it down to experience and don't tell anyone.'

'Even though I hit you?'

Alan shrugged and meant it. An honest shrug was a novel experience. Was this how it felt to be Amelia?

'It was a misunderstanding. Yesterday was full of them. I came with a warning for Rafael. If I'd been looking for trouble, or looking to make it, why would I have bothered to come?'

But, thought Reuben, why would you have come at all, unless... Calculation, however, corrupted the purity of the decision he had reached overnight. He coughed behind his hand and said, 'Before we go any further...' He stopped.

'Yes?'

248

'I want you to know that you're free.'

'Free?'

'Unconditionally free. To go, stay, whatever you want. But I would like you first to hear my side of the story.'

'Free,' Alan repeated. He smiled. 'It *is* Independence Day,' he said. 'But do you mean it, Reuben?'

'You have my word.'

Free. Alan considered this. Reuben was saying that he could drive back to Belize, completing a journey which had not been without its dangers. He would not, however, have completed his quest for Amelia. And that had been the journey's purpose. The dangers he had faced – Pudney on *The Mary May*, Reuben on the *milpa* – he would have faced for nothing. But were there new dangers in continuing and could Reuben be trusted not to be among them? If he were free, then he was free to stay too, but if he were to stay it would only be in order to see Amelia and Reuben would want to know why he was staying. If he were not to go now, he would have to speak to Reuben. Alan decided to risk it.

'Reuben,' he said, 'I repeat: I don't want to make trouble. What I want most is to get on a plane to England. But before I do there's something I have to settle. I have to see Amelia.'

'And that's why you came here,' said Reuben.

'Yes.'

'And the warning about the pirates: is it true?'

'I'll give you more proof of it. I was indirectly led here by them. I had a tip-off, you see, that I would find Amelia by following the pink car. That's how I found George Bourne, then this place and that's how I'm still hoping to find Amelia.'

'She's due this evening,' said Reuben.

'Here?'

'Here.'

'And Bill?'

'He should be in Belize City, winding up the house. Bill's been in the States and she met up with him in Mexico. It's cutting time. They'll soon be clearing out back to the States. So you know about them?'

'Amelia and Bill? I didn't at first, but I...' He hesitated, wondering whether to tell Reuben about Wyler Fuller's letter.

'Amelia told you?' Reuben supplied.

'No. I guessed.'

'She didn't give much away, did she?'

'No,' said Alan, but at the same time he thought: in the beginning she did give away a few grains of truth and now those grains are growing tall. Aloud he continued, 'But all the same, enough got given away for this place, and her and Bill's connection with it, not to be a completely kept secret. For example, my tip-off about the pink car . . .'

Offered a second chance, Reuben couldn't resist asking, 'Who gave you the tip-off?'

Alan thought of telling him, then remembered that Mike had wanted their conversation kept secret. How many more secrets would there be?

He hesitated and said, 'I was told in confidence. But the point is that someone knew . . .'

'Mike Sharp,' said Reuben.

Alan looked at him.

'Why do you say that?'

'Mike knows most of what's going on.'

'Oh? Was it Mike, then, who told you that Amelia was more than Bill's lodger? You remember, on the cay, when you hinted to me she was "spoken for"?'

'Ah, the cay!' Reuben's eyes were inward seeing. 'Hell,' he said, 'how I miss the sea! That was my last trip before I got caught up in this craziness . . .'

'Craziness? You call it craziness?'

'Oh yes,' said Reuben, 'this isn't my world. The first time I saw the *milpa*, with Bill, I couldn't believe it. He called it his "secret garden". And he needed a header for it. His had done a runner. And Bill had saved my father's life. So . . .'

'How do you mean,' Alan interrupted him, ' "saved your father's life"?'

Alan listened as Reuben told him about the radioiodine. 'So you see,' said Reuben, 'by St George's I'd already been drawn in. A few days before I'd driven Bill up here and that's when he told me they were married.'

'Married?'

Reuben looked at Alan.

'You didn't know they were married?'

'Of course not!' Alan burst out. Amelia's power to hurt extended even – most of all – to her absences. 'They were pretending to be landlord and lodger, for Christ's sake! *Involved*, yes, I guessed they were involved in some way. But married! I had no idea.'

'Their cover, Bill called it,' said Reuben. 'But with me, he broke it. With you, she certainly seems to have played her cards close.'

'Cards and cover,' said Alan, 'don't come much closer. Wouldn't you say?' As his tension over Amelia strengthened with this new revelation, so he relaxed towards Reuben. 'Cards,' he continued. 'And the card game looks like poker, but really it's Dirty Liz. It's Dirty Liz pretending to be poker.'

'Dirty Liz?'

'In the States they call it Hearts.' Alan explained the game, then said, 'The winner in Dirty Liz is the most pathological liar playing.'

Reuben said, 'From what Bill told me, I would guess that secrecy is the biggest thing between them. A sort of fantasy. Bill idealises her but he worries too, not just about her, but her and him. I would think that's why he asked me to keep an eye on her, I was trying to do that on the cay, but I guess my heart wasn't in it. I looked in at Regent Street several times, too, but she was never in. Then it was time for me to come up here and I thought she would come too, but she never did. All the time she must have been with you.'

'She was with me,' said Alan.

'It doesn't surprise me,' Reuben said. 'But it would be a big shock for Bill.'

'I would know,' said Alan, 'just how he felt.'

'Are you planning to tell him?'

Alan hesitated. He said, guardedly, 'A little truth would blow the house of cards down, wouldn't it? But what would you think, Reuben?'

'Me?' Reuben paused. 'My opinion doesn't matter. I've told you, you're free. But if you want my opinion, I think both of you have been deceived, you and Bill, the difference being that he doesn't know. And he's such a fantasist that he won't want to know. It may be hard to believe, looking at the *milpa* out there, but Bill's an innocent. He did save my father, too. And now he's sick. He went to the States for a check-up. But why not speak to Amelia first?'

'What time is she due here?' asked Alan.

'This evening. I don't know exactly.'

'What if I waited for her?'

'If you want.'

A doubt occurred to Alan.

'How do you know she's coming?'

'Easy. Someone picks up mail in Belize City. There's a telephone in Trinidad. That's been one of my jobs as the header here, keeping in touch.'

'I see ...' Alan paused. 'And who picks up the mail? Mike Sharp?'

Reuben smiled. 'Now then, that would be nice and neat, wouldn't it? Don't worry, she's coming.'

'I have your word?'

'You have my word. So long as she keeps hers.'

'Reuben, that's no word at all.'

Reuben laughed.

'She'll be here. I'll tell her in Trinidad. But before I go there, tell me, have I lost my touch or doesn't your stomach really hurt?'

'It hurts, Reuben.'

Reuben, for a moment, was downcast.

'I shouldn't have done that,' he said, then looked up. 'But let me tell you why I did it ...' And he told Alan about the roses, the whole story, the first time he'd told it all and the first that Alan had heard of it. Alan listened not just in silence, but speechlessly, as it grew upon him that this man of another race, this virtual stranger, was also virtually his brother, the bond between them a childhood which colonialism had distorted. In the nursery, Reuben's mother had been his maid, part of the alleged family, but all ruined for a few roses.

'I'll never live that down,' said Reuben. 'My mother at the asylum window ...'

'Live it down, Reuben,' Alan said, 'Live it down.'

'And you know what two of the obscenities were that she screamed? Our names.'

'Our names?'

'Yours and mine. Reuben and Alan. Our names.'

252

'Jesus Christ!' Alan passed a hand over his eyes.

They talked, then Reuben asked, 'Do you forgive me?'

'There's nothing to forgive.'

'No. I want you, please, to forgive me.'

'Very well, if you want it, I forgive you. And you? Can you forgive my family?'

'I forgive,' said Reuben.

'It's Independence Day.' Alan smiled. 'Today we've both begun to live something down.'

'The past is dead,' said Reuben, and held out his hand. 'Peace.'

'Peace,' Alan said as they shook hands.

The day was a water-clock which worked on sweat. Time was inside you, to be sweated out. Hours seeped by. Minutes were the units which measured the births of fools. One was born every minute and Alan was beginning to wonder whether he had not, his lifetime ago, accounted for one of those fool-units. His underpants clung damply to his crotch. He had prickly heat. He thought of getting back to whatever degree of 'civilisation' was represented by Belize City. Certainly the *milpa* was not 'civilised', but it *was* fascinating, as a snake is fascinating.

In the evening cool, time started to speed up with the imminence of Amelia's expected arrival. Soon, too, the growers should be back. All day they had been mysteriously away. Alan lay on the camp bed and switched on his Sony. He tuned in to the local station and opened one of the beers, well warmed now, which Bourne had given him. He drank it while listening to a Dutch-made programme, "This Wondrous World". It was followed by a long-winded announcement of a used refrigerator for sale, an Eskimo. Then the call-sign: '*Esta es Radio Belice, la voz de la nación naciente de Belice en Centroamérica ...*'

*Naciente* – being born. Nations have a lower birthrate than fools, but are not necessarily the less foolish. He looked at his watch. Six. Soon it would be time for the Independence ceremony in Belize City. A minor royal was on call. There would, perhaps, be bugles and drums to beat a tattoo. The Bloody Damned Fools would march. There would be stirring words from a dais, a salute of guns, the governor in his plumed

253

pith helmet. Spotlit, the Union Jack would be lowered for the last time. The abstract composition of crosses would be replaced by the new flag carrying, like the old colonial emblem, the likenesses of human beings – the one flag in the world to have people on it. Then the call-sign would be redundant. Belize would no longer be *naciente* – *being* born – but *born*.

The ceremony had been the intended highlight of his visit; he was going to miss it. But hadn't Reuben's story of roses been his own, private independence ceremony, a deeper insight into the centuries of colonialism about to end? His independence had been unveiled.

*Naciente!*

A few more fools were born. Then, the sound of her approach masked by the radio and his concentration on his thoughts. Amelia was standing in the doorway . . .

Amelia had the gift of aggrandising her surroundings. Sometimes she did it by zooming in on a detail like a politician kissing a baby, press-ganging it into some impression of sweetness and light which she wished to make, but more often her technique was to ignore. Her manner was one of powerful concentration on the object of her attention and powerful indifference to everything else. She could have cold-shouldered the North Pole. The effect was to seem to create her surroundings as she went along, like a good actress who can suggest with a minimum of means that a cheap touring set is ancient Rome. Even the doorway of a dope farm's *cohane choza*, if she was standing in it, and if you were obsessed with her and also soft in the head from twenty-four hours of solid sinsemille sniffing, could be transformed into something grander.

Alan got up from the camp bed to meet her. Today she wore blue. Madonna blue. Her espadrilles were blue and her simple cotton blouse, open at her throat around which she wore a delicate chain. It was gold, only a little darker than her skin. She had on her hip-hugging jeans which had once been dark blue too, but which had since been worn, washed and sun-faded to a sky colour. Alan drank her in and already the pious anger he had felt, faced with the reality of its object, had lost it

254

monopoly of him. She was smiling. Alan turned off the radio and at once she got the first word in; just as Alan knew she would have the last word.

'That suit is filthy!'

'Trust you, Amelia, to start on a sartorial note. Haven't we more important things to discuss?'

'Have we?' she asked lightly. 'It's going to be a little complicated. You've certainly complicated things by coming here. And,' she added reproachfully, 'I did tell you not to follow me.'

'But I did follow you, didn't I? And I found you.'

'Yes. Reuben told me how.' She pursed her lips, and for a moment seemed puzzled. 'But I don't understand.'

'You don't understand!' he burst out. 'I think I'm the one in need of a few explanations round here. Your "landlord", for example. Who is he? Apart from being your husband and a dope-grower.'

'It's not like it looks, Alan,' she said quietly.

'Oh no? What's that out there, then? A herb-garden?'

'It's not like it looks,' she said again.

'No? Well, I think that it didn't use to be how it looked, but now it's exactly like it looks.'

'No.' She shook her head. 'It wasn't then and it isn't now. Don't be angry, Alan. You got caught up in our cover, that's all, and if you hadn't broken it,' she continued, pursuing what was to Alan a warped logic, 'you'd never have known I was lying, would you? What I still don't get, though, is how you broke it.'

'I followed my nose,' said Alan. 'This place stinks to high heaven, and the smell of bad faith and broken promises leaves quite a trail.'

'I made you no promises.'

She spoke stiffly, dutifully, as though under oath. With difficulty he controlled himself and said, 'Amelia, you are a pathological liar. For example, you are *not* called Amelia. That's one of your lies and an even bigger one is the lie that you love me. Do you call this charade we've been through love? I don't even begin to know you, not even your...' He hesitated, then coldly decided to wait: he would leave her name until later. 'All along,' he went on, 'the reality hasn't been love, or me. It hasn't even been you. It's been your herb-garden; that. Why didn't you just

255

grow it and go home? Why did you drag me into this?'

'I took precautions,' she said, 'not to drag you in. And you're looking at things the wrong way round.' Her tone was one of sweet, patient reasonableness. 'Of course, I shouldn't have involved you, but I got involved with you. Because I couldn't help myself. Because I love you.'

He stared at her, for the moment lost for a comeback. Did she really believe what she said? Was it, even, true? Or only that he wanted it to be true? He remembered Bourne's riddle of the two Cretans: she was perhaps both in one, a much harder riddle to crack. He felt, suddenly, very tired.

'Please Amelia,' he said, 'Amelia or whoever you are, please spare me the last-reel stuff. When you love someone you break your cover for them.'

'But not until the last reel,' she said. 'And that's what this is. Love isn't always the same as truth, either. Sometimes it's telling the same lie under the same cover. And now we have the same lie to tell, don't we?'

'Ah!' He nodded, as if in control of a situation in which, in fact, his mind was spinning. 'You mean Bill, or whoever he is. You don't want him to know. You want us to keep *us* secret from him and that's who we'll be: the entity that keeps that secret. Amelia, this is pathological. It's crazy!'

'Look at it like this,' she said calmly. 'If you had known all along I was married to him, would you have told him about us? It's not his fault that I couldn't help being unfaithful to him. And anyway we're going soon, back to the States. It won't be long. And there's something you don't know, Alan. He's dying.'

'Dying?' Alan paused, momentarily bewildered by this new development – if it wasn't a trick: if Amelia didn't play with death as well as life . . .

'Dying,' she repeated. 'He has cancer, a year to live if he's lucky. He told me in Valladolid. And can't you see that if he knew about us it would destroy him? He mustn't know. And there's something else too, Alan, I wasn't going to tell you this but now I have to . . .'

But suddenly Alan could not stand it any more and stepped towards her. He took her shoulders, one in each of his hands, and gripped them hard; and it was as if, under his touch, she lost her command and ability to lie. Her shoulder muscles were

256

pliant, sacrificial in his hands; her arms fell helplessly to her sides; her eyes closed. Roughly, he shook her.

'Listen, Amelia,' he said. 'It's over, do you hear? The lies between us are over.'

She swayed slightly under the grip of his hands. She said, her eyes still closed, 'But this is the truth! I'm telling you the truth!'

He used his grip to shake her again.

'Tell me your birthday.'

She opened her eyes.

'My birthday?'

'Tell me. The truth.'

'Sagittarius,' she said. 'But why . . .?'

'*When?*'

'December.'

'What day?'

'The seventh, Alan. I was born on the seventh.'

He let go of her then and stood back, and it was as though, all the time he had known her, he had seen her through an enlarging glass and was only then, for the first time, seeing her at her real distance.

He said, 'You're telling the truth, Amelia. It was December the seventh. A baby girl came from her mother's womb and she had on a Vedal Cap. Her father was waiting for her. Now it is a little later and the baby's being held over a font of water. A priest is there. He is naming her Amanda Holiwell.'

'How do you . . .?'

Her eyes were wide and she had backed away as though from sorcery. He knew that he had spoken the trickster's name and broken her power.

He said, 'Her father was waiting and he watched her ripen under his eyes. Down the road was a big grain silo. It was Bement. It was Bible Belt. It was undo your daughter's dress.'

'Don't,' she said, and now, from staring at him, she covered her eyes. He hated himself but hurting her was too good and he couldn't stop.

'It was pluck the petals off your daughter one by one,' he said. 'Finger them to shreds, petal after petal, love, truth, honesty, friendship, fellowship and trust in life. Until none were left. Like a rose, a ruined rose. And you can't put petals back. It was ruin your daughter forever.'

'*It's my life!*'

She kept her voice down, but it was still a scream, as his steel cut home. Her eyes were hard now, cornered. 'My life,' she said again and, ashamed, he looked away and heard her say, 'You're not talking about a porn movie.'

Miserably, he nodded, still avoiding her eyes.

'No,' he said. 'It isn't a porn movie. It's your life.' His voice was flat, hard. 'Your life,' he agreed again. There were some moments of hurt silence between them, but already Alan knew that the habit of their relationship was reasserting itself and starting its healing work, and that whatever Amelia (as he could not help thinking of her) had done or was still doing he would, in the end, protect her.

She asked, 'How did you find out?' He looked at her.

'He always sent you roses on your birthday. You told me that. Well, he sent them one birthday too many and used his charge card. There was a journalist here called Wyler Fuller who became interested in Bill and he asked me to look into him. I didn't, but he did. I won't, but I suspect he will. This is a crime you're involved in, Amelia, and someone is on to you.'

Amelia had put her hand to her mouth.

'I remember those roses, but I didn't know he'd used his charge card. God, how stupid! Bill's so unworldly, it's stupid!'

'Detail, Amelia. That's what breaks hearts and necks. Detail.'

'And he's dying,' she said, 'and I'm ...' She paused, and seemed to be bracing herself. Alan noticed her tension.

'What?' he asked. 'What are you?'

'You're right about roses,' she said. 'You can't put the petals back. But you can grow a new one. A whole new rose ...' She left it hanging and Alan knew then that she held in reserve a truth to trump any of his.

'Your new rose. What do you mean?'

'I have to tell you, Alan, because Bill ...'

She stopped.

'Go on. Tell me.'

'You should be pleased. You always talk as if people were doomed, as if you were doomed. But under all that you love life. It's just that you don't live it very decisively. You may have been born in the wrong place and I was born to the wrong father, but everyone gets a second chance. We can be born more

258

than once, Alan. You asked me about my birthday, but a woman isn't only born. She gives birth too.'

(*¡Naciente!*)

Carefully he asked, 'Amelia, are you saying what I think you're saying?'

'On the cay ... you remember I wanted to throw my birth pills in the sea?' He stared at her. 'Well, I'd already thrown them.'

'You're pregnant, Amelia?'

She didn't reply at once, but watched for his reaction.

He put a hand to his forehead and said, 'Jesus Christ, Amelia!' and she knew that her calculation of his responses was correct, and that among them was the profound pleasure she had counted upon.

She said, 'I haven't had my period. And Dr Abb, the doctor in town, says so. And I know so and that it's yours, from that very first time between us on the cay. But Bill thinks it's his.'

'And it isn't his? It really isn't?'

'The last time with him I was still on the pill. But he wants to believe and because he's dying he wants to believe all the more. I would tell him the truth, but how can I tell him now? And it was my decision, Alan, and mine alone, and I take all the responsibility for it. You don't have to worry.'

'Responsibility, Amelia? You? You never took a responsibility in your life.'

'And you, Alan, take so much doomy responsibility in advance that you never take a decision. That's where we're different. I take the decision first and then take the responsibility for what I've decided. You take all the responsibility but for what?'

'You should have asked me,' said Alan.

'You'd have said no,' Amelia replied at once.

Alan considered this, then conceded, 'Yes, I would have said no. And shouldn't that concern you?'

'Your permission,' said Amelia, 'was making love to me. That showed what you wanted. You'd never have made the choice. But it didn't matter, because I had chosen you.'

'Oh Amelia,' he said, 'pirate, hijacker, born criminal...'

'If women waited for the permission of their men before having children, the world would be a very empty place.' Amelia looked at him. Her eyes were challenging him. She said, 'I

259

couldn't wait for you, Alan. Life flies by while you wonder how to live it by the rules. But I chose you, I joined you in and you don't need to do a thing. Yes, I'm a pirate. I stole your love for me before you could kill it and kill mine, and now your love is inside me, growing, a whole new rose. And everyone's happy. I have the reality, you have the truth you say you live so much and Bill has the illusion. Kill his illusion if you want, but take the responsibility for killing his spirit before he dies. And if you do that, Alan, he may want to kill me and that'll be another responsibility for you. Do nothing and you're free.'

'But Alan, they can't be pirates!'

'Why not?'

'One of them's run away with the Consul's wife. She's on their boat with them.'

'The Consul's wife?'

'Yes, the US Consul's wife. The last people dopers or dope pirates would go anywhere near is the US Consul and you don't go much nearer than the Consul's wife, and you aren't telling me that the US Consul is a dope pirate!'

'Then that means...'

They were lying across the camp-bed mattress, which Alan had heaved from the bed onto the earth floor. They were becalmed after making love. Amelia had just asked Alan whether it was really the pink car which had led him to the *milpa* and had accepted his explanation that it was. She had not, she said, believed it when Reuben had told her in Trinidad. Now she did and in her mind too, as in Alan's, the same suspicion was beginning to form. Alan saw her eyes widen, fearfully, as she looked at him.

'Christ,' she said. 'What *does* it mean?'

'Exactly.' Then Alan told her how he had seen the three Americans in Raul's Rose Garden, on his visit there with Mike Sharp, and how Blackjack, who was with them now, had wanted to speak to Mike about 'Belize breeze'. He told her about his misunderstanding with Pudney and Pudney's question, 'How much do you know?' and Pudney's assumption that he had come on behalf of a husband; how he had exploited the mis-

260

understanding in his meeting with Pym in the pink car and the fat man's remark, 'He's blown the whole thing.'

He said, 'It isn't just that one of them is involved with the Consul's wife, Amelia. In some way they're *all* involved with *the Consul*. And that suggests...' He stopped. What did it suggest? It wasn't just his uncertainty that stopped him, however, but his observation that Amelia was becoming increasingly agitated. She sat up on the mattress.

'But they can't be narks...', she said, and told Alan about the independence concession given to Belize by the United States following the death of Manuel Zuniga. 'That was a reason we came here,' she said. 'Because the US wasn't going to interfere. If there are narks here the US is breaking its word and...' Now it was her turn to stop. Alan waited, in the half dark of the *choza*, letting her calculate for herself her nation's likely perfidy in the matter of its independence concession. Independence. He looked at his watch. The ceremony would be starting about now.

He said, thoughtfully, 'But Amelia, isn't that just the sort of thing they *would* do if denied open interference? Plant a few undercover agents? And wouldn't a perfect cover for them be as dope pirates? Come on, Amelia, you're the expert on cover.'

'But they're supposed,' she said, ignoring the dig, 'to be spear fishermen.'

'That could be cover for them being dope pirates and that in its turn could be cover. Double cover.'

'Jesus!' she said, and now Alan detected real alarm in her voice and sensed that she was struggling to restore what, for her, was normality; and sure enough she said, 'I don't know. There's no proof that they're DEA. This could all be in the imagination.'

'I didn't come here in imagination, Amelia, I came here by following them. And they're really interested in Zuniga's Hardware and the Consul's wife is really on their boat. This isn't imaginary. It's real.'

'And...' She hesitated.

Instinctively Alan said, 'And something else is worrying you.'

She looked at him. 'What makes you think that?'

'Come on, Amelia, please. Admit it. Mike Sharp is worrying you.'

261

'Reuben told me you had guessed about him,' she said, 'and he'd guessed that Mike Sharp tipped you off. Yes, Mike Sharp is worrying me.'

'What if he used me as a cut-out to find out about the people in the pink car? Or what if they found out about you through him, accidentally, and he was feeling guilty? Or he might be working for them as well, playing both ends against the middle. It might have been his way of tipping *you* off.'

'That's what I've been wondering,' said Amelia. Now she looked still more troubled.

'Certainly,' said Alan, 'he was doing *me* no favours.' Then he remembered something and said, musingly, 'Or perhaps it was a favour of some sort. Pudney didn't register anything in particular when I mentioned Mike Sharp to him.'

'I don't like it,' said Amelia. 'I don't know what it all adds up to, but I don't like it.'

'And Bill?' Alan asked. 'What would he think?'

'He wouldn't like it either,' said Amelia. 'But I'm not going to tell him. How would I explain why you went to this man . . . Pudney's boat?'

'You just have to mention the Consul's wife,' Alan objected. 'He'll see the connection.' But she shook her head, firmly.

'No. There's no need. You don't understand. Bill saw the *milpa* as some sort of image of something. Then he got uneasy about it, then he got ill and now there's the baby. When he hears about dope pirates and the journalist, it'll put him off the *milpa* even more. If he thinks they're narks, the mood he's in, he might try to talk to them, but in two days we can be away from here. I'm the only person Bill needs to tilt the balance and get him out of this and now, with the baby, I'm minded to do just that: do the cold chain and split.'

'The cold chain? Amelia, I don't understand . . .'

'Peurifoy. Remember? In two days it's full moon – flying night. We're flying in the cold chain.'

Alan could hardly keep up with her.

'Are you telling me . . .?' he began, but she overrode him.

'There's a guy called the Zig-Zag man. He's in the MAF, right? That's the Marijuana Air Force. When he brings the cold chain in, we can take his plane out if we want and leave the dope uncut. There'll be no crime to answer, Alan. It's like I told you: the *milpa* isn't necessarily what it seems. We're rich enough to do what we want with it. Do nothing.'

'Are you seriously telling me that stuff out there isn't going to the States?'

'Bill doesn't want it to,' she said, 'and neither, now, do I. The *milpa*'s a little like you, Alan: a little too slow. Life's overtaken it...'

It was early on the evening of the following day, and Bill and Rafael were walking the perimeter of the *milpa*. Rafael was showing 'Mister Bill' round and doing most of the talking, excitedly pointing out this or that plant, the especially tall and strong ones, the few stunted disappointments. But Bill's mind was on other things.

He stopped and asked, 'Where's Reuben?'

'In Trinidad. He said to say he was coming up.'

'And Pedro?'

'Resting,' said Rafael. 'Two days, three, we start cutting. He'll be here night and day.'

'Ah yes, cutting...'

'Then we watch out for pirates,' said Rafael.

'Yes,' Bill answered abstractedly. Amanda had told him about the pirates. But, he was thinking, if there is no cutting the pirates will lose interest. The point of piracy was that you let others do the work for you. If this *milpa* were allowed to go to seed they would find another one to plunder. The pirates were just the excuse he needed, a last straw like the news that Wyler Fuller was on to them. He was grateful to Alan Palmer for bringing his own irresolution to a head – he would go and thank him, when Rafael finished his guided tour.

They walked on, Rafael proudly airing the dope know-how he had picked up from Pedro. It reminded Bill of a visit he'd made to a Texan cattle ranch. Then, too, his meat-packing plant manager had spoken like Rafael of pounds weight, stock, strong and stunted steers – ultimately, money to be made. But the *milpa* had started out in his mind as a symbol of renewal. The money had always been incidental, except that it took a rich man to buy symbolism on this scale – and, if he abandoned it, lose it

263

on this scale. He had started it to realise himself, not assets, and that – the real investment – had been amply repaid. The real book of the *milpa* was spiritual and it already balanced. He did not want his incoherent rebellion against business to turn into a business.

'. . . and this one,' Rafael was saying. 'Look at her! A week ago she was small, then we put the Miracle around her and look . . .'

'That quickly!'

'That quickly. They do their living in a hurry. And Pedro says . . .'

What had fascinated him had been the image of the living plant, the seed and seedling, the life and growth – not the dead, saleable bud. First his conscience had begun to rebel, then reality, in the shape of the Big C in himself, then the child – the little c – his child, in Amanda. He hoped it would be a son; he knew it would be.

Of course – it struck him only now – her call to him about the cold chain had been a clue to her broodiness. Children had been on her mind, but she'd kept it to herself until Valladolid, as though, guessing his bad news, she had come armed against it with good. A surprise, timed to shock him back into a sense of life's sweet symmetry. It wasn't only the Big C that had metastases or multiplied cells; a child was a healthy secondary, a live coal carried from dying fire. And with the child, Amanda too had come to her senses and thought like him of abandoning the *milpa*.

'And this one,' Rafael was saying. He had reached above his head and was pulling down for their inspection a bud of spectacular size. 'A pound she weighs maybe, or more . . .'

Looking at it, Bill could think only of something the specialist had told him – that marijuana was the best antidote to the nausea of radiotherapy. He could expect to end his days on a cloud of dope smoke: medicine for the journey. Perhaps he should take from the *milpa* his own supply for the States, a medicinal amount only: that had a certain symmetry, too.

So did the cold chain. It would not pay for itself, as he had at first intended that the *milpa*, his parody of business, should do. It would be a gift. Symmetrically, he would celebrate the life of his child by saving the lives of children.

Suddenly he was sure that he wanted the *milpa* to end uncut. He didn't want it to turn into a mini industrial complex, the buds manicured and sun-dried, pressed in trash compacters and packed in pigtail buckets. He wanted it to run to seed. The Zig-Zag man was coming and it was time to go home.

The cutting which interested him now was the cut-and-run kind.

'And over here, Mister Bill,' Rafael was saying, and starting to move on. But Bill laid a restraining hand on his forearm.

'It's okay, Rafael, I've seen enough for now.'

'You're sure?'

Bill read the disappointment on the young man's face and said, 'Forgive me. I'm a little tired. Perhaps if I go and see the Englishman now?'

'You're the boss, Mister Bill. I come with you?'

'No. I'll go alone.' He started towards the huts, leaving Rafael where he was, staring after him. Then he remembered something, and turned. 'Oh, Rafael, perhaps you'd do something for me.'

'Say the word.'

'Get Pedro up here, would you?'

'Tonight?'

'Now. I need him right now.'

Rafael's face showed alarm.

'Something the matter, Mister Bill?'

'Nothing. Tell him I've got the money and I want to pay him.'

'Now?'

'Now.'

Amanda was sitting with Alan Palmer at a trestle table outside the growers' *choza*. They were laughing together at something and if they had held the tableau a second longer Bill might have wondered at the easy complicity of their laughter; but Alan saw him and, with a brief wave in Bill's direction, made three company. Bill, before, had not taken to Palmer, but Amanda had won him round with her account of how friendly and supportive of her he had been during his absence, how compassionate at Pascó among the children; and if he was, as Amanda had told him, 'a little sweet on her', well that was easy enough to understand and, now she was with child by him, to

265

forgive. And Palmer had brought warnings of the pirates and Wyler Fuller.

So it was quite warmly that Bill held out his hand. The Englishman stood to take it, uncertainly, displaying the embarrassment of his race. As for himself, Bill felt beyond embarrassment. He took the Englishman's hand and said strongly, 'Alan, thank you for all you've done.'

'It's nothing.'

Alan shifted his stance slightly and looked at the ground. Bill said, 'It's a hell of a lot!' and hearing his robust tone of voice Alan had to remind himself that this man was supposed to be dying. But looking into his face, there sure enough under the tan was a yellowish tinge, like old white paint or paper, and seeing it Alan thought, There's no doubt about it. He's dying. I can't do it to him.

'So,' he said, 'you're pulling out...'

'Yes.' Bill turned and gave the *milpa* a look at once ruthless and wistful – the look one reserves for one's failures. He turned again and said, 'What a waste and what a fool you must think me. But I miscalculated, Alan. A failure of moral imagination. And then when I looked into myself I saw – I've told my wife this – none of your "enriched unconscious". I saw *absolutely nothing!*'

Alan said, 'I know you didn't like it when we spoke about the Box Man.'

'Perhaps I was envious. All I saw in myself was a needle spinning, a needle boxing the compass. But you saw the image of the Box Man.'

'I don't understand.'

'It's another story,' said Bill. 'Let's just say I was a bloody fool, a little bit out of my box. Never mind, I've learned. A little late in the day, but I've learned. Because I got ill, you see, and my wife became pregnant.'

'She told me,' said Alan. 'Congratulations. I mean...'

'And then I knew,' Bill said. 'Life supplied the answer, life and...' He was about to say 'and the fear of death'. But instead he chose, 'And of course you helped, with your news of the pirates and this journalist...?'

He glanced at Amanda. She said, 'Wyler Fuller,' and then, 'But see what else Alan's done. Show it to him, Alan.'

266

Alan handed Bill a white, unsealed envelope addressed, Bill saw, to Wyler Fuller.

Bill said, 'Is this the insurance policy I think it is?' (Insurance for her, he was thinking; I won't be needing any.)

Amanda said, 'That's it.'

Bill took out the letter, and read:

Dear Mr Fuller

Please excuse my failure to get in touch with you but, quite simply, I soon discovered that there was nothing to get in touch about. I got to know Bill Brandl a bit and, on the pretext of wanting to do some sightseeing, travelled with him to the north of the country to look at an irrigation project. He told me he was a philanthropic adviser and himself a small-time philanthropist who was thinking of putting money into the project. He has some sort of foundation in New York. The daughter by his dissolved marriage whom he mentioned to me on that trip is doubtless your 'Amanda Holiwell', since she too lives in Illinois. (He said I might like to meet her and I think he was sizing me up as a second husband for her!)

You told me you could not believe in Bill Brandl. Well, neither can I. He is *unbelievable*. (Or was, until he returned to the States.) Do you have many such people in the States? To me, coming from cynical old Europe, such a wide-eyed, blue-eyed, naive and sentimental idealist is almost incredible, and one of the things about him which I found most unreal was his hand-pumping, gee-whizzing genuineness.

So much for my budding career in journalism. May yours continue in full flower.

With best wishes
Alan Palmer.

'Thank you again, Alan,' said Bill, although he wasn't at all sure that he liked the references to naivety and sentimentality. He put the letter back. 'The stuff about irrigation is just right. I'll see it gets posted. Hey! Reuben!'

Reuben had appeared at a corner of the *milpa*. Bill put the letter on the table and went to meet him. 'Reuben,' he called, 'how've you been keeping?' Alan and Amanda exchanged glances behind Bill's back, and Alan mouthed the question, 'Does he know?' She nodded. In Trinidad she had primed Reuben with the necessary news – that Bill was ill, dying, and that she 'and Bill' were expecting a child. Not knowing Reuben's unease about the *milpa*, she had made no mention of Bill's. As Reuben came to the table, however, Bill's arm about his shoulders, his unease was apparent. Amanda was alarmed. Was Reuben about to spill the truth?

She greeted him, before he turned to Bill and said, 'There's something I have to tell you.' If Bill had been looking at Amanda at that moment he would have seen her stiffen.

'Go on Reuben' said Bill.

'Well...' And he hesitated.

Amanda said, 'Can it wait, Reuben?'

Quickly, Reuben looked at her and then at Bill again. 'The thing is, Bill, I've been here two months now. I feel I've done enough.'

'And you want to pull out...'

'I want to pull out.'

Alan saw Amanda's relief.

'Reuben,' said Bill. 'We seem to have come separately to the same conclusion. I'm pulling out, too. We're going to abort the *milpa*.'

'You're serious?'

'I'm expecting Pedro this evening and I'll pay him his money. Tomorrow we go back to the States.'

Reuben was looking from one to the other of them.

'I don't get it.'

Bill said, 'A sudden change of plan, that's all. Tomorrow night is full moon. Originally I commissioned our pilot to come next full-moon night, when the dope would be cut and ready to go. Then I said to come tomorrow night, too. The cold chain couldn't wait another month. And tomorrow I'll cancel the second flight.'

'The cold chain?'

'You weren't at Pascó, Reuben, so let me tell you about the cold chain...'

*

From the clearing, Pedro and Rafael watched the Americanos go. The Englishman was driving the Transit; Reuben, on his trail bike, was their outrider. The Transit lurched and bumped across the clearing, following Reuben; then they were on the track towards the road which led to Milepost 60, in dense bush, nothing of them visible but the occasional glimpse of lights. The clearing was drained of colour by the full moon. By contrast, the surrounding bush looked darker and more impenetrable than on ordinary nights.

Rafael turned to Pedro.

'Do *you* understand, Pedro?'

'The Americans are crazy,' said Pedro. 'But if they pay for their craziness we can't complain.'

'He really paid you everything?'

'Everything.'

'For nothing?'

'We worked hard.'

'But the *hierba*. He said to let it go to seed?'

'Yes.'

Rafael shook his head in disbelief.

'The dope business is *loco*.' he said.

'Your father thought so.'

Pedro turned on his heel and started towards his pick-up. He called Rafael to join him.

'Don't I stay tonight?'

Pedro stopped and turned to him.

'We have our money,' he said.

'But all our work. We let it go to seed?'

It was the waste which Rafael found absurd and hard to endure. Pedro felt so too but, philosophically, shrugged in answer to the younger man's question and said, 'Maybe. Maybe not. I think about it.'

'Crazy,' Rafael said again. He joined Pedro and they started walking together, then Rafael stopped again and looked at the moon. '*Lunático!*' he said.

'You think *this* is *loco*,' said Pedro. 'Well, in the Sixties...'

Just before midnight they reached the agreed stretch of the Orange Walk Highway. It was recently built, straight and

269

smooth, a real road, the best in the country. It was good enough for light aircraft to land and in the back of the Transit, along with the luggage and Reuben's rifle, were forty car breakdown lamps. It took about fifteen minutes to place the lamps equidistantly along either side of the road, ready, when the time came, to be switched on to make a flare-path. Then the highway would become an improvised runway. The Zig-Zag man was expected at one.

'Why's he called that?' asked Alan.

'After the rolling papers,' said Bill. 'He's a real marijuana nut, a NORML activist and everything, none of my crises of faith. But tonight he's on a mercy mission.'

'And he's going to land *here*?'

'Sure,' said Bill. 'He's landed on worse surfaces. He'll be landing on a worse one in the States.'

'I don't mean the surface. I mean that this is a public highway.'

'Only,' said Bill, 'there isn't any public. And who's going to be here this time of night? Probably more planes than cars use this stretch of road.'

'Really?'

'It's a dope airstrip, practically. And we're not doing dope. We've nothing to be afraid of.'

Alan fumbled in his pocket to find his cigarettes. He and Bill were in the Transit, which was parked, like Reuben's motorbike, near a few low trees on the savannah off the highway. Outside, Amanda was talking to Reuben. In the moonlight, their voices were crisp and carried easily.

Alan heard Reuben say, 'I can't wait to get back to the sea.'

He shook a cigarette from the pack. In less than an hour from now, Amanda was due to go and, because of the need to keep Bill fooled, they could not spend these last minutes together. Instinctively, since Bill's arrival, to keep up the deception and to insulate themselves against the coming goodbye, they had maintained a distance between them. As the minutes ticked by, so the tension mounted. There was tension too between him and Bill – at least, Alan felt it. He lit his cigarette.

There was an awkward silence, until Bill asked, 'Are you happy with the money for the Transit?'

'The hire? More than happy,' said Alan. 'I told you, you gave me too much.'

'Forget it,' said Bill.

They were silent again. Outside, Amanda laughed at some remark of Reuben's: not a forced laugh – she sounded perfectly happy. To take his mind off her, Alan asked Bill, 'How does it feel?'

'To be leaving?'

'Yes.'

Bill's face said that that question had no easy reply.

'A mixture of things,' he said, 'among them relief and hope. In the States, you see, I got lost in a sort of . . . inner jungle. It's strange that I had to come here, to real jungle, to find my way out of it.' He was warming to his subject. 'It's like . . . when there's too much civilisation you make a wilderness in your own mind and then, to reaffirm the civilised values, you have to go back to the wilderness those values originated from. This was my wilderness. I'm relieved I found my way. I'm leaving like a criminal, but I've done nothing wrong.'

Alan said, 'And hope?'

'Hope? Oh, that I'll live to see my child.'

'But of course . . .' Alan started to say. Bill interrupted.

'I haven't long. Amanda must have told you . . .'

'Amanda,' said Alan, and in the tension and embarrassment of the moment couldn't stop himself going on. 'I can't think of her as anyone but Amelia.' He bit his lower lip, realising that his remark carried a certain payload of emotion. But he didn't know about her last line of defence.

Bill looked at him – a sympathetic look – and said, 'You're a little sweet on her, aren't you?'

He recognised her signature at once, but asked, 'Sweet on her? What makes you think that?'

Bill laughed quietly, understandingly – but he didn't understand.

'Well, you weren't to know we were married,' he said. 'And the child was a surprise to me, too. Women are full of secrets.'

'They certainly are,' said Alan. He drew on his cigarette.

Bill looked at his watch.

'Half past,' he said. 'Peurifoy should be here by now.' He called through his window, 'Where's Peurifoy?'

'He'll be here,' she called back.

Alan opened the door on his side.

271

'Excuse me,' he said, 'I know I'm smoking but I could do with some air.'

Bill said, 'Me too.'

Alan got out, slammed his door and walked towards her: Amanda, the woman who lied, Amelia, the fiction who told the truth.

Then he stopped. He thought he was hearing things. The highway, under the moon, was a ribbon of silver light and, to match it, he thought he had just heard a silver sound, chimes, like musical bars struck with a delicate hammer. *Ding-di-ding-di . . .*

He listened, then, hearing nothing more, called to Amanda, 'Did you hear that?'

She turned from Reuben.

'What?'

'Did you hear it, Bill?' asked Alan.

'I heard nothing.'

'Listen,' said Alan, 'all stay still and listen.'

A few moments then, distantly again, *ding-di-ding-di . . .*

They all looked at one another, wonderingly.

Amanda said, 'What's *that*?'

'It sounds like a tune,' Reuben said.

'It is a tune,' said Alan.

Bill said, 'Out here?'

'Peurifoy,' said Amanda. 'Could it be Peurifoy?'

'Ssh!' Alan instructed them. The sort of sound it was, its tune, reminded him of something, but he couldn't remember what. There was a problem of context. They were on a savannah, but he wanted to think of a leafy English suburb, fairgrounds, seaside resorts. They all listened. Then, nearer now:

Ding-di-ding-di-ding-di-ding
Di-ding-di-ding-di-ding-di-ding

Alan said, 'I know it!'

'What?' said Amanda, 'What is it?' They all looked at him.

He sang, quietly, 'Boys and girls come out to play, The moon doth shine as bright as day.' They were staring at him, uncomprehendingly. He said, 'It's an ice-cream van.'

Amanda put her hands together and said, 'Peurifoy! Oh, this

272

is wild!' Her eyes were shining.

'Ice-cream?' Bill asked, and turned to Amanda. 'I don't get it.'

The cold chain,' she said. 'Peurifoy told me he knew of this old ice-cream van for sale in Puerto Barrios. He must have bought it and ferried it over for the cold chain.' Alan heard the excitement in her voice and thought, it's a sensation for her, just as I, once, was a sensation.

He said, 'A full moon and a loony tune.' Amanda rounded on him.

'No. It makes perfect sense. Don't you see? He's used his wits. They can get ice-cream to the bush. Why not vaccine? He's *done something*.' Alan said nothing and for a moment her implicit accusation of him burned the air. Then she said, in a tone suggesting that her fun had been spoiled, 'I'll switch on some light so he can see us.' She went to the Transit and turned its lights on, then rejoined them, facing east. A minute or so, then the ice-cream van came distantly into view, perhaps a thousand yards away down the Orange Walk Highway.

Peurifoy was driving by the moon, whose light, against the night's warmth, suggested cold. On the front of the ice-cream van was a tannoy and from it came a tune designed to tempt the mind to thoughts of coldness and refreshment:

Boys and girls come out to play...

The van was white, like an ambulance, but from its serving hatches on either side came trickles of coloured light, like sundaes or fruit flavourings:

The moon doth shine as bright as day.

Bill thought of the dream he had had on the *milpa*, when he had felt 'the ice' – the fairground and pleasing, meaningless music.

'God,' he said aloud, staring down the highway: then something which would stick in Alan's mind – 'It's so innocent!'

Otherwise, no one spoke. The van drew nearer, then turned off the highway on to the savannah towards them. Now they could see Peurifoy by the dim glow of its dash. He waved to them, matter-of-factly, and they, like entranced children, waved

273

back. The nearer the van came, the less of an apparition it seemed – the less *impossible*. It was painted with cartoon characters and stylised motifs – cones, flakes, ripples, whirls and whorls and lollies on sticks. Then it was beside them, and Peurifoy had switched off the power and was dismounting. Amanda applauded him, clapping her hands, and called to him.

'Jay! That's brilliant! You're *brilliant!*'

'What do you think of her?' he asked, half turning towards the van. He was grinning. Amanda hugged him and kissed both his cheeks, while he, his arms loosely around her, recognised Alan and nodded to him.

Amanda stepped away and said, 'I think it's wonderful, Jay.' Peurifoy was quite calm, a technician doing a job. He stepped towards Bill.

'And you, sir, must be William Brandl.' He held out his hand. 'Well, I want to thank you for the wonderful thing you're doing tonight.'

Bill said, 'All because of you.' It was like a performance – everyone was brilliant and wonderful. Bill took Peurifoy's outstretched hand in both of his, then introduced him to Reuben, who asked, 'You drove from the south in that?'

'From Belize City,' said Peurifoy. 'And the day before from Punta Gorda. She goes well. And' – he turned to Amanda – 'I adapted her freezers for the cold chain. All for a thousand quetzals. She's pretty beat up, but on the BM that's only four hundred bucks.'

Alan stood slightly back from the rest of them, as they crowded round the ice-cream van, marvelling at its being in this place, listening to Peurifoy as he explained how it would be his mobile cold chain depot in the south.

Then Bill looked at his watch and said, 'It's time for the lights'. He hugged Amanda. 'Almost time to go home, honey.'

They split up into two parties and went to different ends of the runway. Amanda and Peurifoy making up one party, Alan and Reuben the other. Bill remained behind at the Transit and, from there, watched as the teams in turn split up, one to each side of the highway, then walked towards one another, switching the breakdown lamps to red flash as they went. The lamps were at forty-yard intervals and soon the stretch of highway started to become, as it was popularly known, 'the Orange Walk

Runway', the lights flashing out of synch, bathing the road in intermittent red. Now the moon no longer shone 'as bright as day' and much of the starlight was blotted out too. Bill imagined the road as the scene of some dreadful accident, the red lights flashing, ambulances and fire-engines: the hi-tech, hi-speed north. It was five minutes to one. Bill climbed into the Transit and drove to the far, western end of the improvised runway.

He was joined there by Amanda and Alan, and soon by Peurifoy in the van and Reuben on his trail bike. They would be going separate ways and this was the parting of them. Bill and Amanda unloaded their luggage, and Reuben his rifle, which he strapped to the back of his bike along with his own bundle of things. His plan was to sell it in Belize City, where he would be bound. Alan would drive the Transit south to help Peurifoy. Bill and Amanda would take the plane. It seemed hardly possible, a plane from the north touching down in this remote place, and Peurifoy was first to voice the improbability:

'The cold chain's coming *here*?'

'You bet it is,' said Bill. 'The Zig-Zag man won't let us down.'

'The Zig-Zag man?'

Bill explained the reference, as he had done earlier to Alan, who then said, ' "From northern sky big silver bird brings new zac stranger." That's from a poem by the Premier.'

'The Premier writes poems?' asked Amanda.

'He does and "zac" is Maya for a white man. Well, the latest zac stranger is the Zig-Zag man.'

'And what's his big silver bird?' Peurifoy asked Bill.

'It's silver, but it isn't big. A Lockheed Lodestar with the seats ripped out.'

'A Lodestar! But a Lodestar's ancient! And he pilots it all by himself?'

It was ten-past one. Peurifoy discussed the Lodestar with Bill, who knew the plane from the war. Alan was struck once more by the keenness of Peurifoy whenever he talked technology. He seemed to have an almost boyish love of it and Alan wondered whether it was not that, rather than love of his fellow men, which lay behind his enthusiasm for the cold chain. The American's name had a romance ring. Perhaps the cold chain was the gleaming sword with which he intended to zap the primitive south. The conversation about the Lodestar usefully filled in and numbed the time before goodbye.

Then they heard the plane.

Amanda was first to hear it, then see it – a silver speck under the moon: a Lodestar. She had called the arrival of Peurifoy's ice-cream van wild – this was wilder still. They stared up at the sky, watching as the plane wheeled in a wide arc towards them; then, the pilot evidently catching sight of the flare path, it tilted sharply and started to lose height. It flew almost directly above them, at a few hundred feet, and Amanda, caught up in the occasion, waved to its silver underbelly. Discreetly, she took Alan's hand and squeezed it. The plane made a wide circle, then, from the east, approached low over the runway, as the Zig-Zag man got the feel of where he was about to land. It roared above them, with deafening engine noise. Another circle, then, lower this time, it made the same approach, flaps up, lower, to make a perfect three-point touchdown perhaps a hundred yards from the runway's eastern end. They all cheered to see the plane safe, hurtling towards them, slowing, braking, taxiing at leisure to their end of the runway. They saw the Zig-Zag man in the cockpit. He grinned and waved and gave a thumbs-up sign before, slowly, turning the Lodestar round so that its nose was pointing east ready for take-off. The wind from the propellers was flattening the grass to the ground and their hair to their heads. Then the engine was cut. The propellers were still feathering when Bill went to the cockpit window and, reaching up, welcomed the Zig-Zag man with a handshake.

Alan heard, 'There won't be a second flight, Zig-Zag...'

Bill turned then and called, 'Okay everyone. Let's make it quick.' Peurifoy drove the van up alongside the Lodestar, where Reuben and Alan waited by the passenger door. There was a heavy tread of footsteps from inside the plane, then a *clunk* as the door was unlocked, then opened. The Zig-Zag man was pale and fair-haired and in his mid-twenties, and, from the erratic gleam in his eyes and his taut, nervous smile, his zigs and zags looked to be those of crazy paving.

Dispensing with the preliminaries he said, 'Okay. Let's move,' and at once started to drag a cardboard box to the door. It was lightweight, but large, and Alan and Reuben between them had to manoeuvre it out of the door and to the ground.

Peurifoy said, 'These are the syringes. Let's do the cold stuff

276

first.' By then the Zig-Zag man was already pushing the first of several isothermic cases – 'cold dogs' Peurifoy called them – to the door. Meanwhile, Bill and Amanda were bringing their luggage from the Transit.

Piece by piece the cold chain was transferred to the van. As each cold dog was loaded, Peurifoy opened it and looked at the monitor card inside, to check that the indicator window hadn't turned blue and that so far the chain was unbroken. The cold inside the cases, as it met the night air, formed a light mist at the serving hatches, as if Peurifoy were cooking something in his ice-cream van. Soon everything was off the plane, and Bill and Amanda started to load their luggage.

They had thrown the first few cases aboard when the Zig-Zag man stumped back down the plane from his cockpit and said, 'There's a fuckin' car on the runway!'

Everyone stopped.

'It's parked there, goddamn staring at me!'

Reuben was first to speak. He said, blankly, 'A car?'

'Yeah. Do I have to spell it out? CAR. And it's in my way.'

But already Alan for one had guessed that the Zig-Zag man had omitted to mention the most salient feature of the car, a feature which like the others, he was able to check by stepping back from the Lodestar's fuselage and looking under its wing along the road. Sure enough, it was the 'shrimp colour shark car' of Mr Fruit's description. It had crept up to within a couple of hundred yards of them and blocked the Lodestar's take-off path. They stared at it, each hoping that the car's intent was friendly, each knowing or guessing that it wasn't. As yet, its headlamps were off; then, rhetorically, they were turned on, pinning them in a blaze of light. 'Guns' was now the thought at the back of each of their minds and, vulnerable though they felt in the light, they did not dare step from it.

'Jesus,' whispered the Zig-Zag man. 'This is more than a piece of traffic.'

'The pirates,' said Reuben. The Zig-Zag man looked at him.

Peurifoy said, 'You mean they've come to bust the cold chain?' He looked at Bill, who shook his head.

'No', he said. 'Dope pirates.' The Zig-Zag man gave a low, cracked laugh befitting the situation.

'They've come to bust *us*,' he said, 'but there's nothing to bust.'

277

Bill said, 'No, but I wonder if they know that.'

It was all happening very quickly, a matter of seconds.

The Zig-Zag man asked, 'Bill, you know these people?'

Bill said, 'No, but it looks like I may have to get to know them.'

Alan glanced at Amanda. Her arms were by her sides, her eyes closed as though devoutly, as they had been when he met her in the hut. Madonna blue. Her lips moved and he lipread her as saying 'Oh no, oh no . . .'

Alan said, 'Maybe they're agents.'

'Agents?' The Zig-Zag man glanced sharply at him.

Bill asked, 'Why do you say that?' and, in the circumstances, his tone was strangely calm, like a professor picking up on a student. Alan opened his mouth to reply, but at that moment Reuben, looking up the road, said, 'Something's happening!'

Peurifoy muttered 'I don't get this . . .' before he and all of them concentrated on the pink car.

Now someone had opened the front passenger door and was getting out. Alan guessed from his size that it was Pym. He stood behind the door, using it like a shield. The red flare path flashed like a cordoned-off area, and the Lodestar with the headlamps trained upon it was like somewhere a gun-happy wacko had settled in for an all-night siege. The red lights now seemed to be warning innocent bystanders to beware. But they were the innocent bystanders. This was the cold chain. It was a mercy mission. Shortsightedly, Alan saw the man he supposed to be Pym raise something to his face, and now his amplified and distorted voice came crackling down the road:

'MR BRANDL . . .'

'Dope pirates,' said the Zig-Zag man, 'with a bullhorn?'

'WE NOW YOU'RE THERE. COME OUT.'

'That guy is American.'

'IT'S TIME WE TALKED. LET'S TALK.'

And then:

'IF YOU WON'T TALK, WE GOT GUNS . . .'

It isn't easy to be subtle over a bullhorn, but Pym was managing it. His tone was one of teasing reasonableness. Now the Zig-Zag man was scared too. He swore and withdrew into the body of the Lodestar, while Alan, Reuben and Peurifoy edged closer to its fuselage. Only Bill and Amanda stayed where they were, and Alan saw that although Amanda's eyes were open now, they were glazed and empty, the eyes of someone going into shock. He grabbed her hand and pulled her closer to the plane. Bill turned away from the pink car and came after her. He took her hands and kissed her on the lips.

He said, 'It'll be okay. Don't be frightened. I love you.'

She said, 'I love you, Bill,' and although her voice trembled she had reaffirmed his cover – and cover is for the living.

He said, 'Good' and stroked her cheek, then kissed her again. He said to the rest of them, 'Get her on board and see that she stays there. I'm going to . . .'

'COME OUT, BRANDL. OR DO WE COME AND GET YOU?'

No, thought Bill, stay away from my people, my wife, our unborn child . . . Stay away from the cold chain. He made up his mind and steeled himself. He stepped under the Lodestar's wing and around its engine housing and left propeller into the wash of light. Here they had isolated him from the rest in a place without protection. They could see him clearly here and kill him if they wanted. The headlamps dazzled, the red lights throbbed, the moon shone. He had been here before, in the war, under dangerous moonlight, and if he had then been defending a way of life here he was defending life itself – a child and a cold chain. The knowledge gave him courage. He walked a few steps up the road towards them, then stopped. He cupped his hands to his mouth and called, 'Here I am. What do you want?' He waited, but no answer.

The red flare path flashed.

'Who are you? What do you want?'

'THAT'S IT, BRANDL. KEEP COMING.'

Bill cupped his hands again.

'It isn't here!'

'KEEP ON COMING . . .'

The beams of the headlamps intersected to form a dazzling vortex. He knew he must go down that vortex and hope that it would spit him out again, safe. He owed it to the people behind him. He owed it to the cold chain and his child. To protect their freedom and safety he must imperil his own. Unless they planned to use him as a hostage . . . No, they had said that they wanted to talk. It was *him* they were interested in. He preferred, however, to keep their interest at a distance. He tried once more.

'Here I am! Talk!'

A pause, then:

'WE TALK OVER HERE.'

Okay, you bastards. Bill squared himself up like a target. *Geronimo!*

He started up the road and to his surprise it was no more difficult than going home from a good party once the decision to go has been taken. The party had been fun, it was still fun, but a condition of the companionship had always been that he would go and be alone again. He was tearing himself away when things were at their best, but had he stayed on he would only have misbehaved. Sooner or later, the killjoys had to be confronted.

He walked towards them and hummed, under his breath, 'Boys and girls come out to play. The moon doth shine as...' Now he had passed the point where the beams intersected and no longer dazzled, and could see them, the man behind the open door of the car, the man in its back, the driver low over the wheel looking at the Lodestar through binoculars.

He stopped and said, 'You're wasting your time. There's nothing for you here.'

'Come closer, Brandl. We can't talk like this.' To Bill, the man's own unaided voice didn't sound one hell of a lot more human than the megaphone.

He said, 'You know where the dope is. Take it. Burn it. It doesn't interest me.'

The man said, 'What interests us, Brandl, is you. That's why we've come out here. To talk to you.'

Bill said, 'Well then, talk. Who are you? What do you want?'

The flare path flashed.

'My name's Pym. Charlie Pym. And this is Peter Pudney. Call him Peter, Bill. Call me Charlie. And that's Al. Call him Al. And you, Mr Brandl?'

Bill said, 'I am an American citizen. I'm protected under the laws of the United States.'

'And required,' said Pym, 'to obey them.'

'I've broken none,' said Bill. 'You know I've broken none.'

'This is Central America,' said Pym. 'And you're a dealer in contraband.'

280

Bill said, 'If you call life-saving equipment contraband...' but Pym interrupted him.

'If it comes in under the cover of darkness, it's contraband,' he said, then laughed quietly. 'Don't worry, Mr Brandl. We watched you unload those boxes and we guess they aren't heavy enough for ammunition or guns. They don't concern us, Brandl – or do I say Blythe?'

They knew his name, which meant they had done research in the States, which meant...

Bill said, 'It wouldn't be the first time a philanthropist has used a false name.'

'A philanthropist, Mr Blythe? Is that a fancy name for a doper?'

'I'm not a doper. I've done nothing,' said Bill. 'This is fun, but I've a plane to catch.'

'You're catching no plane, Mr Blythe. You're coming with us. We're going to have that little talk and we're going to take our time. Now step this way.'

'There's nothing to say.'

'Step this way.'

'Where's your authority?'

'Pointing at you.'

Through the open window of the passenger door, Pym was aiming a pistol at him.

Pym said, 'The plane can go. The people there can go. But you stay. Run and I shoot – I shoot to kill. Run and no one gets out. Now *move*!'

Bill was shaking. His voice was shaking as he asked, 'What do you want with me?' and, obeying Pym, started to walk towards him.

Pym said, 'We're paying a little visit to your dope farm, that's all. Then you can go.' The man in the back of the car, meanwhile, had slid over and opened the door behind Pym.

'Burn it,' said Bill. 'Bring a case against me. But let me go. I'm a sick man and ...' Pym, the pistol in one hand, handed him the bullhorn with the other.

'Take it, Mr Blythe,' he said. 'Put their minds at rest...'

*

281

Reuben and Peurifoy were flat on the road under the belly of the Lodestar. Alan was in its doorway, looking over the wing and occasionally at Amelia who, in the co-pilot's seat next to the Zig-Zag man, was keeping her head low and watching Bill. They had all seen him walk up the road. Now, over the bullhorn, they heard his voice come drifting back.

'OKAY, EVERYONE, YOU'RE FREE TO GO ...'

Pym's statement on Bill's behalf was cleverly engineered. He knew that the surge of relief they would feel at those words would help them to accept the sting:

'BUT I'M STAYING ON A WHILE ...'

Amelia, in the cockpit, put a hand to her mouth and Alan heard her say, 'No!'

'WE'VE SOME BUSINESS BACK AT THE FARM.' A pause. 'IT WON'T TAKE LONG, THEN I CAN GO.' A pause. 'IT'S PRIVATE BUSINESS, SO NO ONE TRY AND FOLLOW.'

Amelia said, 'They're going to kill him. I know they're going to kill him ...'

'REPEAT,' they heard Bill's voice again, 'NO ONE TRY AND FOLLOW.'

'No,' the Zig-Zag man tried to reassure Amelia. 'He's done no dope. He's saved a lot of kids' lives, that's all. They don't kill you for that.'

'DARLING ...'

'Oh James,' said Amanda, 'I'm sorry, please, I'm so sorry ...'

'I'LL SEE YOU IN THE STATES.'

Then they saw him go to the back of the pink car, wave to them briefly and get in. Alan heard Amanda sobbing 'James', then the Zag-Zag man saying, 'There, you heard what he said. You'll see him in the States.' Now she was openly crying.

The Zig-Zag man was abstracted, thinking how lucky he was to get away, hoping the narks hadn't managed to read his Lodestar's markings. He was thinking that he had never carried a cargo of crying woman before ...

The pink car circled on to the savannah, then turned back on to the Orange Walk Highway. It was soon out of the improvised flare path and in the moonlit darkness beyond.

The Zig-Zag man flicked controls and said, 'Okay. Let's get out of here. Wheels up.'

*

Below the Lodestar, Reuben said to Peurifoy, 'I'm going after him.'

He rolled out from under the plane and scrambled to his feet. Peurifoy followed him and when he caught up Reuben was already on the saddle of his trail bike.

Peurifoy said, 'What's he done? What's going on?'

Reuben said, 'There's no time. Get Alan to explain.' He kick-started and the bike's engine burst into life. By then Alan was with them too. He shouted over the engine noise.

'Reuben, what are you doing?'

'I'm going after him.'

'You'll get him killed!'

'They won't see me,' Reuben shouted. 'I won't follow down the road. I'll cut across the savannah. I'll get there first.'

'And then?'

'Watch over him. See he gets out safe.'

Alan grabbed him by his arms.

'Reuben, I beg you. Don't.'

'He saved my father's life,' shouted Reuben.

'Reuben . . .'

'Let go of me!'

'They'll hear you coming!'

'I'll be there first.'

Alan let go.

'Reuben, watch out.'

Reuben nodded and for a moment his eyes met Alan's. Then he slipped the clutch and turned the bike at a right angle to the road. He rode on to the savannah at speed, Alan and Peurifoy watching, and in moments he was indistinct in the half distance. Then he turned in profile to them, his bike less noisy now, riding parallel to the Orange Walk Highway.

Alan muttered under his breath, 'For God's sake, Reuben . . .'

'Alan!'

He turned and saw Amanda at the door of the Lodestar. He ran to her and as she knelt in the doorway he held her in his arms. She was crying. Her face was wet.

He said, 'It'll be okay,' over and over, but the Zig-Zag man was behind her, impatient to go. Alan kissed her, her cheeks, her mouth, her neck, then pushed her from him and stepped back, while she stayed kneeling in mute appeal, Madonna blue, her hands half extended; and if he never saw her again he would remember her in this attitude.

'Write,' he said, 'write.'

The Zig-Zag man pushed in front of her, roughly.

'Time to go,' he said, then shut the door, blotting her out. From inside came a muffled bang as the door was locked shut. Alan stood there a moment, stupidly. Then he felt the grip of Peurifoy's hand on his forearm.

'Come,' said Peurifoy quietly. 'Let's get away from here.' Numbly, Alan allowed himself to be led away from the plane and onto the savannah, where he turned to look at the Lodestar and Amanda in its cockpit, the co-pilot's seat, looking at him, at them, at the country she was leaving, with what despite his short sight he could guess to be a stricken expression. The Lodestar's left propeller started turning, at first with deceptive slowness, then rapidly faster, becoming a blur, then the right propeller, the engines seeming with their noise and power to minimise the misery of departure, making it small and irrelevant. The plane was now tense for take-off and the Zig-Zag man eased the brakes. It pulled away from them, slowly, but Amanda was already lost to sight. Then faster – vee one – down the Orange Walk Highway, faster – Rotate – the plane's nose lifting slightly, more steeply – vee two – taking off and going almost at once into a steep bank taking it away from the territory into which Bill had disappeared. It turned north in a wide circle, gaining height all the time, becoming smaller, quieter, until Peurifoy said, 'Come Alan, let's go.'

'A moment,' said Alan. He wanted to wait until he could neither see nor hear the Lodestar any more and departure was final. Peurifoy seemed to understand his need and waited, until there were only the two of them, the ice-cream van and the Transit, the flashing flare path and silence.

Then he asked, 'Now?'

'Yes,' said Alan, 'Now . . .'


Reuben knew that while they were on the Orange Walk Highway they had the edge over him in speed. His advantage would come when they turned off it onto the heavily potholed dirt track

284

which led to Alfredo's tin tabernacle on the crossroads at Mile-post 60. His plan was to miss out the crossroads and all the tracks bar the last, the fourth leg of their journey, the one which led to the *milpa*.

He knew the feel of the savannah from the country around Hattieville and had done some trail-riding in this area during his time as the header. But he had not done this ride and had to hope there were no major obstacles in the ten miles or so which he had to cover. He rode by moonlight at first, opening up the throttle as far as he dared. Then, when trees appeared to his left and he judged his and the pink car's paths to have diverged enough, he switched on the headlamp and speeded up. The savannah was mostly flat earth baked hard by the sun. The trick was to miss the tussocks of grass, like fret-sawing a piece of wood at speed while missing the knots.

He hit the dirt road on the far side of Milepost 60 at a point which he judged to be perhaps a mile from the even more decrepit track up to the *milpa*. This stretch he took as fast as he could, slowing at the worst potholes and looking behind to try and spot the pink car or its lights. Seeing nothing, he decided he must be well ahead of them. He came to the *milpa* track and turned up it. If by some miracle they had got there first he would run straight into them and be at their mercy . . .

On the *milpa*, Blackjack looked up from his work of sloshing petrol over the weed plants. He had done ten jerricans already and had broken open some bales of straw at strategic places. There were five jerricans to go. He had just heard, in the distance, a throaty whine as the trail bike laboured up one of the steeper sections of the *milpa* track. It was a sound signature he recognised at once. In all Belize there was only one sound like that. In the games of Guess The Car at The South 'Nam a constant had been Reuben's bike. The regulars knew that sound so well that it drew no comment from them, let alone a bet. It was part of Blackjack's intimate world, like the nick in the baize by the top left-hand pocket which he had learned to play around. And, from the Americans, Blackjack had learned that Reuben was working on the dope farm – goody-two-shoes Reuben, incredible but true. He had hoarded the information for future use and it looked now as if the future had arrived.

Blackjack smiled. He set down the jerrican of petrol and

screwed its cap back on. He carried the can the short distance to the edge of the bush where his rifle was propped against a tree. He put the can down there where Reuben would not see it and picked up his rifle. He crouched against the wall of bush where the moonlight didn't touch and waited. At last he had Reuben where he wanted him – on the criminal frontier where his own life had been spent. The moment to take him had come. There was all the time in the world . . .

The pink car's driver, Al, switched off the engine. The block ticked. Bill swallowed and said, 'The *milpa*'s up there.'

'We know where it is, Mr Blythe,' said Pudney.

'You said we were going there.'

'Change of plan,' said Pudney. 'We've sub-contracted out the job of torching it. No need to go up there. You can see it burn from here.'

'And then?' said Bill. 'I can go . . .'

'Change of plan,' said Pudney.

'What do you mean? What "change of plan"? You said I could go.'

'We said you were coming with us,' said Pym. 'Well so you are, all the way to the States. You're under arrest, Mr Blythe.'

'Under arrest?' Bill looked at them in turn. 'What for? On what charge? By what authority? Under what law of what country?' They took no notice of him. Bill protested, 'Come on, what is this? You can't just treat me like a criminal. I demand my rights. I demand to know what's going on and why you're holding me without cause. I demand to be let out of here.'

Pym, looking straight ahead, asked, 'Are you resisting arrest, Mr Blythe?' His tone of voice was chilling.

Bill said, 'I'm simply saying I've done nothing. I grew the dope, true, but I got out of it in time.' It was the plea which he had made several times on their journey and Pym used the same formula to rebut it. Now, though, he spoke with an affected weariness, as if his patience had become strained.

'You got out because of us, Blythe. You ran scared, but we caught you. And now you play the philanthropist. You got out in time? No. We were the ones on time. You were too late and that's why you're here.'

286

Bill said, 'No, I didn't even know who you were. I still don't know.' He had said the same before. Now, though, they responded differently.

Pudney leant across Bill to Pym and said, 'Maybe they didn't tell him.'

'Or,' Pym said, 'they didn't work it out.'

'Or they did work it out,' said Pudney, 'but still didn't tell him.'

'Well,' said Pym, 'they wouldn't, would they?'

'Who are you talking about?' Bill asked. '*What* are you talking about?'

'Your wife,' said Pudney.

'And the English guy,' Pym added. 'They knew where we came from.'

'Alan Palmer? What about him?'

Pudney said, 'Aren't you a little rich to be in the dope trade, Mr Blythe? And a little old? A rich old doper like you, with such a young piece of tail? Who would have guessed about her? Well we didn't.'

'My wife is nothing to do with this,' said Bill. 'Keep her out of it.'

Pudney laughed softly.

'That would be easier to do, Mr Blythe, if she kept herself out.'

'Come on, Blythe,' said Pym. 'You mean you don't know?'

'The English guy,' said Pudney. 'She didn't keep him out, did she?'

Bill said, 'That's a lie.'

Swiftly, Pudney turned in his seat and grabbed Bill by his jacket pulling his face to within inches of his own.

'A lie is it, Mr Blythe?' he shouted. 'A lie?' He used his right hand with its fistful of cloth to chuck him under his chin. 'Calling me a liar?'

'I only mean . . .'

He heard Pym say, 'The old fool doesn't know.'

'He came to my boat, Blythe. The English creep. Looking for your wife. He was hot for her. He told me. And why, Blythe? Because he knew how hot she was.'

Bill shook his head.

'No. That can't be. Not when she's expecting my child.'

287

Pudney laughed.

Pym chipped in, '*Your* child?'

'My child. By my wife.'

Pudney pulled him closer.

'Whose child, Blythe?'

'Your wife,' said Pym, 'but not your child. Your glasses, Mr Blythe.'

'My . . .?'

'Your rose-tinted shades. Give them. Or do I snatch them off your face?'

Bill took them off. His hand was shaking. Pym took the glasses. He said, 'Peter, this is my show,' and Pudney released Bill and let him fall back to the car seat. Pym had put his glasses on. They were too large for his face. 'Gee,' he said, 'You got bad vision, Mr Blythe. Like Mr McGoo. Know why I want your glasses?'

Bill looked into his own shades. He swallowed and shook his head, and, as he did so, Pym punched him hard in the mouth. A tooth broke and he tasted blood from a cut inside his lip. He put a hand to his mouth, but worse than the immediate pain was the knowledge that a psychological border into a country without controls had been crossed and that in another, more dangerous sense, Pym had tasted blood too. 'Because,' said Pym, 'It's bad manners to hit a man wearing glasses,' and he hit him again, and again, Bill trying to duck the blows to his head, his face, his neck. Pudney gripped him then from the back, pinning his arms behind him. Pym paused and said, 'Whose baby, Blythe? Your wife's expecting whose baby?' Bill leant his head against Pudney's shoulder and felt the bruises on his face, his thickened lips, looking at Pym through the blood from a cut over his left eye.

'Mine.'

A fresh rain of blows from Pym. Then, intensifying the attack, Pym reached his hand between Bill's legs and gripped his testicles, squeezed and twisted them.

'A baby?' he said. 'From old balls like yours?' He twisted again and Bill cried out. Pym disengaged his hand and punched Bill in the stomach. 'Whose?' he asked again and Bill knew the violence would escalate until he made the admission they wanted. Pym hit him again. 'Whose?' he asked, then took Bill's chin in his hand and held up his head. 'Who, Mr Blythe? Who's the father of Mrs Blythe's bastard?'

It was hard to say, it was hard to speak at all – but worse, Bill had begun to believe them.

'If you say so,' he managed to say, but Pym punched him again.

'Because it's true. Who?'

'The Englishman,' Bill gasped, 'the Englishman . . .'


The birds began 'talking', as the jungle word has it – chattering like light sleepers woken up – when Reuben pushed his bike into the far side of the bush in order to hide it. Blackjack heard them as Reuben – now that he had seen no car in the clearing – confidently crashed his way through the bush towards the *milpa*. Blackjack thought, This is going to be easy. Softly, he made his way to a point nearer to where he judged Reuben would make his exit from the bush and crouched again, shaded from the moon.

Maybe fifty yards away, a man broke out of the bush. Blackjack tensed. Now it mattered which way he chose to walk. It was Reuben all right. He would know that shape and stance anywhere, and that way of walking, and Reuben was walking towards him. It was only then that Blackjack saw that he was carrying a rifle. Better and better. If anyone found out, and Blackjack intended that no one should, this would look like self defence. And he was working for law and Reuben was with the law-breakers. It was a beautiful reversal of roles. Reuben's footsteps were crunching on the charcoal. Blackjack raised his rifle stock to his shoulder . . .

The evil weed gave off even more smell by night, but there was another smell, too, mixed in with the dope, and just then Reuben smelt the petrol and saw a pile of straw just inside the edge of the *milpa*. He stopped. Something was wrong . . .

Blackjack had done time in Jamaica's Gun Park. Blackjack was so good a shot he could blow the tinamou bird away from the top of the clock-tower tree. Reuben, the black man, was highlighted against the pale green of the weed washed white by the moon. And Reuben had stopped. Now Blackjack had him in his sights.

He fired, and at the report the far side of the bush by the clearing at once came alive with bird cries and whirring wings. The bullet hit Reuben in the left shoulder, ripping through the muscle, shattering his shoulder-blade. He would not use his southpaw again. The rifle dropped from his left hand, useless, as he staggered back under the force of the shot and saw the full moon which long ago his father had told him not to fight.

He still had not hit the ground when Blackjack fired again, a better shot although his target was moving, hitting Reuben's face at the cheekbone, though Blackjack couldn't know that yet. Blackjack was torn between the wish to put his enemy out of the way and the desire that he should know before he died who had killed him. He got up from his hiding place by the bush and, rifle still at the ready, went to the spot where Reuben had fallen. He was face down and, at Blackjack's approach, he didn't move. Warily, Blackjack edged the toe of his right shoe under Reuben's pelvis and levered his body over. He saw his enemy's shoulder and the eyes in his smashed face. Staring at Reuben dead, Blackjack was surprised how little satisfaction he felt. It had been like potting an easy ball.

Blackjack was businesslike. He propped his rifle again by the bush and took the half-empty can of petrol to Reuben's body. He took him by his heels and dragged him several rows deep into the weed. He fetched the petrol and doused the body with it. He returned to the spot where Reuben had died and used some of the cotton wadding from his pocket to pick up his rifle. It was a nice rifle, which he would have liked to own. But that wasn't smart. It was the mistake he had made in Jamaica. Leave it.

No, he had a better idea. He put Reuben's rifle down and returned to his own. He used the wadding to clean fingerprints from it, then went back to Reuben's body and placed it there. Fire would destroy its stock and if anyone got around to anything so fancy as ballistics tests it would look like suicide. Reuben had always struck Blackjack as a potential suicide. And if that fell through there was always self-defence. But all of this was academic, because no one was going to know. On the wrist of Reuben's outstretched right arm Blackjack saw his digital watch. He would have liked that, too, but denied himself, just as he was going to deny himself Reuben's rifle.

He went to the cache of jerricans at the edge of the bush and, taking his time, emptied the rest of them around the *milpa*. When all the cans were empty but one, he made a pile of straw around Reuben's body and poured the last of the petrol over it. He set fire to the straw and quickly stepped out of the weed into the earth alleyway.

The only liquid on the *milpa* was the petrol and the blood in Reuben's body. The straw caught quickly, then the weed around it and rapidly the fire moved inwards, then along the edge of the weed, a slight breeze fanning it towards the centre. Blackjack waited until there was an inferno around Reuben and he was sure that the fire would lay all to waste. Smoke was billowing, a high cloud in the moonlight. Flames were leaping up.

Blackjack said, 'Time's up, tinamou!' and turned from the fire. He started into the bush towards the clearing, the trail and the road where the pink car would be waiting.

Pym took Bill's shades from his own face and broke them in half. He said to Pudney, 'Get the fishing line.' Bill now knew that his life was at stake and started to fight back. He lashed out at Pym and connected with a glancing blow to his cheek, but then Pudney had him from the back by the throat, throttling him, and Pym was punching him in the stomach and chest from so close that Bill, his arms to either side and kicking out wildly with his feet, couldn't hit him. He struggled against Pudney's arm-lock round his throat. 'His arms,' said Pym, 'get his arms,' and now Pym's body was obscenely on top of his, his hands to his throat, as Pudney tried to pin Bill's hands behind him. They forced him round as he struggled, then pushed his knees to the car floor so that he was crouched facing the back of the car, his neck bent and his face hard against the seat. They knelt on his back, one on either shoulder, and forced his arms behind him, twisting them so that he cried out again. Gasping for breath, he felt a nylon line tied tightly, first round one wrist, then the other, hobbling his arms. He cried out that they were stopping his blood flow and Pym said, 'You won't need your blood any more.' Then he called out to Pudney for 'the gag' and Bill heard him say in a kind of ecstasy, 'Okay Blythe, Brandl, Thomas

291

Jefferson, whoever the fuck you are. We're sick of listening to you. Say your piece for posterity.' He felt a length of cloth forced between the seat back and his head, and knew that they planned to kill him and he said, 'Don't, please, God, don't kill me, please...' as the cloth was forced over his eyes, his nose, his open mouth speaking the last words, where Pym pulled it tight, behind his teeth, stretching his mouth in a terrible grimace. They knotted the gag at the back of his head; he could not cry out now, only make a low, animal noise deep in his throat; and, still hoping to reach some pity in them, he moaned behind the gag. Pym punched the back of his head and said, 'Shut the fuck up!' And then: 'We're going to make an example of you, Mr Blythe. How'd you like a little fresh air?'

Pudney opened the door, and together they dragged him out and let him drop to the ground. He lay with his face to the dirt road, gagged but trying to breathe in big gasps, while they strolled a distance apart, confident that he was utterly in their power. He knew that he barely had the strength to stand, let alone to run from them. His hands were numb. He could smell the earth. They had frightened him enough; now they would let him go ... From above he heard Pym say, 'Are you there, Mr Doper man? Turn over.' He did so and their compassionless faces were above him against the moonlit sky, Pym, Pudney, the driver and a fourth man, black, with a rifle, to whom Pudney was saying, 'Blackjack, let me introduce you to James Blythe. Mr Blythe, meet Blackjack.' Bill made a groaning sound and shut his eyes. Pym knelt beside him in the dirt and, with tireless violence, slapped his face. 'Open your eyes, Doper man,' he said. 'It's a swell night.' Bill opened his eyes. Pym bent his head to Bill's and whispered in his ear, 'Blackjack's just come from your *milpa*, Blythe. He just killed *your* black man up there.' Bill stared and shook his head in denial. He tried to speak and shut his eyes, and heard Pym say, 'That's right, Blythe, your faithful servant, Reuben White. You killed him. Corrupted and killed him. *Look at me!*' They dragged him to his feet and turned him to face the bush where the *milpa* was hidden. The full moon gleamed silver on a high cloud of smoke. It seemed to reach almost to heaven, like the smoke from the *milpa* in April, the time of burning. The lower part of the cloud was ruddy with fire, like a sunset under the moon.

292

Pudney said, 'Look at your dream, Blythe, your flaky, doper's dream. *Burning!*'

Pym said, 'Get him in the car. Let's go . . .'


If the tin tabernacle on the crossroads at Milepost 60 was allegedly a house of God it was for a fact a human habitation and the one which lay closest to the *milpa*. Alfredo lived there, the lying, grasping crossroads-dweller whom George Bourne had warned Alan about. For Alfredo, this had been an unusually disturbed night, with the unaccustomed sounds of night-time traffic, the last car only a few minutes ago, and now, outside the tabernacle, Pompidou the green monkey screeching and jumping, rattling his chain.

Grumbling, Alfredo got up from his bed in the central aisle and dragged his trousers on. He muttered and scratched his head, and drank from a bottle of rum and water. What was vexing Pompidou tonight? He was putting on his shirt when he remembered the two hundred US dollars cash which the Americans in the pink car had given him. Quickly he checked under his pillow, found the money there safe and slipped the bills into his trouser pocket.

Doing up his shirt he padded outside in his bare feet. Pompidou was tethered to a stake in the ground, like jaguar-bait, no access to a tree. People said it was cruel to keep him that way, a neurotic bag of nerves. But the more neurotic the monkey the earlier the warning and Pompidou, Alfredo's early warning system, was tonight the craziest that Alfredo had seen him.

He padded towards his monkey, then, suddenly knowing the whole story, stopped. He understood the two hundred dollars and Pompidou's tantrum. He turned to look west, where a dull red glow lit up the sky. He smelt dope smoke. The *milpa* was on fire.

Slowly he nodded his head. Now he had an idea of the sort of lies and selective silence the Americans had intended their money to pay for.

It took more than a high cloud of *milpa* smoke to impress Alfredo.

'Belize broke up bigger circus than this,' he muttered to

293

himself, then turning to his monkey, said loudly, 'What you wake me for this for, Pompidou? It's nothing, you hear? Go sleep now, monkey, sleep...'


At the sea, Pym pushed Bill out of the open door and sent him sprawling on the dirt road. Without the use of his hands, he took most of the impact on one shoulder. Behind him, as he lay there, he heard the slam of car doors and the rattle of metal on metal as the trunk was unloaded. Strong arms – Pudney's and Blackjack's – seized him under the armpits and brought him to a kneeling position. Gravel rash had clawed one side of his face in strips like imperfectly removed paint. Through swollen eyes, he saw the beach a little below him and the sea, which was calm tonight with a muscular ripple of swell. The bulk of *The Mary May* was offshore, a brilliant white under the moon. He smelt the sea and the bladderwrack-smell of the beach, and felt on his face the touch of a breeze.

At Pym's command they pulled him to his feet and as they did so turned his back to the sea. The driver, Al, slammed the car's trunk shut. Pudney and Blackjack dragged him backwards, frog-marching him, onto the beach, Pym leading the way, through the soft sand onto the wet where the surface was firmer; and now the pain from the nylon line was intolerable, his arms were pulled apart and the line cut into his wrists. He moaned behind his gag. The driver, with an armful of rifles, was matter-of-factly following them.

They dragged him further, along the surfline of the beach, past Mr Fruit's darkened hut to the spit and past the trees to where Mr Fruit's dorey and *The Mary May*'s skiff were moored. The land-crabs were out under the moon, but, as the men approached, they scuttled back into their holes.

Pym said, 'Here,' and Pudney and Blackjack let him fall to the ground under his own weight. Pym kicked him in the ribs and told him to turn over. Now they didn't mind if he groaned.

Pym lowered his body on to Bill's, a knee on either side, straddling his stomach. He slapped Bill's face hard with his left hand and said, 'What we going to do with you, fuckhead?' then slapped him with his right. '*Open your eyes!*' Pym shuffled his knees a little in the sand to bring his body over Bill's diaphragm, then lowered his upper half until his head was pillowed in the sand next to Bill's. He said, in a stage whisper, savouring each syllable, 'We're – gon – na – kill – ya!' He moved his head still nearer and Bill could feel Pym's breath hot in his ear, his earlobe in Pym's mouth and Pym biting on it hard, drawing more blood; and above Pym's hot breathing in his ear and the animal noise deep in his own throat – half pain, half horror – he heard Pudney's laughter, as he indulged Pym's little pleasure in life, all too rarely enjoyed – Pym's showtime.

Pym drew himself up and softly put his hands to either side of Bill's face. Softly, he said, 'Open your eyes, Mr Blythe. Open them, doper whore . . .' Bill opened his eyes and Pym, looking into them, called to Blackjack, who came and knelt on one knee beside them, smoking a cigarette.

'Yeah, boss?'

Pym's eyes were still on Bill's as he asked, 'Blackjack, how you keep John Crow from your corn? How you keep the seagulls from your catch?'

A pause, then Blackjack said, 'I guess you shoot them.'

'But you can't shoot 'em *all*, can you?'

A pause.

'Then . . . you shoot one. Hang him up so's the others see.'

'That's right! And you keep America clean of dopers the same way. You don't put a doper in jail with his own TV and attorney and his Hostess Twinkie defence. You kill him and hang him up in a newspaper, so all the other dopers can see and know what to expect. You call up a nice tame newsman called Mr Wyler Fuller and spin him a nice detailed story how this doper got killed by dope pirates. And the only people know different don't know for sure and they can't say a thing. They guess the truth but can't prove it and that's even better, because the word gets around that maybe the pirates were US agents. Peter, you see any holes in that?'

'No holes,' Bill heard Pudney say.

'It hangs together?'

'It hangs.'

Pym punched Bill in the side of the face. He said, 'I hate you, Mr Blythe. You're the trash drags a great country down. We're going to hang you up, make an example of you.' He looked

295

away from Bill to Blackjack. 'Blackjack, we paid you? We paid
you good?'

'I'm happy, Mr Pym.'

'Like to earn a little extra? Say, twenty dollar? Like to beat
up on some white trash for twenty dollar? Then he looked at
Bill and said, 'No, I got a better idea.' He raised his head and
called, 'Al!'

'Yeah, Charlie?'

'You got the ignition, Al? Bring me the car's ignition.'

Al had loaded the skiff and was waiting by it to paddle them
back to *The Mary May*. He walked over to Pym, rummaging
in his pocket for the pink car's keys. Bill heard a slight metallic
rattle as he handed them to Pym, and saw a glint in the moonlight
as Pym held them delicately between thumb and forefinger.
Theatrically, he rattled them a little to make a chiming sound.

'Blackjack, how'd you like to be the proud possessor of a T-
bird?'

'A T-bird? T-bird, boss?'

'The car, Blackjack! The beautiful pink T-bird...'

'Yeah? What I got to do?'

'A death, that's all...'

'Death?'

'Buys you a T-bird.'

'Oh, I don't know...'

It was like a game show. Blackjack licked his lips.

'Snuff the doper,' said Pym, 'the car's yours. You snuffed
someone already tonight. And don't forget, the doper knows
you did. Think about it. You want that he goes and tells?' Pym
rattled the keys again. 'A T-bird, Blackjack, a T-bird...'

'Yeah...' said Blackjack. They were looking at him.

'What? You will?'

Blackjack nodded.

'It's a deal.'

'Good guy, Blackjack. You'll go places. Great, we got us a
death.'

Bill was on his back in the sand. The moon was huge. This
wasn't real. It was in his mind, as the *milpa* had been, his
marriage, the cold chain and the child. He could put it out of
his mind, as he could obliterate the moon by shutting his eyes.
He did so. These people weren't real – not people at all, but

296

phantoms. Only by partaking of his reality, his flesh and blood, could they become real and how could they partake when they were only in his mind? It was only in his imagination that he heard the tiny pop of the clasp which held Pym's sheath knife and now, opening his eyes, only in imagination that he saw the brief flash of a blade in the unreal moonlight.

Pym was about to hand the knife to Blackjack when a smile stole onto his face. The smile hesitated, then decided it was safe to stay. It widened and made itself comfortable on Pym's face.

'No,' said Pym. 'I got a better idea . . .' He sheathed the knife again, as Blackjack said, 'Why not just shoot the guy?'

'Make too much noise,' said Pym. 'Wake people. No, Black-jack' – he pointed to Mr Fruit's steel coconut spike, point upwards in the sand – 'Spike him and you got the car . . .'


Mr Fruit awoke early and looked out over the bay. It was empty. The Americans had gone.

He did his twenty press-ups and ate breakfast. It had been a noisy night. From his bed he had heard the arrival of the pink car. *The Mary May* had gone; then, soon afterwards, the car. At one point he had thought of getting up and speaking to the Americans about money. They had promised him nothing in addition to his daily sweetener of ten dollars, but in justice he deserved a bonus for all his help and advice, all the blind eyes he had turned, their use of what was, after all, 'his' bay. But some instinct had stopped him from confronting them.

After breakfast he went to the spit. Bill was where they had left him, gagged, hands bound behind him, head thrown back. His eyes were staring. Mr Fruit's shock was only momentary; then, dispassionately, he took the scene in. From the blood and what looked like brain matter on and near his coconut spike he could guess that the Americans had used it to smash the man's head open. Around his head was a blood-stain which seemed too small for the wound, because the blood had soaked deeply into the sand, to branch out and blossom under the surface. Other scraps of bloody matter were here and there about the clearing, and Mr Fruit guessed that the land-crabs had been dining and breakfasting on the man, as they did on waste pieces

297

of the fish which he gutted at this spot.

Mr Fruit even took in a detail, a nuance, which properly speaking was not there. The expression in the dead man's eyes was not simply appalled. Somehow, his eyes seemed also to be seeing something – so intensely that you thought it must be there. But it wasn't. Perhaps, though, it *had* been last night, when he had died. Mr Fruit thought of the full moon. Had the man, at the moment of death, been opening his eyes wide, filling himself with its light? What was he seeing? No. Fanciful guesswork was not for Mr Fruit. He was a survivor, and to him one detail, undoubtedly real, dominated the others.

Pinned to the dead man's jacket were two one hundred US dollar bills.

A handsome tip! They were pinned to the left lapel. Mr Fruit crouched by the body and unpinned them. His fingers trembled. The bills were crisp. He held them, individually, up to the light. They were real. Satisfied, he folded and pocketed them. He stood up and at once, despite himself, the same fancy crept into his mind – that the dead man's eyes were seeing. Involuntarily, he shivered. It was nonsense. The sun was bright and warm, and in his pocket were two hundred US.

He turned from the body back towards his hut. Behind it, in the usual place, he would bury his money. Then he would wait by the road until a car came. It might take a while, but one would come. That was a mathematical certainty, to be counted upon, like money or the sun.


After the Orange Walk Highway Alan in his Transit had followed Jay Peurifoy's ice-cream van to the south to help with the cold chain. Arriving in the afternoon, they had been busy until late evening immunising the children of Pascó. After work, when it was dark, they had learned over Alan's portable radio that an American had been murdered and that William Brandl's body had been found.

'They murdered him,' said Peurifoy. 'The guy who brought the cold chain, they murdered him . . .'

Alan was silent. He had half expected and feared this. Now he was wondering what had happened to Reuben. And Amelia –

had she made it safely to the States? Where was she now and how would she find out about Bill?

'*Why?*' said Peurifoy, 'the bastards...' Then, remembering, he turned to Alan. 'Reuben said when he rode away that you could explain.'

'Yes Jay.'

They were in Alan's Transit, parked just off the road at Pascó. A sick child, asleep, was in the back with his mother. It was late and Alan was tired. So was Peurifoy. But Alan knew it was time to talk now and began, quietly so as not to wake the child, to brief Peurifoy on the whole complicated story as far as he knew it. Alan would be leaving Belize soon: it was important that Peurifoy knew.

He told the American how Bill and Amelia had hidden their identities and the fact of their marriage under fake names, and grown a marijuana *milpa*. How knowing nothing of this he had got involved, or entangled, with Amelia, whose real name he had discovered only by accident; and by then she was carrying his child, the child Bill thought was his own.

He told how gratitude, when medicine brought by Bill had saved his father's life, had drawn Reuben in too; and how he feared now for Reuben, who had followed Bill to the *milpa*.

'But the *milpa* was inland,' Peurifoy objected. 'Bill's body was found on a beach.'

'I'm counting on that,' said Alan. 'Maybe he missed them, or they missed him. Maybe he's safe.' And he told Peurifoy then about the roses, and how he hadn't known that Reuben had hated him and how they had made their peace.

Amazement was on Peurifoy's face.

He asked, 'Who are the men who murdered him? Can you tell me that?'

Alan explained that they had seemed to be spear fishers at first, then dope pirates; then how a suspicion had grown, because of the independence concession and because one of them had run off with the Consul's wife, that they might be agents. Peurifoy nodded and said:

'They sound like agents to me. And I think the police and the Belize government would agree.'

'But the cold chain?' Alan asked. 'And Reuben, if he's all right? And Amelia, his wife? Bill brought the cold chain, but he was also involved in drugs. And as things are now the cold chain is also a kind of crime. You know that.'

'He was murdered.'

'And he's dead,' said Alan evenly. 'But Amelia isn't. She was involved in the *milpa* too. And Reuben. Murder may be the worst crime, but it isn't the only one. Whatever justice we might be able to win for Bill, Reuben and Amelia would be bound by it too. Would he want that?'

Peurifoy's morality of stark choice had not been designed to deal with ambivalences like these. He shook his head, perplexed.

'Weird,' he said, 'weird. He did drugs and he did the cold chain too. How was it the same man?'

'But the cold chain won,' said Alan. And for now, he thought, that would have to be Bill's epitaph. 'Stir things up,' he continued, 'and you could bring a great weight of unwelcome attention to bear. Enough to break the cold chain. And would he want that, either?'

Peurifoy, with a reluctant nod of his head, seemed to accept the common sense of that. Then he looked at Alan as though for guidance and asked, 'What do we do?'

'It may seem,' said Alan, 'like ingratitude to Bill, but really it's the reverse. We do nothing, or nothing yet. We do the cold chain first and we find out about Reuben. Then we see...'

Two days later at Pascó, in the clearing, Peurifoy glanced up from his work and asked about Amelia.

'Do you love her?'

'I wanted to,' Alan said at once. 'I hoped that I did. I thought that I might.'

'That's talking like a lawyer,' said Peurifoy. There was a slight clink of glass as he counted the doses of vaccine in an isothermic case. He said, 'It's unconditional. You do or you don't. That's all.'

'You don't understand, Jay. But Amelia did. She was just as defensive as me, more so with her fake name and her lies. We were both immunised early. The same cold chain had got to us both. We were never going to catch love incurably, only in mild bouts of an old illness.'

'I don't want your images,' said Peurifoy. 'Look at these people here and forget your fancy images for ever. Love is the cure. Don't pervert it and call it a disease.'

300

The cold chain was completed that day, and Alan said goodbye and left Pascó. His first step, back in Belize City, was to book a flight for Miami, where perhaps he would be able to contact Amelia – Amanda Holiwell – in Illinois before flying on to England. His next step was to visit Reuben's boat-hire on the Southern Foreshore. The trail bike wasn't in its usual place and a glance told him that the office was shut. He asked in the car-hire a few doors down: Reuben had not been seen.

Reuben's boat fell and lifted in the oily swell. Alan tried the door of his office. It was locked. He peeped into the office through a dusty pane of glass and saw that the desk was clear but for the stalk of a dead flower and a few leaves. Where was Reuben? There was something final about the room's emptiness, the boat's, but Reuben knew this country and perhaps was biding his time in the north. He had been, where Belize City was concerned, a missing person for months, and Alan could not alert the police before he knew more.

Mike Sharp was another problem. His roots here were tangled and deep; he was dangerous. No, he did not relish the possibility of meeting Mike. What could they talk about now, what might he ask Mike and how could he explain? So he collected his ticket and settled his bill at the Bayman Hotel, and kept his head down over the few hours until it was time to go. He would leave it to those who lived and belonged here to work things out.

The taxi arrived on time to take him to Stanley Field airport. With tremendous relief, Alan put his luggage into it, then himself. In minutes they were out of the city and on the airport road.


It was the second day of TV in Hattieville. The satellite dish and set had been delivered from Stanley Field and installed by Blackjack on the roof and in the bar room of The South Vietnam. It was the most difficult electrical job he had ever done and the first for many years, but watching him do it people realised that he had not lied in his claims to have trained as an electrician. Blackjack had for the first time, and at the most dramatic moment in Hattieville's history, become a useful member of the community; and, in Reuben's absence, with the wonder of TV

301

killing stone dead the feud between the two Vietnams, Hattieville was more of a community, a real community, than it had ever been.

On the roof of The South 'Nam, Blackjack had adjusted the dish until pictures appeared on the set in the bar below, fuzzily at first, then sharply defined, soundless at first, then speaking. People had stared, open-mouthed. The wonder of it! Rays sieved by the dish from the sky, pictures pirated out of thin air! And the money – the low white mansions with clipped green lawns, the buildings, the cars, the clothes! Awe-struck, they saw it on the screen, the sitcoms, the game shows, the ads. The TV had been on continuously since its installation and already was regarded as a sort of altar on which, unfailingly, rich and enviable gods would appear at the touch of a button. The satellite dish was a tourist attraction – people came from Belize City to see it. Aimed as it was at the geostationary satellite serving Chicago, Mayor Jane Byrnes and the Chicago Cubs were already household names in Hattieville.

In the rather more backward Belize media, the murder of Bill Brandl had been reported, but no one in Hattieville knew that they owed their unexpected windfall to the philanthropy of the dead American. The satellite dish and TV set seemed to have come from thin air just as the pictures did. Nor had anyone, at least in Blackjack's hearing, thought to enquire where Reuben was – had he not been away for weeks? Not even Reuben's father had asked yet. Blackjack wondered what had happened to his body. Had Reuben been burnt to a cinder in the *milpa* fire? Had the other dope growers found him and, fearing his body might incriminate them, hidden or buried it? Blackjack wondered if he should visit the *milpa* and find out, or wait until the jungle reclaimed the land. And even if Reuben's body were found and there were an autopsy, how could it be proved that he, Blackjack, had been on the *milpa* that night? He had swapped rifles, and thrown Reuben's in the sea.

Still, however, Blackjack was worried. There was a sudden burst of canned laughter from the TV. He looked around The South 'Nam's bar at the rows of gawping people and muttered under his breath, 'Like chicken on a roost.' He got up and went outside to where his T-bird was parked. He patted its hood. Pictures on a screen were unreal, but not a car. It could take you places and Blackjack planned, now, to take a drive and clear his mind of worry.

The American, Pym, had provided him with a scribbled fake receipt for the car made out for several days before the real ownership transfer. Blackjack had known that it was part of the Americans' plan that they should be held responsible for the murder which, in fact, he had committed. How, in this wilderness country, would anyone go about establishing the real facts? The only witnesses to his act had been the Americans, and the Americans had disappeared and wanted to be blamed for the murder. The one strong proof that he had had links with them was his ownership of their T-bird. He had disposed of Reuben's rifle – but he could not so easily renounce the pink car. Had he not earned it, with murder? Was it not his bounty?

People might suspect him, but they could prove nothing and he had ridden out their suspicion of him before – with less to play for, too, than a T-bird. It was, anyway, too late. Even if he disposed of the car, it would be known that he had owned it. And Reuben, his enemy, was gone.

No, the way to handle this was to show himself shamelessly to the world, get into his car and drive it where he chose . . .

It would be Blackjack's misfortune that he chose that moment to go for a drive. Alan was then on the airport road, in the back of his taxi, the slipstream sucking away the smoke of his cigarette, feeling free but also faintly as if he were skipping the country.

He rehearsed again the arguments he had put to Peurifoy. He could go to the authorities and tell his somewhat fantastic tale. He could implicate the Americans, whoever they were, and his 'babyhood buddy' Mike; but Reuben (if he lived) would be implicated too, and Amelia, and the cold chain. And would they even believe him? There was a risk, too, of implicating himself and of his having to stay, to stand trial or bear witness. And he was now desperate to go. All the arguments, selfish or selfless, told him to do nothing. He puffed his cigarette and told himself he was doing the right thing. Nothing.

Then he saw the pink car. In the heat haze, it seemed to be

standing still, but it was heading fast in the opposite direction to his down the airport road, towards his taxi. He ducked and slid across the seat, his head down, pretending to the driver that he had dropped and lost and was looking for something. He was tired of keeping his head down. But slyly, he positioned himself so he could see but not be properly seen and as the pink car passed he saw Blackjack at the wheel. Now, on an instinct, he knew: both what had happened and what he was going to do.

Reuben was dead. He did not know how he knew, but somewhere, somehow, Reuben was dead. His plane was in half an hour and he wanted to go, but he could not leave until others knew too. He felt sick of betrayal and fear, the lies of the past and present.

His driver turned off the airport road onto the approach to Stanley Field, past the Harriers at Airport Camp (under camouflage, like everything else) and into the airport forecourt. Alan got out and helped him unload his luggage.

Then a man walked out of the airport building. Alan looked at him. His face was black, but splashed and streaked with a milky, off-white colour, like two-tone ziricote – as though someone had taken offence and poured a cup of coffee over him, and the stain had stuck.

It was the Box Man. He knew that face from his childhood glimpse. He had taken his helmet off. The Box Man had faced the world.

'That's the Masked Man you're seeing,' said the driver.

'But why did he take off his mask?'

The driver laughed.

'Independence Day. He throw it away.'

'But why?'

'Ask him yourself.'

Why not? There was the delivery tricycle. The Box Man was climbing onto it. There was time. Why not ask him? But for some reason Alan didn't.

'My guess,' said the taxi-driver, 'is he don't feel ashamed no more. Hey, you want to miss your plane? My fare is ten dollar.'

Alan paid him. It was rude to stare, but he had to. The taxi-man drove away, past the slowly pedalling Box Man – as he had once been.

304

Images. Peurifoy had been right. The time of images was over. There was something he had to do. Alan picked up his luggage and walked into the airport building. The tiny telephone directory covered the whole of Belize. In it he found the number he wanted and dialled.

A voice answered:

'Belize City police.'

'Listen carefully. I'll be in touch again, but here's a tip for you now.'

'Who is this?'

'I haven't got long. It's the murder of the American...'

'Go on.'

'There's a guy who calls himself Blackjack.'

'Who is this talking, please?'

'Blackjack. Have you got that?'

'Yes.'

'He's driving a big pink car. Here's what you need to know...'